FIVE BLACK SHIPS

Napoleón Baccino Ponce de León, born 1947 in Montevideo, is a literary critic. *Five Black Ships*, his first novel, received the Novela Casa de las Americas Award in 1989. He loves the sea.

FIVE

BLACK SHIPS

A Novel of the Discoverers

NAPOLEÓN BACCINO PONCE DE LEÓN

TRANSLATED FROM SPANISH BY NICK CAISTOR

PICADOR

First published 1994 by Harcourt Brace & Company, New York

This edition published 1997 by Picador
an imprint of Macmillan Publishers Ltd
25 Eccleston Place, London SW1W 9NF
and Basingstoke

Associated companies throughout the world

ISBN 0 330 32822 0

Copyright © Napoleón Baccino Ponce de León 1990
English translation copyright © Harcourt Brace & Company 1994

Originally published in Spanish 1990 by Editorial Seix Baraal, S. A., Barcelona

The right of Napoleón Baccino Ponce de León to be identified
as the author of this work has been asserted by them in accordance
with the Copyright, Designs and Patents Act 1988.

3 5 7 9 8 6 4 2

A CIP catalogue record for this book is available
from the British Library.

Printed and bound in Great Britain by
Mackays of Chatham plc, Chatham, Kent

PART I

In the year of our Lord Jesus Christ fifteen hundred and nineteen, I, Juanillo Ponce, native of Bustillo del Páramo in the kingdom of León, accompanied my master Don Juan to his estates at Monturque, near Córdoba, that faithless city. And since fate decreed that this noble lord, the most kind and generous master imaginable, whom God grant a place in purgatory (lust being a minor sin), should die a few weeks later in the arms of love (as one might say), I resolved to press on to Sevilla to ply my trade as a jester, and, if possible, to try my luck in the New Indies recently discovered by the great Admiral. While I was in that noble city of your Highness's realm, using my wiles to entertain the seafaring rabble for nothing more than a crust of bread, I learnt that an expedition was being fitted out for the Spice Islands, and I set my mind on joining it.

To my misfortune, I presented myself at the Colonies' Office, where I demonstrated my wit and skill to the officials charged with taking on men for the expedition. After much laughter and boisterous merriment at my recounting of past exploits, they agreed to hire me as jester of the fleet. At the same time, they warned me that the fleet's course and final destination was a secret that I should learn all in good time.

I found myself in such great need, having had only scraps to eat since the death of my master, and being obliged to sleep with the stars for roof and the ground for a pillow, that in return for money in the hand I promised not to press them for any further details, convinced as I was that we were headed for a place that would make us all rich.

How could I have imagined, Sire, the black fate that was in store for us? It is truly said that need has the face of a heretic, and although I am as Christian as any man—apart, that is, from the little slice of my foreskin thrown to the dogs on the seventh day after my birth, which no vows can ever replace—I was at that moment in the grip of a necessity felt by all the faithful, including any prince or pope . . . that is, to fill my belly from time to time, so I felt well satisfied with what your officials gave me, and drove all doubts from my mind. .

And at once I set about spending all I had earned from selling my soul to the Devil—because the man your Majesty appointed as our Captain General was the very devil, even if less of one than the others, in particular the man who, with your Highness's consent, was to usurp all his glory. Thanks to the money I received and to my own talents, I managed to survive in the city of Sevilla until that day, August the tenth in the year fifteen hundred and nineteen, when I embarked with the others on board the *Trinidad* for that fateful voyage round the entire world.

Now that the hounds of need are clamoring round me yet again in my old age, and I am no longer able to raise laughter with my arts—for who wants to employ a jester who has reached the sad tail-end of life?—I made up my mind that before I died I would acquaint your Majesty with the many wonders and hardships we saw and suffered throughout that journey, the great amount of pain and hunger we had to endure, as well as the myriad marvels and joys we experienced, so that in your noble retreat your Highness might learn of and reflect on the way our princes' ambitions and caprices affect the destinies of those of us who stumble blindly through life at the whim of powerful men.

If the precise and truthful account of all our misfortunes—an account which your own chronicler Pedro Mártir de Anglería completely distorted with the sole aim of glorifying your Imperial Majesty, and which that wise gentleman from Venice Antonio de Pigafetta silenced or amended for the same reason—should perchance touch your Majesty's heart, may it please him to bear in mind that in his native village of Bustillo del Páramo, your Juanillo is now forced to live in abject poverty, when once, as jester to the great fleet of the Moluccas, he contributed as much to that enterprise as our Captain General did with his obduracy.

And perhaps this might lead your Highness to intercede before your son, our beloved Felipe, so that he restores the pension I was robbed of, simply for telling nothing but the truth in the villages and squares of our country.

Such an act would not only make reparation for the many ills caused by your decision to send that fleet to the Spice Islands, but would also do justice to this our noble profession of making people laugh, forgetting our own sorrows in order to help soothe those of others. What could be more useful in this world than a Francesillo, a Perico, or your humble servant Juanillo, by profession jester?

ALL THE rumors that had spread through the squares and taverns of Sevilla were suddenly silenced; all the angry gossip against your Imperial Majesty died away in awe at the sight of the huge sails unfurling in the breeze, casual as a dream.

Everything appeared to stand still for a moment. The river stopped in its flow, the sun in its climb up the heavens, the clouds as they drifted by. Birds hung suspended in the calm sky. On the far bank, a shepherd and his flock looked like porcelain figures.

The voices faded out one by one; nobody moved. Time seemed to have been brought to a halt, and we might all have stood there transfixed for an eternity had an artillery salvo not broken the spell.

The mighty roar of the *Trinidad*'s cannon rolled through Sevilla's streets and squares, then echoed into the distance, conveying the news of our departure to the remotest villages. Its thunderclap startled the doves, who flew off in terror from every courtyard and tower in the city.

Slowly the dock came to life again. Everything recovered its essence in the flux of time, and started to slip away from us.

Tearful mothers, wives already lonely, astonished infants, indifferent onlookers. The gleaming towers with your Majesty's flags fluttering above them: all began to slip away.

The great cathedral, the fortresses, the city walls, its hundred towers and spires, all the red tiles of Sevilla fell behind us.

Everything began to move, to glide away, while we, motionless, allowed our world to be stolen from us.

That morning, no one among us could be sure where all those things falling away from us were headed.

A second cannonade, from the *San Antonio* this time, was the signal that the whole fleet had left berth. Almost simultaneously, a peal of bells from all the city's churches jangled the air with their wild clanging.

Now the river slid beneath the ship; the earth turned.

Sevilla had gone, replaced by a succession of empty fields, with now and then a low hill. Dusty olive groves. Plowed earth. Solitary palm trees swaying here and there in the breeze. More villages.

San Juan de Alfarache, fertile in vines, appeared on the starboard bow.

It looked deserted, apart from a few children perched on the ruins of an old Moorish bridge, fishing. As the ships passed, the children dropped their rods and ran to the top of one of the buttresses to wave. They stood there until the last of our five ships had gone past, then rushed back to their lines. We could see them larking about, laughing, without a care in the world.

In the vineyards outside the village, men with huge baskets on their backs straightened for a moment to watch us go by. Three youngsters treading grapes in a vat next to a wooden shed raised their arms in greeting, without pausing in their work.

Women among the rows of vines popped up one by one, their heads turned to the river; a moment later their black figures with white headscarves, like a flock of birds on plowed furrows, bent again to the grapevines.

Then open fields again, dotted with cattle, and soon the white village of Gelves, again on the starboard bank. The river shallows forced us so close to the village we could almost touch its walls, sniff the fragrance filling its cool rooms, its wardrobes.

Our sails stirred the calm air; their shadow flitted across the walls, darkened every room.

The ships seemed to be gliding along the dusty main street of the village lined with low white houses and their empty flowerpots. Yet no one was outside to greet our passage, apart from a group of old men dozing in the sun beside a stockyard wall.

An old woman in black was shelling beans, piling them in her lap, letting the pods drop into a basket at her feet. She followed the ships with her gaze for a while, her hands continuing mechanically with their task . . .

Two more old men, seated at a chessboard, one wearing a homespun woolen cap, the other a battered leather hat. A third man was leaning against the wall. None of them seemed aware of the presence of five ships sailing past only a few feet from where they were taking their ease.

If we had stretched out our arms we could almost have touched them. Even then we would have made no impression on their enclosed, shut-off world.

Then white Gelves was lost round a bend in the river.

The wind puffed out our sails, the current caught our hulls, and images of villages and fields rushed by as swiftly as in a dream.

We passed Coria, village of doves, before anyone living there had time to peer out at us. Only the loud cooing of the doves, the river making for the sea, the black ships gliding on like moving shadows in the bright sunlight.

Next came shady La Puebla, peeping timidly through its willows and poplars at the junction of the Repudio and the main river. A bounding dog barked furiously at the ships; a young man in a tavern doorway stared at the fleet going by, then at the empty river.

Further downstream we passed fields of dusty red earth, a plowman following his oxen. A grove of slender palm trees swaying in the breeze. A shepherd, who waved at us.

Now the river was full of twists and turns, winding between

low hills and olive groves. Windy Trebujera showed in the distance, surrounded by salt flats.

The wind carried our shipboard smells out over the deserted countryside. The ships smelled of freshly scrubbed wood, tar, hempen ropes, sail canvas, the new bronze of our fittings, the leather protecting the masts.

Our crammed holds smelled of sacks of flour, wineskins, the cheeses filling the racks and already turning rancid, sides of bacon and hams hanging from the beams, strings of garlic and onions nailed to the blackened ribs of our hulls, honey, vinegar, oil and lard.

The ships were also redolent with our fantasies. Fantasies of cloves and cinnamon. Of islands waiting to be discovered. Of salt seas to be conquered. And rancid dreams, the plagues and hungers that destroy them.

Somehow this fetid stench seemed to have preceded us to Sanlúcar, where the first stage of our journey ended.

I AM duty-bound to inform your Majesty that we spent twenty-nine days in that stinking port of your realm without a single letter, message or emissary arriving at our ships to raise our spirits or answer any of the thousand questions we were beginning to ask ourselves.

We had set sail from Sevilla without our captains, and now, a whole month later, they still had not appeared to take command of the fleet. Sun and rain bleached the blackened timbers; the weeks of waiting corroded our dreams, yet not a single person, not one relative or friend, nobody from the town paid us the slightest attention.

It was as if our ships were adrift on some unknown sea, without ever having left the docks of Sanlúcar.

It was as if we were long since dead, or else complete strangers in that place. Foreigners. As if we had some dreadful disease they were all afraid of catching. That is how the people of Sanlúcar regarded us, and their disdain became a real torture. They placed leper warning bells around the neck of each and every one of the heroes your chronicler Pedro Mártir de Anglería has described, so they would not mistake us for any of the other seafarers wandering the streets and taverns of your royal city. The moment we, Don Fernando's men, crossed the threshold of an inn, a net of silence would drop over us. In the markets, we paid three times more than anyone else for the rottenest red meat or the most shriveled vegetables. In the brothels, none of the women were ever available for us, although we could see them waiting, out in the courtyards, languid and bored, for nonexistent clients. Not even the dogs came near our ships; they turned their noses up at our scraps.

During those weeks that we waited, I often wondered what singled us out from the other strangers roaming Sanlúcar. It was only months later, Sire, that I hit upon the answer.

We were infected, it was true, and by a disease far worse than the plague or leprosy; we were infected by our dreams. And the others were afraid they would catch the sickness.

They knew that the germ of dreams can spread as quickly as the plague. They knew it can be caught from cups and plates. That it clings to sheets. That it sticks to hands. That it infects any eyes that glimpse it, any mouth that kisses it, any ears that hear it, so that the eyes no longer see, the ears no longer hear, the mouth utters nothing but lies.

Yet had this epidemic not already spread to the four corners of your kingdom? Could it be said that we were the only ones infected? The only ones hoodwinked by a proclamation that promised gold and spices, but made no mention of where the fleet was bound or how long the adventure was to last?

Were there not over two hundred and fifty of us who had rushed to sign up for that mad undertaking? Who willingly agreed to set sail into the unknown, to a destination shrouded in secrecy? Because in all truth, what did the Moluccas mean to us? Nothing more than a name. A foreign name that each of us molded to his own dreams, bewitched by its exotic sound without regard for its precise meaning, as if we already foresaw that in Portuguese this word could only mean "crazy," which is what we all were.

But were we any crazier than our captains? What need did

those worthy gentlemen have of going in search of yet more gold? Did they have the faintest notion where they were leading their men? Did the captains know the course they were setting for the fleet?

Did your Highness know? Was your Highness aware of where he was dispatching us all?

If men of such noble lineage, the richest and most powerful in all Europe, were themselves infected with this sickness that neither priests nor barbers could cure, if the bishop of Burgos, who had inveighed against Cristóbal Colón, now bestowed his blessing on our venture, how could we be expected to resist?

We were mad, yes, just as Ruy Faleiro and our Captain General, Don Fernando, had always been, just as you yourself were, your Imperial Majesty, and the high officials at the Colonies' Office, and Bishop Fonseca, and Don Cristobão de Haro, who financed the expedition.

Mad like the men who caulked the ships, or those who filled them with more provisions and trinkets than any other fleet before us. Mad like the women who sewed the sails with loving fingers, the smiths who forged the bronze of all our fittings, the carpenters who shaped our masts while neighbors looked on in awe and children frolicked around them. And what about all those left behind by a son, a father, a husband or a friend? Did they have the slightest idea what they were part of? Did the woodcutter know, when he felled the lofty oaks that gave birth to our black ships? Did the Jewish women know, as they set about rolling the huge candles, laughing and chanting their prayers? Did the blacksmith in his ruddy darkness have any idea of the destiny awaiting all the burnished bronze hoops piling up in his yard? Could the carpenter imagine that the mast he was planing out in the street would one day cleave through distant skies, until a storm brought it low and left it to wash up onto some uncharted beach, rotting in the sun and becoming home to all kinds of vermin? Did the newlywed bride perfuming her fresh linen with quinces know whether she would ever see her husband again?

In my humble opinion, not even Don Fernando himself

knew where we were headed, however much he tried to fool everyone by claiming he was keeping the secret quiet for reasons of security.

And yet, although so many of us felt this way, we stayed aboard ship waiting for our captains, eager to unfurl our sails in the wind, caring naught for reasons, portents or warning signs.

Not even that absurd, unexplained delay could discourage us, though not all of us were the bravest of the brave (I myself, I must confess, have been scared of my own shadow since I was a little boy). There were many more who felt the same as your Juanillo, especially since we had reasons to spare for going around cringing like whipped curs, and new concerns pressed in on us day after day. Yet none of this was enough to quench the force of the crazy dreams driving us on. Nothing could have. But as I have told you, Sire, those were uneasy days—rumors gripped the fleet and held it in their sway, without regard for rank or station.

The name on everyone's lips was Ruy Faleiro. It was he who had devised our destiny and that of our ships and the ports we were to call at, the seas we were to cross. He traced it all in fine lines that interwove to form strange drawings, transforming everything into tiny numbers and complicated formulae that only he could decipher. And yet it was constantly rumored that this Portuguese cosmographer, the inventor of our course, the man responsible for all our navigation charts, would not be setting sail with us. Some claimed Faleiro was an astrologer, a person adept at calling up spirits, and that through the art of black magic one of these familiars had shown him the tragic destiny in store for the fleet, which was why he had feigned madness to avoid leaving on the voyage with us.

On the other hand, Master Morales, the fleet's surgeon, insisted that Faleiro had been crazy from the outset. He said he heard it from a trollop who slept with a high-ranking official at the Colonies' Office to earn some money, and did the same with Morales for pleasure. The trollop claimed that the official said that the cosmographer had lost his reason three years earlier when his little four-year-old daughter suddenly died. Morales said the official told the trollop that Faleiro had such a high-strung inquiring mind that, either because of this cruel blow or by the will of God, he had been cast down into the depths of madness ever since. And indeed, Faleiro had shown so patently that he was not in his right mind that you, Sire, named Don Juan de Cartagena to replace him as second-in-command of the fleet. On learning of this, Ruy Faleiro installed himself in the Colonies' Office in Sevilla and refused to move until he was restored to his post. And Morales said the trollop said the royal official said it was a pathetic sight on our day of departure to see him pacing up and down the courtyard, which until the night before had provided a rowdy shelter for adventurers from the four corners of Europe, but which now lay deserted and silent, littered with scraps of food and bits of paper that the wind pushed to and fro, rustling like dry leaves. Wrapped in the black cape he always wore as a token of mourning, Faleiro shuffled across the vast empty yard, rousing himself at the cannonades from the ships to proffer dire curses against the traitor Don Fernando and all those who had taken advantage of his knowledge for their own benefit, and calling down the blackest of fates on every one of them.

Such were the rumors concerning Ruy Faleiro, and though at that time they were no more than gossip, our captains' delay in arriving and the lack of any firm news were sure signs that something untoward was happening. And when the captains finally did appear, the cosmographer was not among them, though the whole venture still relied on his plans and calculations, since Don Fernando and you yourself, Sire, judged them to be accurate.

The condition of our ships also gave rise to all kinds of tales. Martín the Cooper, an old seadog who had accompanied the great Admiral on two of his journeys, claimed that the ships Cristobão de Haro had equipped were old galleons which had been refitted. He swore the *Santiago* was one of the ones the Pinzón brothers had used. That the ribs of the *Trinidad* were as soft as butter. That a walnut shell was more solid than the *Concepción*'s hull. That the *Victoria*'s rigging was less trustworthy than a woman's promises. That the masts of the *San Antonio* would come crashing down with the first sea breeze.

But nothing fires men's imaginations, feeding both fears and hopes, like the idea of the unknown.

So there was much talk of the hyperboreal zone where, according to the all-knowing Aristotle, it never rains and is so hot that the waters of the sea boil, steaming ships' planks until the hulls fall apart. There were tall tales of dreadful sea monsters that rise up from the steaming waters south of the Cape of Good Hope to trap and crush ships as if they were no more than pieces of sugar. And talk of the creatures of the antipodes, who live with their heads underneath their bodies. Of men who have one eye in the middle of their forehead, with which they can see the future. Of others with an eye at the back of their neck to see the past, who are slaves to the former. Of women with the heads of sows, and others with mares' nipples who roam the jungles driving all explorers wild with their exquisite bodies and virgins' faces. Tales, too, of the men-plants who have a single foot rooted in the ground so that they cannot move, and who are born and die at the mercy of sun and rain. And of course there are also women with reptiles' bodies, who slither along like snakes; men who bark instead of speaking; children who govern empires and treat their elders as if they were children; and also—why not?—passionate Amazons with a single breast who compel men to satisfy their desires; queens in ivory and jade palaces who conceal their nakedness with gold dust; princesses who protect their virtue behind a fine mesh of diamonds, their delicate sex gleaming there, untouchable. And last but not least, in the Spice Islands, where it is said we are heading, there are cloves, pepper, saffron and cinnamon to make us rich on our return, to bring us titles, government appointments, countless honors.

But your Majesty must not think it was only the common seamen who spent their time in this kind of gossip, where their dreams and fears merged. The officers on board were equally full of doubts—and none more so than the man whom a fickle destiny turned into the person who usurped the glory reserved for my master Don Fernando. Although you will not believe it, during those days that swarthy little man, whom I have no need to name since all the honors and gifts you have bestowed on him show that you know him only too well, was one of the expedition's bitterest opponents. That clown told all and sundry that the geatest Spanish fleet ever assembled to sail for the Indies was nothing more than a costly plaything for the powerful. He even dared tar your loyal servant Aranda, Cristobão de Haro and Bishop Fonseca with the same brush. And, he said, who were we with our ridiculous dreams and childish fears but puppets on invisible strings, governed by the whims of a few crazy men seeking to please their rich masters so that these latter could have pepper on their tables to add savor to their meat, and cloves and cinnamon to spice their wine, while all we would get to drink would be water that stank to high heaven as we roamed lifeless seas and deserted lands until we finally reached the Spice Islands, where they would do away with us. Hunger and perils would be their allies, he said. They were not interested in bringing men back to their homes because, once they had achieved their goal, each one of us would be a hindrance, a dead weight for ships built only to carry cargoes of cloves and cinnamon.

So throughout the month we waited in Sanlúcar, left to our uncertain destiny by the captains, our hopes and fears sprouted like mushrooms inside us. They bred like rats, swarming all over our ships, climbing the rigging, crawling into the holds, and at night sneaking into the forecastle where we were all pretending to sleep.

IN VAIN did your humble Juanillo attempt to keep everyone happy with his songs, his jokes and a thousand tricks which had always worked before, but which he was destined to see fail time and again during our expedition. As the days went by in Sanlúcar, it became harder and harder to raise a smile from any of those men weighed down by the uncertainty of a future none of them could clearly discern.

Twelve sensible men deserted under cover of night, itself less dark than our doubts. Twelve men who succeeded in returning to their homes, to the land where they were born. Twelve brave men, say I, who had the sense to renounce their dreams while they still had time.

The rest of us stayed, awaiting the arrival of our captains. And when they finally did arrive, we were so dazzled by the pomp of their armor and their banners that not one of us had the courage to desert.

A THICK cloud of dust in the distance heralded the arrival of the captains.

As they rode through the sunbaked hills, they looked like insects driven on by an unknown force. Their armor flashed in the sun. Their lances and pennants were like antennae waving in the dust. Men and their mounts made an indistinguishable whole, with arms and horses' legs advancing together in formation. Overwhelmed by the desolate landscape, the column of men looked minute.

Two hundred and thirty-seven men, weapons at the ready and wearing helmets despite the intense heat, were drawn up on either side of the town bridge to greet them. Tension was etched on every face. Our impatience only seemed to increase the sun's fury on our heads. Weapons hung even heavier on our weary shoulders and backs. Our feet ached. Our hands were scorched.

The road disappeared behind a bare hill. The column vanished. The blinding light made the stark landscape even more forlorn.

After a few minutes, which seemed like centuries, the column came into view again at the crest of the final hill. They were scarcely a hundred yards from us now, and we could clearly make out their features.

At their head, proud against the white sky, came Don Fernando, a truly godlike figure. His clashing armor, the green velvet cape around his shoulders, the mighty haunches of his steed, all gave him an inhuman, supernatural air. His head peered out from its iron shell. One hand in a chain mail gauntlet directed the column behind him.

Level with him, four horsemen whose shields and lances bore the Cartagena family's golden phoenix on a purpure ground transported the litter in which the Inspector General of the fleet was carried. Behind heavy velvet curtains fringed with gold we could glimpse the motionless Don Juan. His breastplate was covered with a fine shirt of Flanders lace decorated with the cross of Santiago. Despite the rigors of the march to the port, there was no sign of fatigue on his face, no trace of dust on his clothes.

Behind Magellan rode Gaspar de Quesada the Fair, his legs sheathed in iron but his chest bare beneath the straps of his weapons. Bronzed by the sun, gleaming with sweat, he seemed carved from the finest wood of the Orient. From nearby, he looked like a Greek warrior; from afar, he seemed like a noble tree at the height of its strength. At the crest of the hill he turned his childlike face back to seek out his page in the midst of the column: Luis del Molino, dressed all in black, followed his master like a dark shadow.

One of the first pennants to breast the hill was that of the diminutive, astute Juan Serrano, his face concealed beneath a broad-brimmed hat glittering with hawk-bells.

At a sign from Don Fernando, the column halted. Among the waving lances and pennants of his escort, we could make out the figure of Don Luis de Mendoza, fragile in appearance but thunderous of voice.

The column was at a standstill. The air, too, seemed motionless; the silence was unbroken. From within his iron shell, the Captain General surveyed the squat houses of the town and, in the port beyond, the five black ships.

Then they started down the hill toward the docks. The castle of Medina-Sidonia cast its vast shadow over this stretch of their march, dulling the gleam of their weapons and suits of armor, their harnesses, their steeds' sweating flanks. But this relief for our weary eyes lasted only a moment. They soon reemerged into the sunlight, now only a few yards from the double line we had formed.

All at once the horses' hooves began to thunder across the paving stones of the bridge. The calm of the morning air was shattered, filled with the smell of sweat, dust, iron, horses. The captains went by, almost brushing against us. Our eyes could scarcely take in the thousand details flashing past: a green, frothy bridle, the shaft of a lance stained wet by a sweating hand, a glittering sword pommel, an ironclad knee, another hand clutching a saddle, smooth, shiny haunches, a well-turned hoof. Nor could our ears register all the competing layers of sound: the clatter of hooves, the creaking of harnesses, the clinking of the soldiers' coats of mail, the tinkling of Juan Serrano's hawk-bells, the clash of metals, the rustling of silks, the soft swish of velvets, the snorting of horses and the voices of the men.

I stood rooted to the spot beside one of the bridgeheads, striving to glean from the captains' faces some sign of what destiny awaited us. I could tell nothing from Don Fernando's harsh, expressionless features as he passed arrogantly by me, leaving in his wake a piercing smell of iron that slowly permeated the overcharged morning air. Beside him rode Juan Serrano, his eyes hidden beneath his hat brim, as if protected by the enchantment of the hawk-bells adorning it. He stared straight into our eyes, but we could not return his gaze. Don Juan de Cartagena nodded briefly and graciously on all sides. A scent of Oriental perfume swathed his litter, the only feminine touch among all the sharp, acrid odors. His smile was enchanting too, a mixture of tenderness and cynicism. Gaspar de Quesada's rough-hewn, childish features breathed confidence into the watching crews. Further back, I felt a strange sense of pity as I caught the shy hazel eyes of Luis de Mendoza.

The column made its way between the first houses of Sanlúcar. The streets were deserted. Behind doors left ajar, the townspeople spied on the passing riders. Beyond the thin shafts of cold white light projected into the gloomy interiors, we could dimly make out furtive, deer-like eyes. Silent behind screens, the women of the town watched the procession of these adventurers whom they both feared and admired, so different from their own husbands, more like gods than men. As the column trotted past, old women in black crossed themselves and muttered prayers. The sound of flashing hooves reverberated through dark, silent rooms. As Don Fernando's eyes roved from door to door, his expression became even colder. Serrano rode beside him, glancing anxiously at the shuttered balconies. Juan de Cartagena's smile froze on his lips.

BEHIND OUR backs, a new and thicker dust cloud swirled across the plain toward the bridge. The quiet was shattered again, this time by a furious cacophony of mooing, bleating, squawking and the thud of animals' hooves across the bridge.

A sudden smell of fresh dung invaded Sanlúcar. Its life as a port was interrupted; freed from the pervasive stench of the sea, the whole town smelt like a huge stable, its identity submerged beneath this invasion of animals and plants.

Shouting and galloping furiously from side to side, the horsemen tried to control the shapeless mass that threatened to overflow the path like a river in flood.

Ah, your Highness! If only you could have seen how the poor, motherly cows bumped clumsily against the bridge as the dogs snapped at them, crashing into the marble posts in their terrified flight. If only you could have seen how the panic-stricken sheep rushed hither and thither in a huge flock, some instinct telling them they must stay together even though they had no idea what was going on. In their midst, a sow with sagging teats threshed wildly about, searching for her litter. Herdsmen and animals all rushed blindly on, as if some obscure force were driving them toward the bridge. Behind them, the carts lumbered onto the scene. One of them was full of white hens, their nervous heads darting between the bars of the cages. Then more carts carrying orange and lemon trees and fully grown olive bushes planted in barrels. And cabbages and other vegetables growing in boxes. And earth. A black, crumbling earth that my master had ordered brought from the northern woods near the Portuguese border.

This was to be the floating kitchen garden that the Captain General hoped would ward off the terrible effects of scurvy. All the greenery added an outlandish note to the landscape parched by drought.

Solitary, taciturn at the head of this immense column, Don Fernando made his way aboard ship.

IT TOOK us until well into the evening to find room for all the animals and plants on the ships, which my master's plans had converted into veritable Noah's arks. Even then, the loading was not complete until three days later, when a long barge floated down the river, giving off a strange glow. As soon as the lookouts spied it, many of us climbed the rigging to watch as the mysterious boat drew near. The light coming from this low, broad craft was so dazzling that we were unable to discover its secret until it drew up in the shadow of our flagship. Then, finally, we saw that the reason was its cargo, and the reflection of the sun's rays on it: heaped in the barge were thousands of mirrors of all shapes and sizes, different colored glass and crystal beads, twenty thousand hawk-bells in three sizes, two thousand tin bracelets and two thousand bronze ones, ten thousand fish-hooks and four hundred dozen German knives, plus fifty dozen pairs of scissors, two hundred colored caps, and countless lengths of woolen cloth. All this merchandise was to be used for barter or to pay any ransom.

Yes, this was to be our currency, Sire, in the lands we were setting out to discover. These were the gifts our civilization was offering, in exchange for which we would receive the most precious treasures nature had bestowed on the other peoples of this earth. And the strangest thing was that these worthless hand mirrors and hawk-bells piled high in the barge did completely turn the heads of those people. The glass beads, the bolts of garishly colored cloth for their kings, soon came to seem more powerful than their gods, their wise men, their traditions. Any single one of the thousands of bells we took with us in our holds became worth more than a man's life; whole villages were sold to us for a handful of them.

If you had witnessed this, your Majesty, you would have agreed with my master when he said that after our voyage the world would never be the same again. That is what he told us once the loading was complete, when he finally announced the start of what he called "the greatest undertaking ever known to man."

With these words Don Fernando put an end to the anxious twenty-nine days we had been waiting since we left Sevilla.

The sun and rain had dried out the black timbers; our noblest dreams were beginning to rot like the cheeses in our holds, and yet every one of those two hundred and thirty-seven men was overjoyed because the fleet was finally about to set sail.

And set sail we did. On the morning of September 20, 1519, we weighed anchor.

The day dawned tensely, with a leaden sky and a steel-colored sea. I can remember an almost unearthly silence, despite the profusion of voices in many different languages. The boatswains shouted orders, and the men swarmed over the ships like insects; the caged birds fluttered desperately against their bars; the animals were in an uproar, and yet my ears failed to register any noise. It all seemed to be taking place in some old engraving, and the uniform grayness of all objects under the overcast skies made the similarity all the more striking. Everything was gray that morning; only slight differences of shade made one thing distinguishable from another. The ships looked like shadows as they glided out of the bay on a sea which, though apparently asleep, was only biding its time, lurking like a wild beast in ambush.

There was no wind in the narrow channel so the ships had to be towed out to the open sea by rowboats. Perhaps because they were so heavily laden, the five ships seemed reluctant to leave the port, and we struggled to get them underway.

With their sails furled, the riggings looked as bare and sad as a forest in winter. The masts and yards formed a countless succession of crosses in the sky above the fleet.

Once the five ships were outside the bay, the sails were set at last. No longer gleaming white as they had been when we set off from Sevilla, they were gray and drooped in the absence of any breeze. Yet, little by little, the fleet slowly began to move by its own efforts.

Then a sudden squall blew up. Black clouds raced across the sky, and waves whipped up around the ships. The masts began to creak, bending like reeds with the force of the wind. The mainyards groaned and swiveled wildly in their hinges. Some dried-out ropes snapped as the sails billowed out, recovering their whiteness. Driven on by the wind, the ships' prows dipped beneath the waves, then emerged triumphantly a moment later, water streaming from the decks.

We all looked back at the coastline which the careering ships were rapidly leaving astern. The huge stone bulk of the duke's palace stood out black against the blue-gray sky. In the distance behind it, we could barely tell where the sky began and the hills ended, covered as they were by clouds that hung about them like shreds of dirty cotton. Down by the shoreline, the houses of Sanlúcar seemed lost and threatened by the somber landscape. There were only a few curious townspeople watching as we left from the deserted docks; although they had so cruelly rejected us, I think everyone on board was beginning to miss their presence. To envy them as well, because that inhospitable town suddenly seemed to us, launched on the immensity of the ocean, like the safest and warmest of lairs. A lair for wild animals, for we were like animals torn by a blind, irresistible force from the natural world we belonged in.

By midmorning we had lost sight of land. The fury of the wind was so great we had to take in the sails and heave to. Even so, the waves drove us forward on the course Don Fernando had set. The wind blew from astern so strongly that the ships seemed to be soaring in flight like royal eagles.

"We will never return," a voice beside me murmured. "Never."

With the passing of the years, I myself have come to the conclusion that in truth our voyage was one from which there was no return. But be that as it may, let your Majesty now cleanse his nostrils of the gentle perfumes of the silks and velvets of his court, and breathe instead the incomparable tang of the overpowering salt sea air which seeps into everything. Let your Majesty Don Carlos close his eyes to the powdered secretaries, the pink-cheeked ladies who grace the Italian marbles and Oriental carpets of his palaces, and in their place fill his mind's eye with the image of five black ships hurtling toward the edge of the known world and beyond. Let the smarting salt and the roar of the waves fill his ears; may he even experience in his own guts the unforgettable sensation of seasickness. And if it should please him, let him this once not add cinnamon or cloves to his wine, pepper to his meat, saffron to his pheasant stew, or mint or ginger or . . .

PART II

NEXT, Sire, you will find us drifting somewhere along the equinoctial line on a forest of waterlogged oaks.

What a strange enterprise is this, your Captain General's, which spares neither ancient trees nor even the earth of Spain that gave birth to them.

Your Majesty has condemned more than a thousand lofty, strong oaks to rot in the incessant rain that falls in this part of the boundless ocean.

Vast amounts of rich earth, nourished by other rains, other suns, and generations of fallen leaves and centuries-old bones, have been torn from their natural surroundings by this crazy scheme and set adrift on the sea.

Our fleet is like a real island full of oaks that will never send forth shoots again (or perhaps they will), lost in the midst of this indifferent sea that cares nothing for our dreams.

The *Trinidad* contains the best of the oak forest of Corpes, its beams enclosing thousands of years of frustrations and hopes.

They recover their memory and talk without speaking of their history in this strange quiet, this ancestral humidity, this warm mixture of marine and plant vapors. Trapped between planks made from the branches that gave them life and now constrain them in a blackened surface wounded by nails, bolts, oakum and tar, the rails and the keel talk as they live out their last moments, unable to accept final death. They talk of men like wild beasts stretched out in the shade of their first foliage, men who at night cowered like birds in their nests, but who during the day became fierce hunters armed with stones. The ribs of the *Trinidad* remember other men who arrived one day wearing shining bronze and armed with sharp metals that even the now seasoned timber of the Corpes forest could not withstand; men who wore red plumes on their eagle-like heads, and who spoke a strange, musical tongue that sounded like the rustle of leaves in a breeze. There were no women with them, no children, no dogs. One night was all they spent in the forest, and they were not afraid. These were the first men without fear the oaks had known, and they in their turn began to be afraid. So they grew stronger and stronger; they toughened their wood so that the metal these fearless man brought could not cut into them. Their efforts were useless. The men kept coming back with weapons that were always too sharp for the oaks, however hard they had grown. Many of the trees were toppled; others were burned. And the men without fear built the houses they spent the night in from the wood of these oaks.

Yet the Corpes forest still grew. To protect itself from cattle and to hide from men it became thicker and thicker. As it grew and flourished, each tree thought itself safe hidden among the others: yet all of them together were merely increasing the size of the forest until one day it would catch the attention of the men who built the *Trinidad*. But before that day when the wood began its transformation into an island, the support for our unfortunate destinies, countless suns and rains passed. Many men and women came and went, like the two young girls whom the counts of Carrión deflowered at the foot of what is now our mainmast. The two girls lay there all night, perishing with cold, their clothes in tatters, robbed of the jewels of their honor, all their hopes and dreams shattered.

The huge trunk of the mainmast protected the two girls, who themselves were the origin of a tree of kings. The next morning Alvar Fáñez appeared. In his wrath at the Carrión family for the outrage they had committed against his cousins, he drew a cross in the trunk of the tree with his sword, and swore his vengeance by it.

That afternoon, wounded by the Spaniard's sword, the oak multiplied. When it had produced more than a thousand full-sized trees, and countless smaller ones, your Imperial Majesty cast it into the sea, to rot along with its men and its rats, its memories of the earth, the rain and the sun; its nostalgia for leaves, birds and animals.

The *Trinidad*'s mainmast still bears the mark of Alvar Fáñez's anger, as well as the scent of the rich perfumes Ximena wore when she bade her daughters farewell in the fortresses of Valencia. Forever impregnating our mainmast, they resist the smell of resin and the salt that effaces and rubs out the past.

But why talk only of the trees, when the men themselves have roots that go back many years into our land? Yet here you have them, your Majesty, floating on what were once strong oaks and are now fragile timbers, waiting in vain for a wind to drive them on and for a proper course to follow.

WE HAD left the Canaries behind us and were steering down the coast of that fantastical world known as Africa when we were surprised by a dead calm. For almost sixty days the ships were stuck in a sea that was as thick as mortar.

The men took this as a sign or premonition, as if the gods were opposed to our foolhardy venture. Fear and discontent grew day by day, fueling senseless plans for mutiny. The uneasy calm bred tragic consequences.

Juan de Cartagena, cousin and foster brother to the all-powerful bishop of Burgos, was the most troublesome. The captain of the *San Antonio* was not only second-in-command of the fleet but also Inspector General for the Colonies' Office. As such, he demanded to know what the Captain General's plans were. Above all, he wanted to know why we were plying down the coast of Africa if our intention was to head west across the Atlantic.

But my master remained deaf to all his demands. He sent

his envoys packing, and refused to disclose his intentions. His attitude only served to further exasperate the Spanish captains, who had been suspicious of him from the start.

Although the black bulk of the *San Antonio* stayed with the rest of the fleet, Don Juan openly defied Magellan's authority. At dawn, when each ship should have hoisted flags with the Captain General's colors, the *San Antonio* showed only those of your Imperial Majesty.

At night, the *San Antonio* did not show the stern lights as it should have according to the instructions given before the fleet left Sanlúcar, which stated that each ship was to kindle a certain number of lanterns corresponding to its tonnage. In this way, Don Fernando hoped to keep the fleet together and to know the exact position of each vessel, since he was afraid there would be plotting against him.

Don Juan's ship was the largest, and so was supposed to light five lanterns at nightfall. But since we had been stranded in these lifeless waters, Don Fernando had been unable to tell where the *San Antonio* lay at night, and woke each morning with the secret fear of finding it gone.

In the early hours of the morning, when for some unknown reason the sea began to stir and an occasional wave moved beneath the *Trinidad*'s hull, Don Fernando was roused from his sleep and sat watching in the darkness until dawn arrived. He gazed expectantly up at the sky and, as the stars began to fade, left his cabin and went up on deck to wait for the first glimmerings of light that would permit him to see exactly where the *San Antonio* was. He even spent entire nights trying to guess its position by means of the stars its masts blocked out, but there were four ships around the *Trinidad* and it was impossible to tell for sure which was which, except perhaps for the *Concepción*. Gaspar de Quesada's ship gave off a powerful aroma of fertile earth, shady trees, a well-watered sunny garden. This smell attracted many birds which, thinking it an island, settled in its rigging and made their nests there.

Don Fernando's fears lessened on moonlit nights because then he could make out the silhouette of the other ships on the polished surface of the waters. When the moon was high in the sky, they looked as though they were carved in stone; when its red disc first appeared over the horizon, it seemed they were made of ivory. They were like objects endowed with a secret meaning that Don Fernando could not grasp; he spent hour after hour staring at them, as though trying to discover it.

DURING MANY of those nights, also unable to sleep, I kept my master silent company. And although your servant Juanillo may be very bold, and permit himself certain liberties that his profession excuses, never once did he dare try to distract Don Fernando de Magallanes from his nightly musings.

The stillness in the air, the cloudless sky, the *Trinidad*'s gentle rocking, all created a pleasant sense of well-being in my mind. I used to enjoy trying to imagine the close but invisible presence of the African coast by the exhalations that reached the ship from there.

Some days I could make out a mountain that is called Sierra Leone, but on many others it disappeared in the mists. Its presence was more definite at night, when a slight land breeze confirmed the closeness of its vegetation. I could distinguish how its smell changed as the hours went by between the sun's setting and rising. Its perfume was strongest soon after the evening rainfall, which dampened the ever-present reek of the sea and brought out its own smell. It was like the fragrance of a passionate but contented woman; a sweet, undefinable odor that exuded from its skin, left shining by the rain. The perfume became heavier and warmer as the moon rose in the sky; by midnight it was like musk. Then, as the breeze dropped in the early hours, the coast seemed to slip further and further away. Sometimes at first light I could see the summit of the mountain, but its perfume had already been engulfed again by the terrible stink of salt water: a male, aggressive smell, as strong as that of a fighting man.

In the uncertain light of this early hour, the huge outline of the *San Antonio* seemed blacker than ever; its lengthy shadow loomed over the stern of our own ship. This was the moment for the Captain to go to sleep, without so much as wishing me good night. At the same time, life began to stir once more in the oaken innards of the *Trinidad*, identical with each passing day.

The days we waited for wind were filled with nothing but boredom. They dragged by slowly, exactly the same. Nothing happened. In the grip of inactivity, the men wandered around like ghosts, stripped of all will. No speeches or promises could lift them out of their homesick melancholy.

That was when your servant Juanillo's skills did more for their state of mind than any eloquence or passion from their captains. Your Count of the Spice Islands made up stories, for the most part equally spicy, like the story of Melibea who, after having tasted her stepfather's member between her legs and her father confessor's in her mouth, went on to caress more than one of the ladies at court to such effect that she fulfilled their wildest desires. Not content with that, your Majesty, she is said to have fallen in love with a bull, and to satisfy her lust for the animal she had an apparatus built in which she knelt on all fours covered in a heifer's hide. The bull, kept from any contact with females of his species, would charge the grotesque apparatus and thrust the burning iron of his member inside.

If, Sire, you could only have seen your noble Argonauts stretched out on their backs on the deck in the sun, their own members so erect beneath their trousers that they looked like another fleet of stout masted vessels, raised and launched by the wit of Juanillo Ponce!

They also liked to hear the tale of Duchess Rosinalda, who was besieged in her castle by King Cacavus of Hungary. Every morning as she walked the battlements she could see her men dying, and feared not only for her own inheritance but for the lives of her daughters, who had already been betrothed to the future kings of France and Hungary. She sent word to her enemy that she offered him her body in return for a treaty that would guarantee the lives of her daughters and allow her to continue to live in the land and castles that were hers. The king replied that he considered the treaty unfair, as no woman could be worth so much. Rosinalda did not dismay, but began to walk the battlements naked in full view of the Hungarian army. And so artful was she in demonstrating her charms that the besieging army was thrown into confusion. Whenever Rosinalda uncovered a breast, the fighting stopped. The men in the vanguard stood stock still as if they had been turned to stone, while those in the rear disobeyed their orders and rushed to get close to the wall. Even those in charge of guarding the attackers' camp, driven wild by the scent of Oriental perfume and milk given off by Rosinalda's breast, abandoned their posts. On other occasions, hiding her body behind a turret, she showed off her snow-white buttocks. At the sight, the Hungarians began to fight each other, causing many casualties. On the third day, the duchess gracefully lifted her red velvet skirt and impudently showed them her sex. The tuft of black hair, framed by a kind of tiara of pearls and partially veiled behind a transparent gauze glittering with diamonds and rubies, shone like the most precious of jewels. This was too much for King Cacavus: he sent word to the duchess that he would lift the siege if he might only possess her body.

That evening the king entered the castle at the head of a magnificent column. He was shown to the duchess's bedchamber, where his prize awaited him.

But Rosinalda was a virtuous woman who had sworn to be faithful to her husband, a Crusader away in Jerusalem; and she intended to keep her vow. So she daubed chicken's flesh under her breasts, smeared her sex with mutton fat, and then put on her finest attire. In her apricot robe, she looked like a fruit ripe for the plucking, but she stank to high heaven. When he saw her, although he was immediately aroused, Cacavus was so abashed by her beauty that a sense of respect halted him in the doorway. "Come and enjoy your reward," Rosinalda whispered in her most seductive voice. Cacavus rushed to the bed, throwing off his weapons and straps, his jerkin and his boots, and flung himself upon her. But no sooner had he sunk his fleshy Hungarian lips between her breasts than the stench made him start back. He tried to conceal his repulsion to avoid wounding Rosinalda's pride. He tried to overcome his nausea because he was still excited. He tried to imagine only that bejeweled sex he had seen from the foot of the ramparts, and moved his hands down toward it. The duchess made no protest. She allowed him to remove her underskirts and underlinen, allowed his fingers to play with the pearls of the tiara. "Do you like my jewel-box?" she whispered. Cacavus, almost beside himself, said, "Yes, yes, oh yes!" "Then kiss my jewel," Rosinalda commanded him. Cacavus, who needed no further encouragement, buried his face in the thick tuft of hair smeared with mutton fat. But the stench was so awful he could not go on. All at once he got up from the bed, put his jerkin, his straps and his boots back on again. He stood stiffly to attention and said:

"My lady, Cacavus has no right to make love to you in this way. You are free, and owe me nothing in exchange."

At which Rosinalda, to continue her game, began to purr at him like a cat. "Oh, Cacavus, how could you leave me now? Make me yours! Take me! My jewel belongs to you!"

"I deeply regret this," the king said, "but for the sake of your honor and mine I must leave now."

"My odor, did you say?" Rosinalda asked, with feigned indignation.

"No, duchess, for your honor," Cacavus retorted. He left the room in a fury, shouting insults at his men, and galloped off out of the castle. None of them dared ask him anything, although they were amazed at the short length of time he had spent in the duchess's bedchamber and could tell by his anger that something had gone amiss.

The king ordered his men to lift the siege, and at dawn they marched from the region. Cacavus had not said a word about what had happened, but as he passed in front of the castle, he shouted out, "My God, how these Lombard women stink!" and spurred on his horse.

Following orders from Sánchez de Reina, who must still be roaming the South Seas somewhere, our boatswain banned these stories of mine, even though they had been well received in courts and salons, in cloisters and churches. But the men begged to hear more, and the fleet's fool could hardly refuse.

Apart from these moments of relaxation and some demonstrations of skill with the arquebuses that helped pass the time, we spent the rest of our days overhauling the ships, which is as useless an occupation as rain falling on the sea.

Because of the damp atmosphere and the sea mists, all our metalwork turned rusty and the wood of the yardarms swelled, which made it hard for them to swivel on their hinges. The furled sails became coated with fungus; the bronze fittings with verdigris. However hard the men struggled to scrub it off in the morning, it always returned overnight. Even the steel of our swords turned dull and black, no matter how we tried to keep them polished.

Our presence on the ocean and that of the objects which made it possible was permanently threatened. Everything seemed possessed by an inexplicable desire to regress to an earlier state that would inevitably mean our downfall. Shot through with the damp and the poison of this endless calm, wood and iron refused to obey us. Masts, yards and other timbers that until a short while before had been docile to man's touch were now swelling, growing, twisting out of shape as though trying to regain their natural state. The bronze of our fittings, the iron of our cannon, the steel of our swords all seemed to have rebelled against our orders.

Every day we had to begin again the same struggle against the vegetable or mineral order of the world that surrounded us and on which we depended. The days spent scrubbing wood or polishing metal were all exactly the same; we lost all sense of time passing and our wait came to seem eternal.

"That's your job," Francisco Alba told us, "and you have to do it. No matter if it has no purpose. That is the way of life at sea. Besides, it keeps you from thinking."

IN THE midst of this calm, the struggle for power was unleashed with the violence of a storm. The arrogant Spanish nobles whom your Majesty submitted to the authority of a

Portuguese adventurer tried more than once to free themselves from this usurper.

One morning, after we had been becalmed for many days, Juan de Cartagena, cousin of the bishop of Burgos and Inspector General of the fleet, came aboard the flagship.

What on earth had driven a man like that to embark on this adventure of ours?

Cartagena had no need to go to the Moluccas for spices; he already had them in abundance on his table, brought by the eastern route. He had no need to sail to the Indies in search of gold, nor for new lands to add to his possessions, which were already so vast that in the thirty years of his life he had never managed to visit them all. Nor did he need the expedition to prove his honor, because in the battle of Alfácar, where he had lost both legs, he had covered himself with glory. He was not a hotheaded youth like Gaspar de Quesada, or a madman like Ruy Faleiro. More than anyone else, he loved the soft life at court. He enjoyed its silks and velvets, its gold and marble, its wines and succulent dishes. He always went about perfumed like a lady of the court and took care to dress with grace and elegance. What was it, then, that made this cripple take to the seas, to explore unnamed oceans following a route he had not been told of, in search of a destiny to which he was equally blind? And yet from the first he had wanted to be part of the expedition, so much so that he eventually persuaded his cousin, Bishop Fonseca, a man of great influence, to advise your Majesty to appoint him Inspector General of the fleet on behalf of the Indias Company in place of Ruy Faleiro. Juan de Cartagena did his utmost to win this high appointment, little thinking it would be a fatal choice.

One morning, as I said, Juan de Cartagena came aboard the *Trinidad* without warning. He was accompanied by the cosmographer Andrés de San Martín and four of the ten servants whom the Inspector General had brought with him on the voyage. They were the ones who helped lift aboard our ship the heavy, luxurious chair on which Cartagena was seated.

Our pilot Esteban Gómez led them to the quarterdeck. Don

Fernando was sitting there consulting some sea charts, clad as ever in his armor. Ever since the winds had failed us, the Captain General had retreated into a silence as impenetrable as the iron he used to protect his body from any possible attack.

Don Juan's servants carefully placed his chair on the deck and withdrew. Andrés de San Martín cleared his throat. Don Fernando did not deign to raise his eyes.

Cartagena was wearing a fine Flemish shirt, a green velvet cape draped over the arms and back of the chair, and breeches of the same cloth. The sun glinted on the clasps and golden brooches which closed the trousers where his legs were missing. One hand rested on the jade pommel of his sword; the fingers of the other were drumming impatiently on the arm of the chair.

San Martín whispered something in Esteban Gómez's ear. The latter nodded, then went over to Don Fernando. He muttered a few words to him, but the captain said, still without looking up, "Who did you say was here? The Inspector General? I do not recall having sent for him."

Esteban whispered a few more words in his ear.

"Very well," he conceded, "since he is here, let him speak."

Visibly struggling to contain his anger, Cartagena said that he had come in the name of the Indias Company to demand the reason for this lengthy detour which had cost us two months' sailing time, exhausting the ships' supplies and the men's spirits. He said the doldrums had spoiled the water in its barrels, rotted the food in our holds, and infected the minds of the sailors, whose only thought was to return home. Our drinking water, our food, our dreams and our hopes had all been poisoned. Everything had been lost because of the senseless route we had embarked upon. If we were really aiming for the Moluccas by the western route, as some had been claiming, why were we sailing south, thus adding the threat of Portuguese ships to the rigors inherent to these latitudes? Could the Captain General possibly be unaware that the king of Portugal had sent vessels to the Cape of Good Hope to intercept our fleet before it entered the Indian Sea? Did he intend to take on López de

Sequeira's warships? Did my master not perhaps know that the viceroy of India possessed a very powerful fleet which was more than capable of sending our ships to the bottom of the ocean, men, goods, and all? My Lord must have known this, Juan de Cartagena went on, since he himself had fought alongside this Diego López de Sequeira. Could all this have been a trap aimed at destroying this vastly expensive undertaking? He declared himself unwilling to continue to obey Don Fernando's orders until he was properly informed of the fleet's route and plans. The two of them should discuss these matters together. Had not the King, on May 5, 1519, instructed the officials of the Colonies' Office to require the Captain General and Ruy Faleiro to write down the course they intended to follow, so that a chart could be drawn up with all the calculations of latitude and longitude that Faleiro had made, and a copy of it could be given to each of the pilots? And yet neither he, Juan de Cartagena, nor the other captains, nor any of the pilots had any notion of the fleet's intended course. He repeated that he was no longer willing to tolerate this situation.

Cold, calm, without once lifting his gaze from the charts he had been studying, the Captain General raised his head slightly out of its iron shell and replied: "Like everyone else, the Inspector General of the fleet is required to follow me."

Don Juan fell silent for a moment. Uncertain, he pushed both hands down on the arms of his chair. "Follow you where?"

"The royal decree to which you refer lapsed in July. The plans for the fleet are secret. A secret between the King and myself," the Captain General replied, staring him straight in the eyes for the first time.

"A secret which puts at risk the lives of two hundred and fifty men, and in which the interests of the Indias Company, which I represent, are at stake," Cartagena retorted, trying to control himself and appear as calm as his adversary.

"Like any other member of our crews, the Inspector General is bound by a contract he signed. What difference does it make whether he knows our course or not?"

At this bold challenge, Don Juan hesitated. Shadows from

the rigging drew lines across his delicate face. A few clouds obscured the sun, reducing the glare a little. Don Juan insisted: "Is it not sensible to want to know the route the fleet is following? We have been stuck in these sterile waters for many days now: was that also in the secret plans for the fleet? Was it in your plans, Captain? What is to happen next? How are we to escape from here? In which direction are we to head? Tell us, Captain, or have you no faith in your men? Do you believe only in your instruments and the course Ruy Faleiro mapped out for you? Does what I am asking not make sense?"

Now it was Don Fernando's turn to hesitate. He knew the men were frightened and rebellious. He knew from his own experience how terrible the effect of these doldrums could be. He knew all about their slow poison, how madness could suddenly engulf a ship that was trapped without wind. He was also aware of the air of natural authority Cartagena displayed. He mentally assessed his strength: three of the five ships would follow the Inspector General; he could count only on Serrano in the tiny *Santiago*.

What the Captain General would decide was a complete mystery to us all. Would he yield to Cartagena's threats, thus sacrificing his authority? Or would he try to impose his will? And if he did, should we stay faithful to him or go over to the Inspector's side? Which of the two would come out on top: the all-powerful Don Juan or the bold Portuguese adventurer, Don Fernando? If the fight breaks out, whose side should I take? That was the question each man was asking himself, because only one thing was certain: those who chose wrongly would face punishment and reprisals.

SPEAKING OF punishment and reprisals, permit me to inquire once more, your Highness, why your son Felipe, a lord as tall and strong as a tower, should vent such fury against someone like myself, who stands no higher than a washstand? Why do his powerful Hapsburg lips quiver with rage at your humble servant, who has done his house no ill? It cannot be denied that Juanillo talks too much and spices his stories with the odd white lie to bring out their flavor, but does anyone take him seriously? Does Felipe, as blond and blue-eyed as a cherub, as seductive as a nymph and as saintly as Pope Joan, pay any heed to the braggardly lies of a dwarfish, hunchbacked buffoon? Is it fitting for a man like him, wise as an owl, cunning as a fox, valiant as a lion, to hunt down a weasel? What if I have been known to go around talking nonsense just to earn a crust of bread? They were only harmless jokes, innocent tittle-tattle. I said, for example, that in Leganés there is a boy by the name of Jerónimo who is the emperor's bastard son, conceived by Don Carlos in the belly of a Flemish washerwoman who was in charge of cleaning the royal underwear, and who became pregnant because one day she put on a pair of his drawers to see how it felt to be a king, but your Majesty loved her anyway because she was both passionate and clean, and the boy she bore him was his favorite. Or I said that the empress Isabel died giving birth to a child with a calf's head, and that Felipe was also born with a calf's head but the royal surgeons tried with all their skill to make it look human, and what they found most difficult was the fact that the horns kept growing back, and they were unable to do anything about his jawbone, either, which is why he still has the face of a cow. Or that Don Luis de Quijada, also known as "Whalejaw," was Felipe's real father, because they both have such enormous jaws, though Felipe's is undoubtedly the larger of the two. Everyone knew these were only jokes and laughed at them in all innocence. So did the members of the Holy Inquisition, who interrogated me on Felipe's orders. They laughed until they were fit to burst, your Highness, and then they turned serious and began to question me about the expedition. That was when I realized I had not been brought before them on account of my little jokes. No, they wanted to know why I went round claiming high and low that what your chroniclers had written was stuff and nonsense. And to know why I spent my time searching out my former companions. Why was I looking for them? For what reason did I inquire about Beatriz, Don Fernando's wife, and why did I style myself Count of the Spice Islands? They also wanted to know whether it was true I was writing a lying chronicle of the voyage and trying to sell it to the emperor. When I denied everything and swore by God who is three in one that none of it was true, that I had forgotten the voyage long ago and had no reason to wish to remember it, they replied: You are a whoreson Jew, we will teach you not to lie to us. This went on for some time, with them insulting and threatening me, and me swearing my innocence on the ashes of my unknown father, until they threw me into a dungeon and for three days didn't give me so much as a cup of water to drink. After that, they began their interrogation all over again. They asked me the same questions, I gave the same replies, and they threw me back in the same dungeon and again refused me even water, except for a few sips between their questions and my replies, since I was so exhausted I couldn't speak. This went on something like four thousand times, until one day they said I could go free if I signed a declaration. All I could think of was saving my skin, so I signed the piece of paper they thrust at me without reading it. Then one of the judges or wardens or what have you smiled cynically at me and told me no longer to bother claiming the pension I had been given for taking part in the expedition, as by my own hand I had declared that I had never been on any such voyage to the Spice Islands. When I protested, he read out what I had signed, and a list of survivors from which my name was missing. And I should take care not to complain, he added, because if I did I could be hanged or made to repay all the money I had been receiving over the years under false pretenses. I couldn't believe what he was saying and asked to see the list. But my eyes failed me, and I couldn't read it properly. When he showed it to me again, I counted the names on my fingers: one was missing, and that one was me.

That was how my name and all references to Juanillo Ponce, made Count of the Spice Islands by the grace of Don Fernando de Magallanes, my master, disappeared from all the lists and chronicles, your Highness. That was how I was stripped of my pension and my identity. Your Juanillo became a ghost. That voyage was the central point of his whole life, and all of a

sudden his part in it was denied. That is why I spent what
strength remained to me looking for the other survivors. I
needed them to vouch for my existence. I found a few of them,
and learnt from them all that was left of our glorious voyage
around the whole world. But that is a story I shall leave to the
end of my account; what matters now is something else. Not
a single one of my former companions recognized me. Some
received me politely, others with compassion, and some answered my questions at length; but to all of them I was a
complete stranger. Threatened by the Inquisition, or whoever
it was who tried me, they all refused to acknowledge that they
knew me. Left thus to my own devices, I said to myself: The
only person who can save me is Don Carlos. He must believe
me. He must know who I am. Surely your Highness will recognize the Count of the Spice Islands. Don Carlos will restore
my name to the lists and renew my pension. And if it is too
troublesome to change the lists of names, then at least let me
have my money again. With this in mind, I set to work writing
this account of our journey, which continues as follows:

FRANCISCO ALBO, the *Trinidad*'s boatswain, was watching
Don Fernando anxiously, as though to anticipate his orders.
The three other officers adopted different but equally cautious
attitudes. Esteban Gómez was looking at Cartagena. Juan Bautista was staring at his own feet. Gonzalo was gazing up at the
rigging and the sky beyond it.

The boldest of the crew had climbed onto the shrouds and
yardarms to get an unimpeded view of what was happening in
the sterncastle. The *Trinidad* looked like a vast old tree filled
with birds.

I was about to take refuge in the hold until I could see how
things would turn out when I heard my master's reedy voice
piping out from somewhere inside his armor. He was standing
up now, and shone in the sun like some pagan idol.

"Aren't you afraid, you cripple, to come on board my ship
and try to stir up my men to mutiny?" he asked.

"I must warn you that at this very moment the *San Antonio*'s cannon are aimed at your ship; and beyond them, you would doubtless have to face the guns of the *Concepción* and the *Victoria*, too," Don Juan replied, attempting a smile.

"What would you tell your king? That you rebelled against his power? That you disobeyed my orders? That you betrayed me? Or perhaps that you were envious, that you wanted to keep all the riches for yourself, that you needed every clove and stick of cinnamon for your own table? Or would you confess that you had become afraid, that as soon as you had embarked you feared for your life and could think only of returning home? Well, I'll tell you what I'm going to do with you: I'm going to cut out your tongue and hang you from the mainmast so that everyone can see what happens to traitors. Arrest this man!"

"Captain!" shouted Andrés, who had remained silent until this moment but now tried in vain to intervene.

"You wouldn't dare!" Cartagena challenged my master.

"The death penalty for anyone who tries to defend him!" Don Fernando retorted.

"Roque, Joan!" Don Juan said, calling his servants. "Take me back to my ship! I won't listen to this madman anymore!"

"You no longer have a ship," Don Fernando replied in a deliberately measured tone.

The Inspector General opened his mouth to reply, but the words could not get past his teeth. Instead, they rolled back into his throat as though he were choking on them. All his attention was concentrated on the icy blade of steel that seemed to be burning a black line across the soft, perfumed skin of his throat.

THAT NIGHT the Captain called me to his cabin. He was stretched out on his bunk, still in full armor. Beside him, sitting on the floor with his legs crossed, was his slave, Enrique.

Don Fernando had brought him as a boy from Malacca, and he was in the fleet not only as the Captain's personal attendant but also as our interpreter. My master was very fond of him, and Enrique returned his affection with doglike devotion. It was he who first tasted all the Captain's food, and at night he slept outside his door, a fearsome dagger in his hand. He only came out on deck when the Captain did so; the rest of the time he stayed shut in his master's cabin. Of course there was no shortage of gossip that Enrique sometimes acted as a woman for Don Fernando—an old seafaring custom the Captain General was said to have acquired during his long spells aboard ship—but I for one never believed it. Don Fernando was too concerned with the future to give in to any other kind of necessity: he barely even ate. Those rumors, like all the others that circulated about my master, were unfounded, perhaps inspired by envy or jealousy. I must confess, though, that after two months at sea, that submissive, oiled slave did have his attractions.

When I went in, Enrique looked askance at me as though my presence upset him. The Captain said he could not sleep and wanted to hear me recite a ballad. He particularly enjoyed the one about the adventures of the Infante Arnaldos, and he would have me repeat it hundreds of times, interrupting me whenever he felt the need to correct my accent or the intonation I put on different words.

So I sat down at his feet like a loving mother and began to reel off the verses. He listened with half-closed eyes, then suddenly burst out. "I'm sorry," he said, and when I looked up at him in surprise, he went on, "I regret I had to act in that way, but I had no choice."

I was about to comment, but before I could do so he signaled me to continue with my ballad. When I reached the verses in which the sailor tells the Infante:

> *My tale I will only tell*
> *to whoever goes with me*

he interrupted again. "Cartagena is a good man, but he's living in the past. He's a dead weight I'll have to get rid of."

His words cut like steel. We both fell silent, and Don Fernando shut his eyes.

"Recite me the ballad once more," he said after a while.

When I had finished for a second time, he seemed to have fallen asleep. He lay there without moving, breathing deeply. The iron covering his chest moved rhythmically up and down. As it rose, it caught the reflection of the lantern hanging from the cabin ceiling and then fell back into the shadows of the tiny chamber; up and down, over and over, as though it had a life of its own.

"What do you think Beatriz is doing now?" he suddenly asked.

"Beatriz, my Lord?" I asked him, in some confusion.

"My wife. What do you think she can be doing now?"

His question took me by surprise. "I don't know, my Lord."

"And little Rodrigo? Do you know my wife is expecting another child? Perhaps she has already had it. Tell me about them."

"I don't know them, my Lord."

"You're a poet, aren't you? Close your eyes and tell me what you see."

I hesitated, but it was obvious he was waiting to hear what I had to say.

"In Sevilla, the day is dawning, and . . ."

"She isn't in Sevilla," he interrupted me. "But no matter, go on."

"Well, it is dawn . . . A balcony stands open above an empty square. Inside the room, dimly lit by the first uncertain light of day, a barefoot woman paces up and down, hands clasping her stomach, which is round as a ripe fruit. Next to her bed stands Rodrigo's cradle, carved on your orders from the same wood as the *Trinidad*. The woman is rocking the cradle gently, just as the waves rock our ship."

"I like that," the Captain said. "Did you know my son is called Rodrigo after Faleiro? We used to be great friends. But then he went mad and your king removed him from the expedition."

"So it's true what they say?"

"What do they say?"

43

"That all the calculations and measurements for our course were made by a madman."

"He thought I had something to do with Don Carlos's decision. But it wasn't true, though there were pressures on me. He was my friend."

"They also say he was an astrologer who dabbled in the black arts."

"When they appointed Cartagena to replace him, I suggested Faleiro's brother Francisco be made captain of one of the vessels. I knew he was the only person Ruy would agree to confide his secret method to."

"It's said he feigned madness so as not to leave with us because his familiar had shown him the fleet's dreadful destiny."

"I needed to know how he observed east-west longitudes, and the measurements he deduced from them, but he refused to show me."

"Is he really mad, Captain?"

"You don't have to worry about that. But tell me, what is Beatriz doing?"

I hesitated. I would have liked to know more about our course and the man who had designed it, but my master was not really listening to me, and I was frightened of angering him if I insisted. So I went on with my story.

"She is watching over her peacefully sleeping boy. She is thinking how much he looks like you, and she smiles. Then she walks out onto the balcony and stares up at the sky where the last stars are fading. I think she is imagining five black ships speeding through the waves. In her mind's eye, she sees the *Trinidad* proudly leading the way, then she imagines her husband in his cabin awake, thinking of her. She imagines how on his return she will take both children to greet him. There she is at the waterfront watching the ships enter port, the air filled with the fragrance of the spices in their holds. A royal deputation has come to honor you. 'Can you see the King over there?' she asks Rodrigo. 'Where is my father?' the child would rather know. 'I can't see him, where is he?' he insists, as the *Trinidad*'s huge black shape nears its berth and the shadow of its giant sails sweeps over the heads of all the people waiting there, dimming even his Majesty's glittering crown."

"Isn't his father there?" Don Fernando asked me.

I shuddered, shaken by a sudden premonition.

"Why don't you take your armor off, my Lord? You would be more comfortable, and would find it easier to sleep," I said.

"I cannot. This armorplate protects me from everyone."

"Do you know they say there is nothing inside it?"

"What do you think?"

"I think there's a great man inside."

"So you see why I can't take it off," he answered. Then he asked again, "Isn't his father there?"

" 'There he is!' the mother suddenly shouts. Her voice chokes with sobs. The boy cries out and waves his arms. The crowd bursts into shouts of rejoicing. The cannon of the fleet rend the warm morning air," I told him.

NEXT MORNING a meeting of the captains was called. Cartagena had been declared a mutineer and arrested. He was to be replaced as captain of the *San Antonio* by Antonio de Coca. Don Fernando's pennant was hoisted to the top of the ship's mainmast. He accepted the idea of placing the Inspector General in Luis de Mendoza's custody. Any further uprising would be punishable by beheading. Everyone seemed to agree, and the meeting broke up in great haste. All the captains appeared anxious to return to their ships. For the time being at least, the power struggle had receded into the background. Everyone's attention was concentrated on the breeze springing up.

The first sign was like a shiver in air that had been still and windless for many days. Then there was a vague sensation of relief on the skin. All our senses were on the alert. Gradually what we had felt became a reality. The sea slowly began to undulate; the first wave slid beneath our hull. The timbers began to creak gently, the masts to vibrate. Some birds flew off the rigging of the *Concepción*. Though the captains were talking, their words were empty; they were like unfurled sails waiting for the wind. Sitting bolt upright in his chair, Cartagena's nostrils flared, as though he, too, were trying to detect the first signs of a change. Yet all the captains pretended to be unaware of the signs, and headed back to their ships in silence. A short while later, a fresh, steady breeze trickled like honey over the decks, stopping all the men in their tracks with its unexpected caress.

That night the breeze grew into a strong wind.

As though touched by the invisible hand of some strange god, the timbers of the *Trinidad* roused themselves from their deathly slumber. The whole ancient oak forest of Corpes came back to life. The old ship, still and silent for so many days and nights, shook itself and began to creak through all its length and breadth. It creaked from keel to bowsprit; the boards of the deck creaked, and so did the ribs of this exotic plant grown out of the earth of your kingdom. The beams holding up the deck cried out. The masts and all the tackle shouted their thirst for the adventures their makers had destined them for.

The following morning the sails swelled out like the bellies of the mothers who gave birth to us only so that we could undertake this mad adventure; the rigging that had hung limp for so long stretched taut in the wind. The ships were no longer immobile islands that refused to obey any of the pilots' orders, but began at last to speed through the waves, heading south on the course my master had set for us.

Not even Cartagena would have wished for land at that moment, had he been given the freedom to do so.

ONE MORNING we lost sight of the Pole Star. The news that we had crossed the equator ran like wildfire below decks.

Fortunately, and thanks be to all the gods—mine, my mother's and all the others, alive or dead—nothing happened. The waters did not steam and boil our timbers or make the hulls come apart at the seams, as we had been told they would. No abyss opened up to swallow the fleet, and after four days' sailing we spied the Cape of Good Hope in the distance. At latitude 23°30′ south, we changed course from south to due west, heading for Verzino's land, which the Portuguese call Brazil.

But the change of course only increased our disquiet. We did not know how to use a compass, to read pilots' logs or charts. We did not have the faintest idea whether the earth was shaped like a pear, a grape or a radish.

What were the Captain General's real intentions? we asked ourselves. If our destination was the Spice Islands, why were we now heading for the Indies Colón had discovered? If the rumor that Don Fernando intended to sail west to the Spice Islands were true, what in heaven's name were we doing mixed up in his crazy scheme?

None of the officers had any inkling. The chaplain went around steeped in melancholy, as though he regretted ever having left his peaceful parish to embark on this wild adventure. The cosmographer maintained a stubborn silence. We were all afraid, but it was a sterile, useless kind of fear that only made us more malleable to Don Fernando's whims. So we let ourselves be led ever onward without so much as a protest.

DURING THE two weeks of the crossing, the wind blew steady and strong from astern without once failing us. We crossed the ocean as swiftly as a dream, only halting one morning because of a thick bank of fog.

For fear of colliding with some invisible object, we struck sail. For two hours, guided by lanterns, we grouped the ships, then strung them together with strong cables. Perhaps Don Fernando was genuinely worried that one of them might become lost on this unknown sea made doubly unreal by the fog; or perhaps he was more concerned with preventing anyone who was against him from taking advantage of the opportunity to escape.

The fog was so thick that the men in charge of roping the ships together could hardly see their own hands in front of their faces. It persisted for hour after hour, until a kind of collective blindness completely altered the natural order of things.

This is the curious effect that prolonged fogs can have, your Highness. People forget their normal points of reference and are lost in a feeling of chaos. Even the certainty that the sky is above the sea is open to doubt. Nobody can really be sure where the one ends and the other begins. The same is true of the ship: it is impossible to tell where it finishes and what comes beyond it. The complicated geography of timbers and ropes, which becomes so familiar after a few days' sailing that one follows it almost unconsciously, suddenly reverts to the labyrinth it seemed on our first acquaintance with it. After being immersed in this fog for some time, all previous knowledge becomes useless. Any platform, box or barrel can be taken for a ceiling, or vice versa. The sterncastle can appear at the prow, or change places the whole day long. Any slight contact, any stumble or unexpected noise is enough to create total confusion, to destroy all sense of order. With this terrible blindfold on our eyes, even the outlines and limits of our own bodies are lost. This white cloud makes everything uncertain, confused, chaotic, insecure, even though the sun may be shining only a few feet away, with everything as clear and bright as usual.

We had been lost in the fog for several hours, perhaps—because even one's sense of time becomes distorted—when a cabin boy named Francisco began shouting that a huge ship was gliding past, so close to the *Trinidad* that if we stretched out our hands we could touch it.

At first we thought one of our own ships had broken loose and was drifting toward the flagship. We were convinced it would crash into us, so we all peered in the direction Francisco was pointing, trying in vain to make out the form of the vessel he was describing.

But the sails hanging stiffly from the arms like gray shrouds amid shreds of fog of the same color, the rigging and ropes swinging loose, tangled all around the masts, the spars that gave the whole scene the desolate look of a forest in winter, the ship's hull, covered with all kinds of barnacles and seaweed, like one of those old spars of timber that have floated in the sea for years, each of these details—and we were no longer sure if we had heard them from Francisco or had glimpsed them through the mist, but they came together in our imaginations —gradually filled our minds with another kind of fear. I mean that we were no longer afraid of a collision with a ship from our fleet.

Then we all began to shout and wave lanterns, but there was no reply.

"Perhaps it's a caravel . . ." someone said after a few minutes, breaking the spell that had kept us all silent.

"It could well be, from the boy's description," agreed Martín the Cooper, an expert in ships.

The questions came thick and fast.

"Who could it be?"

"Perhaps it's the Portuguese."

"Or it could be Cristóbal Colón, still trying to reach the Indies by sailing west," a mocking voice called out.

"A phantom ship? I have heard tell of them . . ."

"Don't you think we should board it? They might be in trouble."

"Perhaps it's filled with gold and spices?"

"But there could be the plague on board. The holds stinking with pestilent corpses . . ."

"If we don't intercept it now, we'll lose our chance forever."

"I'll jump aboard it!" shouted Francisco, who seemed to be speaking from very close by, though we could not see him at all through the fog.

"Come back!" Blas warned him. "If you do that, they'll hang you!"

There was no reply.

"Come back, I say!"

A few seconds that seemed like centuries went by before we heard Francisco's voice again: "Wait, it looks just like the *Trinidad*, but it's completely empty! There's nothing here. Nothing, you hear? Only rotten timbers, crumbling ropes, rusty bronze tackle. But there isn't a soul on board, there isn't even a single cup or spoon . . ."

His voice grew fainter and shriller, like a tiny child's.

"It's the *Trinidad*!" he repeated. "I swear by my mother that it's the *Trinidad*! I can read the bronze plaque at the foot of the mainmast! It says *Trinidad*!"

"He's gone mad," Albo said.

"Where are you?" Blas shouted, stumbling around, not knowing which way to turn. "Francisco!" he shouted over and over, like a desperate mother who has lost her son in a crowd: "Answer me, Francisco, you whoreson!"

Little by little his shouts faded, then died out completely.

"What's going on?" someone wanted to know. "What is going on?"

Nobody answered.

I was as silent as the rest, paralyzed with fear. Then I heard a clanking behind me. It was Don Fernando, enclosed as ever in his iron breastplate. Parts of his armor were covered with a greenish sheen, and where the polished steel did shine the fog had condensed in tiny droplets. He looked exactly like one of those huge tropical turtles, with a tiny, sharp reptile's head. Even so, when I sensed his calm presence beside me, I grasped his hand fearfully.

The group of men slowly dispersed. Each of them slipped off silently into the mist.

Silence had fallen on all your five ships, Sire, strung together like beads on a rosary. Stuck inside this white cloud, at some unknown point on the boundless ocean, rocking to and fro with their burden of blind children. Two hundred and more men just like your Highness, not so much regal as real. Thirsty, hungry, with all their weariness, their dreams, their fears. Great and small. Rich and poor. Powerful and insignificant. Pleased to enjoy a good wine, a good woman, a sunny morning or a plateful of food, spiced or not. Fathers, sons, husbands, lovers, solitary bachelors. Men desperately in love, others who are faithless, or cuckolds, or cretins. Men who feel sick, whose stomachs ache, who need to piss every so often, and to cry now and again. Men like you, your Highness, who enjoy fornicating, scratching, laughing and talking nonsense. Seamen, captains, caulkers, boatswains, gunners, coopers, cabin boys, pages and all the rest. And yet to you, your Majesty, we were nothing more than a list of names you could not even read through without feeling bored, unable to imagine a single one of us. Names in a list, numbers on a piece of paper. No faces, hands, feet; no penises or eyes, mouths or ears or asses, or any kind of smell. Simply names and figures in books with black covers, the names of men you imagine must exist because you have heard talk of them, but they are men you have never seen; books compiled for you by other names and figures you have never seen either. And whom you are equally incapable of imagining. All we are is so much shit—less than that, because shit at least stinks. The noble art of governing! I much prefer to stay a jester. Or even a sailor, despite all the dangers. I prefer to set sail, despite the fear and the hunger, despite the uncertainties and mysteries of our adventure; you can see how little of the leader I have in me, my Lord. I prefer to see people's faces, or at the very least their asses, which often amounts to the same thing: I would never dream of playing the role you play. And if I had become Count of the Spice Islands as my master intended, it would have been more a tragedy than an honor for me. There are vocations like yours and mine into which one is born, and which cannot be taught. Although I must admit, Sire, that I have seen you joking and turning somersaults on your august throne so cleverly and unashamedly that you would be the envy of any fool or jester, of Francesillo himself. And what an audience you have! And how you please them! But I'll leave the matter there, your Highness, because it is Juanillo's lot to be a buffoon, and Don Carlos's to be a king. Enough said.

PART III

THE GROUND was hard and dusty, scored with deep cracks that ran off into the thick walls of vegetation on either side of the path. Flowers, plants and branches that had apparently been devoured in a fierce fire were everywhere. Lianas as thick as our mooring ropes hung limply in tatters. The climbing shoots of creepers wove webs round the tallest trees that looked like the shrouds on our ships' masts. Strange fruits blackened by the sun rotted in a deathly silence that was broken only by an occasional distant screeching from the treetops. We found it harder and harder to move forward. Heat and thirst made our fatigue even worse. In single file, without a word, we crossed a dried-up riverbed. Our feet sank into a deep reddish mud where fish lay decomposing.

A sepulchral calm reigned over the whole jungle. There was not the slightest sign of life.

After a few more interminable minutes of marching, we could make out a clearing in the forest. A dense column of smoke rose above the canopy of trees.

The only sound was the heavy beating of a buzzard's wings as it circled overhead.

Nobody said a word.

We kept on going. Some time later we came to a roughly circular cleared space, dotted with black stumps: the remains of trees hacked away and burnt, this time by men.

Your Juanillo looked around him.

In the middle of this clearing won from the jungle stood a small field, surrounded by a few miserable huts.

Nothing was moving.

The village looked deserted.

A dry wind whipped up columns of red dust.

I stared at the modest plantation.

The plants had all withered to an ash-brown color. The stems had nearly all collapsed under the weight of their own overripe fruit. All of a sudden, something moving over near the huts caught my attention. It was a pack of starving dogs, all skin and bone, wandering about, muzzles to the ground. A couple of them were sniffing in vain at a pile of sun-bleached bones, under the others' watchful gaze.

"It doesn't look like there's any water here," Juan Bautista the shipmaster said.

Nobody answered.

He ordered us to pair off and explore the place. When they became aware of our presence, the dogs slipped silently away into the surrounding undergrowth.

The day before, we had disembarked on a small island close to the mainland, in a bay the Captain General named Santa Lucía, because we arrived there on that saint's day. Later, the Portuguese chose to call it Rio de Janeiro.

As soon as we landed we set out to find water.

Although we had stocked up two months earlier in Tenerife, the many days we had spent becalmed off Sierra Leone and the strange route we had taken, first to the Cape and then west across the ocean, meant we had almost run out of water. Our daily ration had been reduced from two cups to one of a dark liquid that stank of the bilges.

To add to our quandary, the patrols sent out the day we anchored to explore the land near the ships came back with their barrels empty. The country was in the grip of a drought; its once mighty rivers were now no more than fetid mud. All our hopes were pinned on this village, which our lookouts had spied from their crow's nests; it was our only hope of freeing our throats and our guts from the thirst that clutched us like the claws of a cat in heat.

But those hopes now seemed to have been dashed, after the long and wearisome trek through the jungle with the sun beating down on us, encased in our suits of armor as a precaution, suffocating from the heat, tormented by the pangs of thirst.

When I saw that the village also seemed devastated by fire, I felt like weeping. Weeping for my fate and that of all my companions, weeping for the Captain and his insane adventure, for everyone as crazy as us in this world. And I would have burst into tears, I am sure, had I not at that very instant heard Juan Ginovés shouting in his incomprehensible dialect, calling us to come and look.

One by one, we ran over to him, then stood like statues, staring into a wretched, shallow well, at the bottom of which was shining . . . shining . . . shining . . . a muddy pool of water reflecting the rays of the sun. We all fell to our knees in the mud, fighting for a place so we could moisten our lips with a hot liquid which looked and tasted like blood, but which we drank avidly.

Once I had slaked my thirst, I became aware of the feeling of being watched, and so did my companions. Yet we could see no one.

Our eyes fixed on the thick wall of vegetation, we filled several barrels full of water, then started back down to the ships.

Night fell quickly, suddenly, on the scorched jungle, filling the narrow path with shadows and making the silence around us unbearable. Not once, the whole way, did we come across any signs of life; everything seemed like a deserted theater, like an extinct, sealed-up world.

When we reached the beach, a huge red moon was rising over the mountains at the far end of the bay.

The heat of the night forced us up on deck to sleep; from

there we could see pinpoints of light: fires lit on mountainsides that had seemed uninhabited.

It was an eerie feeling to be stretched out on the planks of our ship in the center of the huge natural amphitheater of that bay ringed with hills, while a world of unknown beings and things was watching us sleep.

For the next four days we went back to the well time and again without once making contact with the mysterious villagers. Yet every night the bonfires sprang up again out of the darkness.

ON BOARD ship, tension had surfaced once more. Our difficult situation made the men aggressive, and there were frequent quarrels and brawls. One night after we had eaten, we heard voices arguing in the prow. Blas and Martín the Cooper had come to blows, and several of the men were trying to separate them. But Blas was as strong as a horse, and shook off everyone trying to pull him back, flinging himself on Martín again and again.

They were arguing about Francisco's mysterious disappearance. When the fog I mentioned earlier had cleared, your Highness, we looked for him all over the ship, to no avail. We also searched the sea around us, but again without success, so the Captain gave him up for lost and we continued on our way. However, it seemed that Blas, who was inseparable from the boy, blamed Martín for what had happened, claiming it was his talk of a phantom ship full of gold and spices that had made Francisco leap into the void. Martín retorted that Francisco was a fool who saw things, and that of course there had been no such ship, the boy had simply jumped into the sea; so the two of them had come to blows.

After struggling to free himself for several minutes, shouting and cursing the whole time, Blas collapsed, exhausted, into the arms of the men trying to pull him off his victim. As several others dragged Martín away, Blas's huge body shuddered with a furious, stifled groan that suddenly erupted into a violent bout of sobbing. Have you ever seen a man that size cry, your Highness? Blas covered his face with his hands, and the tears dripped between his fingers. All his usual toughness vanished and he became the defenseless child we all are deep down inside, even your Imperial Majesty Don Carlos, if you will allow me to say so, though the dignity of your position may prevent you from admitting it (I would advise you to cry sometimes, to show your noble face ravaged by tears to the whole Council of State, so that the nations you rule may learn that their king can be sad and hurt, can feel as helpless as the lowest peasant or the most despised whore).

After a while the others left, and I was alone with Blas.

"Do you want to talk about it?" I asked him gently. "You don't have to if you don't want to."

He nodded. I sat in silence, staring up at the starriest night sky I had ever seen. Those pinpricks of light, of every size and brightness, from the milky smudges formed by some groups to the sharp outlines of other constellations, with the dark background that gives them a sense of infinite depth—the mystery of it all shook and intoxicated me, made me forget all my weariness. My worries and fears lost their meaning and melted away; I felt myself floating up out of my body high above the earth.

"You were great friends, weren't you?" I said after a while.

Blas seemed to be struggling to overcome his despair. He took his hands from his face, and without looking up replied that it was not that; both of them were from the same village of La Almunia in Aragón, and he, Blas, had protected Francisco as a boy because he felt sorry for him: that was all there was to it. Francisco did not have a father—it was said he was the son of a local priest who left the parish soon after the birth, gravely ill with consumption. His mother lived in a humble stone cottage out by the side of the main road, and it was also said that whenever she saw the cloud of dust in the distance that meant a visitor was coming toward the village, she stood with her naked breasts displayed at the window sill to attract the newcomer's attention. Her breasts were famous for their size, their firmness, and the fragrance of lavender given off by the big, dark nipples that always seemed erect.

Apart from the sudden death of an ox, the lack of rain, how

59

the sowing had gone, and the results of the harvest, the main topic of conversation in La Almunia was Francisco's mother's breasts. "They say the hussy bathes them by moonlight to make the skin smooth." "Last night there were goings on until past dawn. God will punish her." "What she likes is for them to be sucked, hour after hour—they turn as hard as stone." "They also say a wolf comes down from the mountain to lick them, but it's all nonsense." "They spout milk and honey, and ambrosia." For years the stories spread from market to tavern, from the churchyard out into the fields. As a youth, Blas himself spent many a night spying on her window, but it never opened. Yet the number of her children grew and grew. She had an enormous brood, crawling in the dust by the roadside, playing all around her house, buying things in the village for her. Francisco was her eldest. When he reached the age at which boys usually get together and go out to play in the fields or go fishing or bird hunting, he tried to make some friends, but found himself rejected. Humiliated. Their natural desires just awakening, the lads would joke about his mother's breasts, or ask him for a description; and of course, your Majesty, this hurt Francisco deeply. He was a small, dark-skinned boy, with large eyes that always seemed too wide open, as if somehow he had never got over his surprise at being there. Blas felt sorry for him, and once when he came upon him crying, surrounded by several boys his own age who were taunting him with obscenities about his mother, he gave one or two of them a cuff around the ears, and reduced a couple more to tears by saying they would do better to worry about their fathers who were thieves or their sisters who were whores, and so on.

From that moment on, Blas could never get rid of Francisco, who followed him like a shadow—though always at a distance, because Blas had forbidden Francisco to talk to him. But when Blas heard of your Majesty's proclamation offering the earth to all those who followed the Captain on his ambitious adventure, he thought this was the chance, probably the only one, for Francisco to get out of the village and, if they were fortunate, to return home rich enough to take the rest of his family away from the rumormongers to a place where they did not talk about his mother's breasts all the time. His mother's breasts! When Blas went to the cottage to tell her of the plans he had for her son, he could not keep his eyes off them, despite all his good intentions. He fought against it, trying to concentrate on her conversation, but she was a woman of few words, and despite the smoke that filled the kitchen, Blas thought he could detect the exciting fragrance of her breasts, hidden beneath her linen blouse. He could not resist the temptation, and surreptitiously began to glance at them. The folds of the material concealed their shape, however hard he tried to make them out. He began to imagine those two round orbs of smooth warm flesh, their straining nipples, the deep hollow between them, her neck and shoulders. He let the conversation drag on, tried to get close enough so that he might accidentally brush against her. It was as if he were drunk. He went back to Francisco's house many times before we set sail, on any pretext. Once she and Blas passed through a doorway at the same time, and her magnificent breasts brushed his naked torso: Blas felt as though he had been run through by a hundred sharp swords of the finest Toledo steel. One night shortly before we departed, she sent for him: she knew Blas would look after her son, and wanted to thank him for all he had already done and to commend Francisco to his care during the voyage. They were walking along a path in moonlight that painted the woods of the neighboring hills bright silver. All of a sudden she stopped. She seemed on the verge of tears. She said it was Francisco she loved most of all her children. That when he was born she was full of hopes for him. She had been so happy those first few months. She would never forget his tiny red face at the birth, or the way his open mouth anxiously sought out her nipples. Blas thought his moment had come. He had only to make some reference to her breasts. Or to stretch out his hand. It was now or never. But then he recalled how Francisco had followed him day and night like a dog, and it was never. Yes, Blas said, they had been friends, but perhaps he had never realized it. A curse on it, he said, it was all my fault. It was me who brought the boy on this mad adventure. It was me he was trying to impress by jumping aboard that accursed caravel. And that old villain Martín tried to tell me Francisco was an idiot who was lost because he was a fool.

It was true Francisco was not particularly bright, Blas admitted: there was something clumsy about his gestures. But he was no idiot. He was simple, and easily confused; Blas had tried to help him. A great help I was, he said, his eyes again filling with tears. But he won't be any lonelier on the phantom ship than he was in that village full of hyenas. Or any more adrift on a sea of eternal fogs. In La Almunia they would talk of his mother's breasts long after her death, but no one would remember Francisco.

By now the moon had set, and the mysterious bonfires were casting a ghostly light over the black carpet of the jungle.

Trying in vain to imagine what the invisible beings who kept the fires alight until dawn could possibly be like, obsessed by those enigmatic signs whose meaning escaped me, and driven to distraction by visions of the fabulous breasts Blas had described, I spent the rest of that night wide awake.

ON THE fifth day, on advice from the chaplain Pedro de Balderrama, Don Fernando ordered that a mass be held and a cross be placed in the center of the village we had visited.

When the procession set off at dawn, dark clouds were massing in the skies and had already covered the highest peaks. The priest opened the way, dressed in the finest lace with gold and silver embroidery. On his right walked Enrique the slave, swinging a *botafumeiro*, as my master called it in Portuguese, which perfumed the valleys with the holy odor of incense; and on his left went your humble servant, dressed as an altar boy and carrying the Holy Book and a lectern. After us came Don Fernando, noble as a god in his suit of armor; then Don Juan, carried in his fine litter, and trailing the traces of exquisite Oriental perfumes in his wake; then Gaspar de Quesada, the Fair; and further back Antonio de Coca, who was followed by Luis de Mendoza, looking even paler than usual. Three men struggled to carry an enormous cross up the path.

While we were climbing to the village, we heard thunder, and every now and then the dark heavens were lit by a sudden flash of lightning. When we came out into the clearing, the low, ominous clouds were threatening imminent rain. There was complete silence in the village; nothing moved.

Unperturbed, Don Fernando looked around and decided where to position the cross and the improvised altar. The men set to work straightaway, and once everything was ready, we all knelt before the priest, who began to say mass.

No sooner had he begun to chant than the rain started to fall. At first it was a patter of heavy raindrops that smacked into the leaves of the surrounding foliage; then the intensity increased, and soon it became a real downpour like a curtain.

The rain turned Cartagena's velvet cloak a deep purple as the heavy fabric soaked up the water like a sponge; it bounced off Don Fernando's armor as though hitting a windowpane. With an almost imperceptible gesture, the Captain ordered the service to continue.

The priest covered the chalice with a cloth and went on. The captains were all on their knees still, at prayer. We imitated them.

In a few minutes the rain became a deluge. The red earth turned to mud beneath our knees. The noise of the driving rain drowned out the priest's voice; we could barely see the shape of the cross.

All at once the mass came to a halt. The priest seemed to have been paralyzed by some strange vision. Still kneeling, the captains turned their heads to look around, and we could see a forced smile, a mixture of astonishment and terror, creep over their features.

All of us riveted our eyes on the wall of vegetation surrounding the clearing.

Behind the thick curtain of rain, the jungle had filled with a thousand strange, furtive eyes that were staring at us although we could not see them. Men and beasts were watching us from their hiding places, united in their fear of these gods who had come from the sea in hollowed-out boats.

The feeling that we were outsiders, not part of this world,

made us uneasy. We felt confused, unsure of who we were.

Nobody knew what to do.

Nobody spoke.

Nobody could think of anything but to stare at the impenetrable jungle which had suddenly become like a huge peacock's tail.

NOW TELL me, your Highness, does not the person who thus entertains you in your noble but monotonous retreat with the wit, if not the grace, of his pen, deserve at least a drop of your august pity? Is it too much to ask that, after following the thousand and one disasters that befell your bewildered Argonauts, you spare an instant to reflect on the fate of the person who, to the greater glory of your realm, was the first fool of the world entire?

A single phrase from your imperial lips could grant peace to your servant, who now struggles blindly along the paths of Bustillo del Páramo with no more company in his old age than that of his shadow. A single phrase, dictated to a secretary in one of your moments of leisure for the attention of our well-beloved Felipe, instructing him to restore the pension I earned by my efforts; a single phrase from you, so that the Count of the Spice Islands might die with peace and dignity, rather than having to beg for a crust of bread and to sleep in stables amid the dung of cattle and horses. Can the truth be such a sin, that I am punished so? After suffering the countless horrors of that voyage, should I simply accept all the nonsense and lies invented by your chroniclers? For them it's as simple as cooking a stew, once they have prepared its four or five ingredients. But what do they know, Sire, of how each of us really felt as we lived through the four or five historic events they base their accounts on? I would say that the truth lies in the feelings which those of us who took part in the expedition experienced, and which no one else can know, not even your Majesty. Nor can you find this truth anywhere else: it is useless to search for it in archives or libraries; nothing of it is there. That accursed voyage was born with us—someone sowed its seed in us even before we were born. It grew with us like a plant, took control of our minds and actions, and when it died, its roots remained inside us and will go with us to the grave—yes, if your Majesty wishes to know the truth, he must seek it in our graves, must ask the dust of our bones for it, question the worms who have gorged themselves on our corpses.

But while I still have the strength, let me continue with our story.

At that moment, Juan Carvajo slogged through the mud to the Captain's side, and whispered something in his ear. Don Fernando gave the order that no one was to move, and to go on with the mass. Don Pedro de Balderrama hesitated, glancing nervously out of the corner of his eye, then continued with his Latin in a tremulous voice.

A few dogs crept out toward us, ears pricked, necks at full stretch. A skinny mastiff sniffed at the Captain's armor and bared its teeth. Nobody moved. Some monkeys arched through the air, leaping from one treetop to another just behind the altar. The curtain of rain made everything seem unreal.

The rain beat down even harder. A bolt of lightning hit the forest not far from us, followed by the sound of a huge tree toppling over, pulling down others in its fall.

By the end of the mass, the clearing looked like a lake with blood-colored rivulets pouring from it. In the jungle, the lower ground was completely flooded; only a few scattered trees poked out of the waters, offering refuge to all sorts of creatures. The rushing water swept vegetation, branches, dead animals with it; the debris swirled around the tops of the trees then plunged further down into the jungle. The noise of water rushing down valleys and ravines everywhere made it impossible to hear anyone's voice.

As it was also impossible to return to our ships, Carvajo gave instructions for us to spend the night in the village. Soaked to the skin, we all sought shelter in the huts, and Juanillo, taking advantage of his position as jester to the fleet, was able to follow the captains into the large, solid-looking construction that stood in the middle of the others.

All of a sudden, night fell.

And now your Juanillo would ask you, your Highness, if it is not true that women, of any age or condition, were expressly forbidden to set out with the fleet? I can see you nod your august head, the imperial jaw emphatically dipping to your chest. In which case all that I am about to write must be the product of my imagination or my dreams, since surely no one would have dared disobey your orders.

A large fire was burning in the center of the room. Around it, shrouded in smoke and barely suggested by its red glow, I thought I could make out female shapes. They moved like silent shadows, and vanished like a flock of doves as soon as we came in. I thought my fatigue and all the day's emotions might be making my eyes play tricks with me, so I asked Luis del Molino, who was beside me, if he had seen anything. He looked at me in astonishment and shook his head. Yet on the stones around the fire stood bowls of steaming food.

Stiff, exhausted, we took off our clothes and hung them to dry from the roofbeams, then collapsed round the fire. We ate in silence, nobody asking any questions; bit by bit, as we stared at the crackling flames, each of us became an island remote from the others.

The rain was still beating with a furious roar on the palm leaves of the roof.

Feeling the warmth on his skin relaxing his muscles, his whole body softening, your Juanillo surrendered to the caress of the flames, which brought back memories of other fires in his past. The rectangle of the door stood out in the fire's ruddy gleam; beyond it the rain was pouring down, and further away still lay the dark jungle. I could not see it, but I knew it was there, stretching out endlessly, an impregnable mystery. I could feel its presence; I could smell it in the smoke that irritated my eyes; I could sense it lurking in the darkness like the women I imagined hidden in the shadows of our room. I could hear the rain pattering on the pools of water outside, but I also thought I could discern the fitful breathing of young girls huddled like doves in the furthest corners of the hut. Then, in my mind's eye, I saw how the village must look from afar, reduced to nothing more than a tiny dot amidst a vast, unexplored sea of vegetation. Stranded in the middle of this vastness, the huts, the fire, our men, were less than insects: they were nothing at all. Suddenly I felt afraid, very afraid: then the fear itself lulled me to sleep.

I DREAMT that I woke up and everything was silent. I could no longer hear the rain beating on the roof or the fire crackling. Yet I sensed that behind my back, almost touching me, was another person. I tried to open my eyes, but could not; I lay there without stirring. I even ceased to breathe, and could hear the regular rhythm of another pair of lungs as they filled and emptied. An animal, I thought. A dog perhaps. I was unable to get to my feet or move at all. A moment later, I could feel a warm breath prickling the back of my neck. Scared half out of my wits, I forced my eyes open. As far as I could tell by the firelight, the room was deserted except for our men. I lay still for a while, listening to my own heartbeat with my eyes wide open; then eventually I turned over as gently as I could to find out who or what was behind me. And in my dream there was a woman, your Highness. A dark-skinned woman, but not black, more like the Moorish women but with a deeper color. And in my dream she was little more than a girl. Her breasts were pointed like a female dog's; a thin fine down was just beginning to cover her most intimate parts. She was curled up like an animal, with both hands covering her face. Bewildered, afraid I would be accused of breaking your orders, I stood up. As I looked round the hut I saw other women just like her stretched out next to the captains, who appeared to be sleeping soundly, completely unaware of the strange ritual that was about to begin.

I had better remain silent about what happened next in my dream, since I truly fear your son Felipe, a noble and chaste lord who abhors all the transactions of the flesh. I shall leave the details to your Majesty's imagination: there is no mystery about them. They were first performed by Adam and Eve, and with that I have said more than enough.

I woke up excited and confused, with a raging headache. I

had no idea where the women in my dream had appeared from, and even less why they should give themselves to their enemies, but it had been over two months since I had seen any woman at all, so I lay for a long while with my eyes shut tight trying to summon up the dream again, still enchanted by the dying wisps of my vision. All the more so since the images had vanished before I could satisfy myself as the captains had, and I was left with my unsated desire . . .

By the time I gave up, a milky brightness had filled the hut's doorway. A dog stood quite still on the threshold, peering into the room.

Some of our leaders were still asleep. Luis del Molino sat cross-legged, cradling his master's head on his lap and staring down at it like someone admiring an untouchable jewel. He had thrown a cape over Gaspar's naked body; when he sensed I was looking in their direction, he hitched it up over Gaspar's shoulders with a loving gesture.

Hijito (that was what Juan Carvajo called his son, and we all did the same) was sleeping next to his father with the tranquil yet defenseless expression that all children have when they are asleep.

I do not believe I have introduced the boy to you yet, your Majesty, and that is a pity as he was to suffer one of the most dreadful fates. At that time, he was not yet twelve. He had inherited his dark skin and hair tough as pig bristles from his mother, who was said to belong to a tribe that lived in the north of that land. Carvajo had been forced to dwell among them for four years after Cabral abandoned him to his fate. When he was finally picked up again, Carvajo insisted on taking the boy with him. Since then he had looked after his Hijito all alone, not wishing to give him a European stepmother because of his Indian blood. The boy would have suffered too much, he claimed. And I must say in all honesty, Sire, that I have never in my life seen such a loving father, one so attentive to the least request or so willing to make the greatest sacrifices. Carvajo so adored the boy that he spent all his time peering into the child's moon face and trying to anticipate his wishes or to resolve any problem he might have. Hijito was the light of his life, the sunshine of his days, his manna from heaven, and all that kind of thing. They were inseparable and did everything together. If Hijito was playing, Carvajo kept a discreet watch on him; whenever Carvajo was working, Hijito would not take his eyes off him. It was obvious they meant everything to each other and were so passionately bound together that nobody was taken aback at the boy's presence with the fleet. No one, not even your Majesty, would have been bold enough to demand that father and son be separated, especially since Carvajo had joined the expedition so that he could begin to instruct his whelp in the complex art of navigation. Carvajo dreamt his son would one day become one of your Majesty's pilots; perhaps he even imagined fabulous discoveries Hijito would make in the distant future. Be that as it may, on that particular morning the two of them slept alongside each other, peaceful and happy, blissfully unaware of the catastrophes fate held in store for them.

At that early hour of the morning, the heavens were white and polished like the finest porcelain; washed clean by the rain, the air was fresh and clear, full of the raw fragrance of soaked jungle vegetation.

I was enjoying the air's beneficial effects on my still muzzy head when my attention was caught by a number of large bundles lying in the muddy clearing in front of the hut. In that cold, pre-dawn light, my astonished eyes gradually perceived all kinds of animals, either tied up or in fragile-looking cages, baskets full of exotic fruit, clay bowls filled to overflowing with strange drinks, food, or grains. All of this was carefully laid out on straw mats and decorated with flowers as if it were an offering.

"What does all this mean?" Don Fernando asked Juan Carvalho (which is what the Captain called him in Portuguese).

"It's a miracle, a true miracle! The Lord has answered our prayers! Praise be!" Balderrama the priest exclaimed.

"It means they think you are a god," Carvalho replied.

The Captain General seemed perturbed.

"You must explain to them that you are no god," the priest broke in, "that there is only one God, and . . ."

"Explain to who?" Carvalho interrupted him.

Don Pedro peered at the jungle all around him and fell quiet.

"They must think it rained last night because you are here; perhaps they think our mass yesterday brought the rain. There was obviously a terrible drought in the country," Juan Carvajo explained, taking Hijito by the hand. "They're offering all they have left, everything they saved for their survival, to the god who has brought them the salvation of rain."

"I'll make sure and take you to my estates when there's a drought there," Cartagena scoffed.

"We must tell them the truth," the priest insisted.

"They don't believe in coincidence."

"Nor does the Captain General."

"Anyway, the situation favors us."

We all stood like statues around the offerings while the sun climbed the sky and a sticky hot vapor began to rise from the jungle.

"What am I to do?" my master asked Carvalho.

The *Concepción*'s pilot gazed greedily at the mounds of food and replied: "Behave like a god."

The Captain hesitated. The silence dragged on uncomfortably.

"Be generous," Carvajo added, a smile on his lips.

"Nobody is to take anything without leaving something in exchange," Don Fernando finally decided. The sun gleamed off his armor, blood-red and gold.

Moments later, that clearing in the jungle became a market between two worlds. A comb was worth two chickens, with plenty of meat on them though they were small and scrawny; a basket of potatoes was exchanged for a hawk-bell. A mirror was enough for four or five beautiful parrots, the kind whose feathers fall out when you throw them in a pot: and God knows how much just one of those feathers was worth in Europe as a decoration for some count's hat! As for the monkeys, your Highness, the monkeys were so funny and cheeky that Juanillo could have become rich, and not had to beg for his pension from your Majesty or his son Felipe, if he could only have taken a few of the little fellows he obtained for a handful of glass beads around the squares and markets of your realm. Everything we brought was a treasure to those invisible beings: I know of one man who got four chickens in exchange for a playing card showing the king of clubs, whereas in Europe I know many people who would not give two figs for the king in person. But that is the way of the world, Sire! And I will forbear from mentioning what the priest took in exchange for his cards showing our Lord Jesus Christ on the Cross, because the list would be too long. His pictures of Eve trampling the serpent underfoot were deemed even more precious!

We traded like this for two days and nights while our superiors debated the need to explain the Christian concept of the world to our mysterious hosts, and to have them discuss and recognize in good faith the dominion of Church and King. No sooner had we turned our backs on the jungle and its hoard of precious goods than our own offerings disappeared, too; by the time we returned with more, the clearing was already decked out with fresh displays of exotic barter. All of it appeared and disappeared as if by the art of magic, while in the meantime the captains debated over how to read the Articles of Faith, whether to have a clerk witness the reading and whether Juan Carvajo should act as interpreter—although the priest argued that this would not be necessary because he had never read that the articles should be translated. Anyway, he said, they could not be clearer, and he solemnly launched into the part where, after calling on the natives to adopt our faith, there comes the prayer: "If you do not do so, or if you should maliciously betray your promise, then I guarantee that with God's aid I shall take up arms against you and go to war wheresoever and in whatever manner I may, until you come under the yoke and obedience of the Church and our Majesty. And I shall take your wives and children and make slaves of them, and as such shall sell or otherwise dispose of them in whatever way our Majesty see fit, and I shall seize your possessions and inflict whatever harm and damage I can upon you . . ."

When the priest had finished, feeling very pleased with himself, and with his plump little hands crossed on his belly, he added, "But of course, we'll have to baptize them all with Christian names."

By the end of the two days we had not seen so much as a trace of these Christians-to-be, despite sending out several hunting parties, so the priest had to do without reading his invitation to the faith. On the third morning we started back down to the ships.

The clearing, which had been churned up into a red quagmire, was left deserted. In the middle, alone, stood the cross we had erected.

WE MARCHED through the jungle down a narrow path bordered by high walls of vegetation that arched over us to form a solid tunnel. The sky was invisible, and the light that reached us through the dense foliage was green, unreal. There were gnarled trees, rotten trunks from which all kinds of creatures scuttled as we passed by, masses of branches inextricably intertwined, creepers climbing round the boles of great trees and strewing the path in front of us, huge shiny leaves that flapped at our hands and faces with their gummy caress, green shoots sprouting everywhere, flowers that opened to show stamens loaded with pollen, fruit that ripened before our eyes. We heard strange sounds from all sides, but could not tell exactly where they were coming from. Monkeys swung noisily through the treetops. The branches shook as if caught by the wind, then every so often there would be a howl, followed by a ragged chorus of high-pitched protests. Sometimes one of the creatures fell into the midst of our column, then scrambled away in terror, swinging its way branch by branch up into the trees. Whenever this odd escort fell silent, parrots and other gorgeously plumed birds started up. The racket grew and grew, at times becoming deafening. Then silence. Until another harsh scream set everything off again. The jungle heat was as wet and sticky as pitch. The march became increasingly unbearable. We were suffocated by helmets and breastplates. The hot metal cut into our flesh, opening wounds that each step aggravated. The mud dried on

72

our boots, making our legs as heavy as though we were dragging along chains. Our feet sank into a thick, warm blanket of rotten leaves, raising a dense, fetid vapor from the jungle floor, a vapor that wreathed our clothes and our bodies and gave us the appearance of phantoms.

The torrential rains had completely altered both the path and the jungle, making it almost impossible to find our way. All our reference points had disappeared. We halted in bewilderment at each fork in the path, unable to discover any of the crosses we had hacked into the tree trunks. The trees seemed to have switched places. Fresh shoots from the creepers spread over everything. The streams had flooded, cascading in all directions. Lakes appeared that had not been there a few days before, ditches and gullies had vanished. That cursed jungle was a maze and we were stuck in it.

By noon we had lost all notion of where we were. Perhaps we were headed in completely the wrong direction, or had been walking around in circles. Every few steps, exhausted by marching in the stifling heat that made it ever more difficult to draw breath, one of the men would collapse. Nobody stopped to help him. He would get up as best he could, stagger on a few yards out of fear of being left behind, then fall headlong once more. At last, Don Fernando ordered a halt.

The officers talked things over. Carvajo wanted to go back to the village, but was not sure he could find the way. On the verge of hysteria, Cartagena laughed at his uncertainty. Gaspar cursed. The priest said his prayers.

Marcos de Bayas, the *Trinidad*'s barber, sat beside me bemoaning his fate. "What the devil is a barber doing in a place like this?" he complained.

Calm had descended on the jungle. Everything was quiet. The silence deepened until it was palpable. The feeling that we were being watched from the vegetation took hold of everyone. Nobody said a word. Little by little, the feeling changed into terror. A blind terror of the unknown. Don Fernando got to his feet.

"Prepare your weapons and open fire," he ordered.

"Open fire on what?" Don Luis wanted to know.

Guns at the ready, we all stared at each other.

I SWEAR to you, your Highness, that even though my mother was Jewish and my father unknown to me, and though I am dwarfish and hunchbacked, with the proof of my conversion plain on my body and a reputation for rebelliousness thanks to my master Don Juan, and with no other profession than that of buffoon and crude jester and no other riches than those offered by your generosity, whereas you are a Christian of ancient stock, son and grandson of kings, robust and elegant, the scourge of Moorish lords, Caesar, Emperor, King of Kings—notwithstanding all this, I swear that it was me and not you whom our Lord God chose to reveal the site of Paradise to our fellow men. Yet in all truth I must tell you, Sire, that when these narrow blue eyes of mine first viewed what was at my feet, I was convinced I was dead, and felt sorely afflicted at the idea, because the one thing I have learnt in all my years of wandering has been to feel a great affection for your Juanillo, in spite of his many defects and vices, just as you must hold Don Carlos in high regard, with all his virtues and great qualities. How could I not think I was dead when what I saw before my eyes as we emerged from the jungle onto a hilltop was nothing less than Paradise? Terrified, I turned to my companions and, seeing them pale and unreal-looking, I thought they must also be dead, and felt so sorry for them I began to cry, out of that irrational attachment we have for this our life on earth; then the salty taste of my tears reminded me of the sea, whereupon your Juanillo, who had always hated anything to do with it, was filled with tenderness imagining he would never again . . . Of course I immediately realized how absurd it was to shed tears, since God the Father created the kingdom of the just so that worthy souls might experience eternal joy, and if men as wise as the ancient prophets or as austere as their Catholic Majesties, your grandparents, got on so well there, then a rascally buffoon like myself would have a fine time. This thought calmed me, in spite of the fact that I could not quite accept the idea of being in Heaven for all eternity, which I have heard is a very long time indeed, and I was afraid of becoming bored, since I have always been restless and of a mind to wander from place to place as the spirit took me. While waiting for the boatman who would ferry our souls over to the other side to appear, I set myself to examining what I, at that moment, was convinced would be my eternal resting place.

Thunderstruck by my unexpected transferral to the other world, I gradually saw emerging from beneath the clouds I thought I was standing on, the most beautiful bay that your Majesty's lively imagination could conceive. This spectacle left me totally dumb (without words to think, rather than speak, since there was no question of talking to the gaggle of dead men who accompanied me), yet wild ideas began to take shape in my mind: that the bay surrounded by its thick vegetation was like a woman's sex, with its narrow entrance and warm insides, calm yet exciting, broad and inviting; that it was like my mother's womb, which I had not wanted to leave so that I would not have to start out on this wretched profession of mine; that if Paradise were the reward for a virtuous life, then it would necessarily be like my mother's womb, and then it was only natural to think that to be born is to die, and that when we give up the ghost we are returning to true life. But, at the same time, if it were true that I had gone back to my mother's womb, then what the devil were all the captains doing in there with me, and how did Don Fernando dare come in all dressed in armor, and why did Juan Serrano not even take his hat off, and how could Don Juan allow himself to be carried in on his litter, and what were all the other men doing there anyway? While all this was going through my mind, my nostrils were breathing in the ancestral perfume of the wet jungle, and my eyes were as sharp as a hawk's as they gazed down on the blue peaks that rose out of the mist in the distance, on the tranquil islands with their coconut trees, on the shimmering green mirror of the waters, the burnished white sands of the coast. Everything was bathed in a warm golden light that reminded me of the honey my mother poured on the milk toast she made for when I was a child.

To tell you the truth, Sire, not even the seductive power of those delicacies my mother made could in any way compare to the effect that Paradise had on me, even though I was stone dead.

From the heights our souls had ascended to, the five black ships looked as small as five seeds floating down a stream; it seemed impossible they could have been big enough for us to sail in. At first I was perplexed that the fleet should be in Paradise too, but then I reasoned that they must have won their place in heaven by virtue of their righteous Christian names, and I was pleased at the thought: We could use them to cross the river Lethe and so avoid having that evil old man Charon beat our heads with his oar. "Just a moment," I said to myself, "this is Paradise, so why should I allow an old scoundrel like him to treat me as if I were in hell, eh?"

I was beginning to feel incensed at the idea that even after death I had to put up with the arbitrariness and brutality of those in command, when a loud explosion shook me out of my thoughts. The sound roared round the valley and echoed off the distant peaks. In my terror (I was afraid this was Almighty God expressing his displeasure at having a newly converted Jew in his kingdom) I turned to rush back into the jungle and hide, and saw the smoking black mouths of four arquebuses pointing toward the ships. "What the devil are you up to?" I was about to shout—convinced that Don Fernando was trying to scare off the heavenly hosts so he could plant your banner and your cross in Paradise, then read the Articles of Faith to the souls of the righteous and require them to accept our religion—when another explosion rang out, this time out to sea. So I turned back toward the bay, where I could see a puff of gunsmoke drifting away from the side of the *Trinidad*.

"They're signaling," a voice beside me said. "That means they heard us."

I was so confused I could not imagine what he meant.

"Prepare to be off!" Don Fernando commanded, leading the way into the jungle.

"Oh, no!" I shouted. "I'm going to wait here for the Last Judgment. Perhaps God in his mercy will choose me out of all the hordes of dwarves and mad beggars who wander about Don Carlos's realm."

"Stop talking nonsense; this is neither the time nor the place for your rubbish," Cartagena hissed as he passed by, his voice tarter than a dried apricot.

I did not know what to do, but since I was afraid of losing my pay or even of being hanged for insubordination, there was nothing for it but to follow the captains, dead, alive or whatever else they might be, and follow them to heaven, hell or wherever, just as I would follow your Majesty if your son would only restore my pension. Those of us born to serve do not have the right to choose when we die, nor where we are to recommend our souls, but are obliged to shift from being dead to being alive, from the kingdoms of this world to those of the other, according to the whims of the powerful.

Years later I learnt from that fellow Pigurina or Pigafetta or whatever his name was—who spent all his time observing what was going on with his arms folded, never so much as deigning to dirty his hands with work, except perhaps from the ink he spilt taking notes, if that can be called work—that the great Admiral Colón had a different theory about Paradise.

As your Majesty must know, according to that illustrious explorer, the world is shaped like a woman's breast, with the nipple pointing upward, closest to the sky. Which is why, that fearless sailor wrote, "ships rise gently toward the sky, and we enjoy a feeling of gentle temperance," with the result that he imagined Paradise to be on that "sweet nipple." What I cannot tell you is whether the great Admiral meant his mother's breast or mine. I think it must have been his mother's, because if Paradise were part of my mother's scrawny teat, it would have little bounty to offer—if it had not been for a wet nurse who, according to an uncle of mine, was a fountain of milk, I would not be here now writing these lines for you. Could the Admiral have met my wet nurse, I wonder?

The whole question seems very unclear, especially since that Pigurina or Pigafetta or whatever did not seem to know which of the two breasts Colón was referring to. This leads me to prefer my theory that Paradise is like my mother's womb over the idea that it resembles the nipple on one of the Admiral's mother's breasts. Enough said.

It also goes without saying that the days we spent in Paradise were the only happy ones in all our hellish journey around the world.

In that Eden, the caulkers forgot the tar for our hulls and the pitch for the ropes; the coopers and carpenters neglected their duties; the seamen did not bother to climb the riggings to sew the sails, check the blocks and tackle, examine the cables and lanyards, or grease the anchor hawsers; the ships' boys did not scrub the decks twice a day as regulations stipulated; many of the men were still asleep and did not appear for the dawn roll call; others, lost in daydreams, forgot to doff their caps at the evening one; at night, the lanterns were not lit on the stern-castles; during the day, the other ships did not raise flags to the Captain General, but he did not seem to mind; despite all this abandonment of duty there was not a single captain, boatswain, master, constable or priest who was able to restore a semblance of order.

On top of all this, the *Trinidad* had turned into a sort of New World Noah's ark. The skinny hens protested at their imprisonment on the stern deck; protected from the sun under an old sail, the pigs we had found on shore kept up a deafening squealing from the lower deck; the monkeys swarmed up the riggings and shrouds; the parrots and toucans squawked and squabbled on the yardarms; the rats scampered about all over the ships in broad daylight; lulled by this plentiful abundance, we spent our time in gentle, carefree reverie.

In all those happy days, nobody remembered the rumors about the expedition; nobody gave a damn about the fleet's destination, about what was behind us or what lay ahead. We forgot all the dreams and aspirations we had conjured up and dismissed during the long weary hours at sea; for us at that moment, only the present reality existed. And more than one person claimed, half in jest, that there could be no better a spice island to discover than this.

But, since the pleasures and delights of our life of toil cannot be relied on to last, since they are the charms of a fickle lady, and since the joys of this earth are, precisely because we enjoy them, only ephemeral, whereas the torments of the other world, which always await us, are nothing less than eternal; and since the world is full of deception and our lives are like rivers flowing out to the sea and all that kind of high-flown stuff which poets use simply to tell us that, more often than not, this life of ours is a heap of shit; well then, those happy days in the bay of Santa Lucía vanished like the morning dew on a meadow. And the fault was mine. Something that I, your blabbermouth Juanillo Ponce, Count of the Spice Islands, could not keep quiet about, made our Captain General decide to leave that Garden of Eden as quickly as he could.

One evening, during those brief moments of intense calm that follow the angelus, as all the colors fade and the smells of nature stand out sharp and clear, I was leaning on the rail of the poop deck watching the red of the sunset drain from the horizon when my nostrils sensed something unusual.

It was a strange smell, which had nothing to do with ships. It reminded me of the fragrance of gardens in Sevilla, so at first I thought it must be a memory. But it was too strong and real. I could clearly distinguish the smells of earth and of dung. The unmistakable perfume of jasmine wafted through the still air. It was then I remembered the *Concepción*, rocking at anchor like a shadow close by us, which Don Fernando's wish for greenery had transformed into a floating kitchen garden. I recalled how once before, when we had been becalmed off the coast of Africa, I had noticed a similar aroma. This time, though, the smell was much stronger and more precise. No longer did it have to battle against the stench of the sea; we were surrounded by the most exuberant vegetation which exuded all kinds of fragrances, and yet the smell from the *Concepción* stood out clearly. As I have said, Sire, my Jewish nose sniffed nothing less than a garden in your city of Sevilla.

I turned my eyes to take a proper look at that ship, which I had almost come to disregard, so familiar was its presence.

And I saw the rigging hanging limp from the yards, like the lianas we had seen so often in the jungle. I saw the iron and bronze fittings covered with verdigris. I saw seaweed growing all over the hull like a beard, and making the ship look even more plantlike. I saw the tops of trees crowding its gangways, as tall as the sterncastle. I saw thick branches poking out of the hawseholes in the prow. I saw feelers from climbing plants sprouting from the mouths of cannon and portholes as they sought the sun . . .

I ran to my master, who was supervising the lighting of the lanterns atop the stern.

"Just look at the *Concepción*," I said to him in a low, quaking voice, knowing he did not like to be disturbed.

Don Fernando looked at me blankly. I clutched at his arm (the cold of the iron made me shudder) and repeated, "Look at the plants, my Lord. They have taken over the ship."

He simply smiled and stroked my head gently—he was capable of unexpectedly tender gestures like that, which always brought tears to my eyes.

"I don't have the time now," he said. "We can talk later." Then, seeing I had no intention of leaving, he added softly, "Go on, be off with you."

The worst thing about this profession of ours as builders of illusions, creators of dreams, is that nobody takes us seriously when we are being serious. Nobody listens to our warnings or advice, however accurate it may be. In this we resemble that lady of old, Cassandra who, though she could foresee the future, had been cursed by lord Apollo so that she could not convey what she saw to her family: everyone laughed at her, and she was forced to become a silent witness to the fall of her house.

I was about to leave the deck, thinking, "The devil take him, then," when my stupid obstinacy made me try once more.

"Listen to me, Captain," I begged him. "This isn't a joke. Look over the rail on the port side and you'll see with your own eyes what's going on. And you can have me flogged if I am lying."

He looked down at me in surprise. Reluctantly, he took

two steps to the side of the ship, then stood there watching the shadows of night rising from the depths of the bay to engulf the *Concepción*; as the darkness grew, so the aroma from the ship increased in intensity.

"It's as if the wood in its timbers were growing again," I said.

The next morning, from our skiff, the Captain General, the ship's master, our chief carpenter and the boy Felipe all stared in mute astonishment at this strange form of plant life swaying on the sea a few yards from us. As we drew alongside, the greenery towered above us, blocking out the sky.

The *Concepción*'s boatswain, Joan de Acurio, and the master, Juan Sebastián, received us. Acurio was a pleasant, cheerful fellow, with huge heavy hands that were always as warm as doves. But the ship's master seemed to me to conceal a grain of hypocrisy behind an attitude of false modesty and fawning manners that led everyone—including my master—to believe he was a simple, harmless man.

"Where is the captain?" my master wanted to know, sweeping the deck with an anxious look.

Wherever we looked all we could see was vegetation. It altered and confused the whole shape of the galleon. Here and there oranges glowed, bathed in the soft dawn light. Lemons peeped out of dark foliage. Olives shone like jewels, branches bending under their weight. Thick roots pushed through the sides of barrels, bursting the rotten iron hoops and spreading across the deck. The scent of thyme, parsley and basil perfumed the morning. Eggplants of all kinds, and melons, Don Fernando's favorite fruit, carpeted the quarterdeck and twined around the mainmast.

While we were staring at all this, amazed, a smiling Gaspar de Quesada appeared in the doorway of the sterncastle.

The captain of the *Concepción* had the golden locks of his mother, a lady from a noble family of Bruges, but not her rosy pink skin; Gaspar was dark, like his father the count. His big, almond-shaped eyes were a steely blue, in sharp contrast to his tanned skin, which glistened with sweat. He had an open, candid look that was powerfully attractive to both men and women. His finely drawn features, with high cheekbones and a rugged chin, seemed the work of the most skillful of craftsmen. There was no doubt that his was a truly fine head: strong and noble as an antique marble bust. A real work of art worthy of being placed on a porphyry pedestal by your Highness.

"What on earth is all this?" Don Fernando demanded before Gaspar even had the chance to greet him properly.

A blank look came across the childish features of the *Concepción*'s captain. He did not seem to have understood the question. Soon, though, his frank smile had reappeared.

"It's your garden," he said. "What do you think of it?"

"Throw it all in the sea. I don't want a single plant left."

Gaspar looked puzzled.

"They cannot be tamed, my lord," Acurio put in. "Ever since we've been here they've been growing so quickly that it's no use trying to cut them back. There's been no time to transplant them or even to pick all the fruit."

"Get rid of them," Don Fernando repeated, this time addressing himself to Joan de Acurio. "I'll leave Juan Bautista, the carpenter and Felipe on board here. You must make the ship seaworthy."

"Do you really want everything thrown overboard?" Gaspar de Quesada asked.

There was a silence while my master ran his eyes over the strange floating plantation.

"Unless you think you are capable of steering an island through the ocean . . ." he replied with a mocking smile.

"But you said about scurvy . . ." the captain of the *Concepción* protested, the smile gone from his face.

"I prefer to take my chances with death," Don Fernando replied, turning his back.

All of a sudden, as if he had remembered something important, the Captain General looked around again. "Everything but the soil," he said. "Keep the soil."

When we were back in our boat I could not contain my curiosity.

"Why the soil, my lord? Isn't there enough of it in the worlds we are to explore?"

"Not soil like that," he whispered in my ear. "It's from Oporto."

When I looked at him none the wiser, he added: "I want to be covered with it if I should die during the voyage."

WORK ON cleaning out the *Concepción* began that same morning.

Men swarmed up the shrouds and rigging with brushes, tarring the ropes or greasing the pulleys; others descended into the bowels of the ship with nails and oakum; the carpenters' saws buzzed, blows from the coopers' hammers shaped and stirred the ship's planks; the blacksmith's hammer rang out on the anvil like a peal of bells. And whenever there was silence for a moment, a hundred nimble pairs of hands could be heard rhythmically stitching the sail canvas with waxed yarn.

All this started before first light, when the ship's boys began to heat the tar in a huge cauldron set up on deck, and went on until almost midnight, when the blacksmiths were still shaping iron and bronze as patiently as ants by the glow from their forges.

The bustle of activity was such that, had your Majesty been able to see us that day, you could not have helped thinking that those two hundred and more men were anxious to set off in search of their destination.

Not even Juanillo himself, despite all his efforts, could escape from that frenetic labor. Because I was so small and light, I was placed in a rickety trestle and hung overboard at the *Concepción*'s waterline.

Freed from the weight of Don Fernando's pastoral dream, a broad band of the *Concepción*'s hull was now visible, festooned with seaweed and other parasites. Since there was no possibility of properly careening the hull, I was sent down to scrape as much off as I could.

There, at the farthest reaches of the ship, hidden by the hull's bulge from the boatswain's eyes, I was able to discover many aspects of our adventure that have escaped the other royal chroniclers, who have arrogantly disregarded the explorer's true task.

Take the different kinds of seaweed, for example. Some of them were like lettuces but of a deeper green, dark and soft like moss; others were round and fleshy and reminded me of Joan de Acurio's fingers, like scraps of leather sticky to the touch; still others resembled deer antlers, or fragments of red coral, or oak leaves in autumn, or the down of women's pubises, or angels, roses, feathers. All these silent fellow travelers were like stowaways on this ship of fools. And if you had looked more carefully among this strange flora, you would have spotted goose barnacles with their waving fingernails, and barnacles, armorplated like Don Fernando and clinging to the hull as fiercely as he did to his dreams. If you peered even more closely, your nose pressed against the planks, you would have been rewarded with the sight of a host of tiny sea lice, slowly but implacably gnawing at the timbers, as slowly and implacably as the sun gnawed at our crazy hopes with each new day. And the senseless desire of all these creatures that drove them to be part of our adventure.

ON THE eve of our setting sail again, insistent rumors of revolt began to spread once more. According to these rumors, Juan de Cartagena was plotting with Luis de Mendoza, with the probable support of Gaspar de Quesada. It was said that the go-between was Sánchez de Reina, and that the trouble this time stemmed from Don Fernando's refusal to allow any women on board. But rumor had it that there were women hidden in one of the *Concepción*'s holds, where they satisfied the needs of the plotters and other officers of the fleet. None of us had seen them, or had any idea of how they had got there, but Martín the Cooper, who always knew these things, claimed that there was the unmistakable smell of women's urine in the *Concepción*'s bilges. It was impossible to tell if there was any truth in all these tales. On the surface everything was quiet, with nothing to interrupt the shipboard routine we had recently settled back into.

Don Juan was not involved in the preparations, but spent all his time under the awning he had set up on the poop deck of his ship. The Inspector General spent whole days there in a hammock made from plant fibers that he had obtained by bartering with the natives. It was slung between the mizzenmast and the stern lantern, which sat atop a fine, brightly colored carving of San Antonio, the ship's patron saint. Protected from the sun by one of the extra canvases we had brought in case the sails needed replacing, Don Juan lay, richly dressed as ever, absorbed in reading *The Prison of Love*, his favorite book. From time to time, overcome with emotion, he would close the pages, and play a few plangent notes on his guitar.

Don Luis de Mendoza spent most of his time in his cabin, stricken by an illness which by that point left him little respite. With each of his fleeting appearances in public he looked worse. The black shadows beneath his eyes had sprouted like mushrooms. His large black eyes sank further and further into their bony sockets. The skin of his face had the color and consistency of wax, and seemed likely to tear apart at any moment like an old, worn-out silk shirt.

According to Filiberto the Fairy, page to the *Victoria*'s captain, Don Luis's chest had a bone that stuck out like a scrawny chicken's; in the silence of the night, the sound of the air struggling to fill his lungs was like the plaintive whistle of the wind as it swept through the empty streets of Filiberto's village.

The lad kept watch over his master every night, and with the slow march of the hours the desperate bellows of Don Luis's chest filled the whole cabin so that Filiberto, unable to take his eyes off that strange creature lurking beneath the Dutch lace of the captain's shirtfront, found it increasingly hard to breathe himself. He would shut his eyes, stand up, turn his back, but still be obsessed with the agonizing sound, while the air of the cabin smelt of poultice and seemed never to reach his own lungs.

Sometimes in the middle of the night the noise began to seem like the final death rattle. Then Don Luis would haul himself up, clutching at the bronze rail fixed to the top of the bed, his whole body juddering with the effort. He would break out in a cold sweat, a grimace of terror on his face. Time stood still: Filiberto could sense death circling around them, waiting to strike. And yet, after a few seemingly endless moments, the wheezing of air in Don Luis's lungs would start up again.

The humidity of the tropical air only served to exacerbate an illness the *Victoria*'s captain had suffered from since childhood.

By contrast, Gaspar de Quesada seemed full of life. We would see him striding round his ship, hard at work with his men the whole day long. Clad only in blue velvet breeches, his powerful body tanned by the sun and glistening with sweat, he looked like one of those spirited Arab horses that cause such a stir at any parade.

To see the Spaniards like this, nobody would have credited any of the rumors of plotting. Only Father Sánchez de Reina's comings and goings between one ship and another could have raised any suspicion, but he seemed so peaceable and good-natured that it was hard to believe he might be involved in any sedition.

Therefore, as I have already said, in my opinion any talk of there being women on the ships was simply a slur invented by the sailors (surely nobody would dare contravene your orders?). All I can add, between the two of us, is that during the time I was hanging alongside the bulging belly of the *Concepción*, careening her sides, on more than one occasion I heard Sánchez de Reina's reedy voice, together with the booming tones of Chaplain Balderrama, outlining the principles of our Christian faith to an invisible congregation. It seemed to me they were not talking to each other, but addressing a third person, although I never heard any other voice. Both of them mentioned Sodom and Gomorrah, the seven plagues of Egypt, and many other disasters illustrating how God behaves toward anyone who rebels against His command. So convincing were they that as I lay on my trestle in the shadow of the ship's hull I began to work even harder, lest any slackness on my part should draw down God's wrath on my head. If their sermons were in fact directed at the women who were supposedly hidden in the hold, those unfortunate creatures must have been delighted by the plain, straightforward way in which the priests explained such things as the Holy Trinity, Reincarnation, the Ascension and other similar trifles. They also warned them about Hell, doubtless showing them pictures like the ones I was shown when I was converted. I can see the images to this day. Legions of the damned with their heads barely rising out of a sea of fire, like harvesters in a field of corn; men and women with disheveled hair raising their hands to heaven to implore a forgiveness they will never be granted; serpents and devils and all kinds of the most gruesome scenes. And up in the Heavens, the good Lord seated in glory among the clouds, surrounded by the hosts of the righteous, nearly all of them with long white beards and dressed in white robes, a look of utter boredom on their faces, while a gang of chubby angels hovers around, keeping the flies off this venerable assembly.

It was while I was hanging there, imagining how stupefied those imaginary women must be by all these complex matters which were, moreover, pronounced in a language they could not possibly understand, that the crazy idea of baptizing my pet monkeys came to me. After all, I reasoned, if they had to help me in my work, why should they be denied the right to enter Paradise? I was none too clear about Paradise, in fact, since the monkeys had been living in Paradise until I came along and took them from it so they could join our adventure, which had little to do with heaven . . . but anyway, I felt I should give them that opportunity, and afterward they could do as they wished with their souls.

I was wondering whether I should read them the Articles of Faith, how I should explain everything to them, and what Christian names I should baptize them with, when something underwater caught my eye.

It was a kind of plant with violet-colored leaves that swayed to and fro as if caught by a breeze.

I had never really studied the seabed before, but in that bay it was like an exotic garden seen through a glass pane. While I was working out how to explain the Holy Trinity to my monkeys, although I had never really understood it myself—"it means that you have three monkeys, but in fact there is only one of them, but that one is three in one"—I was staring like a village idiot at the blue or red flowers on the rocks of the sea bottom, and at some huge crabs that scuttled off in terror at the sight of the *Concepción*'s shadow, looming like a premonition over their strange marine world. The fish did not seem at all frightened, though, and came in dense silver, spotted or striped shoals like heraldic emblems to investigate the shadow of my trestle, swimming round about it with the grace of a troupe of dancers.

The seabed was also littered with all sorts of shells, some of them shaped like spindles, others like breasts, or meringues, or combs or Chinese lanterns; still more in the shape of cornucopias, meatballs or turds.

The ship lay motionless above this world, separated from it by nothing more than a thin, fragile layer of glass. Yet the shadow of our vessel weighed on all its silent creatures, darkening the sun in the middle of the day.

THAT AFTERNOON, in a simple but moving ceremony, I baptized my monkeys with Christian names.

It was shortly before the angelus, and I was back on board the *Trinidad*. I took advantage of the chaplain's absence to borrow his habit. I donned the amice, the alb, and even put on the spare chasuble he kept in a trunk, then went out onto the gangway to offer the sacrament to my animals.

Among the monkeys there was one who, although not the largest in the group, was undoubtedly the leader, because he spent the whole day frenziedly trying to keep all the other males off his territory.

He would scamper up and down the imaginary border he had traced for himself, baring his teeth and emitting bloodcurdling howls whenever any of his male companions came near. If one of them trespassed on his territory, he would maul and bite him furiously. I am not sure what it was he was defending so ferociously—perhaps he was simply demonstrating his power—but be that as it may, his kingdom was no grander than a small area of the gangway where they were all caged, and his subjects no more than a few other monkeys identical to himself. And his lot depended on me, while mine depended on Don Fernando, and Don Fernando's on your Majesty, and . . . Yet those wretched animals had no awareness of this, and tore each other to pieces over a tiny, meaningless space, prisoners on a ship over which they would never have any control.

I refused to baptize that particular monkey. I simply hung round his neck one of our cheap mirrors, which at that moment reflected the ruddy splendors of the setting sun. Then I took the paw of one of the others who was always fighting with him, and who was remarkable for the way in which he never admitted defeat but always returned to the fray. I draped a velvet cloak I had made from some scraps around his shoulders, and baptized him Juancito. Then I blessed another monkey with the name Mendo; he looked wizened and sickly, with big weals on his ragged fur. The prettiest one was Gasparico, of course; then there was another one who often slipped into the disputed area while the others were fighting for it. Once he had gained access (usually by climbing along the ship's rail) he would imitate the leader's conduct in defending the territory. He would copy all the leader's threats to an invisible enemy, and scamper up and down the gangway until a growl or warning cuff from the master put him to flight. Him I called Sebastián.

While I was busy in this way, a large group of curious onlookers had gathered, leaving the mass on the poop deck to come and see what all the laughter was about over the more modest ceremony I was carrying out. The crowd was so enthusiastic I decided to baptize all my birds as well. I had two crows with jet black plumage and bald heads, whom I decided to name Fonseca and Cristobão. I called a pair of buzzards I had brought with me the Hapsburgs: they were the first to go into the pot when we ran out of food during our long winter stay in the bay of San Julián. I also had a talkative, hysterical parakeet which I christened Juanita la Loca, and an elegant yellow and blue parrot I called Isabelita.

My idea delighted the crew, who were able, for a short

while, to forget the sorrow we felt at having to depart again. The master of the ship, Sánchez de Reina, was not pleased, however: he called me a Jewish heretic and denounced me as a thief to the Captain General. Don Fernando was angry with me too, and not only gave me a stern lecture but ordered that I be given ten lashes, which could easily have been more, he warned me. But from that moment on neither Don Fernando nor anyone else could prevent the crew from calling all the animals by the names I had given them.

"How about eating a Hapsburg?" they would say. "Let's wring Cristobão's neck," "Juancito will come to a bad end," "Mencito is going to die on you," "I'll kill Sebastián one of these days if he doesn't stop his thieving," "What a pretty boy Gasparico is," and so on and so forth.

PART IV

Driven onward by strong winds, we sped south.

As we left the shoreline, the seagulls and other coastal birds dropped away; only a few frigate birds hung motionless high above our masts, like children's kites.

Perhaps our ships, seen from above, also looked like kites hanging over the boundless surface of the sea.

A school of dolphins led the way, diving and leaping in front of our prows, accompanying the headlong flight of our ships as singlemindedly as playful dogs that run and jump in front of their master's carriage without ever once being struck by the horses' hoofs. The dolphins swam in formation, rising out of the waves, then dropping back into the water one by one, only to flash upward again a moment later, as sharp and shiny as swordblades in the sunlight. They never fell behind, but flowed along like a cavalry regiment sweeping over the crests and valleys of a rough terrain.

But such was our haste that after a few hours they could no longer keep up, and eventually they gave in, pausing to lift their charming heads out of the water and watch us speeding on.

The ships were like birds tormented by a strange anxiety. They dashed across the sea as though to catch the wind with their wings, scarcely touching the water, their hulls turning one way, then the other, as if in a dance: showing first their dark undersides, then their whitened backs. Occasionally they crashed into the water like black stormy petrels landing clumsily on the waves; the timbers shuddered from keel to crossbeam. An instant later, they were skimming the crests again, almost without touching the water, leaving a thin creamy wake behind them as, sails reefed, they seemed to shoot skyward, gliding majestically over the surface of the ocean like huge albatrosses.

With each day the coastline changed. The vegetation receded inland, the beaches became wider and more desolate.

On the sixth day out, someone announced that we had left Portuguese territory behind, and we cast anchor to give ourselves a brief respite.

What a strange boundary that was, your Majesty. A cape populated by huge granite whales, their backs covered with dark brown, furlike seaweed and rising only a few feet out of the foam. An odd landmark indeed, this group of peaceful stone whales, whose hard backs shone among frills of spume finer than any Flemish lace. Backs over which water had cascaded in silvery streams since time began.

Beyond this cape lay immense sand dunes. Seagulls wheeled in lazy circles above the dunes' indescribable desolation. Opposite the wall of sand, in a sort of bay closed to the south by a rocky point, stood two small, gloomy-looking islets. The wind had carved a host of towers out of the gray rock; moaning, it wove its way through them as if through the turrets of an abandoned castle. Grouped on the shore, or dragging themselves along through this ghostly landscape, we saw hundreds of those dogs of the sea known as sea lions or seals. Their cry was a sad howling that lent a note of foreboding to the bleakness of the coast.

The sky was overcast with dark clouds, making the whole landscape look as if it were painted in shades of gray. From time to time the clouds parted and the rays of the setting sun bathed the enchanted isle in a red glow that only made it seem more unreal.

Don Fernando sent some men in the longboat to hunt a few of the sea lions so we could taste fresh meat, as we had exhausted our stocks. He told the men to kill as many of the creatures as possible because their skins are very valuable in Europe, where they were first introduced by the explorer Torres.

I did not want to go with them; for some reason I had taken it into my head that a disheveled old woman lived on the island, hobbling along pursued by the pack of sea lions, and lamenting her solitude with heartrending cries.

The next morning we raced off again under full sail. We passed more rocky points, more endless sand dunes and forlorn beaches on which no man had ever set foot. I thought to myself: what kind of realm is this, where there are neither men nor women, nor children, cows, pigs or hens; where there are no voices to be heard, no laughter or weeping or protests; where the smells of sweat, shit and sex are completely lacking. What the devil does Don Carlos want this deserted kingdom for? I asked myself. A place where there is nobody even to pronounce the king's name, let alone love or hate him. A kingdom as silent as a house suddenly abandoned, as untouched as a room left closed after the death of a loved one, as solitary as a cot forgotten in a loft.

A few miles further, the waters began to take on a strange red tinge. Andrés de San Martín took this as a portent. He said it was the color of betrayal, and everyone remembered the Spaniards and their intrigues, although perhaps he was referring to a different kind of betrayal, of which we were all both the victims and the perpetrators.

The water turned redder and redder. We were sailing between huge clumps of water lilies torn from the jungles by rivers in flood, water lilies that drifted past us bearing a cargo of monkeys and all kinds of other creatures.

"This is Solís's river," Albo said.

On the tenth of January of the new year of 1520 we caught sight of a sheltered bay surrounded by sand dunes and dominated by a hill we called Monte V (do not ask me why; it is still a matter of great debate). Although this seemed a quiet and protected spot, ideal for us to rest up in, we went on instead in a northerly direction up the great river.

The other ships signaled to us, asking where we were headed, but Don Fernando paid them no attention, simply ordering the captain to press ahead under full sail. He was very excited and active, constantly rushing from the prow, where he could observe the river, to the stern, where he kept a keen eye on the other ships of our fleet. He gave everyone orders, attending to the tiniest details of our shipboard routine, and even taking a hand himself in some of the maneuvers. His nervousness was so plain to see that we all felt something important was about to happen. Most of the crew were worried about a possible ambush by Portuguese ships intent on blocking our progress; this river seemed like a perfect place for it. They were also uneasy because this huge river, whose far bank we never even saw, was where the natives had killed Solís in a most horrible manner. If the royal pilot had ended his days in a pot like a chicken, what might lie in store for simple sailors like ourselves?

Your servant Juanillo tried to calm his fears by telling himself that perhaps those savages would prefer succulent Spanish flesh—for which they had already developed a taste—to the scrawny nondescript meat of a converted Jew. Bolstered by that specious argument, I attempted to instill a little more courage in my companions as well.

"Who says that Don Solís is dead? Haven't you learnt to pick out the truth from official lies?"

They all looked at me, perplexed, so I carried on: "What do you expect their Catholic Majesties to tell you? That he took off with a native woman as soon as he landed, and wouldn't hear another word about discoveries or navigating? Can't you imagine the chief royal pilot preferring an easy life of pleasure, stretched out in the warm sun, to one of armor and constant worry? What do you expect the Crown to say? That he gave up his God and his king and all his dreams of grandeur for a dark-skinned beauty with ebony breasts and soft mosses, petals and other moist charms? I reckon he is neither dead nor eaten by cannibals: he's out there in those hills somewhere, naked and content, better off not only than any of us but than the Captain General, Don Juan de Cartagena and all the rest of them put together."

And then, to clinch the argument: "Do you know they say that Don Fernando's great friend Francisco Serrano did exactly the same? Yes, Serrano is a wise man who had the sense to renounce ambition and the craziness of the spice wars. After fighting the sultan of Malacca alongside Lopes de Sequeira, he set himself up on one of those paradise islands with the king of Ternate's daughter, and still lives a carefree life of plenty there. He might not have been the most heroic or noble of the conquerors, but he was the happiest and wisest of them all."

By this time, none of my listeners was laughing. One of them asked how I knew all this.

"It was the Captain General himself who told me," I answered. "He's got letters with him from Serrano, inviting Don Fernando to join him. There are only two of them, but he has read them hundreds of times. I myself have read them. You should hear how Serrano pictures the quiet peaceful life he is leading. It is really moving. Sometimes I even think that is where we're heading. The Captain hasn't said as much, but whenever he mentions Francisco Serrano there is a kind of longing in his voice; he closes his eyes as if in a dream."

"Do you think Don Fernando intends to retire to an island like that?" they wanted to know.

"I must ask him sometime," I replied. "You never know; we are always discovering new things about people."

AS WE pushed our way through the islands of floating vegetation, the going was slow. Lianas and leaves compacted together in their long journey down from the jungles made a solid carpet for terrified monkeys and slithering snakes. There were also hundreds of frogs and toads whose noisy croaking at night made it hard to sleep. The vegetation parted in front of the ships, then closed again behind them, leaving no trace of their passage. As we lost the direction we had come from and headed into the unknown, we were like another huge plant among the many, like one of the ancient rotten trunks caught up in this green slimy mass and carried along by the current of a river that, we imagined, was flowing out to sea, as we toiled against it. Whole trees floated past us, all kinds of birds clustered in their bare, forlorn branches. There were parrots of every color under the sun, white and pink herons, an occasional stork; without exception they looked exhausted, their plumage filthy and ragged. Dead animals drifted downstream too, bloated like wineskins, looking as though they were about to burst. And one evening we saw some household utensils being swept downstream. Two or three clay pots, some matting, a rudimentary plow caught in the roots of a sinewy plant, and even a stone idol, staring at us expressionlessly, as frogs dozed like flies on its enormous head.

It became increasingly difficult to make our way up those dark waters with their hidden dangers, but Don Fernando would not hear of turning back. In the daytime we kept our fears at bay, or imagined we were doing so, but at night they grew and grew until they blotted everything else out. First there was the silence as night fell, broken only by the constant thud of logs and vegetation hitting our hull. Sometimes this was nothing more than a dull thump, at others it was a crashing sound that rocked our timbers as if they were about to split open and smash into a thousand pieces. Nothing happened though, and we waited with bated breath for the next crash, searching in vain for some indication of when it might occur.

After that, a cold moon whose light had nothing in common with the one that bathes the streets of my village of Bustillo del Páramo climbed the sky and filled that unreal meadow my master called a river with ghostly reflections. With sails unfurled to no effect, our fleet resembled the birds we could see waiting to die, perched on the branches of trees carried downstream by the current. Then, too, there was the deafening croaking of the frogs and, whenever they fell silent, the scrambling sound of all kinds of creatures swarming over the sides of our ships. In my terror I tried in vain to take refuge in my memories, but it seemed as if Juanillo Ponce's memory had also floated off downstream or had been submerged beneath all the vegetation, like the waters of the river itself. Scared half to death, I would spend the rest of each night saying my name over and over until I finally fell into an exhausted sleep around dawn, only to be awakened with a start every time Don Fernando's footsteps resounded on the deck above my head. My master spent all night pacing the decks; his iron steps sounded like the ticking of a clock measuring out our hours.

On the fourth day—after not once retiring to his cabin for three days—with discouragement and exhaustion plain on his face for all to see, Don Fernando ordered Esteban Gómez to put about and head back down the river we had struggled so long to conquer. Nobody knew how many miles we had traveled. Andrés de San Martín took bearings for a longitude from the conjunction of Jupiter and the moon, but the result made no sense according to Zacuto's tables or Juan de Monte Regio's almanac.

This news alarmed the men; only Don Fernando seemed unconcerned by it. "Tell the other ships we are going back," he instructed Francisco Albo.

"It's for the best, my Lord," San Martín agreed.

"For the best," my master muttered, a sad smile flitting across his face.

We cast anchor once more in the sheltered bay at Monte V. A tense calm, which presaged no good, reigned.

Don Fernando now spent all his time shut in his cabin trying to decipher nautical charts that seemed more incomprehensible to him by the day. Everything had looked so simple and straightforward when he and Faleiro were poring over maps and measurements before we set out; but now he did not understand a thing, and the harder he tried, the more details escaped him. The radii of the nautical projections blurred in front of his eyes until they became a spider's web he felt caught in like a tiny fly. At times, in his frustration, he cursed his former

99

associate, accusing Faleiro of having kept vital information from him. At noon one day, exhausted by his efforts, he stopped and rushed out on deck with his astrolabe to see if his own measurements could provide him with some key to unlock the secrets of the tangled mass of lines that governed our destiny.

No one dared suggest anything until Don Fernando had given fresh orders. All kinds of rumors abounded about the future of our expedition.

The priest Sánchez de Reina, who to all intents and purposes had taken over the chaplaincy of the fleet as a result of Pedro de Balderrama's weak nature, was one of the most worried. He took Cartagena's side, feeling linked to the Inspector by his longstanding friendship with the bishop of Burgos, and he was concerned about the secret plans he thought Don Fernando might be hatching. He spent the whole day leaning over the starboard rail staring down at the red waters of the river. He thought he saw God's hand behind their disturbing color, and he also saw it as a warning about his own fate. In his despair, the priest let himself drift off into the distant memory of a morning thirty years earlier, the morning he had arrived, bursting with idealism, to take charge of his first parish.

He had been very young then, with the wan features of a seminarist and the gaunt physique of a saint. But he was ambitious, and thought that he would soon become a bishop and then, with time, might even reach the position of a venerable cardinal in the church of Christ. All his dreams were quickly shattered by the poverty of his parish in La Mancha and the indifference of his parishioners. He tried in vain to cling to his hopes and illusions. The daily struggle to get by wore away his dreams just as the cold winds of the high plateau wore smooth the stones of his church; the years buried and hid them just as the yellow dust of the fields around the village covered everything that stood in its way. He had no idea when it was that he gave up dreaming. He only knew that he began to see things differently. He let himself be absorbed by the routine of sermons, evening walks around the village's four streets, regular meals, and his trivial conversations with the villagers. Even the feast days he celebrated became identical after a few years. He put on weight. Grew old. Became respected, even loved. He forgot about bishops, cardinals and other princes of the Church. He was happy. Then all of a sudden the cathedral of his youthful dreams seemed to rise again out of the dust like the landscape after the October rains. Thanks to his Majesty's expedition, he might find himself a bishop in the Indies, or even chief prelate of all the newly discovered lands.

From the moment he learnt he was to join the fleet, Sánchez lost all interest in the life he had been leading for thirty years in Argamasilla de Alba, and which until a few months earlier he would have sworn he would continue to enjoy untroubled until the day of his death. He gave up hunting and his games of cards with the village barber and the local squire. He suddenly lost his taste for wine, and even began to go off his favorite dishes. He silently cursed the fierce sun of La Mancha and secretly detested the wind and the dust. He took to avoiding the villagers; he was even reluctant to say mass for such clod-hopping peasants whose furthest horizon was the outskirts of the village.

Yet the afternoon that he left there were tears in his eyes when he looked back at his church. He was choked with emotion as he received the best wishes of his flock. Many of them cried too, especially the women. The old people could not understand what he was doing, and the young envied him his opportunity.

There were warm embraces and handshakes, provisions for his journey, recommendations that he take great care and return home soon. All of this turned Pedro Sánchez as soft as butter, and were it not for the fact that he had promised the bishop of Burgos, he would have given up his crazy idea there and then and leapt into the arms of his housekeeper, who was trailing behind his cart along the road to Ciudad Real like a ghost. The priest turned round more than once to wave goodbye to her and urge her to return to the village, but it was useless. The dark haggard figure with whom he had spent so many years, sharing what had perhaps been a sacrilegious and never-confessed love, still followed him beneath a sun like molten lead. The white village gleamed in the distance, with a group of villagers huddled by the last house, still waving.

Above the village roofs he could make out the belltower of his church. Just at that moment a stork flew off from it with beating wings.

"Let's be on our way," he said to his sacristan, who also served as coachman. "Get those mules going."

''Now I won't be able to go back. Even if we return to Spain I can't go there," he said. "Another priest will have taken my place: a young man full of ideas; nobody will remember Father Sánchez anymore."

I didn't know what the devil to say to him. There was a pause as we both looked up at the sky to watch a seagull gliding a few yards away from us.

"I can still remember the names of all my parishioners, every couple I joined in marriage, every dead person I bade farewell with tears in my eyes, every child I baptized. The first one was a girl: they called her Encarnación, then she became Encarnita, and now she is Doña Encarna. Surrounded by children of her own. A big fat woman. And the last—how could I forget him, when he was the son of my friend Quijana (or could it have been Quesada?—it's strange that even though we were such good friends I have doubts about his name: to me, he was always 'Alonso' and I was 'the priest'). Anyway, we called the child Alonso, too. His father said the boy would become a soldier just as all the Quijanas had done since the days of King Sancho. I remember he was a small skinny baby who accepted the holy water without so much as a protest. That day there was a great celebration in the Quijana family home. The local wine flowed freely, there were suckling pigs and turkeys to eat, cheeses, nuts and everything you could wish for. Alonso's father was a good man. He was honest, a good friend, always willing to lend a hand, and a good Catholic. We used to spend the afternoons together, either in the sacristy or in the tavern. We had spent so much time together we didn't even need to speak to each other anymore. I would say my rosary, and he would sit there chopping toothpicks out of bits of wood with his knife; he used to make hundreds of them and give them to his friends. Or sometimes he would doze beside me, or leaf through a prayer book. We scarcely moved even to brush off flies, but sat there without a word, keeping each other company. The day I left he came to say goodbye with little Alonso in his arms. He stood in the doorway watching me pack my things. He didn't say anything then, either."

Hearing all this, your Juanillo was as silent as Quijana had been, yet from that moment on I felt a secret esteem for the priest. He was not a bad man: he made some mistakes, of course, but which of us has not? Well, anyway, who's to say if his friend is not already dead from loneliness and boredom, or whether little Alonso has turned into a bold, resourceful youth? How would I know, your Highness? Why do you make me say these things? The saints preserve us!

I MUST confess, Sire, that the disputes among the captains are not only hard for me to relate now in these pages but were painful at the time, when I was a being of flesh and blood stuck among that handful of lunatics roaming the high seas in our four wooden tubs. Even then it struck me as tedious and unnecessary for our superiors to be intriguing and plotting to win power when all of us were completely powerless. The real power (I know you're thinking I'm about to write, "lay with you, your Highness," but you're wrong) the real power lay with the sea, with those unknown lands, with those boundless jungles, or up in the sky, in the sun that continually scorched our skins, in the rains, in the winds or the lack of them. Everything else was an illusion: our ships, our navigational instruments, our sea charts, our determination to arrive somewhere. Only we ourselves believed in all that. It was only we who were impressed by the size of our fleet, the scope of our ambitions, the persistence of our dreams, the power of our captains. To the sea, the jungles or the wind, we were nothing at all, less than a handful of tiny ants clinging to a twig in the midst of the vast ocean, as much at the mercy of those forces' as ants, and perhaps even more so. But nobody seemed aware of this. Yet we were all frightened, with a kind of constant, ubiquitous fear that seemed to spring from the very marrow of our bones, and perhaps that was our way of being aware.

This was not true of your Spanish captains. They were so much more concerned with winning control than with any thought of the fate of the fleet or its crews that they seemed to have lost all interest in where the ships were heading or even the reason behind the voyage. Their demands to see Don Fernando's charts became less frequent and insistent. They now seemed hardly bothered at all by the secrets he guarded so jealously, even though this had been their main bone of contention at the start of the expedition. Their indifference did not reassure Don Fernando, but threw him into a thinly disguised despair. Perhaps he felt even more alone and responsible, as if his own convictions had been reinforced by the clash with other people's disbelief. Now that he could not count on that opposition, his own faith seemed to waver. He had only himself to rely on. He alone had to decide whether to pursue his plans. It was no use questioning the stars with his astrolabe, no use wearing out his eyes trying to decipher Faleiro's charts. They could give him no answer. So one evening he sent the skiff over to the *San Antonio* to fetch her pilot Andrés de San Martín, a cosmographer by profession and an astrologer by repute.

The Spaniard came on board just as the sun was sinking into the muddy waters of the river. A reddish glow softened the outlines of all the objects around us and the features of the expectant crew. The evening silence, broken only by the call of a distant bird returning to its nest, closed in around us.

We all stood stock still as the pilot walked the length of the deck. It was as if the *Trinidad* were carrying a cargo of statues for the king's gardens. San Martín's footsteps rang out across the ship. As if abashed by this array of silent witnesses, he hardly raised his head as he made for the Captain General's cabin. Inside the cramped room, dimly lit by a single lamp hanging from a beam, Don Fernando was standing waiting for him beside a table strewn with parchments and instruments. I could not hear their voices, but I saw them exchange greetings and then saw my master indicate that the pilot be seated. My natural curiosity led me to draw closer so that I could see properly what was going on.

The cosmographer's eyes, big and gentle as a doe's, were now scrutinizing a parchment. He followed the traces of the nautical roses nervously, paused at the places where they converged, concentrated his attention on numbers and other annotations written in tiny handwriting. Every now and then he glanced up to intercept Don Fernando's somber gaze, then shook his head and bent over the chart once more.

The only sounds came from the *Trinidad*'s creaking timbers and the river rushing under its black hull. The shadows lengthened; the first stars appeared in the leaden sky.

"Well," the Captain said, "what do you think?"

The cosmographer apologized. He said the charts were too difficult to follow, that they must be based on different calculations than the ones he had been trained to use; he was very sorry, but he was not sure he understood them.

Don Fernando went over to him and laid a hand gently on his shoulder. "Don't be frightened," he whispered, "sometimes I get confused myself."

At this unexpected sign of tenderness the cosmographer turned to the Captain General with moist eyes and smiled wanly.

"We're heading for the East by sailing west, aren't we?" he asked timidly. "And the fleet's destination is our point of departure, except that you intend to reach it by heading away from it," he added in the same subdued tone.

Don Fernando asked if that surprised him.

San Martín hesitated. "Nobody has ever done it before," he said.

"But we will! You and I will manage it," the Captain replied. "We will prove the Spice islands can be reached from the west, and we will return with our ships laden with pepper, cloves, cinnamon, saffron, ginger . . ."

Andrés de San Martín seemed dumbfounded. "What about this huge continent that stretches from south to north, from pole to pole, blocking our way? Are we looking for a strait through it then? Do you really think one exists?"

"I don't think it," my master said, "I know it."

The cosmographer's eyes returned to the chart. His fingers groped along the lines as if he were blind. "No lands are marked on the map beyond Cabo Frío," he said. "Where does the Captain think the strait is to be found? To the south? So we'll be heading further south?"

Don Fernando nodded.

"Without any points of reference? Sailing blind?"

"Not blind, no; I have my instruments."

"May the Good Lord help us," San Martín said, looking in vain for the crucifix which hung over the captain's bunk on every ship (in Don Fernando's cabin it had been replaced by an astrolabe).

"Were we supposed to find the strait here in Solís's river?" the cosmographer wanted to know.

"We were supposed to make sure, one way or the other," my master replied.

"So, then you don't know exactly where it is?"

"I know the strait exists, and that we will find it."

"Where do you situate the Spice Islands?" the cosmographer asked, while his small, nervous hand groped across the parchment's seas as though to feel where they were.

There was silence for a few moments. The expression on Don Fernando's face hardened. "Anywhere," he said.

"I don't understand why you sent for me," Andrés retorted, his face aflame with anger or shame, or a mixture of both. "If the Captain General does not want me to meddle in his affairs, I shall leave," he added, trying to regain his composure.

"No, stay."

"I cannot be of any help to you."

"Perhaps you can. You are said to be a fortune-teller."

"I thought you were against my science."

"I am in favor of everything that might be useful to me. And against everything else."

When their discussion had reached this point, I was no longer able to control my bowels; fear had set them writhing inside me like a knot of vipers. I ran to the latrines to avoid soiling my trousers. Phew! I can assure you, your Highness, fear stinks. It has a stench as foul as death, and sometimes even worse, although of course it has the advantage of being only temporary rather than lasting forever. Of course, since you never chew on doubt, but always on pheasant or phoenix, and never drink fear, but only wine with a pinch of cloves and cinnamon, you can know nothing of these particular perfumes. I have even wondered whether kings do in fact shit—if you, in all your majesty, go and squat over a bucket and strain like the rest of us, if you take off your layers of ermine, silks and velvets with your own hands or whether a pageboy has that task and the added honor of wiping the royal ass. Is there a special place reserved for these functions among all the gold and perfumes of your palaces? I am truly confused about this, because it seems to me that with all you swallow, guzzle, gnaw and consume—and always the best and largest portions—it would make no sense for you to do only the eating and the rest of us to do all the shitting. But one never knows, the lot of a common sailor is as different from yours as that of an ant is from a lion's. A bit of hard tack and a cupful of stinking water is enough for us to leave the ship's latrines a foul mess (and I must say that the stink the officers make is hardly worthy of their exalted position); and yet one can never tell if the same is true of the powerful such as yourself who rule the world from dry land. However that may be, let me say that if you do not have the habit, you should try it, because it is good for the mind as well as the body. Whenever I visit the latrine, for example, I find myself as much at peace as if I had been to mass. But like everything else in this life, one has to know how to make the most of it. To continue with my own example, whenever my belly starts to rumble I know what's to come, but I take care not to rush things, so that the feeling of relief afterward will be all the more pleasurable. If, on the other hand, you are constipated, that can only be of value for the affairs of state and your subjects, since while you're squatting or sitting over the bucket waiting for something to happen, you'll be able to see things more clearly and will make decisions you would never have been able to make anywhere else. It may even be that you start to meditate—even a king could acquire that habit if he went to the latrine often enough—in which case it could truly be said that God is on our side, all praise be to him. As for me, seeing that I seldom have anything to decide, as others have always decided for me ever since I was born, I tend to spend my time in the latrine meditating on my fate and other equally interesting topics, and it is as though my guts were doing the thinking and not my brain. That is precisely what happened when I overheard the conversation between Don Fernando and Andrés de San Martín. No sooner had I learned of the plans for the fleet than my stomach started to churn. Hearing the Captain General consult Andrés as a fortune-teller rather than as a pilot was enough to send me running, and not because your Juanillo is a great lover of science and an enemy of magic, nor because San Martín was particularly inept at it—the members of his family had been the advisers of kings, and it was well known that their prophecies always came true, even though it must be said that although the San Martín family read the future in the stars like an open book, they were never able to foresee their own tragic destinies.

The truth is that I spent too long in the latrines, in spite of the nauseating smell that filtered up from the hole we used to wash the urine down into the bilges. I should have realized that if the smell was not overpowering, it could only mean that the timbers of the hull were allowing enough water in to put the ship in danger of sinking—I recommend a similar method for you to determine the health of the Ship of State.

The fact is, I spent too long down in the latrines and did not hear what Andrés de San Martín prophesied. By the way, did you know he used to wear a big, broad-brimmed hat with a feather, and a cape with a blue silk lining that had the constellations embroidered on it in silver thread?

"Is that you?" he asked without turning around.

In answer I shook the bells on my bracelet.

No lights were lit in the cabin, but two broad beams of moonlight shone in through the windows. One from the port side struck Don Fernando full in the chest. The other shone across the whole room, picking out fragments of objects in the darkness. In its path lay half a trunk, the tin disc of an astrolabe, the bottom part of an hourglass, and a white circle that moved to and fro across the floorboards as the ship rocked back and forth.

We both remained silent for a while.

"I checked the list of provisions with Odoardo today, and I can assure you there is nothing to worry about," Don Fernando finally said.

I said nothing. He went on with his monologue.

"We're not exactly overstocked, but we won't go hungry either."

I remained silent. I felt he was beating about the bush, and that I should say nothing until he began really speaking his mind. I was in no hurry. I knew that sooner or later he would crawl out of his suit of armor like a caterpillar out of its chrysalis, and turn into a gaudy butterfly as he fluttered among his memories and my inventions. It had happened before when the two of us were alone in his cabin.

He watched the river flowing by, still without saying a word. I was watching the sand slipping through the glass. His slave Enrique moved around in the darkness like a cat.

Several minutes went by before he decided to break the silence.

I cannot now remember exactly how our conversation went. I have no wish to invent it, as I have done before now and will again whenever necessary. Suffice it to say that he continued with his evasive talk, and I with my silent provocation, until he reached the point of telling me how he had met his wife Beatriz in Odoardo's house. Did your Majesty know that when she first saw him she was overcome by a strange premonition? It was as though a huge black bird had flapped its wings in front of her face for a second, stirring up the calm air. Months later when she told him about it, Don Fernando had laughed at her, yet sometimes when they were together he experienced the same absurd feeling. As if wings were beating at the warm air. He rejected the idea as crazy, but it kept coming back.

He was talking intently of these things to himself, then he suddenly said out loud:

"It's odd, but Andrés de San Martín also mentioned black birds that blocked out the sun."

From there on, I can remember our dialogue as if it had taken place only a few moments ago.

"An ill omen?" I suggested gently, fearful lest my question spoil his metamorphosis.

"It was in the look."

"Did he say something bad?"

"There was fear in the eyes."

"You shouldn't put too much store by it."

"The eyes of a frightened young girl."

"He has always liked to talk too much."

"Of a girl who refuses to grow up."

"An astrologer should be more sure of himself."

"I don't think I wanted to grow up either. So we tried to create our own world, cut off from reality."

"Andrés de San Martín is a loudmouth," I said, although by now I suspected we were talking at cross purposes.

"I had them cut out his tongue," Don Fernando said, collapsing onto a bench.

The sudden clatter of his armor shattered the silence that still clung to the dark corners of the cabin. I did not say a word. I was imagining the gaping, bloody mouth. A dark cave, dead forever. An empty house. A tomb.

Something crashed against the hull and the whole ship shook. Neither of us moved. When everything was still again, he said, "Tell me about her."

"Why did you do it?" I asked, trying to recover from the shock.

"She must have given birth by now."

"Why?"

"Now he'll have to keep his prophecies to himself. I'll be the one who dictates the course of events."

"And the course of the stars?"

"The stars are no more than points of reference. A reflection at the tip of the astrolabe. Do you think she has had it?"

"Had it?"

"I'm asking you if she has given birth," he said, his voice becoming imperious.

"I was thinking of something else. I've no idea. I don't want to talk about that."

"That's your job. You're the fleet's chatterbox."

I hesitated. I didn't know what to do. I could think only of San Martín, and my mouth and teeth ached.

"Well, if you want to be lied to, I'll oblige," I said defiantly.

He looked at me anxiously.

"In Sevilla it is the hour when the doves have not yet left their nests, when the outline of the orange trees is still black, and the light from the lanterns on the palace walls is guttering. I see a dark figure appear at the end of a narrow street. It's an old woman, who scuttles across a tiny square. She has the neat, tidy look of a midwife, wearing her spotless starched white headscarf like a cap. She is looking up at the only lighted balcony in the square. The shutters are wide open . . ."

"I enjoy your descriptions; you are a good poet," Don Fernando said.

"Listen then. The shutters are wide open even though it's so late, and behind the windows a lamp is shining. It's the same balcony as before: do you recognize it?"

"Yes, you're right, it's the same one. We were happy there."

"Did you make love with the window open onto the square, with the warm breeze wafting in the scent of orange blossoms, and all that kind of foolishness that young lovers go in for?"

"We were happy and we were sad. We were a family."

"Why did you leave then?"

"You know why. Don't torment me."

"Tell me again."

"Because the sea was part of me too. However far I left the coast behind me, even in the middle of the dusty plain of Sevilla,

I could hear it, and in those early morning hours its roar drove me mad."

"So you risked everything: wife, children, your own happiness."

"I am a sailor. A navigator."

"A treasure hunter, more like."

"What is the old woman doing, the one in the cap?"

"She has stopped at a door and has lifted the knocker. Can you hear the sounds echoing round the sleeping square?"

"Is it closed? What is the door like?"

"The same as the front door of your house."

"You've never been there."

"I'm a poet, aren't I?"

He smiled.

"Go on," he said.

"Now there's the sound of hurried footsteps on the stairs and someone opening the door. Can you see who it is?"

"It's our maid. What is going on?"

"I don't know yet."

"Do you think I should have stayed with her?"

"You know the answer to that."

"Say what you think."

"I'll tell you: I think the sea is for madmen. Sensible men stay on dry land. Their own land. Putting down roots among the bones of their dead and the skin of their companions. But enough of that. Let's go up the stairs with the old woman. The maid is leading the way. At the top there's a landing, then we go into a room. The air inside is filled with a scent of herbs. There's a lamp on either side of the bed . . ."

"You said there was only one."

"That was from outside, from there I couldn't see both of them. There's a woman stretched out in the bed. When she turns to look at the old woman there is pain etched on her features. She doesn't say anything, but her eyes are asking for help. Pleading for it. The old woman goes over and uncovers the woman, who by now is groaning loudly."

"She's very delicate, you know. You'd realize that at once

if you saw her. She has narrow, bony shoulders with freckles on them. She also has freckles on her chest. And you can see the outlines of her bones under the smooth skin. She doesn't have a strong build. She's fragile. When you hold her you get the feeling you could break her. I like that. It makes me feel strong. But go on. What's happening?"

"The woman's breathing is becoming faster and faster, heavier and heavier. Her legs are writhing. Good God, look at her belly, swollen like a mainsail that's about to tear apart!"

"She's thin. She has skinny legs like a young girl who's grown but isn't yet entirely a woman. She's a fragile thing, although she tries to appear so strong."

"I think they are very much alike. Both of them try to hide their weakness. She builds glass walls inside. He shuts himself in a suit of armor and lets himself be guided by a madman's calculations and listens to prophecies from the mouth of a mute."

"That's enough."

"I'll wager she hides behind her laugh, which often sounds false. And that she sometimes chatters away emptily."

Don Fernando tried to smile, but his face was still sad.

"One of those people for whom each day is a shipwreck. Today it's you she clings to, tomorrow her son, the day after a cooking pan or a new gown. Anything that will help her stay afloat. Any fleeting dream. Like you."

"You're cruel. I should have you thrown overboard. But come and sit here."

Frightened but fascinated by such a contradictory character, I obeyed and curled up between his knees like a cat.

"Now tell me," he said in a voice scarcely louder than a whisper, "what is this belly you spoke of?"

"It's a ripe fruit. A giant melon. It's throbbing. I can't see what it is exactly. But it's growing. It seems to be swallowing the woman. The room. The square; the whole of Sevilla. It fills all the fading night. The day just dawning. Oh, my God!"

"The shadow of my departure stalked the house. It lay in wait at night in all the darkest corners of the room," he said.

"Didn't she try to get you to stay?"

He shook his head.

"Perhaps she didn't say so directly, but was being subtle, the way women are when they want to achieve something."

"No; it was a joint idea."

"Would you have given up the Spice Islands for her?"

"Don't you understand? It's a dream we shared right from the first moment. A secret between us that helped defend us from reality. That saved us from common mediocrity. That helped us overcome all the minor setbacks."

"Minor setbacks lead to great defeats. And great dreams end in black and blue."

"Keep your wisecracks to yourself and go on with what you can see."

"Do you know what I can see at this very moment? You and her like two children. You are hiding in a toy house, sitting next to each other, holding up a book of maps. Neither of you says a word, but you point out the blue seas and she follows your finger while outside there's the noise of a storm, and the wind makes the walls of your frail shelter tremble. The noise grows and grows, the wind roars louder and louder, but you two do not seem to care as you slowly turn the pages—so slowly it seems that time has stood still."

Don Fernando's face darkened. He looked confused and puzzled.

"Let's go back to your room in Sevilla," I said. "Do you remember that enormous belly? Now the old woman is plunging her hands into it. She presses her ear against it. Comes and goes. Busies herself. Gesticulates. Gives instructions. The woman clings to the bars of the bed. Does it have bars? Oh, that's stupid of you! A bed with no bars! Well then, she clutches at the pillows. She tears the linen embroidery in her struggle. Her legs are doubled up. Her sex (if you'll permit me) spreads like the night. The lips of her sex (if you'll permit me) open like a flower. I don't know which flower. Perhaps it's a vegetable—a cabbage. A huge pink cabbage with black tips and a scarlet heart, opening to the morning dew. The belly is going

114

to explode, I tell you! Look at the old woman! She's bustling about all over the room. She gives the maid orders. The woman stuck to the enormous belly starts to scream. Calm down! Everything is normal, everything is fine, the old woman nods. She presses with both hands, with all her body and soul, on the belly. Careful, it will burst! The screams die down. The woman clenches her teeth. Her face turns red. The veins on her neck stand out like blue rivers from the effort she's making. Her body arches and tenses like the bow of a crossbow. On the point of firing. The old woman—some old woman!—straddles the huge melon."

"I swear I'll have you hanged!"

"I'm sorry, but that's what the old woman is doing. She is shouting like a boatswain: 'Now, now!' From her toothless mouth she shouts, 'Now, now!' And out of the sex which has devoured the window and the dawn beyond it, the lamps, the bed, the old woman, the maid, the walls of the room, there comes the head of a tiny, filthy, furry creature, uglier than a monkey, sticky and smeared with blood: the future viceroy of the Spice Islands, master of three quarters of the globe, lord of two oceans, latest in a long line of navigators, who are a race of giants. Now all of him is out. There you have him. Smaller than a piglet. Slimy as a jellyfish. Pink as a sausage. Tied to the mother ship by a thick cable that the old woman is about to cut with a pair of scissors. This I cannot watch! A spurt of blood gushes out. The old woman holds one end of it between her fingers; with the other hand she smacks the baby's bottom. Nothing. She tries again, harder. Still nothing!"

"A curse on you! What's the matter? Isn't the child breathing? I can't hear him crying!"

I hesitated for a moment. An icy chill had spread through my bones.

"The old woman tells them to open the window! She takes the future viceroy by the heels! Shakes him; lifts him into the air. She shows him at the balcony as if to an invisible crowd. Then slaps him again . . . and a sharp cry like the squeak of a mouse flies out of the window into the square, sweeps through the narrow streets of Sevilla like a wind searching for the port, rides down the broad back of the Guadalquivir, crosses the ocean until the waves of the New World cast it up on a beach, then forces its way through jungles, down rivers the color of blood, glides like an albatross above five tiny black ships, until it pours into the Captain General's cabin just as the sun pours in through a window open onto the countryside."

The Captain lifted a cup of wine to his lips. Two large teardrops brimmed in his eyes and slowly slid down his cheeks. He buried his head on his chest as if to hide, and the teardrops fell onto the iron of his armor with a sound of breaking glass. Outside, the river had stopped flowing, as if it were asleep. Inside the cramped room, the slave Enrique turned over the hourglasses with silky gestures.

A silence thick as honey oozed from the walls and slid across the cabin floor.

"Call the captains and the pilots and tell them we are heading home."

Don Fernando was slow to respond.

"It's too late," he said finally.

"Did San Martín tell you we will never return?"

"How do you think I can possibly hear someone who's dumb?"

"That's why you had his tongue cut out."

"There was no place for his plan in mine."

"His plan? What a fool you are! Can't you see that what he was showing you was the universal plan? And that's written up above us in the stars: you can't twist that to suit your own ends."

"Could you go back for me?"

"Right now," I said. "What is your message?"

"That everything will turn out as she and I planned, whatever the stars say."

"What, have you nothing more tender to say to a woman who has just given you a son? Come on: whisper something in her ear."

He hesitated, then smiled. He was struggling with the inhibitions imposed by the dignity of his position. His cheeks flushed and he hid his face. Then he said, "Tell her that underneath this armor I can still smell her perfume on my skin. Tell her that beneath this steel covering I keep her warmth as my only treasure."

"Now I understand why you never take your armor off," I said sarcastically.

He laughed.

"Tell me though: Which of the two are you really?"

His face immediately became serious once more.

THE NEWS of San Martín's sudden dumbness spread like the plague through the crew. Fear filled us with invisible sores that dripped pus into our hearts. What had happened to the astrologer? What did fate hold in store for us? What did Don Fernando plan to do next? Questions such as these poisoned our blood. I pretended to know nothing: what, in fact, did I know? That the Captain had had San Martín's tongue cut out because the horoscope he had drawn up went against his own plans. But what did that horoscope say? What were the prophecies Don Fernando refused to listen to and wanted to hide from everyone else? That we were sailing to the east via the west. What did that mean to me, who knew nothing about navigation? That the Captain was looking for a nonexistent passage to a nonexistent sea. That he had given the name of the Spice Islands to his crazy dream. Things like that were too much for my poor village idiot's brain. I had become the fleet's jester for the simplest of all reasons: the need to fill my belly. So to hell with the Captain General and his imponderables. To hell with the other captains and their boundless ambition. I do not understand them, your Majesty. Just as I do not understand you, nor your son Felipe who has so taken against me, as if it were worthy of a king to fight over a crust of bread, a few crumbs, with the most wretched of his subjects. I understand nothing of these great things: great ambitions, great dreams, great loves. None of that is for the likes of me, who cannot see the forest for the trees. I'm a simple man who is content to follow the dictates

117

of his senses. A plate of steaming hot food. And lots of it. An easy woman. Strong as a plow horse: I won't have anything to do with fragile women. And if she's lecherous as a ewe, frolicsome as a mare, so much the better. And a big pitcher of wine. It's easier and less dangerous for me to get drunk with wine than with crazy dreams as our captains do. And I don't harm anyone. I don't uproot an oak forest centuries old and send it sailing the seas aimlessly. I don't cast more than two hundred poor wretches onto the sea either, men who would much prefer to stay on dry land if they could only get enough to eat there, because they are sick through and through of the sea. It horrifies them, they are afraid of it. I don't weave treason like a spider or threaten any necks with my steel blade. I don't leave pregnant women on shore or ask fools to keep me in touch with them. I don't leave behind desolate mothers to wander like shadows through empty palaces that are too big for them. I don't rip out tongues that tell the truth. Or confide in an idiot who tells me lies.

So, since I didn't understand them, I contented myself with observing them, and kept my mouth tight shut in order to keep a tongue in my head. After all, what use is a dumb jester, how could he use his freedom to say what he likes with no tongue? How could he speak out fearlessly without his mouth clapper? How could he dissolve the boundaries between nonsense and knowledge, between life and art? There would be no point me dressing up in the finest fawn damask with slashed taffeta sleeves, just to make monkeys or billygoats dance. How could I lend my puppets voices, or imitate birds, mimic ministers or prelates, or even sing? Perhaps a dumb astrologer can get by, I don't know, but a dumb buffoon would never do.

THE NEXT morning we began making ready to set sail again. We were leaving once more. Setting ourselves in motion again. As if that were our only aim in life. As if our whole destiny consisted in constantly moving on. And always blindly. Without ever knowing where we really wanted to go.

And once again there was a meeting of the officers, exactly

as before; and exactly as before orders and instructions were given; the same things were discussed, exactly as before, and the same things hidden; and in the end we all had the same things to do, exactly as before; and all this as though it were the very first time.

So we set off again, still heading south. The oak wood on its way once more. Headed for nowhere. Headed for regions lit by sickly suns. For everlasting ice. Wandering madmen.

The further south we traveled, the harder the winds blew. The fleet was like a herd of wild horses, black and shiny with foam, galloping madly toward nowhere. In the grip of an unreasoning need to plunge onward, in circles, without respite.

The pilots could scarcely control their ships. They were afraid that the sails would be torn asunder. That the rigging would snap, and the shrouds burst. That the masts would fall as though chopped down with an ax.

Don Fernando gave orders for the rigging to be tightened, the shrouds to be strengthened, and proudly watched the masts creaking and groaning as the wind bent them. He laughed to himself at the white sails displaying their defiance to the sky.

The temperature dropped a little every day. The cold penetrated our flesh and lodged itself in our bones. An icy wind blew the length of the deck, roared down the gangways, soughed into the sterncastle. Some nights it was so strong that it ruffled clothes on their racks, sent hats spinning on their straps and made the candles gutter.

The sea became rougher, with taller and taller waves. It boiled and surged under the ships. Reared up like an animal. Furious waves ranged themselves against our prows. They unleashed their anger in billows of spray that washed over our decks. They tore at our timbers. They threatened our dreams and grew inside each one of us in the silence of the night.

Clouds covered the sky, black as shadows. Pregnant with cold, swift as birds. The sun barely shone in that ashen sky, all its fires spent. It was more like the moon seen through a dirty pane of glass. A sun for the blind.

The distant coastline looked like the walls of a gloomy prison. High bare cliffs. Solid rock gouged out by the claws of the sea. At their foot, an occasional paltry beach of black sand. Beaches where flocks of sea lions yelped their fear. Beaches where penguins stood motionless in their eternal wait, and from where birds spread out like a giant fan, flying over the ship with their lugubrious cries like a witch's curse.

Day after day for two months. Anchoring in every bay. Exploring each river. And every bay was identical to the one before, but less sheltered, colder, more inhospitable. And every river a fresh disappointment.

Then one day in mid-March, when it had become impossible to go on because the fiendish black waves seemed on the point of staving in our battered hulls, and the wind was bludgeoning our masts and spars, with the sails already reduced to tatters; when prayers had taken the place of shouts and orders; when the icy cold and blackness of those seas had installed itself in the very marrow of our souls, filling us with fear and self-loathing; when it seemed we must have reached the bottom of the pit and there was no point even arguing anymore because it was so obvious to everyone that the only thing to do was turn back; at that moment we heard rumors that paralyzed us all, sent our stomachs churning, made us sick with fear; news like red hot coals on our eardrums; news that rattled our teeth and made our hair fall out, sent our spirits plummeting to our boots, and burst their seams open: Don Fernando had decided we should winter here.

AT FIRST we could hardly believe it was true. "Nothing but gossip," the eternal optimists among us said. "You'll see that in a few days he'll decide to turn back," the sensible ones said, still thinking that reason was bound to prevail. "We'll die of hunger, cold and loneliness," the rest of us asserted. Deep down, none of us really thought he could persevere with such an idea, so with the last remnants of our candid innocence we set to work on the far from easy task of stripping the ships so they could be beached.

In that vast desolate landscape we looked no bigger than ants, coming and going from the fleet anchored in the bay, carrying on our backs everything we could remove to lighten the ships. Crazy ants transporting everything to the anthill we were going to make our winter quarters in. Toiling feverishly like ants, but with the secret hope that Don Fernando would countermand his order at any moment.

But he did not. Days went by as we bustled between holds and decks, decks and longboats, longboats and the beach; our anthill grew and grew, and no new order came.

While we worked like machines robbed of all will, the captains roamed their empty ships like recent widows.

On board the *Concepción*, which now looked like a garden scorched by frost, Gaspar de Quesada the Fair wandered like a shade, obsessed by a dream he recounted to everyone he met.

He had dreamt of his castle in Carpio, close to Medina del Campo. He saw himself crossing the courtyard followed by his faithful squire Luis del Molino.

In his dream, the sun blazed down on the barren fields around the castle. The light was so strong it blurred the outlines of the landscape, while a hot wind gusted into the yard.

The captain of the *Concepción* hurried, in his dream, to escape the fury of the sky and, followed by his squire who carried their arms, entered one of the castle's ample halls. The hall was dim and even cool at that early hour of the morning when the sun did not beat down on the castle walls.

Then, in his dream, Gaspar sank into a chair and flung back his noble head. The silence in the room, broken only by the buzz of an occasional fly, made him feel sleepy. He closed his eyes and gave in to the sensation. He fell asleep, and in his dream dreamed another dream. In this dream he saw his dead mother stroking his head in greeting, as did all those who were close to him, even his squire Luis del Molino, whom his master allowed such liberties. The truth is, Sire, that Gaspar's head was so powerful it fascinated everyone. It was not enough to admire it, one had to touch it, as one does certain statues. In this dream, in Gaspar's dream, the countess prolonged her caress as if she were giving it a special meaning her son was unable to fathom.

"I had a nightmare last night," she says. "About your voyage. It was horrible."

Gaspar smiles affectionately, and in the dream his boyish expression stirs his mother's heart.

"Don't go!" she begs him. "Don't go; stay here. We'll talk to your father. The dream was too awful."

"Come now, Mother," he replies, "you shouldn't believe in such things."

The countess sits down beside her son, and he takes her two hands in his.

"What did you dream?" he asks her in his dream. "Tell me, it will make you feel better."

The countess frowns. She asks her son why he is covered in dust and sweat.

"I have been practicing swordplay with Luis," he says unconcernedly. "He's no good with a sword, but he'll have to learn so he can protect his master."

"Do you plan to take him with you?" his mother asks, her face anxious.

"Of course. He will be my shadow," Gaspar says.

"That's enough," his mother replies. "When are you leaving?" she asks gently after a pause.

"Four days from now," Gaspar replies in the dream within his dream. "But don't worry, Luis will look after me. I will come to no harm. When I return you'll be the mother of one of the most famous men in the kingdom."

"You're already the best, to me," the countess says. "And the most handsome."

"What about that dream of yours?" he asks.

All of a sudden his mother disappeared and Gaspar woke up into his first dream. The hall was empty except for Luis who was standing behind him. Gaspar tried to stand up, but something prevented him from doing so. He struggled, but could not get up. He tried to move his arms but was unable to. He tried to talk, but his voice failed him. Finally he woke up. He was in his cabin on board the *Concepción*, trembling and bathed in sweat. Luis del Molino was beside him.

"You had a nightmare," Luis whispered.

"A dream within a dream," Gaspar replied.

ON BOARD the *Victoria*, whose black hull looked like a coffin afloat on the turbulent waters of the bay, Don Luis de Mendoza could feel death creeping into his body the way night creeps into an empty house and takes it over.

The treasurer to the fleet was wasting away in the shadows of his cabin. He hardly had the strength to get out of his bed anymore. The icy wind pierced his lungs like jagged slivers of crystal. Loneliness, the immense loneliness of the dying, sank its fangs into Don Luis's soul as it distilled the bitter honey of a few memories in the red glow from the coals of his burner and the vapors of strange herbs. Perhaps he looked back longingly and saw himself asleep in the sun, the air still, and time standing still, then watching as a lizard cautiously poked its nose out from some stones. There were other boys like himself in those endless days of summer, but he could not make them out now. There was a mother too, with a mother's smell, close by in a house that in those days seemed everlasting. Perhaps there was also a busybody of a grandmother who never seemed to rest but was always out and about trying to change the whole world. There was an older girl he was secretly in love with. Also a leper he spied on in the woods, terrified, a leper who sometimes crawled in through his window when he had nightmares. A drunken, well-meaning priest who delved into all his evil thoughts. An old horse. A father who was only a blurred image. A new pair of boots. A fat black hen that looked just like his grandmother. And above all, there was time, an abundance of time. Time to play. Time to dream. So much time he did not even know what it was. Until one day he began to notice the hourglasses. It was only now he realized how much he hated those glass bulbs filled with sand. He had gradually seen how they crept in and took over everything; and nothing, his sleep in the sun, his house, his grandmother, his mother with a mother's smell, his child's games—none of it could last forever. Except the hourglasses.

And now, shut in his cabin like a chicken in its egg, he may have wished he could summon his page Filiberto and have him smash all the hourglasses, but he knew it was too late.

He looked at his waxen face in a mirror and knew it was too late. He examined his bony hands. Used them to touch his eyes sunk in their sockets. Listened to the painful whistle of the air trying to reach his lungs. Heard them wheezing like a flawed pair of bellows. And knew it was too late.

He was convinced he was about to die, and black thoughts filled his mind. He could feel a desire for revenge swelling in his tortured breast. He had nothing left to lose, which made him the chosen one. All the fear, anxiety, hatred and despair floating in the atmosphere entered his veins and inflamed his senses. He was obsessed with the idea of a posthumous gesture. It gave him no rest. He would have his revenge on the hourglasses through Don Fernando. He would pit the time he had left against the Captain General's time. Perhaps in the clash between them, all the hourglasses in the world would be smashed.

At the same time, from the empty, all but dismantled *San Antonio* came the sad sounds that Juan de Cartagena wrung from his guitar. The Inspector General was at a loss. He watched everything going on around him with disdain, and sought refuge in his music. He missed his palace, his silks, his liquors and the smooth-skinned ladies of the court, but unlike Luis de Mendoza he felt certain he would return there one day. Something in his eyes told me so. A secret determination shone in them whenever he looked at the *Trinidad*, a determination that seemed to swell with the sounds of his music. In that desolate landscape, his tunes seemed as much out of place as his perfume was different from the stench of the sea.

By contrast Juan Serrano was hard at work. His ship, the *Santiago*, was at anchor in the open sea outside the bay, and was the only one not to have been unloaded or dismantled. Don Fernando had given him the task of continuing on as far as possible to the south, to explore. But rumor had it that his real mission was different. According to the men, the Captain General had ordered him to take all the young native women and abandon them on the coast, far from our camp. They had apparently been transferred to the worthy Portuguese captain's vessel from their hiding place on board the *Concepción*.

My feverish imagination brings those poor ghosts back to life. I lament their fate. I rail and rebel against what they were made to suffer. Poor ignorant creatures, I tell myself, blithely unaware of the destiny in store for them. Who picked off their lice and bathed in their communal baths, calling on their gods for help. Who begged for them to send rain, not knowing that after the rain had come, nothing would ever be the same again. Poor unfortunates, I think, whom the rains brought only evil. Betrothed for marriages that never took place because they were offered to other gods who had come from the sea to bring the saving rain. Scarcely more than girls, torn from their world and impregnated by your imperial dreams, by the crazy ambitions of your henchmen, by your castles, your cathedrals, your squares, your God, and your language. A language they never managed to learn but which they now carry within their tiny bellies as round as melons. Fecundated like exotic flowers with pollen carried from distant lands on the limbs of your ironclad beetles. Cut off from the trunk of their lives, and now abandoned in a lonely spot somewhere in this empty world because food was short and the Captain General did not want any more mouths to feed. Too many mouths, as simple as that. And all the officers agreed because those tiny bellies were growing and soon there would be eleven mothers who would be little use for their pleasure. And soon there would be eleven little ones, one of whom would perhaps sport Gaspar's golden locks, another Don Juan's perfumed skin; and there might be a girl with Serrano's eyes, another with Sebastián's languorous gestures; nobody wanted to see that. They would learn to say: mama, church, sword, Spain, and fear; nobody wanted to hear that. So they all accepted the Captain's way of thinking. That neither the women nor their children should survive. That they must die, sooner or later. That they should fall ill with the cold, just as my monkeys had done, and no sugared wine was able to revive them. That is how the captains thought; they decided that was how things must be, then dismissed it from their minds. They would not question the past. There is only one way to see everything: the way the gods from the waves see it. But are not all gods alike, wherever they come from, impregnating us mortals with their madness and then abandoning us on a beach in this empty world? Yet there are still men who wish to seem like gods. Not me. I prefer animals. They are so peaceful, as an old man in my village used to say. They don't stay awake all night and moan on about their guilt, said the old man, who called himself a philosopher though the rest of the village said he was a madman. They don't confuse me with all their talk of duties toward God. Not one of them is unhappy, or obsessed by the crazy need to possess things. None of them kneels in front of another, and none of them forces any other to kneel before them. In the whole world, not one of them is more knowledgeable than another, or thinks himself more decent, the old man used to say. That tramp spent hours lying in the grass observing them. I learn from them, he would say. And we all laughed at him.

IN SPITE of the cold and the fleet's unrest, Don Fernando was determined to celebrate Palm Sunday properly. He ordered a mass said on shore, and invited all the captains, pilots and officers to eat on board the flagship.

To protect us from the harsh weather, mass was said in the half-finished winter shelter. The wind snatched away the priest's voice, snuffed out the candles, ruffled and tore the pages of his missal.

Immediately afterward there was sherry, nuts, raisins and honey as a reward for the common sailors. Everything gave off a powerful smell of earth, sunny gardens, familiar streets and noisy houses; there was a strong scent, too, of warm sheets, Sunday best, devout old aunts and blooming young girls.

There were also humorless jokes, unenthusiastic laughter,

pointless conversations: there's nothing like the sherry from such and such a place, what about the pinenuts from somewhere else, they're unbeatable; all that's nonsense because the raisins from there are every bit as good as the ones from here, if not better; and all these matters debated passionately over and over until everyone grew tired, as if it were really important to settle the issue.

At a certain point in the celebrations, the captains, too, wanted some questions settled. "Weren't we supposed to be headed for the Spice Islands, that southern paradise caressed by the sun and perfumed with the scent of cloves and cinnamon?" Don Luis de Mendoza said, wanting to know what we were doing here instead, wretched, sick and frozen to the bone, wasting away while we waited for the winter to end, when it was plain that winter was the only season there was in this forlorn part of the world. "What has happened," he said, turning pale, his hands shaking with agitation as he struggled to breathe, "is that Don Fernando has not obeyed his instructions." "Back in Sevilla, Álvarez claimed," Sebastián added, "that Faleiro had refused to accompany the Captain General because he absolutely rejected the idea of heading south around Africa, which is the natural route to the Spice Islands."

From his litter, Juan de Cartagena protested that your Majesty had granted him the right to be lord of the first fortress they found or built on any lands they discovered, and that therefore one should be constructed at the mouth of Solís's river. "Also," Gaspar put in, "the Portuguese fleet, which failed to catch us there, could do so easily now, and with our ships dismantled we wouldn't stand a chance." "There's no fear of that," Sebastián retorted, "because we are the only ones who would venture into these regions; nobody else would dare sail in these seas, down coasts like these, which don't figure on any map and therefore do not exist. If the Captain knows where the passage through to the South Seas is, why doesn't he take it? I tell you it's because he lied about it, and even managed to take in the emperor, who is a foreigner and too young to be able to read his men's innermost thoughts." That is what Sebastián said, adding, "Don Carlos will trust anyone except a Spaniard; sooner or later he will regret it. But why doesn't Don Fernando tell us his real plans? Why are we following this senseless course? Why are we allowing ourselves to get stuck in this endless winter? Why? Why?" Each one of them had his "Why?" All of them demanded explanations from Don Fernando, explanations he only wished he could provide, to himself and to his men.

So, seeing the tension increase and the celebrations turning sour and sad, your Juanillo, in his efforts to be worthy of the pension your son later denied him, did as you have heard he did, and went and picked up a scythe that was lying there among other tools and agricultural implements. Raising it above his head, he began to run round in circles brandishing it and shouting:

"Here, my lords, begins the dance for one and all in which I, Death, do warn all living creatures of how short life can be!"

My words brought their arguments to an end. All eyes and ears turned to me. I began my song:

> Come and join the dance
> all those born in this world
> whatever their station . . .

Everyone reacted to this old rhyme with a kind of instinctive fear. The silence deepened as I circled them; some gave a sickly grin, others hid behind their companions; no one was able to look me in the face. Pleased by my sudden position of power, I went around pointing at each one in turn, until I finally stopped in front of Gaspar. I can remember that a ray of sunlight filtered through the planks of the shelter's roof, its wan light setting the captain of the *Concepción* apart from all the rest, exactly as a painter concentrates the light in a picture on its main subject.

> Gaspar the Fair, courageous and bold,
> Come join the dance without being told

128

I said, placing the scythe above his head.

He stared at me like a startled child. He could feel everyone's eyes fixed on him. He was bewildered, not knowing what to do. I insisted, shouting, "Gaspar, Gaspar." Other voices joined in, timid at first, "Gaspar, Gaspar . . . ," then the whole room began to shout: "Gaspar, Gaspar!"

Suddenly I noticed someone pushing his way through toward me. I found myself confronted by that madman Luis del Molino, who pounced on me like a hawk, sword in hand: "Dance with me, I'm his shieldbearer." So then your Juanillo ran away scared, with Luis's heavy blade whirling around his ears, while everyone laughed and shouted, "Take that, Death!" and, "Let's see you use your scythe now!"

So I started laughing too, and began to skip and turn somersaults as I ran, then to walk on my hands. Everybody cheered and applauded.

Luis del Molino was at the far end of the room, and to get my own back I picked up the scythe again and ran over to Juan de Cartagena, who sat immobile on his splendid chair.

> *All-powerful Count, there's no need for fear,*
> *Although you've no legs, I won't leave you here.*
> *Throw off your cape and join in the dance,*
> *Even on stumps you'll be able to prance,*
> *You mustn't refuse, it may be your last chance.*

Everyone in the room fell silent again, waiting to see what the Inspector of the fleet would reply.

"I'd be happy to dance if the Captain General joins me," Don Juan said.

A roomful of tense faces turned toward Don Fernando.

"I don't think the Inspector would make a good partner," he said.

"The best you could find," Cartagena retorted. "Although of course there are many others who wish they could dance that dance with you."

"Then I'll choose someone else," I said, sweeping round

with the scythe. "You all know that money and rank mean nothing to me. You will all come to the same in the end. So be ready; don't let yourself be taken unawares."

"Why not ask Don Luis?" Juan Serrano said, his face half-hidden beneath his hat brim. "I don't think he would refuse."

Serrano's cruel joke drained the color from my cheeks. I could not bear to raise my eyes lest I meet those of the *Victoria*'s captain.

"I think I'll take a caulker," I said. "Or better still, an armorer. Or perhaps the surgeon. No, a storesman would be the best. Or even a pageboy, as they are meant to serve. Or a ship's boy, because they have to try everything first and take the lead so they can gain experience. You choose, it's all the same to me."

"Take a priest," someone shouted.

"A king, more like it," another one said.

"Ask Don Luis," Serrano insisted.

"I'll leave him for last," I replied.

"No," Mendoza said, appearing by my side. Deep in their sockets, his eyes shone like two iridescent beetles. "Take me now. It's better that way."

I hesitated, sorry I had ever started the jest.

"It's only a game, my lord," I said eventually. "A stupid game." And then, seeing he was still at my side looking so serious, "Anyway, where has my lord ever heard that Death was a man, son of a Jewish mother and an unknown father, dwarfish and with no foreskin?"

No one appreciated my joke, but everyone stared at me strangely, so I burst out:

"Death is an old crone, I tell you! Don't you know that she's fickle and treacherous; that she'll open her legs for anybody? That she promises a better life, but instead gives you only dust, worms and shit? Death is a great whore, friends. Nothing more than a bitch who only looks up to the mighty. You say she carries them off as well? That's as may be, but only once they've had their fill of life, when they expect no more because they've had it all. And for every single great

130

person she takes, ten thousand poor wretches die, for whom the pleasures of life have never begun, because there never is any pleasure for them. Those unhappy thousands put all their faith in tomorrow, because anyone born down below has nothing else to hope for; all they can do is wait and wait, until the moment when Lady Death appears to tell them that time must have an end. You tell me death is the great leveler? Nonsense. A hoax invented by the rich to console the poor. Because I tell you that if Death were of the same low station as you, then in a twinkling of an eye the world would be free of the high and mighty, and hell would be crowded with counts, dukes, kings, bishops, lords, rich merchants and farmers. Since that is not the case, and hell is full of poor people while the others are still firmly established in control of the ship, that must mean that Death is on their side as well."

I was so caught up in my protest against the injustices of death that I didn't realize I had been left all alone.

The shelter was empty. The wind scattered the ashes and swept away the remains of our Resurrection feast, while the shadows lengthened and deepened in the corners of the room.

A sudden panic swept over me. I couldn't hear a single voice and was terrified that I had been abandoned there to my fate. I rushed out onto the beach, shouting, "It was only a game, friends! Nothing more than a game!"

AND YOU, your Highness, what did you make of my game? Wouldn't your Majesty care to dance with Juanillo? I'll wager Don Carlos is very light-hearted, just dying, as they say, to be one of the crush. If that's true, follow me, but remember that I make no distinctions for anyone.

So let the king arise from his throne without waiting for the end of the speeches or a sign from his chamberlains. Let him cross the hall without listening to his ministers' advice, his courtiers' flattery, his clerks' intrigues. Let him wave away his escort of guards; for once, let him walk alone down his palace's long, mazelike corridors. Stride on boldly; do not stop however curious you may be to know what lies hidden behind those doors that have always remained closed to you. Do not let any of those mysterious empty rooms deflect your attention with their siren song, my lord. Let your footsteps carry on unfalteringly down the high, dark corridors, echoing and multiplying. Then, when you have crossed the threshold of the spacious room at the far end of which lies your bed with its purple canopy (as befits one of your exalted position), make sure you dismiss all your fawning hangers-on and devoted servants and remain entirely alone. Then take off your royal garments—our clothes are nothing more than the masks we wear—and, as naked as you were when Juanita la Loca brought you into this world to govern and conquer it, start to dance. Twirl on your tiny feet. Shake your majestic buttocks. Break into a sweat. Dance. Let the king dance too: it is hardly right for everyone else to do it for him. Dance like a Gypsy woman, turn somersaults like a clown. Dance round the four corners of the room. Round the whole world. Dance because we live. Dance because we dream. Dance because we die. But above all, Majesty, dance all alone.

PART V

Tᴇʟʟ ᴍᴇ, O august Majesty, have you ever been under a table observing the feet of those present while you follow their conversation? No? Well then, more's the pity, because it is no good thing for a prince to see the world only from his throne, or only by looking into the faces of the throng of adulators in his court, who powder and make themselves up for hypocrisy. Underneath a table you see things differently. You can see how nervous some feet are, the way a leg moves here, a pair of knees bobs up and down there, or spot a hand's furtive gesture. You can judge the sound of words without the risk of being taken in by the speaker's face, and you will learn much more about men and the affairs of state than from all the speeches, all the scandals you see or hear from high on your platform of purple velvet. Take the word of someone who has spied on life from every corner: what little knowledge I have has always been acquired while I was under a bed, hidden in a wardrobe, peering through a keyhole, concealed behind a chair, or underneath a table. It is the same as in the theater, your Majesty: you can either enjoy the play from the balcony, and truly believe that the young fellow on stage is a woman, and the other young actor a powerful king, and that they are indeed loving or betraying each other; or you can go backstage and find out that the fragile, tormented young woman is in fact a gruff sodomite in disguise, and that the passionate king's wife is busy cuckolding him with her lover under the very boards he so majestically treads while spouting his speeches on the concept of honor. You will learn that between this poor man, the pederast, and the wanton woman there is no jealousy, love or even hate; nothing but their wretched trade. If you were to do this, perhaps you would feel as I do, never knowing which of the two versions to prefer, or which to take as real, unsure where life ends and the theater begins, such is the sense of unreality they create.

Take Don Fernando's feet, for example. Watch how he crosses them, left over right, then right over left, shifting all the time. You would learn that underneath the table your ears pay more attention to the metallic scrape of the chain mail protecting those feet than to all the statutes and provisions of the royal agreement that the notary León de Espeleta is reading. You would also see the mutineers more clearly, and be able to tell from the way their legs are placed, from the mud caking their boots and the parlous state of those boots, a badly bruised knee or one bare foot, what is going through their minds. And you would better understand the stony silence they all fall into when Don Fernando begins to speak, and you would see how his fingers twist under the table as he says up above that he feels pity rather than hatred for those who have betrayed him.

And while the constable reads out the names of all the prisoners and the charges against them, you would see that forest of legs tremble as one, waving like a field of wheat in the breeze.

Beyond them you would see another row of legs, very different from the first group. These belong to those who have not been accused. Straight legs. Strong knees. Relaxed feet. Clean boots. Legs that move unconcernedly or resolutely when Don Fernando talks of mothers saying the rosary in the bustle of their kitchens, praying to God for their sons; while he talks of long nights, beds that are too wide, houses too big. And wonders what he could tell those mothers, those wives.

Then under the table the priest Pedro de Balderrama joined his hands together in silent prayer. Juan Serrano played with his hat, and the sound of the bells on its brim added an incongruously playful note to the somber proceedings.

One pair of legs gave way. The knees hit the ground and, a few paces from my hiding place, a face dropped like a fruit from a tree—the face of someone who until only the day before had been a friend, but who was now unknown to me. No hand stretched down to help him. The legs next to his instinctively shied away.

The Captain General was insisting that not even the memory of the guilty ones would provide solace for those they would leave behind, because their deeds had stained all memories of them: everyone would know they had lost their lives through treachery rather than acts of bravery. As Don Fernando was speaking, the notary nervously rubbed his hand on his thigh and Odoardo rapped his knuckles against a table leg. No, Don Fernando insisted, crossing his legs and swinging one of his feet only inches from my face, he could not prevent old women from muttering as the mutineers' mothers went by, nor men from falling silent whenever one of their brothers or perhaps their father entered a tavern, the silence making the wine taste sourer still. Not even the captains who bore such illustrious names could escape this, the worst of punishments, because they too had brought dishonor on their families, had besmirched their names.

At this point Gaspar's legs, solid as tree trunks, began resisting the weight of their chains, came alive and rattled the fetters. Without a word, the captain of the *Concepción* was calling to be set free and handed a sword.

Beneath the table, one of Odoardo's hands reached for the pommel of his own weapon in response.

The Captain General traced patterns in the sand with the tip of one foot.

The priest fiddled with his rosary beads.

"What is the sentence of the captain of the *Concepción*?" a voice asked above the table.

The constable clasped his knees with both hands. He said in an even tone that Gaspar de Quesada had been found guilty of treason and of the murder of the ship's master Juan de Elorriaga. Both of these crimes carried the penalty of death, to be carried out when and how the Captain General thought fit.

"In the prime of his life," someone muttered.

Under the table, Don Fernando's hands showed not the slightest sign of trembling as he slowly announced that de Quesada would be beheaded. There and then. In front of them all.

A silence vaster and deeper than the ocean told hold of everyone present.

Gaspar's legs seemed rooted in the sand when the Captain called on Luis del Molino and told him, "You are the one who will wield the sword. The one who will end your master's life. It was he who taught you to use a sword for treason."

At this, everybody's feet became agitated like ants whose anthill has been suddenly destroyed.

Luis del Molino fell to his knees. Gasped that he could not do it.

But above the table, the Captain General retorted, "Yes you can, because that way you will save your own skin. If you don't, both of you will lose your heads, and that would be a stupid waste."

"I promised his mother I would take care of him," Luis del Molino protested, still in an absurd position, on all fours, as though he no longer had the strength to stand up.

"All you can do for him now is give him a sure and loving blow with the sword," Juan Serrano said, toying with the bells on his hat once more.

The chaplain's fingers clutched at the rosary.

Above the table, someone softly begged the Captain to show mercy.

"Nobody would show me any," he replied. "Not even you, I think."

"Let's move on to the others," Odoardo said. He was so short his feet barely brushed the ground, and when he spoke they swung up in the air.

"Everyone shall have his turn," Don Fernando promised. "But first the leader must be punished. Let Luis del Molino prepare to carry out the sentence."

Time seemed to stop, waiting for him to respond.

He finally raised his head. His face was covered in tears. Sticky with snot. Smeared with sand.

After he struggled to his feet I could only make out his legs and his right hand, which took the sword someone thrust at him.

Its blade flashed on a level with his thigh, and I thought that only now was day dawning, and that this must be the longest dawn of my life. Longer even than the summer mornings when I was a boy back in Bustillo del Páramo. I was about to escape back into my memories when I saw several pairs of steady hands and feet, no doubt belonging to the group of men who had not been accused of anything, go over to Gaspar and release him from his chains. He offered no resistance. It seemed almost as if he had already left the scene; his legs were no longer the sturdy trunks they had been, but were like two dried-up branches that could easily be hacked to pieces. Then I saw him walk off to the sea's edge, alone and docile, without any escort. As he drew away from the table, I could see all of him, a tiny figure upright in the distance.

They had taken off his breastplate and shirt. As he stood there in the midst of the foam, with bare chest and hair streaming in the breeze, he looked like an ancient idol greeting the rising sun.

Yet he was no more than a child, your Highness, a big, clumsy child staring out to sea so that he did not have to see whether his squire, Luis del Molino, was already standing behind him like a shadow.

A heavy silence weighed down on everyone and everything on the beach.

The wind had dropped; so had the sound of the waves.

With his back to the others, Gaspar sank to his knees. His head drooped like a flower on its stem.

Gaspar de Quesada, the Fair; it was you who, like a fool,

set all this in motion. Goaded into it by Luis de Mendoza, who had nothing to lose, and by Juan de Cartagena, you took over the *San Antonio* with thirty armed men under cover of darkness. Then, haranguing the crew, telling them they were lost and reminding them of how Don Fernando had treated them when they had wanted to know where the fleet was headed, you demanded they hand over the faithful Álvaro de la Mezquita, the Captain General's cousin, who at that time was captain of the ship once commanded by the Inspector of the fleet. We must teach Don Fernando a lesson, they say you said, so that he learns to respect the will of the Spaniards who are the natural masters of the fleet. Then you strode up and down the thronged deck like a swaggering bull among a herd of cows, until Juan de Elorriaga, the *San Antonio*'s master, came up and asked you in measured, almost gentle tones, in the name of God and your king, to return peacefully to your own ship. This is no way to settle your affairs, they say that unsuspecting fellow said to you when he refused to hand over the captain. Then, blinded by fateful destiny, you clenched your teeth and rushed at Elorriaga, dagger in hand. Death left four holes in his body as he fell to the deck in a pool of his own blood, which the moonlight turned to silver.

The blade swung up like a great bird in lumbering flight. The silence deepened still further.

Beneath the table I could see Odoardo's big shiny leather boots.

The chaplain, wearing sandals over thick black socks.

The notary's battered court slippers.

Juan Serrano's hat hanging silently from his hands.

Don Fernando's ironclad feet.

The constable's rough, blemished boots.

All the legs were tensed now that the jury had stood up.

With the sword poised above his head, we heard Gaspar ask, "Is that you, Luis?"

"A nightmare," Luis murmured.

"A dream within a dream," Gaspar replied.

No more was said, because the sword had already begun

its descent, searching out his neck like a passionate lover, and nothing and nobody could detain it now. I shut my eyes tight and told myself that this was the time of day when Vicente's rooster begins to crow outside my window, when Justino lets the sheep out of their pen, when Filomena kneels to blow life back into the fire, her eyes still sticky with sleep and her sex with lovemaking, when Fermín the sacristan washes himself noisily out in the yard, kicking and cursing the ducks and hens, the time when the bed is at its warmest, when the coffee Almodóvar brings from Granada smells its richest, when the fire offers most comfort; the time of day when one can wander awake through a house still asleep, and the rising sun makes everything seem new, before it all returns to its familiar old existence.

So I lay on the sand beneath the table and started to weep. I only wanted to remember my village, I did not want to know anything more of what was going on around me. But I couldn't help hearing fragments of what was being said, which mingled with the fragments of my memories of Bustillo del Páramo. So my mind was a jumble of Doña Herminia's tame cattle and the order to take Luis de Mendoza's body from its cabin on board the *Victoria* and to quarter it on the beach. "You have to take good care of those cows," the old woman said to me, "they're good strong beasts, and if anything happens to them I'll pull off one of those big ears of yours." Meanwhile, the chaplain protested that he could see no reason to profane the body of a dead person in that way, when his soul would pay for his sin for all eternity. And one day, just for the hell of it, driven by the blind urge to do the old woman harm, I took her favorite cow Butterfly to the edge of a gully and began to chase after her and throw stones at her until the poor creature, finding herself trapped, stumbled and fell over the edge. Her neck was broken. You should have seen, Sire, how the old woman cried over her cow's death; she was so upset that not only did she not pull off one of my ears as she had threatened, she said nothing at all, not even a single reproach, which caused me more shame than if she had given me the thrashing I deserved. I could see the cow dead at the foot of the gully, her huge blank eyes staring up, while alongside I saw Luis de Mendoza so helpless and shriveled in death that any cruel boy could have done whatever they wished to him without pity or fear.

He did manage to stop all the hourglasses on the night of the plot, but everything happened so quickly he did not even realize he had done so.

Gaspar took over the *San Antonio* and had the stern lantern extinguished to hide the ship from the Captain General's view. When Don Fernando's eyes searched the heart of the desolate night in vain, he understood at once. He dispatched a troop of armed men to recover the *San Antonio*, and at the same time sent the constable, Gonzalo Gómez de Espinosa, with six secretly armed men and a letter for Luis de Mendoza on the *Victoria*.

Mendoza received them in his cabin, which still reeked of herbs and the apothecary. His hands shook as he took the letter. His eyes shone like an animal at bay as he read the message:

"Palm Sunday in the year of our Lord fifteen hundred and twenty. On board the *Trinidad*. To the most honorable captain of the *Victoria*, treasurer of the fleet, Don Luis de Mendoza: I kindly request your excellency to accompany the bearer of this letter to the flagship in order to discuss a matter of great interest to you."

A smile came to his bloodless lips, as if to say, "You will not catch me like that," but as he crumpled the letter and threw it defiantly on his coal burner, he felt the icy chill of a dagger piercing his throat. The air bubbled out of the wound, making it impossible for him to speak. He felt no pain, and could not believe that the last of the hourglasses had been smashed to smithereens, its sand filling him with dread. He could not believe it until he saw Gómez de Espinosa looking down in horror at his bloodstained hands.

And when your Juanillo, overwhelmed with horror, tried to summon up Filomena crouching over her tub brazenly washing her sex, slowly rubbing soap on with one hand, while the fingers of the other moved up and down, coaxing it into bubbles, his ears could not help but hear how Don Juan de Cartagena had been found guilty of sedition.

"Is it not true that you sought to take command of the *San Antonio*, which Gaspar de Quesada had briefly seized for the rebels?" a voice, which might have been that of the constable, asked. And Juan de Cartagena replied that he had, your Majesty, and that he would do so again. But the priest Sánchez de Reina, when accused of misusing his position to instigate the rebellion, swore he was not involved. He insisted he was innocent, Sire. And begged them to show some mercy. "In the name of God, that's enough blood," he sobbed.

"Enough blood," my master agreed. "Both of them are to be left to their fate on the shore."

Tipped out of his litter, Juan de Cartagena dragged himself along like a crippled dog between the cluster of legs which moved apart to let him through. The Fleet's Inspector made a superhuman effort to crawl along on his hands and elbows. Nobody tried to stop him.

Filomena always performed the same ritual, with the door of the privy left open. She laughed at the faces I made, and once she had rinsed herself she threw the water onto the fig-tree—to make the figs taste better, she would say.

THE FIRST act ended with Gaspar de Quesada's splendid head stuck on a lance, and the pieces of Don Luis de Mendoza's quartered body being washed in and out by the waves. Don Fernando carefully planned the next scene.

He announced that while Don Juan and the priest Sánchez were being locked up, the judges should consider the punishments to be meted out to the other plotters.

The only sounds to be heard were the judges' whispering and, when they fell silent, the distant rumble of the sea.

Then after a tense, interminable wait, Don Fernando called for the next prisoner.

It was Sebastián. At that moment, the glorious circumnavigator of the whole world was so cowed he could hardly stand or lift his gaze to look at his accusers. He would not have been able to support even the weight of the laurels you were to crown him with years later.

"Sebastián," the constable said, "you stand accused of conspiracy and treason. You have been found guilty, and are condemned to pay with your life how and when the Captain General sees fit, in accordance with clause five of the royal agreement which bestows these powers on him in the name of God and the king."

"Let him be beheaded here and now in the presence of us all," the Captain decreed.

A shudder convulsed the master of the *Concepción*. Ashamed of himself, he clasped both arms tightly, trying to conceal his fear.

"Captain," said Juan Serrano, "I think this man was led astray by his superior, but he's a good sailor and we'll need him. I suggest you spare his life and postpone his punishment until we return to Spain."

"If what you say is true," my master said, "then he's weak, and we have no need of such men on this voyage."

"Hernando," Barbosa put in, speaking in Portuguese to the Captain General. "I think Serrano is right."

"And what do you think?" my master asked Sebastián.

The question took him by surprise. He did not know what to say. His voice stuck in his throat. Totally lost for words was your great circumnavigator, that loudmouth who was so eloquent in boasting of his exploits to you, your Majesty.

"I have a wife and children," was what he finally came out with.

"Reason enough for me to spare your life," Don Fernando replied with a wry grin.

A few of the prisoners laughed nervously. Even Sebastián managed a weak smile, which he soon repressed.

"So, since you have a family, I should give you a second chance to stab me in the back?" the Captain went on.

Sebastián shook his head.

"You see, he himself is saying I shouldn't."

"It wasn't my fault, it was Gaspar; I was against it."

"But you followed him because you thought he would win. As you can see, you chose the wrong side."

"It could have happened to any of you instead of me," Sebastián said firmly, "and I would have spared your life."

"You're too generous, but we aren't," the constable said, "Take him away!"

Then the Captain General called over Odoardo, and whispered something in his ear. Odoardo looked over at Juan Serrano, who nodded, and at Álvaro de la Mezquita, who shrugged his shoulders.

"Wait," Don Fernando ordered the two men about to lead Sebastián off. He crossed his arms on the table, closed his eyes, and laid his forehead in his hands.

All eyes were fixed on him, anxious to catch the slightest gesture which might give some hint of what was going on in his mind; all ears were trying to detect the faintest sign of his thoughts before they spilled out in words.

"Get him to swear the oath of allegiance," he said eventually.

Overcome with emotion, Sebastián burst into tears, and hid his face in his hands. The priest also shed a tear or two, and the notary cleared his throat several times before he could begin to read the oath properly.

Both sets of legs—those of the accused and those of the men who weren't accused—were swaying to and fro as if following the rhythm of a monotonous piece of music.

At that moment Andrés de San Martín burst in, his mouth empty, dark, silent. He fluttered round Don Fernando like a moth, gesticulating at him with head and hands. He was saying no. The Captain told him to get away, but San Martín persisted despairingly. He slapped the table. Pointed at the mute cavern of his mouth. Insisted it wasn't right.

"Our astrologer is very worked up," Odoardo said. "Give him a pen and some paper, it looks as though he has something important to tell us."

But Don Fernando would have none of it.

Apart from this interruption, the procedure was almost exactly the same for all the rest of the accused. The ritual began with the official charge, then the sentence was announced; it was debated, at first a pardon was refused, but then, after fresh discussions among the Portuguese, it was granted. In each case, the final decision included something different, as if to make them all convincing.

By the end of that long day, Don Fernando's magnanimity, demonstrated time and again against a background of absolute power, won him widespread respect and admiration. Everyone forgot his cruelty toward the rebel captains, even the captains themselves. Don Fernando had washed away our doubts with blood. The captains had been made the scapegoats for the fear and despair we all felt, including Don Fernando himself. Now we could all feel that our burden had lightened.

This produced a new confidence in the crews. That very day, many of them expressed optimism at the future of our undertaking, and even declared themselves happy to spend the winter at San Julián before we renewed our exploration.

Don Fernando had won a complete victory, and he knew it. For the first time, as he slowly made his way across the beach to the ships like a huge turtle while the men burst into noisy, spontaneous applause, I saw him smile contentedly. Then, since the weight of his armor was making his progress difficult, I saw him come to a halt, call over his page Cristóbal Rabelo, and take off his iron suit in full view of all, for the first time.

He cut a small figure without it, but that day he looked like a giant to everyone.

WE SPENT the next few days in titanic efforts to haul the empty, dismantled ships out of the water.

We must have looked like tiny madmen struggling with those immense structures that grew and grew as they emerged from the sea. Like insects beneath their colossal sterns or under the fierce outline of their bows. Carefully placing logs under their hulls so we could push them along. Hanging like bunches of grapes from the makeshift levers we tried to lift them with.

146

Hauling away like beetles on the thick hawsers until a wave came and scattered us, then regrouping and starting again. Each time a little higher up the beach, a little deeper into the sand, so that the storms of winter would not snatch them from us.

All this without so much as a curse or a complaint. We toiled away in a loving silence because those massive hulks with their swollen bellies were all we had. Our only possible link with the world we belonged to but had left behind us on a day already far in the past. That is why we loved them, your Majesty. We were gentle with them even though they demanded so much of us. As if they had been frail young women. Dazzled by their graceful lines. By their looks. By the secret parts usually hidden behind the veil of the sea. We took great care with them. We stroked their timbers affectionately. I think we even talked to them. And little by little they yielded. They became more receptive to our loving care. And followed us out of the sea, then flopped on their bellies close by our shelter. Happy to spend the winter with their men, because they belonged to that other world as well, because we were their only chance too. When we had beached all four of them, and strung up all the masts and rigging on a nearby promontory so that it looked like a forest of freshly lopped trees, the cold set in again. It began to snow, and we were forced to abandon them, with one last look of longing. They lay there in line: the *Trinidad*, which had been so lively and now seemed fast asleep, as the snow covered it with its spotless blanket; the *San Antonio*, big and fat like a stranded whale; the *Concepción*, next to the spot where the head of its former captain Gaspar was bleaching on its lance; and the *Victoria*, whose slender lines gave it an adolescent air. The only one missing was the *Santiago*, the smallest ship of all. Don Fernando had sent it on to look for the passage, which he still believed must be close at hand.

AT FIRST, life in the shelter was spirited enough. We defended ourselves against the cold, the solitude, and the feeling that we were in a vast, uninhabited world where there were no dwellings or even footsteps, by talking endlessly. At the start, we

147

rambled on about everything and nothing. Most of the time we were dreaming out loud, as the cold became more and more intense, the wind blew day and night with uncontrollable fury, and it was so dark that we could not properly tell when it was day and when night.

We talked about what we would do when we got back to our homes. At that stage of the voyage, no one doubted we would return. We tried to forget our plight with crazy plans, convinced that when we returned we would find everything the same as when we had left, as though time had only been passing for us, but had somehow stopped back in Spain on the day of our departure.

All our loved ones, parents, wives, children, friends, some pet animal or other, all seemed frozen in a particular position. We remembered them as though they were in a portrait. We spoke of them as if we were describing a picture whose frame we could not step out of. The same thing happened with fields, streams, wellsprings, streets, houses, even objects. We saw ourselves back there in the same way. The feeling of lost, dead time that our monotonous wait created within us only added to the confusion. Time did not seem to go by. There were no days or nights; the winter seemed endless and springtime impossible; the wind was always the same, and so were everyone's faces; the minuscule geography of our shelter, the people we conjured up and the tales we told all began to jumble together. To evoke that other world more clearly and incisively we mixed people, landscapes, things and even feelings, but to no avail. So, as we secretly tired of those unyielding memories, but found ourselves unable to recover the feelings that had brought them to life and were their lost soul, we gradually retreated in silence into our own solitude. Slowly, we began to realize what our true situation was. One day, someone burst into tears. On another, someone else came to tell us that the sails were getting moldy. The weather made it impossible to keep them dry and they were covered with fungus. Whenever the snow melted, it rotted the ropes. Even the ships' timbers were splitting with the bitter cold. The ships were decaying, he said. After that, the silence clung to us even more closely.

Each day made it a little harder to talk. We did try again though, until someone suddenly complained that we had spent months in those godforsaken lands without ever seeing a single human being. Our only company were the crowds of idiotic penguins, standing there in the wind and the snow as if in silent protest at our presence, perhaps mocking us or waiting for us to waste away entirely so they could come and peck out our eyes, tear out whatever was left inside. There are thousands of them, the sailor said, about the size of a five-year-old child at least. He had gone up to them several times, convinced they were not alive. He had imagined they must be some kind of mysterious idols someone had been collecting there. But they were real, they were alive. They even laid eggs. And they were the only creatures that could withstand this weather. They were the lords of these desolate lands. An army of children with bird beaks, just waiting for the right moment to attack. To drive us out of their world. And if they did attack, how were we to defend ourselves against such numbers?

Little by little, our bleak reality began to seem increasingly vulnerable, as we felt ourselves to be at the mercy of unknown, mysterious forces.

I remember that even I was sucked in by that growing sense of unreality. One day while Ginés was trying to get us to picture springtime in his village, I replied, "Winter is the death of everything. The death of hope."

"That's true in part," he said, "everything dies to some extent, to be reborn with the spring. But hope does not die. Because at winter's end the earth, the sun, and the plants are born anew, and so are animals and men, and that shows that hope has remained alive deep inside all things, all living beings."

"What if there were no end to winter?"

"You know that day always follows night," he replied, smiling.

"But here you've seen that isn't necessarily so. Here night follows night. And the same might happen with winter."

Ginés's smile froze on his lips.

"What if this winter doesn't end?" I insisted. "Hasn't it gone on too long already? Wasn't it winter here when we arrived months ago? It has got harsher, that's true; but that is no proof that it may end one day. What if we were in the place where winter has its lair?"

"That's in the north," Ginés argued.

"Don't be stupid. At this end of the world, winter is holed up in the south. That is where we are now, and where we are heading."

"That's impossible," he protested. But he did not say another word, and a short while later he went off silently to another corner of the shelter.

The months of waiting were making everything decay. The ships were rotting and so were the men. Boredom and madness crowded round us like a pack of hounds; we only just managed to stay free of their fangs and black gaping mouths.

Now whenever someone spoke it was not to recall their village or their loved ones. Even their dreams had been contaminated; most of them only wished to be free of this inactivity so that they could set off again on their adventures. Moldering away, they dreamt of roaming the seas in search of distant isles; already they sensed the sun's warm caress on their skin, the exciting aroma of spices in their nostrils. They sang the praises of the seafaring life and bold quests. They waxed lyrical as they imagined the huge sails billowing out and the masts creaking as they responded to the wind; they could feel the ropes tautening in their hands numbed with cold. None of them seemed to understand it was those very same dreams that had brought them to this reality from which they now wished only to escape.

For as long as our forced confinement lasted, nobody asked after the *Santiago*. No one mentioned the ship or named one of the thirty-seven members of its crew, even in a slip of the tongue. It was as though all of us were keeping to a silent agreement. Not even Cartagena in his pit dared make any reference to it.

EVENTUALLY THIS huge, slimy sadness completely took over our souls. We were reduced to the level of animals. We lay there all day ruminating on our silence. Without so much as a thought. We did not even feel fear. We simply let ourselves be, in that unchanging half-light, not knowing if it was day or night because there was no difference between the two. Huddled together like beasts. Unconsciously seeking the warmth of whoever was beside us without asking ourselves who it might be. Because it did not matter. We were all exactly alike. Dumb animals on the floor of our barn. Tamed beasts crouching round a fire. Protected from the harshness of the unknown by make-shift wooden walls that let in the cold and the wind. Above all, the wind. A wind that came from far beyond anything we knew or could imagine. A wind that blared like a herald. A wind that seemed to get under our skins that tangled itself in our beards and hair. That forced its way deep inside us. A wind that blew without pause, until we no longer knew if there was any wind or if we were only imagining it. Why was there so much wind there, your Majesty?

Whole days went by without anybody speaking. Days in which we did not hear a single word from a human mouth. Not even to agree on who should keep the fire going at night, or who would sweep the snow from the roof. It snowed so much the roof seemed bound to cave in. Then it melted and freezing water poured down, drenching our wretched humanity. So whenever the fire began to go out or the roof began to creak and to drip water, we merely stared at each other with a look devoid of all expression, and there was always someone who would get up, stiff with cold, and throw a log or piece of wood on the fire. Or who would leave the shelter and clamber across the roof, scraping at the snow with a spade. And always the wind. And the crash of the sea on the beach. That desolate beach of black sand where Gaspar de Quesada's noble head was putrefying. Splashed by the steel-colored waves of the icy sea. Beneath a sky full of clouds heavy with snow, dark as shadows. Stung by the ceaseless wind that toyed with the captain of the *Concepción*'s faded gold locks.

We did move around our shelter, but so slowly that it seemed we were stuck in one spot. We edged about as silently and imperceptibly as shells on the bottom of the sea. Searching

151

for warmth. For company. Anything. Perhaps to recognize ourselves. We were like processionary caterpillars, which wriggle and band together until they form a tight knot of cocoons.

One day my shuffling took me next to Don Fernando. I realized it was him when I felt the icy touch of iron on my skin. He was stretched out on a mattress in a dark corner far from the fire. Wearing his armor as usual, with his purple cloak over it. I pulled my hand away, the cold of the steel was so intense to my touch that it felt as though it were burning. But above all I felt a sense of pity for him, so I stayed by his side. I sat silent for a while, with my eyes closed. I could hear his breathing, which had the same rhythm as mine, and I decided to stay there. Several hours went by—I have no idea how many, we had lost all sense of time, since nobody bothered with the hourglasses anymore. Don Fernando stirred once or twice, as if to make himself more comfortable beside me.

"It's you, isn't it?" he asked all of a sudden.

"I think so," I said.

After that we fell silent again, without moving. Listening to the wind. And then the snow began to fall once more.

"How could you leave such a beautiful and tender young woman, sitting there all night in her armchair waiting for you?" I burst out, much to my own surprise.

He struggled to sit up, and looked at me, puzzled.

"Can you see her?" he asked. "What's she doing now?"

This time it was not a game, the vision of her came unbidden, in spite of me. The urgency of his question made me think Don Fernando realized that.

"She's fallen asleep in her chair waiting for you," I replied. "She was measuring the silence of the street outside, anxiously interrogating every sound. The noise of a coach clattering toward her, her anxiety growing with every moment, then speeding on by, and finally dying away, until it disappeared altogether. Or the footsteps of a passerby. The sound of heels on the cobbles, of her heart beating loudly in her breast, the steps quick and decisive as they drew closer, her heart beating stronger and stronger, until the sound of the footsteps and the beating of her heart seemed to merge for an instant, and then gradually the steps faded away down the street, and her heart calmed down again. The same thing happens every night, until the street falls asleep in the womb of the night, and she, weary of waiting, rocks herself to sleep in the chair by the window, her last thought that perhaps on the morrow . . ."

Don Fernando closed his eyes, lowered his head until his chin brushed his steel breastplate, and said nothing.

The wind battered the shelter walls. In the middle of the room, lit by the fire's glow, Andrés de San Martín waved his hands in the air and mouthed silent words, trying to say something to his chance companion who could not understand a thing.

"Sometimes I think we're like those puppets of yours, pulled by invisible strings that determine our every gesture but create the illusion that we are free and so responsible for our actions," the Captain said.

"It's easy to think that," I replied, though I was not so sure this was true.

"Only death cuts all the strings. But tell me, how do you know it's her? Is it the same balcony?"

"No, not this time. But it's the same face. The window is smaller, and there's no balcony."

"Why isn't it the same? What's happened?"

"I don't know, but for some reason she has changed rooms."

He sat there, deep in thought. The shadows from the fire settled on his face like big dark moths.

"When I heard she was expecting a child, I had no choice," he said. "I had been nursing my project for years. It had cost me so much effort and frustration to get the fleet together, and just when everything at last looked possible, how could I say I didn't want to go to the Spice Islands anymore?"

"Why not?"

"Because I could not. Because that dream, she, and I, were all one and the same thing. The three of us were chained to each other forever. I couldn't give her up, but I couldn't relinquish my dream either."

153

"So you were a kind of double-headed monster. Half man, half navigator."

"She accepted me as such. The Spice Islands were a dream we shared."

"Do you really think so?"

"Like a child, which brings together and separates at the same time."

"But she loved the man, not the navigator. She loved you, not the Spice Islands. She was frightened of your dreams."

"Tell me about the baby boy. Can you see him in the cradle?"

"I can't see any cradle in the room."

"What do you mean? Do you think he sleeps in the other room with Rodrigo? Isn't he too young to be so far from his mother?"

"I can't see a cradle in the other room either."

"Look more carefully—don't annoy me with your jokes. There must be a cradle somewhere in the house."

"Do you have a room full of old clothes and things you no longer need?"

"The boy can't be there!"

"Do you have a room like that?"

"You're a knave!" he shouted, launching himself at me.

I felt something as sharp as a claw, as cold and rough as a sea creature, fastening itself around my throat. I could not reply, I was gasping for air and could not even cry out: I kicked and struggled while my companions looked on blankly. The stench of dried blood on Don Fernando's chain mail gauntlet made me retch; I thought I could hear Andrés's noiseless laugh, but still I could not get the image of a room full of old clothes out of my mind, a room with an empty, dusty cradle in it, only half covered by a cloth.

"In those final days before we set sail she was like a madwoman," Don Fernando said after a while, as I sat there quivering, freed at last from his grasp, my throat a burning wound as I breathed in air that was like molten glass scalding my mouth and teeth. "She said a navigator like me should never come close to a woman," Don Fernando recalled.

I recovered my voice: "It was odd. I wanted to know everything. I had to stick my Jew's nose into everything, without regard for the consequences. That's why my mother had to beat me more than once, especially when I was determined to find out who my father was, and went round our neighborhood asking everyone, although I never got any straight answers. A friend I used to play with had told me my mother was a whore."

"Never let the fateful song of the sea fall on any woman's ears, she would say to me."

"I had discovered my mother in bed with a Christian gentleman, and since they were both in a position for making children, I guessed that was what they had done previously to produce me, and that therefore this same gentleman must be my father. I did not get the chance to ask him though, because no sooner had they seen me at the foot of the bed than my mother started to shriek and my father ran off out the kitchen door, clothes in hand."

"And never to engender children in a woman's belly, because women belong to the land, not the sea."

"The next time, I took great care not to give them such a fright, but spied on them from behind a curtain. I recognized the man plunging like a colt between my mother's legs as someone who lived in a nearby village. He had a reputation as a learned man, a writer of verses and moral aphorisms, who had seven children with a cold, blond woman who was his wife."

"She said that the only destiny for a true navigator was the oceans' infinite solitude, the bewitching aroma of impossible islands."

"You can imagine your Juanillo's bewilderment. He could not understand how a man could have two wives and make children with both of them, so in order to avoid frightening my mother, I decided to put my doubts to the blond lady. The result was that three days later I found myself in the service of a clergyman who was chaplain and adviser to my first master."

"That will do. No more of that. I didn't mean to offend or hurt you," Don Fernando said. "I'm sorry. You know I have a high regard for you. Tell me about the child."

"I can't. I can't see anything more."

"Because I struck you? Take your time, calm down. We have all the time in the world."

I lowered my head between my knees. He took off his gauntlet, and stroked my hair. Ruffled it.

"You have a strangely shaped head," he said.

"All of us Jews do."

"I don't care what you are. But tell me, why did she say all those things?"

I made a great effort to try to remember all the fragments I had heard.

"Because she had her dreams too," I said tentatively. "Because all of us live wrapped up in our own dreams. Embedded in them. Caught in their nets. The prisoners of their snares."

"You too? What do you dream of?"

"Oh, my dreams would make you laugh. They wouldn't even seem like dreams to you, they're so tiny and insignificant compared to yours."

"But you do have them. Why is that?"

"Because you, I, and everyone else are a little like pilgrims lost in a desert. Dreams are our mirages. Mirages that sharpen our thirst without satisfying it. It is that thirst which tells us we are still alive."

"I hate your project, she told me on one of those last nights ashore. I detest it. Your voyage will destroy everything, she said, and broke down in sobs."

As he said this, Don Fernando lowered his head, which hung like a broken branch. The wind tore at the planks of the shelter, whistling through every crack. Among the huddled groups of shadows I could make out Andrés de San Martín close by.

"When you two were together, when she was cradling you in her warmth and you could smell her perfume, both of you breathing in and out in unison like docile animals stretched out in the sun, did you still wear your armor?"

"Why do you ask me that?"

"You know what I mean."

"She is the tenderest of women. And so affectionate. As

lovable as a little animal. So lovable I was frightened sometimes."

"What were you frightened of?"

"I was frightened of staying on land, resigning myself to
that as my future."

"Because you're one of those who prefer the allure of
dreams, which are sweet to begin with but in the end turn even
more bitter than resignation. Did you make love to her with
your suit of armor on?"

"Don't play the fool."

"Do you know what I think sometimes? That you're like
an onion: beneath one layer there's another layer, and so on,
and so on."

"You don't know me then."

The wind blew in squalls that cracked like thunder in the
distance before they crashed against the planks of the shelter.
After a while it dropped a little, and beyond it we could hear
the roar of the sea.

"Do you hear that?" he asked. I nodded. "Listen well . . .
The sea is an open door, a path disappearing in the distance,
the ship we watch as it leaves port, a woman waiting."

"And the land is a rainy afternoon by the fireside, a steaming
pot, a child asking for affection, fresh warm bread."

"All lit by a flickering candle burning slowly down."

In my ears I could hear the ceaseless, eternal roar of the
waves. I said nothing. Suddenly a hand gripped my arm and
shook it. Andrés de San Martín was beside me. His empty
mouth was opening and closing in futile efforts. His huge black
eyes were trying to tell me something. They were full of fear
or anguish, I could not make out which. His despairing gestures
roused Don Fernando, who sat up again. His face turned grim
when he saw who it was.

"Tell him if he doesn't get away from me, I'll kill him."

I prized San Martín's hand from my arm and signaled him
to be off. All in sign language, as though he were deaf as well
as dumb. The cosmographer slid away as stealthily as he had
approached.

"I can see the house again," I said. "I can't have been looking properly before. I can see the little one now, I was so stupid. There he is, in his mother's arms. Shh! Don't make any noise. Look at him, wrapped in a shawl. Waving his little hands about as though he's fighting something in his dreams. And I'll tell you a secret: that little scrap of a thing is giving off so much warmth that it fills the whole room, spreads beyond it into the street, wafts across fields down to the river, and is carried out to sea."

"Has the astrologer gone?"

"Why are you so afraid of him?"

"I think I made a mistake; he'll never change his mind now. I robbed myself of that possibility when I had his tongue cut out."

"What if he got his speech back and told you something you didn't like again?"

"Then I think I would have it cut off again."

"What did he tell you?"

"Anyway," Don Fernando said after a pause, "what could I offer her? Only the brief pretense of a life on land."

"Love?"

"That's a serious, important word. I don't like words like that."

"I'll put it differently: With you by her side, she feels a little less lonely. And you a little less lost. And both of you a little less hunted."

"For a while."

"All right, for a while. But during that while, she has a reason for facing up to each day. To see it through and look forward to the next one. Don't belittle that. There are many in this world for whom each day can be a far harder and more uncertain journey than this one taking us to the Spice Islands."

"We weren't even together much. I had very little to give her really. Not because I was selfish, but I didn't know how. I have always been very clumsy on land."

"You know you gave her a lot."

"And now she's all alone."

"With a handful of dreams in her apron pocket as her only legacy from you. Those dreams are what she will give suck to her children with, far more than milk. They will help her wash the clothes. Will fill her pans. Will warm her feet. They will be milk, soap, salt and clogs for her. And a stick, too, for her to lean on when her legs give out. And a protecting shield. A roof and a door."

"Like a toy house," he replied. "But that's enough of your words. Words: you twist them about, and you make me catch the disease, so that I believe in them too. But words are empty when the actions that give them meaning are lost in the past."

"But aren't you trying to reach her? Aren't you conjuring up her image through my words? Aren't they transporting you to her side?"

He sat thoughtful for a while.

"Make sure the astrologer is nowhere near."

"What did he tell you?"

"Tell me about the way the child smells. I love the smell of children."

"He smells of apple blossoms on a warm spring afternoon," I said. "And of curdled milk and urine, of course. But the apple smell is strongest."

"And her?"

"She smells of loneliness."

"What does that smell like?"

"Something like the smell of the sea, tar, huge canvas sails."

"And me?"

"You smell of spices. And loneliness. With a touch of apple blossom."

Don Fernando laughed, and that unexpected and unusual sound stirred all the shadows in the room, which turned as one toward the dark corner the guffaw had come from. While the Captain went on laughing and calling me a liar, a barefaced liar, those dark silhouettes began to join in, until the laughter rippled through the whole gaggle of men huddled like animals on the floor of the shelter. The laughter grew so loud that for an instant it even blocked out the sound of the wind and the roaring of the sea. Every one of us laughed, even the soundless Andrés de San Martín.

THEN ONE day the snowfalls ceased. We waited for several days but they did not return. The fury of the wind began to abate, although it went on groaning like some huge wounded beast, and little by little, though we could hardly admit it to ourselves, the days began to be distinguishable from the nights, and the sky was lit with a spectral glow.

One afternoon we were all startled to hear a knocking at the shelter door.

We stared at each other, not knowing what to do. Nobody dared open the door or shout a question. The knocking continued, and without a word Don Fernando signaled for us to see who was there.

Outlined in the doorway against a dirty gray sky were two figures in rags who could barely stand on their feet. We were hard put to recognize those two ghosts as companions of ours from the *Santiago*, and from the way they looked at us, they seemed to find us equally strange. They stood in the door, staring at us, until someone shouted:

"But aren't you Bartolomé . . . Bartolomé García?"

The man he was referring to burst into sobs, staggered in, and collapsed into the arms of the nearest sailor. Both of them were crying like little girls. The one who had remained in the doorway said in a scarcely audible voice, "And I'm Pedro Brito," his eyes searching desperately for a friendly face before he, too, fell to the floor too quickly for anyone to catch him.

They were so exhausted that we could only give them a little hot wine with sugar before they fell into a deep sleep.

We took turns all that night watching over the two inert forms stretched on the beds we had laid for them next to the fire, stroking their heads or just staring at them. No one dared wake them, however anxious we were to know what had become of the *Santiago*.

As soon as they opened their eyes the next morning, we gave them each double rations. Pedro Brito flung himself on the bowl of food like a starving dog. Bartolomé still seemed to be a long way away. He clasped the bowl as though he were warming his hands on it and stared up at us with absent eyes. Nobody could bring themselves to ask him anything. His gaze came to rest on the Captain General, and he said in a broken voice, "Juan Serrano sent us because he wishes to know who is on the throne of Spain now, so that he can take possession of the lands to the south of here in his name."

There was a moment's silence during which we all stared at each other in amazement.

"So Serrano is still alive? What about the others?" Don Fernando asked.

"Benito drowned. He's the only one who was lost."

"What the devil are the rest doing then? Why haven't they come back as I ordered them to? Have they all gone mad?"

"Captain Serrano told us we had to stay where we were to recover the remains of the ship and its goods that the sea kept casting up on shore. The ship's master Baltasar said that made no sense. That we would perish from the cold and hunger. But Serrano insisted it was his ship and nobody could tell him what to do with it. 'Your ship is at the bottom of the sea,' everyone told him. That only made him angry. 'We have nowhere to go, so we'll stay with the ship,' he retorted. 'But your ship doesn't exist anymore,' the master insisted. The captain pulled out his dagger and plunged it into his arm. 'The next time it'll be your throat,' he screamed."

"But what happened to the *Santiago*?" Don Fernando wanted to know.

"It was about twenty leagues from here, after we had been fishing and hunting seals in a river that he named the Santa Cruz. A storm destroyed all our sails and blew away our rudder. The *Santiago* was like a paper boat that has been in the water too long. She came apart like a melon. When we were boys we used to kick our neighbor's melons to see how they exploded: that's what it was like. She foundered on rocks close to the shore, so we were all saved except for Juan Serrano's slave, who couldn't swim."

"But why didn't you all come back here or send some men in search of help?"

"When the supplies ran out we ate whatever shellfish or roots we could find. All we had to drink was ice, which we had to crush to get a little water. But Serrano insisted that we shouldn't leave the ship. We spent God knows how many days scouring the coast for whatever the sea threw up on the shore, even though we were so weak from hunger. We picked up bits of timber, spars, a tub, a bowl, a wooden spoon. We had to rescue everything and then show it to the captain, who spent hours staring at each object, as if he were trying to reconstruct the whole ship in his mind. We were as dependent on the ship that the waves were tearing to pieces in front of our eyes as when we had been when we were sailing in her. We built a shelter from the bits of flotsam to protect us from the cold and the snow. 'You see, the *Santiago* hasn't abandoned us,' the captain said.

"One day a mast was cast up on the shore, and Serrano said he would use it to make a cross to plant on the top of a nearby mountain so that he could take possession of the land in the name of the king of Spain. The carpenter Ripart had to build a makeshift cross with the few tools he had left. When he had finished and the wind had dropped a little, we went in procession to the summit. What a sad-looking procession we made, your Honor! We were all half dead from hunger; the cold had frozen us to our bones, and yet we filed behind the cross in the unreal, almost violet light of that region. At the top, the captain said a prayer and while a few of us struggled with our frostbitten hands to wedge the cross in between two rocks and secure it with rocks, he began to take possession of those lands in the name of . . . and when he had got that far, he stopped."

Do you know why Serrano, the man who never doubted, suddenly stopped, your Highness? Because, according to Bartolomé, he realized he did not know in whose name he should take possession of those lands. They had lost all their hourglasses in the wreck, and since there is no distinction between day and night in those regions but always the same gray half-light, they had no idea how long they had been there collecting the wreckage of their ship from the beach. So Serrano began to wonder whether Don Carlos was still on the throne of Spain, or if a successor was now ruling, and if so, who was he to swear by? Quietly, he asked the notary, who was supposed to know about these administrative matters. But the notary did not know; he said he had no idea how long ago they left Spain, but that to judge by the quantity of evils that had befallen them it must have been a long time, and therefore he could not say with any certainty whether the captain should swear in your name, Sire, or in that of your successor. Then everyone began to be plagued by the same doubt, and at the foot of the cross they all started discussing who might be the king of Spain. Someone asked why they were suffering in those desolate lands if they could not even be sure they were serving the same monarch who had sent them off on the journey. "We serve the King of Spain, whoever he may be," the notary replied. "But it might be that as a result of war or marriage Spain and its crown have fallen into the hands of a foreign king, in which case we no longer have any monarch to serve. Or that our endeavors are now contrary to the wishes of our new lord." Such were the debates, and all the while the carpenter was awaiting Serrano's oath so that he could carve your royal name on the cross. But the captain could not make up his mind. Finally he sent those two men to search for Don Fernando's camp so that he could settle the matter once and for all.

"So we struggled on foot across empty, inhospitable wastes for you to decide in whose name we are to take possession of those lands."

The Captain General himself seemed plunged into doubt, and all of a sudden Serrano's question no longer seemed absurd to us, but legitimate.

UNTIL ONE morning a pale sun slanted through the thick layers of clouds and filled the shelter with an unexpected brightness. In that instant we ceased to wonder who was in charge of our destinies.

We had grown so used to our meager shelter we thought we knew every last detail of it, but when the darkness suddenly lifted everything changed. We could see the depths of the misery we had been living in, and could not believe it. The floor was strewn with all kinds of rubbish. There were bits of food, nests of straw, a torn mattress displaying its innards, weapons, wooden plates, spoons, a comb, letters scarcely begun, excrement, Hijito's toy boat . . . even the body of one of our companions who had died without anyone noticing. We also realized from the fresh air streaming in through the door just how bad the stench of our lair was. Everything stank of despair. The cold light sweeping into our shelter revealed to us unknown aspects of ourselves. Yet some corners still remained dark, inspiring us with real terror, so we could not wait to get out.

The air outside immediately refreshed us. The sea had regained its true color, and on the distant hills we could see patches of green amid the remaining snow. Bathed in this gentle, new light, the beach we had so often cursed looked almost friendly and welcoming.

Then, without a word from anyone, like sleepers frightened of destroying a dream, we slowly came back to life. And our first thought after all that time was to go and examine the ships.

They were still there. Waiting for us like loving women. They seemed like four black pearls encrusted in the sand and to us they were even more precious. We ran to greet them like crazed young lovers.

They had had a hard time of it. The metalwork was rusted over. The ice had twisted or split the timbers. The scarecrows we had left to keep the birds off the ropes had lost their stuffing and swung sad and bedraggled in the wind like hanged men. We had filled a suit of armor with oakum and left it on board the flagship; it was clanging forlornly against the mast with a sound like a cracked bell. The *Trinidad*'s shrouds had snapped and hung gray and frayed from the mainmast. The birds had not been scared by our silly puppets but had built nests in all the ships; the *Concepción* was full of beating wings, the loving attention of the females and the cheeping of their chicks. The

San Antonio had keeled over where two of the props holding it upright had given way.

But they were intact. They were still alive. They would float again, and that was all that mattered to us. Because we did love them.

We were walking among the ships, staring at them as you stare at a woman you love sleeping beside you in the silence of the night, when we saw prints in the snow. There could be no doubt they were human footprints, which meant that in this world we had been convinced was totally empty . . .

"It's uninhabited all right," Bartolomé had insisted, because they had walked a hundred miles across the land without encountering any sign of human life. But during the following nights back in the shelter, commenting on the discovery and discounting the possibility that the prints might have belonged to another survivor from the *Santiago* because they were far too big, we invented the wildest theories about the origin, nature and appearance of this mysterious being.

Then the footprints reappeared, this time around our shelter. They came from inland, although we could not tell exactly from which direction because the ground was still frozen hard. They crossed to the hut and led from one of its two windows to the other.

We began to feel we were being spied upon. We barred the door and put up makeshift curtains; we spent days and nights on guard without ever discovering who was responsible for the tracks, although they continued to reappear when we were least expecting it.

The questions we asked ourselves were always the same: What was this strange creature up to? Why did it never show itself? Was it frightened of us or was it simply inspecting us as if we were insects in a trap? This last feeling was strongest, because the creature could come and go as it pleased, whereas we were always stuck in the same spot, as in a trap.

HEADING SOUTH again! We were not dismayed because setting off in any direction was better than being stuck in an

165

immobility so absolute it seemed eternal. Anything that meant a change from the present of which we were so weary. So disgusted. So dead in spirit. But now we were putting to sea again and could all feel hope inside our breasts sending out its shoots which clung to our minds and souls like those ivy plants that plunge their roots down among the bones of the dead and cling to ancient cemetery walls.

We did not spare ourselves. Some men started careening the ships until their hands bled, when they were replaced by other hands, until little by little from beneath the tangled mess of seaweed, barnacles, limpets, tiny crabs and small white shells, the stout old oaks of Spain began to emerge once more. Battered by the waves, scoured by the salt and riddled with scars, but still intact and anxious to set off again. The carpenters worked without respite; the sound of hammer blows, the scrape of saws filled the beach. The masts rose up, scrubbed clean, reinforced. The shrouds were tarred; the ropes greased, the cables spliced. The anchor hawsers were changed and fresh ropes and buoys added. The blacksmith spent all night at his anvil repairing chains, shaping stanchions, making fittings and hooks. Bare-chested, his sweating skin reflecting the ruddy glow of the embers, Pedro Pérez shouted at his helpers to bring him tongs, a measure, a hammer; he moved like a supernatural being, picking up a piece of red-hot iron, dipping it into the water barrel, then laying it on the anvil as he whisked off another piece he had hammered into shape. For the moment he was the master, and he reveled in his importance, refusing to rest or eat, his muscles tensed and all his senses fixed on the work before him. We were lulled to sleep by the rhythmic sounds of his hammer, and his blows on the anvil like a peal of bells were the first thing we heard on waking. Whenever the hammering ceased, we could hear the forge bellows roaring like furious beasts in the silence of the night.

The whole bay reeked of red-hot iron, oakum, grease, huge canvases drying in the sun, sawdust, the steam rising from the vats of boiling tar: the smells stuck to our skins and blotted out the salty odor of the sea.

We swarmed over the ships, fitting the shrouds into the tops, hoisting the sails, strengthening the boltropes, greasing the ropes for tacking the sails. As we worked, the intricate network of rigging grew and grew; bit by bit the ships regained their own motley, familiar appearance.

Not a single person remained aloof from the urgent desire to be heading off again.

No one except Don Juan de Cartagena, who was not leaving.

The fleet's Inspector occupied his time observing the huge flocks of birds that swooped down from all sides to pair off and nest on the beach.

Inured to the wind and cold, Don Juan spent each of his last days on the inhospitable promontory that dominated the coastline, observing the birds' habits and writing them down.

"Take me to my post," he would call out to the first person he saw at daybreak.

Most of them paid him no heed; others, irked by the arrogant, authoritarian tone of this man who had once been in command, retorted with a filthy curse or cruel joke. But Don Juan would not give up, and went on repeating his order unperturbed until finally he found someone who, out of pity or habit, would agree to carry him up to his chair atop the promontory.

One morning, spurred on by curiosity, I decided to sneak up and spy on his watchtower.

As I made my way stealthily up, I was amazed at the nests all around me. Conical nests, nests built underground like catacombs, rudimentary nests among the grass, the normal kind in the branches of bushes, nests in the rocks and in the sand, nests everywhere. Nests that had emerged from nothing, instantaneously. Because I can assure you, your Majesty, that during the two months we spent in our shelter there were no other nests in those frozen wastes than the empty ones of our four ships, and no other bird but Gaspar's head impaled on its lance like a stuffed eagle. Everything had been empty and dead. Then all of a sudden the sun began to shine, the days lengthened, and the birds started to arrive singly or in flocks, sure of the direction they had to take to reach their homes.

What mysterious hand guides them to this spot and not somewhere else? I wondered as I went slowly on, treading carefully among the nests. What secret force brings them back to the place where they first saw the light of day, with the sole aim of continuing the cycle of their species? This is where each new generation practices the same ritual as all those before it, I said to myself as I observed the brilliant plumage of the mating season, watching those exotic birds perform a courtship dance like the doves in my village. And the precise way they built their nests, just like the herons in Bustillo. And the hatching of the eggs, which reminded me of the storks in my own country. An obscure, timeless ritual, always identical, and just the same here as in my village. A ceremony none of them could refuse to take part in. A meeting with the natural order.

I was so caught up in my thoughts that I accidentally stumbled and fell onto some nests. A whole multitude of birds immediately sent up a deafening screech, then spread out like a sail in the wind and launched themselves into the sky, blocking out the sun.

Your Juanillo was so taken aback he was about to run away from this legion of enraged angels, when he heard Cartagena's voice calling out to him:

"Don't be afraid; come up here. If you're quiet they'll return to their nests and forget all about you."

"It's not that I'm frightened of them, my Lord," I said, clambering up to him. "I've liked birds since I was a boy, when there wasn't a nest in my village I didn't know about. I used to check them every day, so I could see exactly when the chicks were born."

"Be quiet," he said, silencing my chatter in a voice that was both high-handed and friendly.

Neither of us said a word. One by one, the birds returned to their nests where they settled in flocks of the same species. Each group appeared to have its own well-defined territory, although each one was close to the neighboring species, and within each group the individual birds were packed in together, so that the whole promontory, the adjacent rocks, the beach and the sandbar in the middle of the river all seemed covered with a strange, thick carpet of feathers that rippled and seethed as if the life impulse they had come there to perpetuate was being transmitted among them in every direction at once. All those creatures were beating in unison to produce a sound that was not of this world. Their cries were infinitely varied: some were braying, others clucking, or screeching like old women, or cawing, whistling, caterwauling, cackling, groaning; all of them mixed and superimposed like a hellish chorus. A chorus that reached a paroxysm whenever an intruder strayed into the wrong group of nests.

"There is something diabolic about their cries," I said. "It sounds like the lament of fallen angels."

Don Cartagena was thoughtful, staring down at the *San Antonio* gently rocking in the middle of the bay while her crew swarmed over her decks and rigging. They were hoisting the sails, which fluttered and shook like huge wings as they unfurled, gleaming when the sunlight caught them.

"I'll tell you a secret," Cartagena said. "They are the gods in this godless world."

"That's because this is their land."

"Even those great birds who never settle on it," Don Juan agreed, pointing to an albatross with outstretched wings which glided by on the wind, tilting its body from side to side as it soared up, opening vast vertical or sloping circles, then closing them as it drifted gently down again. "And look at those over there," he said. "They're as clumsy on land as ships out of water. They can hardly move because their huge wings get in the way. Like these stumps of mine," he added, laughing.

Looking down at his legs, I saw he had a book on his lap. To hide my confusion, I asked what he was reading.

"Just a book of adventures."

"A book of chivalry, *Amadís* perhaps?"

"It's an old book about adventures on the high seas," he replied offhandedly. "You know, voyages to distant lands, endless perils and so on."

"Is it true you write about the birds?"

He nodded.

"I thought you were a warrior."

"I was once. Now I am a prisoner, so birds . . ."

"Even as a prisoner you're privileged because here you have all the birds in the world."

"All the sea birds. Don't forget I was a sailor as well. And by the way, how is the work on the *San Antonio* progressing?"

"Will you miss your ship?"

"Did you know that those great seabirds never die in the place where they build their nests? There are thousands and thousands of them here, but you won't see one of them that is sick or old, let alone a dead bird. As if they all knew when the cycle was coming to an end and they had to set out on their final journey."

"To where?"

"To nowhere. That is not what matters. They simply fly off, soaring through the ocean skies, until they fall exhausted on a lost beach somewhere."

I stood there silent and thoughtful as I looked at the birds around us. Cartagena stared down at the ships.

"I've heard you bamboozle the Captain with visions you invent," he said after a while.

"Would you like to hear something about your house?"

"No thank you. Keep your chatter to yourself. This beach is my home."

"Do you know something? You're not as despicable as I thought. At least you're courageous. If it were me who was being abandoned on a beach like this . . ."

"What did you expect? That I would break down in tears and beg for mercy at your master's feet?"

"I would try anything."

"Take the priest," he said. "He wanders around like a shadow, watching all the preparations without saying a word. He looks like one of those crazy old women you see in our villages, the ones everybody makes fun of and the boys throw stones at. Is that a better way? Just look at him."

Absorbed as I was by his words and the birds' antics, I had

170

not noticed Sánchez de Reina who, his habit stiff with dirt, his face crisscrossed with wrinkles, was walking around like a ghost only a few yards from us. He seemed old and lost, like the battered image of a saint in an abandoned church.

"Forget it," Cartagena shouted at him. "You'll never see your parish again! You don't exist for your village anymore." Then, turning to me: "Can you see that colony of gulls down there on the beach? They can fly wonderfully and have no problems walking on land either, but they are more cautious than the great birds up here, they never stray too far from the coast where they have their nests. They prefer short trips to long voyages."

"When I'm a bird, I'll be a gull," I said.

Don Juan burst out laughing.

"Now let me read for a while, I want to finish this book as soon as possible."

I left him without saying anything more, but as I was making my way back down from the promontory to the beach through the birds' pandemonium, I heard Cartagena's voice calling out to me: "I feel sorry for you! You won't be here when all the chicks are born!"

THEN ONE morning after a meeting with all the new captains, Don Fernando gave the order for us to prepare to set sail.

Everyone carried out the complicated maneuvers with such childlike enthusiasm that it was only a few minutes before we were staring openmouthed at the magic of the enormous sails spreading in the wind. It was as though the ships had suddenly blossomed. The sails were white as a woman's breasts, as spotless as the sheets draped from balconies in villages back in Spain, as brand new and perfumed as a bride's trousseau. They hung from the sky like full moons, flapping with the sound of banners held high; they were like Flanders lace delicately sewn on the yards; they were anxious to feel the wind, to swell out like a newlywed wife. You have never seen such a sight, your Majesty. Yet we were not even sailors, nothing more than a handful of madmen desperately in love with those huge sails. We were like bees drinking pollen among enormous petals of white canvas. Nothing, not even the ships themselves, could escape their enchantment. All the rigging quivered, and every piece of timber came back to life, as if the sap were running through their veins once more after the long winter months. The *Trinidad* heeled over and shook like a submissive woman. The *San Antonio* charged the waves furiously like a bull. The *Concepción*, which was in a more sheltered corner of the bay, bobbed up and down gently as if it were in a cradle. The *Victoria* pitched and tossed like a madwoman.

Don Fernando gave orders to tighten the ropes. The pulleys squealed, then all at once the sails filled with wind. The masts shuddered and tensed. The timbers and all the bolts in the hull creaked and groaned as the *San Antonio*, black belly and white wings, led the ships out of the bay.

The sun began to set on the black sands of the beach, seeking refuge in the vast wasteland behind which it could hide from the night.

The priest ran up and down the beach like a phantom, as though he too were looking for somewhere to hide. On top of the dark promontory, Don Juan sat motionless, surrounded by silent birds.

As our ships sailed away, the miserable shelter where we had suffered so much grew smaller and smaller, until it seemed unreal, almost unimaginable. We could hardly make out the lance where Gaspar the Fair's head was rotting, and the crosses we had left to mark the spot where we had buried the dead were like playthings in the distance.

We left it all behind with the same mixture of relief and anxiety that one feels on waking from a nightmare.

THE SAILING conditions began to worsen the very next morning. Dark clouds covered the sky, and a strong, icy wind blew up from the south.

That afternoon the sea boiled up creamy as milk. The spray flew in heavy chunks; the waves washed over the decks time and again.

The *Trinidad* quivered like a willow twig. She seemed about to break in two as she lay poised on the crest of a huge wave. She did not do so, but fell headlong into a bottomless pit, only to emerge again, triumphant, streaming with foam like a horse that has just won a race.

The sea's fury grew and grew until it became impossible to control the ships. The sails began to tear and were impossible to handle. The masts bent like bows, snapping the shrouds and threatening to come crashing down. We had to find shelter or the whole fleet would have sunk. So we headed back toward the coast and, when we spied a wide river, used the last of our strength to steer into it.

As we drew closer, we saw the cross Serrano had not known whom to dedicate to on top of a nearby hill.

Perhaps that was what decided the Captain. Or perhaps he was simply looking for another excuse not to have to face up to the truth, so that he could still cling to his crazy dream of finding a passage through to the South Seas (something which seemed impossible at that stage of our journey). I do not know. What I do know is that . . . only two days . . . only two days sailing south from San Julián. And just two degrees from the strait. (Although of course we only realized that later). He decided to make. Another halt. In the stinking guts. Of winter.

Can you tell me, your Majesty, how you claim to be looking after your subjects, vassals and servants if you allow such a thing to happen? Because one can tolerate other misfortunes like hunger, poverty, wars, or even death if one imagines that they are all part of your Highness's secret design and that everything will be all right in the end. But what I cannot forgive you for is having allowed us to come to a halt again to wait for the rigors of winter to pass when we were only two days away from the strait. Even though I am the forgiving kind. The blows I have received have taught me to make allowances for others, as that is the only hope we, the weak of the earth, can have. I can forgive you for the fact that I was born a dwarfish Jew, with no father and a whore for a mother; forgive you for having to watch my little sister die of hunger and cold when

173

she was only a few months old, and having found myself close to succumbing in the same way all my life; even forgive you for deceiving me, poor fool that I am, someone less than a worm, a simple village jester who had his head filled, his soul corrupted, by a royal herald selling dreams. All that I can forgive: but not the fact that you allowed another halt in our progress, when we only had to go on that little bit further.

Can you imagine any greater folly? Do you have any idea of the grief and despair the decision caused among everyone in the fleet? Do you realize how justified our dismay was? I most humbly suggest you cannot know. Because you were born in pomp and splendor, and I would wager that you did not even come into the world all sticky and dirty as we mere mortals did, but were spotless and proud even then. And that you did not wail when the air of this world first entered your lungs but instead gave your first order. And that you were wrapped in ermine, and the sun was told to keep you warm. And you were given suck by the richest coffers of Europe, but you guzzled so much you almost dried them up, so that a new source had to be given the honor of nourishing you. And that as an infant you played in the Council Chamber with the crowns and scepters accumulated by several generations of your ancestors. And that your every tantrum was taken as a decree which half the world rushed to implement. And that with each whim you built or destroyed whole nations with the same easy carelessness that ordinary children display with colored sticks or clay dolls. And as a young man, with your eyes accustomed to the glitter of gold, your mouth to the taste of spices, your skin to the rustle of silk, your nostrils to the perfume of the court women and your hearing to compliant voices, you inherited a flock such as no other shepherd in the world has known and, not content with that, you sought to increase it. Then when age overtook you, with all your flock gorged on peace, justice and prosperity, you decided that you had done your duty and retired to a silent, white-walled monastery full of peace, with a shady garden and a tinkling fountain, the discreet sounds of Latin, hooded shadows flitting through the cloisters, a simple table offering dark bread and fresh wine, a secluded white cell with only a crucifix for adornment; and there you await without fear your passage into the other world, where a place has been reserved for you at God's right hand for all eternity. Amen.

PART VI

Is ALL this too much for you, my Lord? Then I'll give you some respite, as it is not a good idea to exhaust the person on whose goodwill we depend, nor is there anything wrong in pleasing someone of your stature. Therefore sit back and listen, while I whisper in your ear: The tranquil surface of the sea shone like the emeralds that adorn the empress's neck on grand occasions. Shall I go on? The ships looked as though they were encrusted in a flat, shiny mirror that merged with the sky on the misty horizon. That raging bull which had roared beneath our hulls had turned into a gentle, sweet cow, silent and contemplative under the sun's steady gaze. A deliciously insistent sun, your Highness. Shall I continue? A sun of liquid gold, pouring like honey over our crumpled shoulders. Sliding thickly down the bony backs of each and every one of your Argonauts. Sinking its fine amber needles into our wrinkled, colorless skin. Spreading its burning molasses right into the marrow of our bones. A sun that wove webs of light among the rigging. That polished the masts with the brightest of varnishes. That hung from the yardarms like lanterns at night. Bleached the sails to the color of jasmines. Flooding the decks, spreading its syrup through the insides of the ships. A sun that even ventured into the forecastle, where the stiff mattresses and few clothes we possessed were heaped in damp, sticky piles. Shone everywhere below the hatchways, even lighting the holds which stank like a badger's den. Even peeping into the kitchen with its stale cooking smells, the gleaming rays driving pots and pans mad, sending the cockroaches scurrying off.

At the touch of the scorching honey which the sun poured over the ships just as my mother poured it over my hot toast on childhood feast days, everything came back to life.

Where has all this sun come from, you ask? If I were to tell you, it really would be too much for you, so please do not insist. I have no wish to lose my pension forever after all the effort I've spent trying to regain it. Why don't I tell you about the lack of wind? About the force that tore us one day from the dock with its crying mothers, its already lonely wives, amazed infants, indifferent onlookers. The force that dragged the gleaming towers with your Majesty's flags fluttering above them further and further away. That took with it the great cathedral, the fortresses, the city walls, the hundred towers and spires, all the red tiles of Sevilla. The force that diminished all else. That made it all disappear. The self-seeking, jealous energy for which only the ships existed. The ever-present power we could not escape from even by putting our heads under the blankets because it was there in the flapping of the sails, in the groaning of the hinges and pulleys of the yards, the creaking of the masts, the beating of the waves against the hull. The invisible strength pushing and pulling us, driving us ever onward. The violence that had absorbed us since the moment of our departure. The power whose whims ruled our lives, whose hopeless slaves we were. It had finished. Disappeared. No longer existed. And when it ceased, it was as if the ships themselves had ceased to exist, the whole fleet, our voyage with all its distances and uncertainties. Even the immense, mysterious ocean was reduced to nothing, now that the wind had left our lives, and began to seem familiar to us, now that it had suddenly lost the threat hidden in everything unknown. It was as though we had woken from a nightmare. Life seemed more real, as if it were somehow easier. I am not sure why, but everything did seem easier now that the wind had disappeared. Even the Captain General's plans and Faleiro's calculations seemed possible. The calm sea was as gentle and peaceful as a sleeping child. The sails hung as unruffled as sheets on a summer morning. The ships rocked gently like my grandmother's wicker armchair during her naps. The rigging had slackened, the shrouds were nothing more than rough lines standing out against the blue sky, somehow they had lost the looming appearance of nets about to fall over their victim. And silence, your Highness. Not the slightest sound was to be heard. The hulls did not creak. The masts and yardarms did not grate. Everything was as silent and unmoving as in a painting.

Now you are calm again, so I can whisper in your ear that contrary to shipboard routine and seafaring tradition, we used to swim around our ships. The cold, clear water soothed the blisters the sun had raised on our skins, the salt stung but cured the lumps and swellings the cold damp had brought out on our backs; this newfound ease brought relief to the pangs of hunger gripping our empty stomachs. We plunged like dolphins around the ships' hulls, floated on our backs in the shadows of the lofty sterns.

Where were we? Better for you not to know. Don't ask me for explanations or details, just enjoy these moments of gentle relief. There are certain things I prefer not to mention. Have you forgotten that your son Felipe stripped me of my pension because he said I talked too much? It is a real art to be able to make people laugh, a true artist is someone who can bring a smile to the sternest face. And the truth? The truth is something only fools and children believe in. A mirage that a few crazy men chase after. The illusion of the weak. What do powerful people like yourself care for the truth? Perhaps you would like me to tell you that we were somewhere on the South Seas, close to the equator, to judge by the heat. Does that mean anything to you? That's all I can tell you. That's all any of us knew. Not even the Captain General could be more precise.

How did we get there? Don't ask me to tell you that. Orders are orders, yes. But you're taking advantage of me. Well . . . if you truly so desire. But at least let me tell it my way. And bear in mind that I did warn you. You will not want to hear what I have to say. You won't want me to tell you that everything began in the shelter that Serrano built from the remains of the *Santiago* on the very spot where it had been wrecked. You won't like me to say again that we spent two months holed up there, when we were less than two days away from the mouth of the strait—although of course nobody could have known that then.

What shelter was that? See how you are becoming angry again? What will happen when I tell you that the confused jumble of planks and beams did in fact bear some resemblance to a ship? That it was like a clumsy, rough imitation of one. Like something children might build to play their games in. Why, it even had a mast: a tiny foremast from the top of which flew a tattered flag, with its mizzen, broken like a reed, standing out stark against the lowering sky.

There was even an improvised poop deck, topped off with a glassless, rusty lantern. There sat Serrano, who greeted us in a dignified manner despite being dressed in rags.

Don Fernando and he exchanged embraces. There were tears in their eyes, and they whirled around in each other's arms like two young girls meeting again after many years apart.

Then Serrano invited us to board the *Santiago*. That is what he said. A joke? I don't think so. Look, better to talk of . . . But since you insist, I'll tell you that the roof was low, and seemed about to fall in. It was built from bits of all kinds of timber. Some of them were whole, and curved like ribs so they made a proper arch. All the planks leaned up against the central structure, a huge beam supported between two ship's masts, and were fixed in position by shrouds tied to stakes in the ground. From inside, the shelter looked like a grotesque cathedral or the skeleton of a huge whale.

Would you really like me to go on? Well then, I'll tell you it was very dark in there, which made it difficult to walk among all the timbers and ropes that made it seem like the machinery backstage in a theater. Perhaps that was why Serrano warned us to be careful of the low yards. Yes, that was what I asked myself as well, your Highness: What yards did he mean? It was not long before I had the answer. The central section of the shelter was bristling with yardarms, some of them broken, all of them in a sorry state, which were put to all kinds of uses. A lantern hung from one. Another was used to hang the crew's clothes from. A sail draped from a third served as a partition. Pots and pans swung over here, a string of wretched onions over there.

"Here are the stores," Serrano told us, pointing to a corner where a few empty casks and barrels were piled. Then he invited us to join him on the sterncastle.

See how this has brought a frown to your face?

He meant a part of the shelter roofed over by two sails sewn together. In its center was a capstan without its handspikes, on which stood a carving of the apostle Santiago. Most of the paint had flaked off the statue, and its arm with the sword was missing, snapped off at the shoulder. As Serrano passed by it, he crossed himself, then pushed aside the crow's nest that served as a kind of curtain, and invited us to step into his cabin.

Yes, that was the question I asked myself when I saw a binnacle without its compass, an astrolabe covered with green mold and, in the middle, an upturned foretop that he used as a table with an empty hourglass and a faded parchment on it.

None of us had any idea what to make of all this, but Serrano was busy explaining to the Captain General his doubts about who could be on the Spanish throne, and whether the new king might still support our venture.

Don Fernando cut him short, telling him he should have made for our camp immediately after the shipwreck. But Serrano, scarcely able to conceal his annoyance, went on talking about how he was plagued with doubts and reeling off all the arguments that had crossed his mind when he had found it impossible to claim these lands in your name.

"She was a good ship," the Captain General insisted.

His words were followed by an embarrassed silence, then Serrano stood up and rang a bell nailed to one of the beams.

A moment later Tomé, the ship's master, came in and, to our astonishment . . . No, I had better not tell you . . .

What did Serrano do? He asked Tomé whether he had checked the rigging and tarred the ropes. Then he told him to take personal charge of the soundings and to make sure they were done as accurately as possible, adding, "Write them down."

What did our Captain do? "The *Santiago* was a fine ship," he repeated. "I'm sorry about what happened," he added. What else could he say? He was studying Serrano closely, perhaps not yet sure whether he was completely serious in what he was saying. He did not want to hurt his friend's feelings. He knew how much losing a ship meant to a good captain.

Then he said, "A lot of what you have saved will be useful for us. It is as though the sea which took the *Santiago* from you is trying to give her back . . ." I think he intended to say "in bits and pieces" or something similar. He fell silent though, because at that moment Serrano shouted to Tomé to throw the line.

I am sure there is no need for me to tell you what had become very obvious to us all: that not only did Serrano refuse to talk about the shipwreck, but he could not even admit it had happened. And that all the nautical language he was using about his shelter, and the orders he was giving, were no joke. They were not his way of hiding his sense of shame, but something more: Serrano genuinely believed he was still sailing the *Santiago*.

You ask if he was mad? I am not the person to answer that question. I have seen many cases like his in my eventful life. Take my grandmother, for example: she spent hours talking to her dead loved ones, but was so sharp-witted in everything else she did that her insistence led me to believe, from her endless debates with the spirits, that they were true members of the family, so that I respected the place left empty for them at table or their invisible presence in the fireside armchair. I even greeted—with some trepidation, I admit—my grandfather, dead many years before, and asked questions of an aunt of mine who had died very young and who was the person my grandmother most enjoyed talking to. So although Serrano's attitude shocked me at first, with the passing of the days it came to seem quite natural. The thing was that after hearing him repeat over and over instructions for keeping the decks clean, the shrouds greased, the bronze fittings polished, and seeing the men willingly rush about to obey his orders, well, not only did I grow used to the seafaring language and to this pretense of a life on board ship, but I even began to believe we were really sailing on the *Santiago*. And I must tell you that I was not the only one.

No, don't think we were fools, your Majesty. It's just that when one no longer believes in anything, one becomes as credulous as a child and begins to think that anything is possible. We had been chasing so many mirages since we started out on our undertaking that it was all the same to us now to believe in Serrano. Bitter experience had taught us to be wary of appearances, with the result that anything seemed likely. Since we no longer knew what reality was, we could accept almost anything. Reality had shown itself to be so treacherous, so elusive, so fickle. It corresponded so badly with our dreams, with what we imagined or thought we knew it to be! So it was that during that interminable wait in the shelter, while at night the wind set itself to unraveling the illusion Serrano had so laboriously tried to create during the day, like the frayed remains of our dreams, more than once we all came to hear the *Santiago*'s sails flapping and the noise of waves breaking against its prow.

I'm sorry, your Highness, but you insisted. But stay calm, and listen to your Juanillo, your servant, your son, your child. Here in Bustillo del Páramo it's raining. The heavy drops are splattering on the slate roofs with a sad sound, while the trees outside my window drip fleeting pearls of water. The street is deserted; the whole village is covered by the silvery blanket of the rain, hidden among fields that are turning to mud. Is it raining in Yuste too? I wager that you are in a melancholy mood, gazing out at the empty cloister garden where the vegetation closest to you glistens as though painted in enamel, while further off everything is unclear and dark behind the curtain of rain, and the general impression is sad and forlorn. I wager, too, that the rain has washed the dust from the columns and is dripping from the arches and making puddles in the cloister. I wager again that the monks glide forward like shadows, wrapped in their cloaks and in silence, and that you watch them with little enthusiasm, imagining the monastery wrapped in the shroud of rain, the Vera valley hidden in mist, the tall peak of Tormentos lost in the clouds' dark folds.

HOW DID we manage to leave the shelter? No, I have no desire to tell you about that. I do not wish to relive those dreary months. I want to be able to tell myself they had no effect on me. That I left that prison intact, with renewed energy to carry on. I want to be able to convince myself. I want to forget the cold, the hunger, the fear. Above all, the fear. Why should it be so hard to forget fear? All the rest can be forgotten. The cold fades away, so does hunger, and even the chronic uncertainty that weighs on your soul as though it were a stone: all that disappears, but not fear.

But you insist, don't you, your Highness? You insist on knowing how we arrived at that spot in the South Seas where everything was so sunny and calm.

One day Don Fernando called a meeting of the captains. He was obviously impatient, and did not say a word until all of them had gathered.

"Serrano," he began without ceremony, "you are to be the new captain of the *Concepción*. Gaspar's ship is yours."

Everyone's eyes turned toward Serrano. Only Sebastián, who was trying to hide the disappointment on his face, looked down.

"The *Santiago*'s crew will be divided between the other four ships according to their rank and skills," he added.

As pale as a corpse, Serrano tried to say something, but the

Captain General cut him short. "Clear everyone out of this shack and set fire to it," he commanded.

Serrano, speechless, nodded in agreement.

Don Fernando then announced that his cousin, Álvaro de la Mezquita, would take over as captain of the *San Antonio*. This time it was Esteban Gómez who turned his back on the meeting and stared at the statue of the apostle. Like everyone else, Don Fernando noticed the gesture, but he went on to declare that Odoardo Barbosa was to be the *Victoria*'s new captain, and that all of them should prepare to put to sea as soon as possible. "We've already lost enough time," he said.

"What course are we to set?" Esteban Gómez asked without turning around, stroking the broken arm of the statue. The Captain General replied that we would travel down the coast until we found the strait or until the land ended. "We must find a way to cross into the South Seas," he said. Still with his back to the others, Esteban Gómez asked how he thought it was possible for us to continue on south. The Captain told him he would not give up until the ships had lost all their rigging twice, and only then would he head east to find the Spice Islands via the Cape of Good Hope. At that, Esteban Gómez whirled round and said that we were already more than fifty degrees south and that it was virtually impossible to navigate; the Captain should consider what conditions would be like from then on. Did he not think it would be better to head east straightaway, while we still had enough provisions for the voyage? Because otherwise it would be too late. Could he not see that all the men were weak from cold and lack of food? What would happen if we were caught in a storm, or if there was no wind? Why did the Captain not make up his mind once and for all on the route he wanted to set for the Spice Islands? What were his intentions? Was he toying with everyone? He, Esteban Gómez, was one of His Majesty's pilots. He was sick of so much secrecy and change. First they had headed for the Cape of Good Hope, then they had altered course completely and followed an unknown route that was too far south to reach the Indies. Now, from what he heard, there was still a doubt as to whether they were going west or turning east again toward the Cape. Was the Captain mad like Faleiro? Did he have some secret plan, for Heaven's sake? The gigantic Esteban Gómez spluttered, his face purple with rage.

And the Captain? He made fun of Gómez. He laughed in the pilot's face. He asked why he was so nervous: Could it be he was frightened?

Everybody laughed with him, which only enraged Esteban all the more. The veins on his neck stood out as thick as cables; he lowered his head like a bull ready to charge.

What happened then, you ask? The answer to your question, your Highness, is—nothing. Esteban had to choke back his anger, pacing up and down that strange landscape, with no idea what to do next.

At that, Don Fernando declared the meeting over and made to leave. But as he reached what could be called the door, he stopped a moment and said, without turning around, "We'll sail on to seventy-five degrees south before we change course. Be ready to sail in three days."

This announcement turned the captains and Esteban Gómez to stone. The Captain's bold decision left them all speechless. It dug deep inside them, then went to their heads as quickly as bad liquor.

A few interminable seconds dragged by before the giant Esteban said, almost as if to himself, "This is the end of the world."

That was all. Nobody said anything more; they all began to leave in silence. No, I'm sorry, not everyone: Serrano, looking longingly around his baroque construction, did ask, "Do you think I should burn it?"

But no one answered him.

So, when I saw from the hiding place where I was listening to everything—because a fool has to know what's going on—that all the leaders were going to do nothing, I raced off after my master. I caught up with him as he was crossing Serrano's fake afterdeck and blindly threw myself around one of his legs. He stopped and looked down at me with a mixture of surprise and anger. What did I want? he asked. I told him: Who was he trying to convince with his display of confidence and determination, the others or himself? Go away, he said. Get your hands off me. Leave me in peace. But I would not. He should have listened to Esteban Gómez, I said. He had gone too far this time. But he struggled to free his leg from my grasp, and shouted that it was not true, that for a long time now he had been faced with no choice about how far we should travel. So I said, sobbing by this time, that it was true then that we were going on to the end of the world. I felt his powerful steel-clad hand lifting me by the scruff of my neck and dropping me, while his voice, from somewhere above the iron tower, said, "The ship is the world." Then he continued on his way.

I took my head in my hands and, blind with rage, shouted after him, "Leave us in peace! You're mad!"

"I thought you wanted to be Count of the Spice Islands," he said, disappearing among the tangle of ropes and beams that littered Serrano's shelter.

"The Spice Islands do not exist! And your life is so much shit!" I shouted at him, but he was no longer there, your Highness.

And now, I beg you, let me rest awhile. I'll draw a line of three stars, the Three Marías (the empress María Isabel, María Filomena, my mistress, and whichever other María you wish), and let's leave it at that.

You say I still haven't told you how we reached that spot in the South Seas so full of sun, so empty of wind. You're right, as ever; I promise to tell you later. And just in case, don't forget to repeat your question after the line of stars.

Is IT still raining on San Jerónimo, your Majesty? Here in Bustillo night has come, and my window is a black, sightless frame.

Night in Bustillo smells of damp earth, smoke from fires, eggs and sausages.

What about Yuste, your Highness? Let me guess how it

smells. It must smell of mountain mist, whitewash, incense; it must smell of marble saints.

Yet deep down I think both nights must smell the same; they smell of solitude and silence.

But we could not care less, could we? You and I have no need of anyone apart from each other. Let it rain, let the night spread everywhere, and the damp penetrate our bones (our poor tired bones) or the shadows shoot up like weeds and invade our souls (our poor tired souls); we'll still be here together waiting for the morning sun, I on my side, and you on yours. I telling you how it was we came to arrive at that point in the South Seas where everything was so sunny and calm, and you listening with loving attention, while the rest of the world disappears in the rain and the black night.

WE SET out on the morning of the third day, as Don Fernando had decreed, and after a day and a half's sailing we dropped anchor in a well-sheltered bay.

Andrés de San Martín was suddenly overcome with terrible anxiety. He wandered the decks like a madwoman, pushing his fingers into his empty mouth while he stared at the far side of the bay where we could see a wide channel.

He was so desperate that he rushed to the sterncastle and clutched the Captain General by the hand. He tugged at him the way a stubborn child pulls at its mother when it wants to show her something. Intrigued, Don Fernando let him have his way.

San Martín gesticulated toward the coast, growing more and more frantic as my master shook his head and gestured that he could not understand. It was a curious fact, but, as I have already mentioned, we all behaved as if the astrologer were deaf as well as dumb. Perhaps it was because we felt him to be so isolated from us. The fact is that my master kept gesturing that he did not understand, while Andrés grew more and more desperate. San Martín pointed first at the coast, then all of a sudden took the Captain's hand and plunged it into the dark cavern of his mouth. Yes, Don Fernando's fingers, and when

190

the Captain tried to pull his hand away, he repeated the movement. Then finally he released the hand, and pointed first to the mouth of the channel at the far side of the bay, then to his own mouth, picking up Don Fernando's hand again and pushing the fingers in once more. Don Fernando was so perplexed that he let him do so several times, until finally he burst out laughing and roared, "So that's it, so that's it! Now I understand you. You mean I should go in that mouth over there." The astrologer nodded frantically and laughed as well, though without a sound.

No sooner had dawn broken than the ships were gliding stealthily over the waters.

They looked like towers perched on the curved back of the ocean; from further away they took on the aspect of old ladies with tall lace ruffs nodding their heads as they chattered away to each other; from further still they seemed like toys a child had left beside a high blue wall at the bottom of a garden—the sky rose from the sea's horizon like a blue wall, while the ships slipped one after another down a crack in it, darting in nervously like lizards on a hot, sunny day.

Those waters, never before parted by the prow of a ship, were transparent and cold as crystal and shone like mirrors where the sun's rays caught their surface.

As we progressed along the channel the light became dimmer, and the ships looked like ghosts in the cold astral light. A sense of desolation and a deathly silence reigned over the narrow water way that ran between high rolling hills. A virginal silence, more ancient than man himself. A silence that weighed like a stone on the spirit of every one of your discoverers.

Their faces drained of color, the crews stared at the high mountains that closed off the horizon in all directions, preventing us from gaining any idea of what might come beyond this narrow stretch of water when we arrived in another bay.

The channel became darker and narrower still; but just when it seemed there would not be room for the ships to continue, it suddenly widened out into a bright inlet, off which ran another channel similar to the first.

No one spoke. The ships glided on silently, as though they, too, were dumbfounded by the feeling of intruding into this mysterious world.

Time and again the channels split off; the inlets multiplied, and your powerful fleet groped its way blindly along a labyrinth that seemed to be the product of a crazy god's imagination, designed solely to lead astray anyone who dared to enter his hiding-place, without hope of ever finding a way out. Days and nights went by in this vain search.

Don Fernando spent his time hunched over the charts.

He drew lines out from the radii of the nautical roses, drew circles with his compass to make fresh radii, then, when he had covered his parchment with a whole mass of interconnecting lines, stood there for hours studying it.

As the wind blew the flame of his candle this way and that, throwing patches of shadow and light across the complicated web of lines, Don Fernando's anxious eyes roved to and fro trying to follow its swaying movements.

He scarcely ate, and fell asleep exhausted over his instruments. Then all of a sudden he would jerk awake and at once start erasing his calculations and begin all over again.

The Captain General only left his worktable to go on deck and peer uselessly up at the sky.

Alone in the middle of the night, the astrolabe hanging in his hands like a violin with no strings, he tried to recognize in the distant, star-sprinkled vaults of heaven any of the few constellations which appeared in his astronomical guide. But no sooner did he think he had discovered the Centaur than closer observation showed him it must be Argo, or when he was thinking of some individual stars he knew, he realized from their declination they must be the constellation Sagittarius. After a while he would return bleary-eyed to his cabin, and shut himself in again with his nautical charts.

He was so caught up in his task that nobody dared interrupt his silence, which by now had lasted days, if not weeks. Life seemed absurd, turned in on itself, concentrated around this one man desperately trying to decipher signs that refused to reveal themselves to him.

The powerful Captain General felt like a lost child. A child whose mother suddenly disappears and takes all bearings with her. Suddenly the world becomes an indecipherable hieroglyph because the child has lost all the keys and is stuck in a hole that grows and grows as if it were feeding on itself. A hole which swallows up every certainty, in which all that is unchanging becomes ephemeral, everything ephemeral seems unchanging. The child, overwhelmed by the bewilderment that goes with the disappearance of the natural order of things, has no idea which direction to turn, even though he may be only a few steps from his house, or in a street he has been in many times before, holding his mother's hand, or in the village square where he has played on many an afternoon. And the neighbors' faces, which were so familiar, become strange, distant, unknown, enigmatic masks which say nothing to him. Overcome by panic, the child flees, shutting himself deeper and deeper in his own labyrinth. Wandering like a madman across an absurd landscape.

Baffled in this same way, the officers shouted their orders absentmindedly, while the men cowered in corners to conceal their dismay.

The *Trinidad* seemed like a warren, full of holes where faceless men hid as best they could. In the semi-darkness saturated by the smell of oak timbers, pitch, and the salty reek of the sea, only fragments of human beings were visible, inserted between the timbers like holy images in their niches. A hand, two marble-colored feet, half a blue-shadowed face—that was all they revealed, and without realizing it. Because all that the men wanted was to be completely hidden. To disappear altogether.

When your Juanillo roamed the gangways, he felt the way he had when, as a child, he slipped away from the sacristan and explored inside the crypt which contained the remains of Don Juan's ancestors. Stone statues of a bishop with his miter, a huge warrior with a broadsword crossed over his chest and a young girl with an angelic face filled the center of the crypt. All three lay horizontal, yet did not seem to sleep; their polished stone eyes were wide open like those of some gentle cow. The walls were lined with niches in which marble coffins of all sizes were kept, each with a Latin inscription.

It's strange, but at first I was not at all afraid there. On the contrary, I found the complete silence and the cool atmosphere with its hint of damp rather pleasant. Until one day Death made her presence felt. The door was closed, but I managed to squeeze in through a skylight. Inside, I seemed to detect a sense of uneasiness on the normally inexpressive features of the bishop, the warrior and the girl. There was a loud, persistent buzzing in the air. I couldn't tell where it was coming from until my eyes spotted a swarm of bright green flies clustered around the lid of a coffin that had not been there before. Only then did I become aware of the stench that had invaded the whole crypt.

The moments it took me to clamber up the warrior and escape through the skylight were the longest of my entire childhood.

Now, as I walked along the gangway amidships, I was afraid I was about to run into that same buzzing, which ever since that day I have associated with the stench of death.

At the end of many days (we had given up counting them) of continuous sailing through channel after channel with the disturbing sense that we were going round in circles and constantly returning to the point we had started from, we came out into a semicircular inlet like an amphitheater that was noticeably wider than any of the previous ones.

Two identical channels led off it, one to the southeast, the other to the southwest.

The pilots had no idea which of them to follow. Don Fernando was undecided as well, so he opted to divide the fleet in two. He sent the *San Antonio* and the *Concepción* to explore the first of them, while the *Trinidad* and the *Victoria* sallied into the second. We agreed to meet back at the inlet three days later.

After two days' sailing we had found nothing new. No sign to give us hope that we had discovered a way through. Nothing at all. The landscape was exactly the same, only the silence seemed to have changed: somehow it seemed even deeper than before. And the feeling that we were at the mercy of a higher will that took pleasure in toying with the ships, laughingly hinting at and then hiding its secrets, was even stronger.

We therefore returned to the inlet without further delay, in the blind expectation that the *San Antonio* or the *Concepción* had met with better luck. But neither of the ships was there waiting for us.

Several days of tense waiting followed.

No one talked of the missing ships or the fate of their crews, and this sudden blanket of silence weighed more heavily on our spirits than the most pessimistic conjecture about what had happened to them. It was no easy thing to leave half the fleet out of our conversations; the *San Antonio* and the *Concepción*, their crews and their stories, had always been spoken of, and now all of a sudden there were too many gaps in our dialogues, the sentences were full of holes, and most of what we did say took on a kind of ambiguous double meaning.

By the fifth day we were reduced to silence and spent most of our time leaning over the starboard side or squatting on the yardarms to peer despairingly at the far end of the bay.

The weather had improved and visibility was fairly good, so we could make out a wide mouth of water about two leagues across that disappeared between the mountains. We stared at that empty mouth as anxiously as two lovers who have quarreled; in secret we entertained the absurd hope a mother feels when she has lost her child, but somehow expects to see him come in the door at any moment and so cannot take her eyes off it.

We kept changing the lookouts in the tops. We took turns up in that vantage point from which a ship looks as thin as a knife blade, its crew like insects caught in the web of shrouds and rigging, and the sea like a concave blue mirror.

But we saw nothing. Nothing but the glint of the waters all around us, and the dark shadow of the hills reflected in them.

THEN ONE morning we all woke up with the sensation of a ship inside us. We could feel its presence, even though we could still see nothing. We felt the way a hunter does when he detects his hidden prey, and tenses his muscles and sharpens his senses; he does not know exactly where the animal is, but he is sure that it will crash out of the trees at any moment and dash in front of him.

That was how we felt, until in the distance we heard the creaking of timbers and the faint slap of sails as though some great bird was flapping its wings, stirring up the air. At first these noises mingled with those of our own ships, but little by little they stood out distinctly, making our hearts beat wildly in anticipation. From the tops to the lowest yardarms, men stood straining their eyes toward the horizon. Others were dangling from the sails, hanging like monkeys from the shrouds, peering out from the bow, or pressing together silently amidships like a flock of placid sheep. Everyone in suspense, waiting for the slightest sign.

All at once, half hidden by the dark slope of a hillside, we spotted a set of sails, the whitest, most beautiful sails we had ever seen. They glided toward us with the magical elegance of a swan crossing a pond.

Don Fernando ordered the gunners to fire a volley, and the boom of the *Trinidad*'s cannon rolled over the inlet and up the distant channels; the whole landscape, silent since the beginning of time, sent us back the echo of our greeting.

A moment later the whole of the *Concepción* came into view, as proud and beautiful as a bride.

JUAN SERRANO'S story of what had happened kept us enthralled. A squall had taken them by surprise. The channel had been too narrow for them to maneuver through, and they had been forced to strike sail to avoid losing all their masts. One man had been lost as they did so. "A pulley jammed, and . . ." The current had taken hold of them. Pulled them irresistibly to the end of the channel. "It was Lorenzo. The wind swept him off like a fledgling from a branch." Unable to control the ship, they all waited for disaster to strike, praying to God because they felt sure they would be wrecked. "He was always making plans, fool that he was." But just as the crash seemed

196

inevitable, the current swept them off down another channel that had appeared out of nowhere. "It was impossible to try to rescue him." At the end of that channel they came out into another small bay, where the same thing began all over again: the current sweeping them along, the seemingly inevitable crash, then another channel opening up in front of them. "He was blown off one of the highest yardarms." This went on for three days. They had lost all sense of direction, and had no idea where the current was taking them. "He was a fool."

"Did you reach the end of the labyrinth or not?" the Captain General asked impatiently.

"There was no end to it," the Portuguese captain replied.

"That must be the strait," Odoardo muttered, as if fearful of the sound of what he was saying.

"It might be a river," Don Fernando cautioned.

Everyone was staring at Serrano, who had become thoughtful.

"I did not dare go any further," he said finally.

"What about the *San Antonio*?" the Captain asked.

Serrano explained that he had searched for her for two days. He had sent up smoke signals. Fired off cannons regularly. But there was no trace. So he had set out on the route back. They had put up crosses, leaving the *San Antonio* indications as to what they were doing in pots beside them. He still had no idea how they had managed to find the way back to us. He had no news of what had once been Cartagena's ship.

Don Fernando took the news badly. He scratched his head nervously and said nothing.

Serrano went over to him and held out his hand in a timid gesture. It hovered over the Captain's armor-plated shoulder, then finally settled on the back of his neck in a brief show of friendship.

"She will appear," he said.

There was a lengthy silence. Serrano stood side by side with the Captain General in silent solidarity.

"I can't afford to lose another ship," Don Fernando said.

"I'm sorry about the *Santiago*," Serrano replied. His head

drooped like a faded flower on its stem, setting the bells on his hat tinkling.

Don Fernando looked at him sadly, yet gave a smile and pressed his hand.

"You're the best man I have," he said.

His eyes glistening, Serrano was about to say something, but Don Fernando interrupted him: "Forget about the *Santiago*, will you?"

"What are we to do now?" Serrano asked, nodding in agreement.

At that point Sebastián's voice could be heard. He thought the time had come to head for home. The voyage had been foolhardy enough for the fleet as a whole, but now that there were two ships missing . . . And the *San Antonio* had been the one with the most supplies. It was a crushing loss in men and provisions. Esteban Gómez had been right, Sebastián said. It was time to turn back.

Odoardo thought otherwise. Could he not see we had finally found the way through to the South Seas? They had only to follow the channel Serrano had emerged from. The channel where the *San Antonio* was lost and the *Concepción* had almost been wrecked, Sebastián butted in scornfully. Couldn't they see that those strong currents must come from the different tidal pulls of two huge water masses? Odoardo insisted, ignoring Sebastián.

Don Fernando seemed to be looking inquiringly at Serrano, who repeated, "I didn't dare continue. I was afraid of losing another ship."

Our hope of seeing the *San Antonio*'s white sails and imposing hull faded with each passing day. The ships became a tangled skein of whispered allusions that rustled like the leaves on riverbank poplars, allusions that caught and held us like flies in a sticky web.

The whispers scurried to and fro like hungry rats, like desperate cockroaches. To and fro, almost meaningless, as if avoiding explanations that were too open or explicit for anyone to express them. And around them, on top of them, as if on the naked wood of a frame, we wove a complex pattern of details aimed above all at hiding the ghastly emptiness behind.

Cristóbal embroidered the dark interior of a mosque converted into a workshop. An age-old light the color of oranges shone in through the minaret windows, picking out the arabesques of the friezes and capitals before settling on a group of women silently spinning cotton. Out in the courtyard, another group was busy with the huge canvases stretched out in the sun. With their long needles that curved like scimitars, the women hopped over the sails like sparrows across a snowy square while the fountain splashed merrily in the quiet of the afternoon.

Then it was the turn of El Sordo, who knew a thing or two about carpentry, to take up the frame. He wove a fresh tapestry, this time full of bull-necked men with arms as strong as roots, their muscles tense and their veins standing out as their axes bit deep into the wood. Their blows and their voices echoed through the whole valley; the buzz of their saws sent old people to sleep in the nearby villages; the smoke from the bonfires where they burned twigs and leaves filled the air. Then all at once everything fell still. The noises died away; every movement seemed suspended in midair. The dozing old folk stirred, listening hard to the unexpected silence. A shepherd following his flock stopped and leaned on his crook to peer over at the wooded hillside. Then there was a short splintering sound and suddenly one of the trees, as tall and strong as a tower, began to topple. Amid a pandemonium of branches snapping, birds fleeing their nests and animals rushing to escape, the tree hit the ground with a roar like a thunderclap that reverberated all around the valleys. Then, as the dust turned golden by the evening sunbeams was settling again, while the bewildered animals crouched fearfully in hiding, while the workmen, axes in hand, dried off the sweat and had a drink, and the old people in the villages began to imagine the ship that would spring from this treetrunk which had been huge even in their childhood, on board ship it was Juan Serrano's turn to speak. Perhaps because he was one of the captains, he was the first to utter the words we were so afraid of. "The *San Antonio* is lost," he said. Nothing for it but to start our embroidering all over again. This time it was Esteban Gómez's ship which began to fill the frame, in its fruitless search for a way out of the labyrinth of waters. We pictured timbers rotted by time, tattered gray sails that cast their shadow over a crew of old men. The ship drifting aimlessly, like an abandoned cradle, while the brown-stained sails fell in shreds from the yardarms, dropping like the remains of a shroud on top of the already dead crew. Finally we saw its salt-encrusted hull high and dry on a deserted beach somewhere, like the skeleton of a huge whale.

The frame passed from hand to hand, with each of us adding his own touches of color to the design. We were like young girls entertaining themselves in front of the fire during one of those long wet winter afternoons.

Only Don Fernando remained aloof. He did not know what to think, but he was unimpressed by the words, colored by our fears, that we used to weave this framework around the *San Antonio*'s fate. Perhaps words as stark as "shipwreck" or "death" were going through his mind, or perhaps, when he was all alone, he thought, "betrayal," and wove his own conclusions.

ARE YOU still with me, Don Carlos? Still awake, with my chronicle in your hands? Here it is the middle of the night, and time flows by like a silent river. It flows along the empty streets of Bustillo, slips beneath the doors and between the cracks in the shutters, flows out into the fields and up among the stars. Nothing can stop it; everything turns into a memory in its dark waters. This voyage of mine, this moment we are sharing, the morning that will perhaps come.

But forgive your servant rambling like this; listen instead to the reliable account with which your Juanillo Ponce hopes to steal from time what belongs to it.

Let me tell you how we came to reach that tranquil spot in the South Seas. Let me tell you how life went on and we forgot the *San Antonio* and sailed off in search of the way through the channel Serrano had explored. Beyond the point which the

Portuguese captain thought he had reached, the waters became so narrow that our sails set the foliage of the trees on either side rustling as loud as the wind does. In the morning, we could see drops of dew like pearls, an empty nest on a branch, and nearby the silvery sheen of a spiderweb. One day we discovered a track leading up from the waterside through the trees and decided to follow it. The trees turned the daylight green, and the air was filled with the scents of moss, fungi, time standing still. The track ended in a clearing strewn with flowers and other offerings around some open graves. But the graves were empty, as if they were still waiting for their dead bodies. We could see no footprints or other signs of human beings, although at night bonfires burned in the woods. We found no trace of them during the daytime; it was a completely empty world. We did not even see any fish, except for the carcass of a whale on a beach surrounded by cliffs. And those fires at night. Mysterious fires that accompanied us throughout our journey.

Soon we came to a stretch of water that was not even wide enough for the ships to pass and which, to judge by the snowy peaks all round, was a dead end. But the Captain General sent six sailors in a longboat to explore further. He gave them three days to reach the southern ocean—it could not be further away than that, he insisted—after which they were to come back to us. But two days later we saw the longboat reappear. First we heard the sound of the oars, then we saw the men standing in the boat waving frantically.

At that moment the shouts of joy we had repressed for so long burst from our throats. All our fear and anxiety poured out, swamping all words. Our mouths were like the sluicegates on a river in flood. The men cried and hugged each other, like a gaggle of overexcited madwomen.

Yet Juanillo Ponce found something pathetic in all their rejoicing. None of them seemed to realize what they were celebrating. We had finally gone beyond the point of no return. The Captain General had won, and his victory meant final defeat for the world we had left behind. The world taken from us by the wind.

Troubled, I sought out Don Fernando in the crowd of men.

Even now in his moment of triumph he was not with the others, but at the other end of the ship. All alone. Apart from the celebrations. Still encased in his iron shell, with traces of dirty snow on it. Like one of those statues that stand proud and solitary in their squares at dawn.

And all the while the *Trinidad* was like a noisy aviary in the first light of day, the joyful cries of the men drifting out over the shores of this desolate ocean. Your Juanillo wanted so much to shout at them to be quiet. Not to show our insolent human presence. There we were, crazy interlopers with our leaky tubs and a few torn sails, and we had no idea what we were doing there.

I SENSE that you are uneasy, your Highness. As if you were troubled by the way events are going, or the way that Juanillo is telling you of them here. You seem to miss the thrill of action, and the straightforward organization of facts starting with those furthest away in time and progressing smoothly to the most recent. But in this part of his chronicle, your author's perspective converges on a particular point in the South Seas close to the equator where the fleet has been stuck for ninety days for lack of wind. And from that perspective, which is like a watchtower or the crow's nest of a ship, he seeks to recount all that has happened in the expanse of time stretching out around him. So first he related, from the far corner of the panorama at his feet, how they spent several months in Serrano's shelter at the southernmost tip of the New World, close to the strait between the two oceans which my master discovered. Then the story of how we crossed that strait, our wanderings through its maze of waters. Finally, almost at the foot of this imaginary watchtower, your chronicler speaks of the religious terror which this new ocean and its mysteries caused him. I tell you in all truth that not even cockroaches in abandoned synagogues, or a bird lost in the endless arches of a mosque, or a child on Good Friday staring at religious statues covered in purple shrouds with only their marble feet poking out—none of these experienced anything of what I felt at the sight of that new ocean. An ocean no one had ever sailed before. Which was not shown on any map or nautical chart. Which we knew nothing at all about. Neither what its predominant winds or currents were. Where it began or ended. Nor what creatures swam in its depths.

And yet, after a few days of repairing the ships as best we could, Don Fernando gave the order to set sail north. To escape the cold, he said. To find fresh provisions on one of the lush islands which he claimed were only a few days' sailing away. Or so he said.

At first the crews spent all their time every day running from port to starboard, from stem to stern, silently questioning the blue mystery. They soon tired of this, however, because apart from the fleeting wake the ships left behind them, nothing else ever changed. No, that is not quite true, because as we sailed further north the sky became clearer, the atmosphere brightened, and the air warmed up. Until one morning we awoke and it was like the first day of spring back in our villages when one is very young and can feel all the signs of new life on one's skin, and the sudden fragrances and unexpected warmth pierce the soul, and one is happy, life is good, and everything is possible. Does spring burst into palaces in the same way, your Majesty? No, there is no need for you to answer me. I wager that spring never comes to that maze of dark rooms and icy corridors. Because although the palace windows are large and infinite in number, they are always closed. And the corridors smell only of tapestries. And the rooms of their velvet curtains, the rugs, dust, the walnut wood of the furniture. And your own bedrooms are full of the scent of silk, aromatic potions and medicinal herbs, and also the fragrant corset of canvas and whalebone dropped by some lady in her flight, which you have hidden under your bed. And the queen's rooms must smell of candles, cat's piss, her own frigidity. The empty rooms of illustrious corpses and bored spirits. And the whole palace of intrigues, ambitions, jealousy, endless plotting. Would you like some sound advice? Tell Felipe that next spring he should open all the windows in the palace, even if he has to use an army of men to do so and it takes over a century to close them again. Tell him to let the warm scented air of the fields in. Let the rooms be filled with the scent of mint, lavender and basil. Let the breeze carry the rustling of leaves and burgeoning wheat-fields along the palace corridors. Let the wind cleanse the chapels of the fusty smell of candles and incense, and bring instead the smell of stables. Let the sun scare off the illustrious dead as it does bats, and let them go and hide in the caves of nothingness, as my mother used to describe the Sheol of her Jewish ancestors.

Oh, munificent Majesty, how different the world would be today if just once you had ordered the windows of your palace opened! You could have done so, you had the power to open them all. Now, nobody will do it, not even Felipe, because he is too fearful. He hates all windows, and spends his time closing the heavy curtains and making sure all the shutters are bolted. So many locked shutters it would take centuries to open the windows again.

PART VII

Well, Don Carlos, here we are, you and I, once more at that spot on the South Seas where the fleet was becalmed for lack of wind at the beginning of the last chapter.

Your entire oak wood was drying out under that fiery sun, which withered the sails, splintered the masts, and split the rigging so that it hung like the shriveled shoots of a climbing plant. The ships stank of burnt wood, melted tar, hot canvas, scorched leather, urine. The bilges gave off a nauseating stench that penetrated every corner. Life on board was no more than the beating of our own hearts. Nothing else moved because there was nothing else. No breeze. No flies. No bees. In the vast immensity around us there was nothing but silence. And the sun at its zenith. The sun and silence. A silence that only Don Fernando dared disturb as he paced up and down, his footsteps resounding throughout the boat like the tick-tock of a pendulum in the silence of the night.

Since there was nothing to do, we whiled away the time stretched out in the shade of some sails we had put up as an awning. And we talked. We talked all day and most of the night. We slept little and talked a lot. As if to fill the vast emptiness surrounding us. And the emptiness inside. And that of our bellies. Some of the men put all their effort into recovering a past that was already too far distant, clutching at slender threads which eventually snapped or became entangled. Others were enthusiastic about a future that was also too far away, and traced its outlines in hesitant, unclear shapes. Little by little the stories told by both groups merged into one. Past and future became inextricably jumbled together. And your Argonauts found themselves caught like Penelopes in their own threads.

Here, for example, was Gonzalvo de Vigo, normally a shy youth, recounting for all to hear the story of his summer night's fornication with his aunt Basilia. In his grandmother's corn field no less, your Highness, with Basilia who had always driven him crazy. He remembered how as a little boy he went and said to his mother that when he was grown up he was going to marry Basilia. His mother laughed and told everyone at table, and he almost cried with rage because he could not stop himself from blushing. Even this did not cure him, and he grew up with his eyes fixed on Basilia's neckline, and whenever he could he would fall on the floor pretending he was playing, just to get a look at her legs. And she encouraged him. She would lean over him, all innocence, the top of her blouse gaping to give him a glimpse of her nut-brown breasts. When Gonzalvo was no longer a child, what had to happen did: His aunt was very fond of drinking aniseed cordial, and between the two of them they downed a bottleful. Then the fun began: I'll touch you here; if you touch me there I'll touch you here; and then they went out into the country, into his grandmother's corn field, your Highness.

"Do they have corn in your village?" somebody asked.

Gonzalvo hesitated a second and replied, "I've got the grains here for my grandmother to plant," showing us a bag full of corn he had traded for in Brazil, which he always kept on him.

We all stared at him in consternation. He went bright red, furious with himself.

"The future is a delicate glass that can smash to smithereens if we try to shape it," Ripert the glazier commented.

But for Gaspar Díaz, storeman on the *Trinidad*, the future was something else. A mirror, perhaps. A glass lined with quicksilver in which one tries to capture one's own image. In that glass moon you could see yourself as a little devil nine or ten years old who got together with his friends at harvest-time to run across to a rich neighbor's fields and spy on the women harvesters when they went to relieve themselves under an old holm oak. So, Don Carlos, watch as a sea of golden wheat rippling in the breeze is conjured up before your eyes, with women in black who look like birds among the stubble, and who stifle laughs, shriek and run off when they discover what is going on. And there was the smell of hot earth, grain, dung, lots of flies, and a desperate desire to get closer to that woman harvester who had sometimes stood there showing them her sex with a smile. Until one day Gaspar made his mind up. He was confused; his heart was beating madly in his breast, your Highness. The women were whispering, laughing and shouting something at him that he could not hear. He only had eyes for the one who stood there with her skirts raised. He could imagine his friends looking on, scared stiff. He kept on going toward her even though his heart was beating so wildly his sight became blurred and . . .

"But that's the past!" someone protested.

Gaspar shrugged his shoulders and walked away. Someone else immediately took his place, because as I told you, your Majesty, we talked a lot on those South Seas. We had nothing else to do but wait for the winds the Captain General had promised us, eat our ration of the last of the boiled rice, the only food left, without protesting, and talk. We only fell silent after sunset. When the ball of fire fell into the vastness of the sea, we were all overcome by a strange, almost religious feeling. The silence became even deeper. Even Don Fernando's footsteps which rang out day and night in the empty holds came to a halt for a while. But as soon as night had fallen and the moon rose from the side where land must have been (because there must have been land somewhere), our talk started up again. Yes, we talked a lot. We talked so much we confused not only past and future but the stories themselves.

Like Martín the Cooper, who had stolen Lorenzo de Corrat's first communion, and spoke of the preparations for it in such detail that he bored us all, apart from Lorenzo himself, who listened to him enthralled.

"But the smell of chocolate, biscuits, marzipan; the tinkling of plates and the religious aunts whispering: that's all Lorenzo's story," someone protested.

"It doesn't matter," Lorenzo said, unable to take his eyes from Martín's lips.

So the cooper stayed hidden behind the tall armchairs of a dark room while the old women went on chattering and praying and someone told him come here you'll get your knees dirty, or what a fine lad you've become, he'll be a saint one day, Father, you mark my words.

Even Joan de Acurio, an officer, stole a story from Zubeleta, a mere gunner. The thief told of the innocent joy of a child waiting for him to return from the fields, a boy who ran to meet him, threw his arms round his neck and clung to him, breathless from his run, his cheeks burning from the cold. And the thief lost himself in a maze of someone else's sensations and feelings until Zubeleta appeared. At that he fell silent, waiting for the right moment to return to the tale which did not belong to him and which, unbeknownst to him, was not even true: Zubeleta, who had never known any family except for an occasional cellmate in Valladolid jail, had made up the whole thing.

Yes, we did talk a lot, your Highness. We talked the whole time. As if we could fill that vastness with words. As if we could quiet our empty stomachs with words. We talked the whole day and most of the night. We would only stop at sunset or when whales appeared. All at once the crystal of the waters would shatter, and it seemed that cathedrals streaming with foam were rising out of nothing, as in a dream. At that all of us fell silent. After a while, though, we started up again. We certainly talked a lot during those days, your Highness, but since there wasn't much to talk about, we not only borrowed or stole other people's stories, but traded them, since they were the last things we had left to barter with.

For example, your Highness, Policarpo exchanged a spinster aunt, who gave him sweets if he could recite from memory the verses by Macías El Enamorado she had taught him, with Severino Segade for a rainy autumn afternoon. But not just any afternoon. An afternoon with the sound of hoofs on the flagstones of a square, a blind wall over which the tops of dark poplars peeped, a Romanesque church porch where doves had taken shelter, a carriage pulling up in front of it. The driver climbed down, and Policarpo could see the trails of sweat on the horse's haunches, then heard the heavy thud of the knocker and the sound of saws in a nearby carpenter's shop. And Policarpo spoke, O Caesar, of the smell of the kitchen garden behind that seminary wall (wet earth and vegetables) and the sharp aroma of sawdust he took with him from the square when the priest showed him in through the door. The priest locked the door behind him, leaving his father on the other side. Then he heard the "giddup" and the sound of the mare's hoofs outside in the square, and it was as if his childhood were vanishing into the distance with the sound. Except it was not his childhood, but Severino's; Policarpo had never attended a seminary, or been in that square, or heard those hoofs, the knocker on the door, the sound of the saws in the carpenter's shop—these were all Severino's memories. And of course Policarpo had never smelt that garden, or carried the smell of sawdust with him, or seen the doves taking shelter from the rain under the Romanesque porch, or any of that; he didn't even have a father. Yet for some strange reason he loved that scene; it moved him deeply and, with tears in his eyes, he really felt it belonged to him. Severino Segade, meanwhile, repeated Macías's verses and grew tender over a spinster aunt he had never had.

As I said, we talked a lot during those days, and there wasn't a lot to talk about. But what else could we do in that prison without bars while we were waiting for the winds that would finally take us to the Spice Islands? What else could we do to kill time, forget our hunger, stop ourselves from imagining the powerful fleet as no more than a handful of nutshells lost in the middle of a vast ocean? That is why we talked all the time, stretched out in the shade of the huge sails. We talked day and night, only pausing at sunset, or when whales appeared, or if someone spotted an enormous sea turtle swimming by. When that happened, we all left the shade and ran to the rail to watch the slow, majestic passing of one of those strange dark creatures which seemed embedded in the crystal of the waters. They moved so imperceptibly it seemed they were not progressing at all, as if the sea had suddenly frozen around them. Yet they did move forward. They would skirt the ships without paying us the slightest attention and continue on their unhurried way as if they had all the time in the world. We gazed after them sadly, and when they had finally disappeared from view we returned to the shade and our stories.

We talked of the price of rats, which by this stage of our journey were our only food. We established that an adult male was worth up to three hundred pounds of pepper, to be deducted from the buyer's share of what we found when we eventually reached the Spice Islands. And a pregnant female was worth her weight in gold. That's because there were so few of them, your Highness. And since rats were so scarce and so valuable, a kind of aristocracy of hunters had arisen, who controlled the whole business. It was they who, for a fee, authorized the hunt. Only they, and nobody else, could sell a rat. The ship had been sectioned off into well-defined areas, and I can assure you, your Highness, that the reprisals were so ferocious that nobody trespassed on a neighbor's hunting ground. Whenever you wanted to catch a rat, you first of all offered everything you had for it, and if this wasn't enough (it never was) then you signed a document promising to hand over a proportion of whatever reward you expected from the voyage. It was even said that the whole thing was organized from above, and that several officers were involved, headed by that man Sebastián whom your Majesty named First Circumnavigator of the Entire World. Be that as it may, the organization worked even more smoothly than your own administration, Don Carlos. Spurred on by the thought of their rich pickings, the hunters descended the gangways armed with a club and a sack. They took no lanterns with them so as not to scare off their prey, but dived like cats behind empty barrels, into baskets, or between earthenware jars. They hunted in every corner of the ship except the store where the hard tack was kept. There the pile of sacks once reached the roof, giving off a rich aroma of hearth and warm bread. But that was long ago already. Now all that was left were little heaps of meal full of maggots and rat excrement. This disgusting mess was our only capital. The rats we ate grew fat on it. Thanks to it their young could grow and multiply. That was why hunting was forbidden there, and why the store was guarded by two gunners after a cabin boy had broken this law. He was found scooping up the meal with both hands, and his corpse was left hanging from the mainmast for a week. Yes, your Highness, we talked of him as well, of course, but only for a while. After that, he became part of the scenery. And we went on to talk of other things. Because as I have already said, we talked a lot then. And when we had nothing to talk about, we invented games. Silly games like the one we called: "What Is?" that was also known as "The Tautology of Hunger" or, if you prefer, "A Madcap Dialogue on the Essence of Some Things and Not of Others."

"What is a ship for you?" someone would ask.

"A bowl," another replied.

"A bowl of life," a third added.

"A bowl of wood," the first retorted.

"Trees. A whole wood."

"A pile of timbers."

"An open door."

"A coffin."

"Death."

"And what is death for you?"

"A ship. The last one."

"Another door," Balderrama the chaplain said.

"We can't know what it is until we have gone through it," added Rodrigo, who liked to speculate. "And by the time we do know, we can't tell anyone about it. But I think I would say death was a moment of transition, between this world of travail and the true life. In that sense, it could be said that death is life, couldn't it, Father?"

"That all depends," the chaplain answered, warming to the

subject. "It all depends. It could mean eternal life or eternal damnation, which is true death, that of the soul."

"That's enough," I said, annoyed at all these highflown words. "Death is revolting. It's a foul stench, the buzzing of flies, worms; it's revolting."

"And it is solitude," someone added.

"What is solitude for you?"

"A locked house."

"An empty cradle."

"That's death," I said.

"So is solitude. They're the same thing."

"Solitude is a plant that grows in your breast and puts down such strong roots you can never dig it out."

"A gesture or a smell we can never recapture. A savor lost forever."

"A path disappearing into the distance."

"That's a ship."

"No, that's freedom."

"What is freedom for you?"

"A ship."

"Many doors."

"An untamed animal."

"A child at play."

"Gold and spices."

"A river that forces its way past all obstacles."

"Death is a river."

"No, life."

"And what is life for you?"

"A bowl."

"But we said a ship was that."

"The smell of a good stew."

"A woman passing by who seduces us for a moment."

"I think it's the earth."

"A seed."

"A plow and a pair of oxen."

"That's work."

"And what is work?"

"We were talking about life. What is life?"

"The port awaiting us at the end of every voyage."

"That sounds like death."

"A woman who misses us."

"So does that."

"The child calling for its father."

"Life is good," someone said, dreamy-eyed. Then he ran the tip of his tongue over his inflamed gums.

Although he tried to conceal the gesture, we all saw it, and fell silent.

"Go on about life," the man with the swollen gums said.

"It's a dry, warm bed," another man answered.

"An armchair by the fireside."

"A woman who misses us."

"That is solitude."

"Solitude is the sea."

"The sea is death."

"Boredom."

"Hunger."

"Madness."

"A huge, strange mirror."

"A dream."

"That's what a ship is: a handful of dreams."

"And what are dreams?"

"A woman passing by who seduces us."

"They're like a pack of stupid hounds, dragging their master after a nonexistent prey."

"Like hounds that turn against their master and pursue him ferociously."

"Dogs that bark at night and keep him awake."

"That break all the chains you try to tie them up with."

"That's freedom."

"No, dreams."

"A flower that fades in the sunlight, that is what dreams are."

"That is time."

"Time is an ocean whose shores no one knows."

"A child growing up and making men of us."
"The setting sun."
"And what is the sun?"
"The sun is a forge."
"A double-edged ax."
"A stone crushing our ships."
"A gravestone."
"That is death."
"It's the sun."
"It's hunger."
"And what is hunger?"
"An empty bowl."
"But that was a ship."
"Hunger is a ship waiting for winds that never come."
"A fungus sprouting on the brain."
"A rat digging its tunnels in your stomach."
"A silent, bare table."
"And what is silence?"
"Silence is a stone."
"A gravestone."
"That's death."
"That's the sun."
"The sea."
"Silence is a dead wind."
"And what is wind?"
"A ship."
"A door."
"Every door."
"And the lack of wind?"
"A caged bird."
"A gravestone."
"That's death."
"That's hunger."
"That's our fleet."
"And what is a fleet?"
"A whole forest."
"A pile of timbers."

"A coffin."

"A handful of dreams."

The game always ended with the same question, "What is Maluco?"

Nobody answered that question quickly. It seemed too obvious to say that it was the Spice Islands or that it was the fleet's destination, so we set off again on a sea of fresh questions until our interest in the game petered out.

"Did you know that in Portuguese it means crazy?"

"Don't you think the word has a strange, magical sound?"

"Why do they call the Captain that?"

"Where is it?"

"Who knows? Somewhere or nowhere at all."

"Perhaps it's inside each one of us?"

"Do you think the Captain knows?"

"Is it a dream?"

"A handful of dreams?"

"A fleet becalmed?"

"A ship?"

"A gravestone?"

"An epitaph?"

"Another door?"

WE REALLY did talk a lot, your Highness. But there were things we carefully avoided in all our conversations. Like a ship which, in order to skirt the hazards hidden beneath the innocent surface of the waters, sails round in circles, its crew tense and alert, concentrating on each maneuver. That is how we were when we avoided talking about the lack of food or the lifeless days that had gone by and that we had lost count of, or our return home. Nor did we talk about the growing number of the sick. Nor about Gonzalvo de Vigo, who had been caught dining on Gaspar Díaz's dead body. Gaspar had died without anyone noticing, and Gonzalvo had hidden him in one of the empty stores. That was where they found him, perched over the body like a vulture. But as I said, we did not talk of those things. Hunger was a personal problem. An intimate duel. An

217

individual challenge. Unnamable, like the Hebrew god. Your chroniclers were lying when they said Don Fernando forbade us to speak of the lack of food. The fact was, nobody wanted to. Hunger was our dialogue with God, which each and every one of us carried on in secret. Convinced that to mention it would be to smash down the final barrier, beyond which we would be nothing more than a handful of wild animals, a pack of hyenas.

So we remained silent while we drank our diminishing ration of stinking water. And in resigned silence we chewed the leather chafing gear that was by then our only sustenance, since even the supply of rats had given out. We stripped the masts and yardarms of their leather protection, soaked it in the sea for four or five days, and then chewed on it hour after hour. Even though our teeth ached and fell out of our gums like grains from a ripe ear of corn, we did not complain. We made no comment whatsoever, pretending we were eating leather by choice, and then falling asleep in the midst of the vast calm all around us. Under a sky without a single cloud, bird or even fly. On a sea that was made sometimes of crystal, sometimes of stone, but never of water. Because in all that immensity there was nothing but the sun and silence.

The only person who refused to accept this was Don Fernando. Despite the sun and the silence, he carried out the same ceremony every day.

The ritual began at noon, when he appeared on the stern-deck, astrolabe in hand. He hooked his left thumb through the metal ring, lifted the instrument to his eyes, and with his right hand moved the short bronze arm until the fierce sun of those South Seas was nothing more than an inoffensive glow in the opening at its tip. After that he looked down and read off the sun's altitude as marked on the tin disc. He repeated the same operation three times, then, with the astrolabe dangling from his right hand like a broken shoe or an unstrung violin, he stood staring at the sky for a few minutes. After that he came down on deck and headed for the compass box. He opened it and looked down at the compass for a long while, searching for heaven knows what sign from that magnetic needle. Then his eyes roamed over the objects piled in the tiny cabin. A lamp that was usually lit all the time so the helmsman could see the compass, but which was now cold and moldy. A lodestone for priming the needles. Several richly engraved pairs of compasses. Different sounding lines with their lead weights, to measure water depths. The log, neatly coiled as ever in its container. And there were the hourglasses, some of them still on their shelf, others which had fallen on the table, one with its bulb smashed and all its sand gone.

The Captain General looked this way and that, unsure which of these instruments to use. Finally, unable to choose, he decided to walk along the deck to the midships hatchway instead, and then disappeared down into the hold.

We could not see him, but in the silence his footsteps became a precise code by which we could detect every point and gesture of his painstaking tour. The plan of the hold each of us had in his mind became like a game board, on which Don Fernando was the piece. But this piece advanced without any problems through the stores, whose iron doors were wide open; it also continued untroubled past the cells, where the last water barrels were kept, and that was a bad sign, your Highness. It meant we were losing. Because the piece only stopped at the magazine, full of powder, and at the store with all the goods for barter, still crammed to the ceiling with cheap mirrors and glass necklaces of every color. Then the piece moved on to the furthest recesses, speeding between empty baskets and barrels full of seaweed. The game was over when it reached the foot of the hatch where it had started from. And we always lost, your Highness. However hard we concentrated, we never won. It was as though the dice were loaded against us. But the worst of it wasn't losing, it was not knowing whom we were playing against.

Don Fernando emerged again from the hatchway and continued his tour along the starboard side until he reached the bowsprit.

He was the only person who dared venture beyond the

capstan into the area reserved for the sick. Those of us who were still fit and those who were sick had divided the ship in half, as if a barrier between the two worlds could possibly still have meaning in the situation we found ourselves in. The healthy members of the crew went about their routine without help from the sick, while they on their side went about dying without any help from us. The two areas were well defined, so that whenever someone recognized the unmistakable signs of illness in himself, he would leave the stern without being told to do so, cross the neutral zone between the capstan and the mainmast, and confine himself to the prow. The sick spent all day under cover there. By moonlight we could see their gaunt profiles like shadows. Shadows of what they had once been, torn apart by their illness. Made unrecognizable, cruel and selfish. All this only reinforced the imaginary boundary between our two worlds. A boundary only Don Fernando had the courage to cross in his daily inspection of the ship. Deaf to the insults those cursed creatures shouted at him, he tried all the pulleys, which screeched from their lengthy overexposure to the sun. He pulled on all the ropes to see how flexible they were, though they were stiffer with each passing day. He tested how taut the shrouds were, though by now they hung limply. He whirled the capstan round despite the covering of salt which made it laborious. He examined every inch of the foremast, running his hands up and down it, his fingers pausing like a lover's at every crack in the wood. He swung from the mizzenmast rings to make sure they were still intact. He tried out the pump, making sure no one saw him doing it. Rapped his knuckles on the mainmast in a loving dialogue with its wood. He gazed at the stern lantern, corroded with rust. Then finally, as though his legs or his soul were weighed down, he slowly made his way back to his cabin, disheartened at how the ship had deteriorated and at the continuing lack of wind. Because there was no wind or any sign of it. And without wind there was no ship, because wind and ship are inseparable. What is a ship without the wind that propels it? A ridiculous conglomeration of timbers and cables and canvases, just like the sad shelter Juan Serrano built. A pyramid in whose secret galleries rot futureless and faithless men. A monument to past dreams. That is what Don Fernando was thinking while the rest of us, stretched out in the shadow of the sails, our teeth slipping out as though they were sand in an hourglass, our gums swollen and riddled with ulcers, our entire mouths a shapeless mass of pink stinking flesh—the rest of us talked endlessly. We talked all the time but couldn't bring ourselves to look directly at each other, so the talk went in one direction and our eyes in another. From time to time someone got silently to his feet and walked up to the prow, because a terrible gnawing pain in his stomach had told him it was time to leave. Even that didn't stop our talk; mouths crimson and swollen from scurvy opened like roses in a spring garden.

YOU ASK what was the outcome of all the useless chatter our glorious voyage around the entire world had degenerated into? Yes, O glorious Majesty, Juanillo is well aware that you are bored and impatient, and are cursing this chronicle of crazy chatterboxes and its even crazier author. You want to see action. You want to see your men climbing the rigging, flinging themselves from the spars, tightening the ropes and dashing forward to adventure. You want to hear the sails flapping in the breeze, the splash of waves as your fleet's noble prows plunge onward, the hubbub of excited voices and the roar of cannon; all the talk I have written of, all this idle chatter is going in one of your ears and coming out the other, you're dying of boredom. You are tired of the nauseating stench of the ships, your Imperial nostrils are yearning for the sharp smell of gunpowder, the sickly sweet smell of blood (that's one you haven't found yet in my chronicle) and most of all, of course, the fragrant aroma of spices. Yet I go on bothering you with all this blah-blah as if you hadn't already had more than enough of it. Besides, didn't Pedro Mártir and that other fellow, Pigateta or whatever his name was, deal with this part of the journey, which is taking me so many pages, in a couple of paragraphs? Wouldn't it have been enough simply to say that we were becalmed for several months, that our food ran out completely and we all nearly starved, then take up the story again from the point when the winds returned and we continued on with our journey? Why all this beating around the bush? You've already put up with enough of it, you say, and your all-powerful will wants to see the fleet on the move again. If you could, you would shout the order at me, and have me flogged if I disobeyed. And you must be thinking that in this or the next sentence I am bound to yield to your command, as everyone does. But no, you are wrong, your Majesty. I am deaf to your commands, and I am leaving the fleet stuck in the South Seas for as long as I see fit, while I open a parenthesis in my story.

A parenthesis, your Highness, to remind you that the author of these lines is not God, this or that Muse, or some strange chimera. No, he is Juanillo Ponce, made of flesh and blood like the next man. Therefore, if this tale runs smoothly and gives you the impression of having been written at one sitting, without my having had to stop to eat an omelette or relieve myself in the vegetable patch, then you are mistaken. It is all a lie. Pure invention. Tricks one learns to conceal one's shame, disguise one's needs, camouflage one's inadequacies.

But now I'm growing tired of all this deception. I feel the need to tell you that at this moment my belly is aching, and that for months now my Filomena, the light of my life, has been ill, and that at night I, too, feel the stealthy approach of death in my rotten teeth (as a blind man in a neighboring village used to say). Also, I want to tell you that the story about Filomena is false, that she is a grotesque mask behind which, out of loving modesty, I am concealing the name of the person I really love. It is to her I dedicate this record of our journey, and the only dedication will be this one, at this precise point in the story: "For R., who means everything to me."

That is what I feel like doing, however little it means to you, or however much it may irritate you. Even though it interrupts my flow, or spoils my chronicle. Or leads you to think, he's an idiot, and throw all my pages on the fire, keeping instead the royal chroniclers with whom to while away your leisure hours in the future.

I'm not like them, I know. I have no wish to be. They all carefully hide their own misfortunes, so you can enjoy the spectacle they offer with a clear conscience. Liars, clowns, cowards, that's what your Pedro Mártir de Anglería and the other chroniclers are, although it hurts me to say so—like all poets who invent fables merely to give pleasure, as if they themselves were transparent as the air, all-knowing as God the Father.

It's their fault that you think there is nobody behind the masks. And that the false opulence of costumes tells you nothing. Nor the grimace you take for a laugh. Nor the tambourines and somersaults you see as joy.

Well you're wrong, all of you. Because if you turn to our art when you feel like it, when you have a free moment, or to fill some spare time, whereas the rest of your life you spend working, eating, shitting, loving, having children, suffering, cursing, and dying when the moment comes, then what on earth do you think we are doing when we're not putting on our show? What do you think happened to us between pages 35 and 63? You, who read for pleasure or to help you get to sleep, and when you feel sleepy leave the chronicle at such and such a page, when Don Fernando is about to . . . what do you know of the real story behind that page? How do you know whether, just as Don Fernando was about to . . . the chronicler perhaps had to break off because he was told his mother had died, or because he was shivering with cold and first thing the next morning he had to go out and earn the crust of bread you refused him? That is why, your Highness, I am often disgusted by the flow of my narrative. I am ashamed to think that the peace and protection its continuity offers you is achieved by my hiding my wounds, disappearing behind the mask of words, the faces of my characters, the invented pains of those phantasmagoric creatures who steal through these pages which either delight or bore you. That is why, your Highness, I sometimes feel an overwhelming need to break off my tale as I am doing now and let my chronicle become as rough and ready as life itself.

ARE YOU still there, Don Carlos? Are you annoyed with this servant of yours? I'll wager you're not. That with your Olympian patience you are waiting for this childish fit of mine to pass. That with the benevolence characteristic of the powerful you tolerated this flesh-and-blood Juanillo bursting in upon your chronicle, sure in the knowledge that after this brief interruption everything would return to normal. You are right, you are always right, and in that you are identical to Filomena. "What will become of you without Don Carlos?" she used to say to me. "What will you gain by insulting him? The pair of us will die of hunger, that's what," she would say. "So, be gentle. You don't want to cause me any harm, do you? I would get ill, perhaps even die. So think of me a little, you selfish brute. You don't want me to starve to death, do you?"

"What do you know about going hungry, you greedy witch? You're trying to tell me what it means to starve?" I told her, pretending to disagree, even though I knew she was right. "You don't know anything about hunger," I said. "Nor does his Majesty Don Carlos."

BY THAT time, my contacts with the Captain General had become less frequent. He seemed distant, caught up in his own thoughts. He was not interested in my tales and did not listen to my visions. We spoke only a little, and when we did it was about banalities. He did not find my jokes funny and hardly ever responded to my taunts.

"You true Christians grow beards more quickly," I said to him.

He made no reply.

"I've heard that Siqueira, the viceroy of Malacca, had a fearsome beard," I insisted. "A beard so thick and bushy it grew all over his cheeks up to his eyes and made him look like a wild beast. They say he was just like a monkey."

Don Fernando went on staring at the hourglasses ranged on a shelf at the foot of his bed.

"I also heard that even though he was a soldier, he couldn't bear the smell of gunpowder or blood, so in the midst of battles he would take out a Flemish lace handkerchief sprinkled with perfume and hold it to his nose," I went on, watching to see how he would react.

Although my master had fought as a youth alongside the legendary Portuguese hero, he still said nothing.

He must have been thinking: now there was a brave man. Brave and delicate. He probably missed him. He must have regretted not being under his command rather than in charge of this immobile fleet. But he didn't say so. He said nothing at all. Nor did he take the bait when I said:

"Cartagena was a brave and delicate man as well. Do you think he is still alive?"

Don Fernando did not answer because he knew it was ridiculous to worry about the Inspector General now. His only worry was the wind. And the number of men he might lose from starvation that day.

"You're right," I said, continuing with my monologue. "Best to cast all that into oblivion, that dark, bottomless well into which we throw all the wrongs done to us and all our own errors, in order to go on living."

At that I thought I detected a faint nod of approval, which encouraged me to carry on in the same vein.

"When I was a little boy, wells fascinated me," I said. "I liked to climb onto the rim of the one we had in the backyard and stare down at the calm mirror of water at the bottom."

Perhaps Don Fernando was thinking, that is what this ocean is, a calm mirror of water. But he didn't say it.

" 'Where does the water come from?' I would ask. 'From the sky,' my grandfather the rabbi would tell me, insisting that the well was rainwater. 'From the bowels of the earth,' my grandmother would say, adamant that it was a spring. They could never agree, but I preferred my grandmother's idea because it meant the well was infinitely deep. I spent whole nights awake thinking of it. And whole days leaning over the well, although my mother had forbidden me to do so because she said I might fall in and drown. But that possibility only in-

225

creased my curiosity. I imagined myself plunging into those blind, dark waters. Plunging down and down for years. For so many years that I grew while I was falling headlong, became an adult and then an old man, still plunging downward, because for me that mirror of water had no bottom. Ever since then I have thought of the human mind as a well like that. And of God as one of those turtles people throw down wells to purify the water. What was the well in your house, a tank or a spring?" I asked him.

"I don't know," he replied, with obvious reluctance. "Wells never attracted me. In fact, I loathe them. It's water that's trapped, stagnant."

Now you've given yourself away, I thought. If you're in charge of a fleet that has been becalmed for almost three months, you would hate stagnant water; and I was on the point of making a joke about it when I said to myself, but you're trapped too. And it's costing you your life. Through his fault. He's the one to blame for the fact that I am going to die of scurvy in an unknown spot that doesn't even figure on any map.

"I wouldn't like to be in your shoes," I said. "They'll say of you: He was the man who lost four ships and two hundred men without moving from the same spot. And the worst of it is that your failure will cast its shadow over your loved ones. Your son will have to come to blows to defend your memory, and he will secretly hate you for what you did. Because he will take your failure as a personal slight: you know how children are. And though he will fight for you, he will be convinced deep inside that you failed him. And when he is hitting his best friend, it won't be his friend's face he sees, but yours, and his anger will make him lash out twice as hard."

"Stop attacking me, will you?" he said, sitting up on the bed. "Do you really think you're being funny? Well, let me tell you, you're not. Not one bit. You're pathetic. Sordid. Repugnant."

Realizing I had gone too far, I fell silent, desperately trying to think of something else to say which might fill the void that had opened up between us. As I could think of nothing better, I launched into an outburst:

226

"Do you know what's really repugnant? The smell of fat from that candle. Why don't you blow it out? I hate that smell. It reminds me of churches. God forgive me, but I detest the smell of churches. When I used to be an altar boy for the priest I told you about, I was scared of that smell. It used to make me feel sick. Do you know that I vomited up the host when I was being given First Communion? It was terrible. The priest placed the body of Christ in my mouth with his cold, plump fingers, and I began to taste it and to tremble. Because it was the taste of eternity. My saliva was dissolving the future. That's when I began to feel nauseous. I knew I was going to bring the host up, and I could already hear the indignant reaction of the congregation in my ears. The priest went on with his litany, looking at me with the face of a pharaoh initiated into the mysteries of life and death; when he raised a golden chalice I was blinded by its reflection. Next to him I could see the angelic faces of the other altar boys swinging the censers. And next to me, the terrified faces of my companions as they filed to the altar and knelt in front of it, mouths open and tongues hanging out, awaiting their turn. And above the altar, the feet of the virgin, which looked like a dead person's, trampling a serpent underfoot. And Jesus' hands, bleeding on the Cross, between two enormous candles. All of a sudden I couldn't take any more. I scarcely had time to stand up and rush a few steps away from the altar before I brought everything up at the foot of a marble column. Everybody stared at me, aghast."

"That must have made you feel very bad," Don Fernando said. "I feel sorry for you. You must have had a hard time as a child."

His unexpectedly gentle comment disconcerted me. I didn't know what to do, so I ended up laughing a hollow laugh. I began to shake the bells on my bracelet and pretended to dance.

"Why are you doing that?" he asked.

I said nothing because I had no answer. I had no desire at all to amuse him, but suddenly felt I ought to. I found I had to perform the role assigned me in the script. To accept the mask I had worn over my face so as not to cheat him. But I was still very moved by Don Fernando's open show of affection.

By his sudden interest in me as a person. His taking me seriously threw me into confusion.

"Count Don Juan never took me seriously," I said eventually. "That's why he ended up having such confidence in me he would tell me everything that was on his mind."

"Didn't that make it hard for you?"

"That's our task, as you know. A jester must know how to keep a secret. Because a jester is like a hired friend. People can console and unburden themselves knowing there won't be any consequences, because nobody takes a fool seriously, do they? They can tell us things they wouldn't tell their closest friends, and treat us in a way they wouldn't dare treat their worst enemies. They needn't feel bad about it, because that's what they pay us for. That's why I say that, together with whores, we have the oldest and most necessary profession in the world. And the same happens to us as to whores. There are men who go visit them to do things they think are unworthy of their wives. And I'm not just talking about sex. They go to tell them about their deepest hurts, they cry on their shoulders that smell of cheap perfume, they pour their hearts out to them all night long, and then, goodbye and farewell. So you see, whenever you're tired of me, you only have to say so. You're the one who's paying."

"But I really do appreciate you," he said, patting me on the knee. When I shook my head, moved again by his words, he added, "You shouldn't talk like that. I've become accustomed to you."

"And I to you," I said, stammering. "But I thought that . . ."

"Be quiet," he said. "When you're the Count of the Spice Islands everyone will respect you. You won't have to play the fool for anybody. You'll even have your own jesters, and perhaps you'll grow fond of one just as I have of you."

"I never had any friends."

"You'll have lots of them."

"Do you think we'll reach the Spice Islands?"

The smile faded from his lips. He sat there lost in thought, no longer looking at me.

I knew he thought he had no other choice, and he was right. He could not confront the fleet's backers or the Colonies' Office empty-handed and simply say to them, "I was wrong." Or say that Ruy Faleiro was completely mistaken in his calculations of the width of the South Seas, and that what seemed possible in his maps simply was not. This ocean was immense, perhaps infinite, but Don Fernando could not have known that. Nor could anyone. Nor could he have known that the New World stretched so far south or that, although the strait did exist, it was situated at its southernmost tip. He knew they would ask him why he had not turned back when he realized his calculations were wrong, and he would have no answer. He knew they would blame him for carrying on against all reasonable advice, and for losing so many (how many?) men and ships. He knew they would accuse him of refusing to listen to the advice of the other captains who wanted to return to Spain. He knew that only an abundant cargo of pepper, cinnamon, saffron and cloves could wash his hands of the blood of the Castilian nobles, and he had no such cargo. He knew they would accuse him of treason and sedition. That after stealing the *San Antonio* from him, Esteban Gómez would be one of the judges accusing him of being a murderer. That Gómez would have turned everyone against him and distorted everything that had happened before and after the stay at San Julián. Because the one thing he was certain of was that the *San Antonio* had sailed back to Spain. And that while he was here, powerless, they had probably seized his possessions and left his family in misery. He knew nobody would dare protect them; he knew how cowardly people can be. He knew about the anger being whipped up against him in every house, every town. He was being made the only person responsible for the loss of so many lives. For so many ruined homes. For so many beds that were too big now. So many silent tables. So many children who would grow up hating his name. So many women who in the deep silence of nights that stretched on to despair would curse the man who had robbed them of their son, their husband, their lover. No, there was no way he could return defeated. Nobody would forgive him for that. Only cinnamon, saffron, pepper and cloves could save him. And he didn't have any. He was forced to go on searching for the Spice Islands until he found them, even if they were situated in the lap of death itself.

"I won't even escape revenge in death," he said, as though struggling with a heavy burden. "My memory will be scorned, it will haunt my descendants like a ghost. You yourself said so."

"Don't take me seriously, I was only trying to get your attention. Besides, why be so pessimistic? At least we've come further than anyone else ever did. We've even discovered the passage through to the South Seas, which no one believed in. In some ways the voyage has been a triumph, hasn't it?"

"What do you think?"

"That we're on the right route, we'll reach the Spice Islands, and I'll become a count, so they'll say of me, 'Here comes the count, a man to take into account.'"

"I have to tell you I don't know how far this ocean stretches, nor how long it will take us to cross it once we get the wind back. I'm so confused that I'm not even sure we can reach the Spice Islands by this route."

"I know that," I told him.

He looked at me in surprise.

"But I'm not worried. Know why?"

He shook his head.

"Because I know that the Spice Islands are on the other side of the line they call the horizon," I said, putting on an air of great conviction.

Although he shook his head a second time, a smile began to spread across his features.

"Is this another of your jokes?" he asked.

I climbed up on the bed beside him and whispered in his ear, "The Spice Islands are just over the horizon."

We both sat there in silence. The ship was barely swaying. The sun sank into the lifeless waters and shadows invaded the cabin, concealing compasses, instruments, hourglasses. All at once both of us became aware of the sword propped against the wall.

"Do you know what?" he said. "If we return home in triumph, I promise you I'll turn that sword into a plowshare, and make our oars into yokes for oxen."

"You know I don't believe you. But even so, I'd enjoy working the land with you."

"Do you know how to build a house?" he asked after a while.

His strange question left me perplexed. I didn't know what the devil to think. I thought of our tiny ships stuck in the middle of that curved blue mirror whose limits nobody knew, and the question seemed even more absurd.

"A house where?" I asked in the end, for the sake of saying something and to see what he was driving at.

"Where do you think?"

"In the Spice Islands, perhaps?"

"I said a house. Well, do you know how to or not? Have you ever built one?"

His tone was so anxious that I hesitated to tell him the truth.

"A house made of wood or stone?" I asked.

"A house ought to be made of stone. Leave wood for making ships."

"You mean a fortress?"

"No, you don't understand. Don't you know what a house is? If you don't know, how can you build one?"

"And you do?" I said curtly. I was beginning to be annoyed by his question, which I thought was merely to poke fun at me.

"I don't know how to build one but I've been giving it a lot of thought and I think I know what a house is . . ." he replied in all seriousness.

Something in his expression told me that however absurd this preoccupation of his seemed, it was both sincere and genuine.

"I think you have to start with the foundations. You have to measure the floor area on the site you've chosen and then dig the foundations. You can use the earth you remove to level the ground around the house. If you want a solid house you

231

need deep foundations. And they have to be made of stone. You can flatten them with earth or mortar."

Although I had never seen a house built, I imagined this was how it had to be done and Don Fernando nodded his head and seemed so convinced I felt obliged to carry on.

"Once you've dug the foundations and leveled the ground, you can start to raise the walls," I said.

"Which wall should I start with?"

"Whichever you want, it's not important," I replied, anxious to get to the roof and finish this tedious business. "The foundations are the essential thing."

"That's true, but let's talk about the walls. I want them to be very thick. So neither the cold, the wind nor any sound can get through them; I want all those threats kept out of the house."

"All right, let's build the walls. I think it would be best to raise them all at the same time, because if you finished one on its own, how would it stay up? Perhaps you should start with the corners, because they support everything else. The outside corners and where the outside wall joins the inside ones. Do you want them made of stone as well?"

"First of all, get the outside walls finished, then we'll see. Stone on stone until we reach the roof, which must be made of slate."

"You've ended up shutting yourself inside," I said, a knowing smile on my lips.

He shot me a furious look. I tried to make my smile more innocent. The expression in his eyes became less aggressive.

"Your house doesn't have any doors or windows," I said. It was his turn to smile.

"Are you so frightened of the threats from outside?" I asked.

"I'd forgotten about them."

"Is your house your new suit of armor? Are you going to live shut in, enclosed inside it, when you finally hang up your armor?"

"Don't try to annoy me. What's the matter with you? Does it upset you when people take you seriously, or does it frighten you?"

Don Fernando's comment made me think. Perhaps he is right, I said to myself. Perhaps I'm frightened of disappointing anyone who cares for me.

"As you are raising the walls, you should leave the openings for doors and windows. You need to use wooden beams to finish off those openings. I know you prefer stone, but some kinds of wood are as hard and tough as stone, and they make things much easier. Otherwise you would need a very skillful stonemason. Of course there are lots of them. I know one in my village who builds churches, so . . ."

"I don't want to build a church," Don Fernando interrupted me.

"It might not be a bad idea, come to think of it. To build a church, then we can all go in and pray for the wind to return."

"You are not funny."

"But seriously, I know a stonemason who . . ."

"I don't want to hear about that."

"I only wanted to talk about the hearth. Imagine one of those hearths that take up almost all the kitchen, cluttered with pots and pans and blackened by smoke. Where the fire is always lit. With a big fireplace where you can hang cauldrons and smoke sausages and hams. We don't have huge ones like that in Bustillo, but Filomena is from Galicia and she's told me about the ones there. Yes, my lord, a big hearth in the middle of the kitchen with a fire always lit, a pot of stew steaming on its trivet and a cat asleep between an old woman's feet. An old woman who could be your mother, an aunt or simply a maid; whoever you like."

"Your house isn't bad," he said, smiling.

"We can build one for each of us. Yours would be bigger, of course. But we'll have to keep it a secret, because if the others hear of the idea, we'll soon have a whole city built on the sea. Then we could call it the Spice Islands, couldn't we? That way, we would have reached them and returned home, all without moving from here or worrying the lack of wind. You could be king and I'll be the count, and we'll all live happily ever after."

"Help me with my armor," he said, standing up. "I'll see

233

if I can sleep for a while. I've heard more than enough nonsense for today."

As I was loosening the straps of his breastplate, he added, "You can stay if you like."

I WANTED to stay, your Highness. I wanted to stay, because outside the night was like a black, blind sheep, bumping into everything in its path.

Yet I could not, your Majesty. The fact was that even while we were talking I had begun to feel such dreadful pains in the stomach I could barely disguise them. The dreaded moment had arrived. Now I, too, was sick and had to go to the front of the ship. That was what the tacit agreement that nobody dared break required me to do.

So I said farewell to the Captain and made my way to the prow.

I groped my way forward, guided by the pestilential smell coming from there. When I reached the capstan, I paused for a moment. Beyond that point lay a strange world from which there might not be any return. Nobody knows about this, I said to myself. Perhaps you can go on concealing it for a few more days. Not even the Captain noticed. But I knew it was useless, so I continued on my way. It was when I realized how meekly I was accepting my fate that I knew I must really be sick.

A moment later, I heard a voice: "Who goes there: friend or foe?"

The question seemed so absurd to me I did not know what to reply.

In the tense silence that ensued, I could hear the harsh rasping from an inflamed throat coming closer and closer to me, and finally I received a hot blast of fetid breath on my face.

At that moment I tried to run back. It was barely more than an instinctive reaction, but the bells on my bracelet gave me away.

"Is that you, Juanillo?" the voice asked.

"No, it's Juan Serrano," I said almost without thinking,

234

remembering the bells on the Portuguese captain's hat brim.

"Juanillo is here," the voice said.

"I'm not Juanillo. I am his Imperial Majesty," I replied, shaking my bells once more.

But nobody laughed or made any comment.

A huge red moon began to rise from the waters. In its eerie pink glow I could make out the first silhouettes. They were wrapped in rags from head to foot. They slowly closed around me in a circle.

Blurred faces peered at me in the moonlight, examining me. I was studying them surreptitiously, too, trying to find a face or features I recognized. But either because their illnesses had horribly disfigured them or because the light was too dim, I failed to recognize anyone at all that night.

After a short while they had satisfied their curiosity and began to shuffle away as slowly as they had come forward.

I was left alone to witness the most heartrending spectacle. I was searching for a place, somewhere to fling myself down. But the whole deck was strewn with bodies. Some lay on their backs. Others were sitting up. Others were still sprawled in confused groups. The worst cases were in the forecastle. A candle was burning in the center of the cabin, but they all seemed to prefer to huddle in the shadows. In the corners I could see feet that looked as though they had been sculpted in marble, while the rest of the body was swallowed by the darkness. From time to time a voice begged for some water or something to eat. But there was no food to be had in any of the ships. And no water to waste on these condemned men. When the voice insisted a second time, a chorus of shouts howled it down. Then there was silence again.

Still terrified by that horrific scene, I can imagine your Majesty offhandedly tasting the banquet that fills your table to overflowing, discussing how much pepper there is in this dish, or whether another one has too little saffron, and it makes me angry, very angry. Then I feel sorry that you know nothing about hunger. The truth is, Don Carlos, that you know nothing at all about hunger. Nothing. You are more concerned with filling your cannons with gunpowder than you are with filling your subjects' bellies with food. And it's a real shame that you know nothing about it, your Majesty. A shame that none of those fawning courtiers who fill your august ears with flattery and poison should ever have mentioned it to you, so that it's left to me to be the one who must open your imperial eyes. Because I can assure you that if they had advised you just once to go without the chicken broth with milk, sugar and spices that you delighted in for your breakfast, then your reign would have been far more just and great. And your retirement far nobler. And your dreams far sweeter. And your old age more peaceful. Because a monarch can be unaware of everything, except what we innocently term hunger. The fiercest of your foes. Impervious to all cannons or decrees, because it scoffs at them, conquers them all with the needs it creates. It is hunger who decimates your armies. Sinks your ships. Fills the nights with criminals and the squares with scroungers. Who gives priests their authority and power. Who prostitutes women. Turns children old overnight. Who is the father of all vices. Who breeds adulation. Stirs up treason. Tempts with gambling. Condemns to drink. Puts fingers in other people's pockets. Puts the dagger in stomachs. Necks into yokes. The power of hunger is so great it is equal to that of God himself. Because it can give life or take it away. Decide the destiny of souls. Bring about wars. Make victories and defeats. Topple kingdoms. Discover continents. Conquer nations. It is all-powerful.

There is so much truth in what I am telling you that if people could choose their own king, then we would see many monarchs overthrown by their cooks. If Bañuelo promised to serve his famous white sauce, made from rose water, white ginger, almonds and a whole stick of boiled cinnamon, at every table in the land, then his power would extend far beyond that of your palace's kitchen and the imperial gut—it would encompass all the Spanish Empire and the universal gut itself. The same would have happened with Sardinas, Don Álvaro de Luna's master cook, and with Jotxim, the head cook in your grandfather Fernando El Católico's kitchen, whom he held in far greater esteem than he did his devout wife Isabel, who was more dried up and wrinkled than a raisin, or with Lopera, who enticed your mother Juana La Loca with his preserves. And what can I say of the famous Ruperto de Nola, cook to the viceroy of Naples and author of the *Book of Stews*? He knew two hundred and forty-three recipes. Just imagine how he could have/governed, simply issuing one of them by decree every other day: "I, Ruperto de Nola, King by the Grace of My Stews of the kingdoms of Castilla, León, Aragón, Galicia, Valencia, Granada, Jerez, Mallorca, the two Sicilies, Naples, Jerusalem, the Low Countries, the Indies both East and West, etc., etc., having regard for the supreme interests of the Empire and of each and every one of its inhabitants, do decree, in consultation with my ministers, that today Thursday the such-and-such of the year of our lord Jesus Christ fifteen hundred and something, baked eggplant is to be eaten at every table in all my kingdoms. To this effect, first peel several eggplants and then cut them into three or four slices. Then boil them lightly in a mutton stock with two onions. When the eggplant is soft, chop it finely on a board, add some grated Aragón cheese and several egg yolks; stir the mixture together and chop it into small pieces as if you were stuffing a kid goat. Season it with fine spices: ginger, nutmeg, parsley. Return the eggplant to the fire. When it is a golden brown, remove it from the heat, and serve with sugar and cinnamon.

The authorities in every town are to supply the eggplants and other ingredients; the citizens are to follow strictly the indications laid down in this decree for the said recipe.

Any violation of these instructions will be severely punished.

Publish and file as appropriate, etc."

Just imagine the reaction to a decree of that kind, your Highness. There would of course be some who wouldn't want to eat eggplant that day, since there are always a few people who are dissatisfied by nature and who feel it their duty to oppose everything, but for the majority it would be like manna from heaven. And the rich would rejoice as well as the poor, since duchesses would not have to rack their brains thinking of what to serve for luncheon and so would have time free to devote themselves to decking themselves out in all their finery, for the greater glory of your court. People would also go around in anxious expectation wondering what the next decree might bring, and your royal criers would no longer have to shout to make themselves heard, as they do now, when your subjects are tired of hearing phrases they cannot understand and that always end either in deception or in a good thrashing, so they hurry past the criers or simply go on with their own chatter and ignore them entirely. Because I tell you that everyone is tired of promises that always come to nothing, so they turn a deaf ear to all royal proclamations; and yet how gladly they would all listen to a good recipe! Their mouths would water and with tears in their eyes they would thank the heavens for blessing them with such a king. Amen.

PART VIII

WELL, YOUR Majesty, Juanillo can imagine you now. You are in your retreat at Yuste. In your private chamber. You have been placed on cushions, like a newborn baby, close to the window that gives on to the church interior. You yourself ordered the window built in your bedroom wall, and had the other windows, which looked out onto the fields and hills of Extremadura, stopped up. Through the window, hidden from the eyes of the monks behind heavy brocade curtains, you follow the holy offices you proffer day and night for the souls of your mother and sister. Those two recent deaths make your own seem that much closer. And that frightens you. The past rises up against you. Torments you. Accuses you. Has lost all meaning. Seems one huge irredeemable mistake. The all-powerful Caesar Augustus, lord of the whole world, wishes he were a boy again. So that he, who never had a mother, could have one now. So that he, whose mother was hidden for half a century, could hide in her lap. Shut his eyes and listen to her heartbeat. Be lulled to sleep by the sound of that primordial rhythm in his ears. That language without words. Fall asleep while the music flows from her old heart like blood through the veins. Forget the world. Forget himself. But it's all in vain. There is no way for him to recapture the music that death has snatched from him. His mother's heart is an organ without wind. An organ with its bellows punctured. Its pipes blocked with dust. Perhaps you will cry for her, you think, hidden behind your brocade curtain. My poor mother, you think. Torn apart by the struggle between father and husband. Split between those two men who fought over her. They were fighting for Castilla, not Juana, but she was the battlefield for a duel without quarter. The duel between two men who thought they loved her, and perhaps really did. And Juana suffered in secret. Her health broke down in silent protest. My mother was always ill, and I never knew why. Always laid low. Stretched out like a wounded bird. Always with that same expression of infinite weariness. My poor mother, you think, while the sound of the church organ invades everywhere. Now your memories are floating in the organ music, which is like a flowing river: the death of your father when you were six, a father you barely knew, a death that had taken place in a far-off kingdom known as Spain, and yet you cried over him. And you were angry at yourself for crying. At last your mother would take care of you. You would have her all to yourself. But she had loved him too much. She still belonged to him. She blamed your grandfather Fernando, who had nothing to do with the death. And when he found himself rejected, your grandfather's rage grew and grew. Vague news of a war between the two of them. Rumors that she had been shut away. Mad, disheveled. Clutching a dead baby girl that no one could persuade her to surrender, because she wanted to give her suck. Howling naked in the room where she was locked up. Talking with your father's ghost as if it were her doll. It was only later that you learned the truth. She was not mad, but it suited everyone to believe she was. You hated your grandfather for that, but did not have the courage to confront him with it. You wanted to be king. Emperor. She was in the way. You kept her locked up all through your reign. You let the people poke fun at her: Juana La Loca, driven mad by love. Now, within the space of a few months your mother has died and you have abdicated the throne. We are at peace, you think as the monks' prayers drift up to your window. But in the silence of the night you feel your mother calling you. Every night your Highness hears his mother's voice. And your heart leaps. For an instant the king's tired old heart beats with childish joy because his mother is calling him. A mother erasing the past. Driving away death. Yet every night his mother's voice says the same thing. "I had a terrible dream: I dreamt a monstrous giant cat, white as ermine, was devouring my innards." Just remembering that dream fills you with terror. So then you close the heavy curtains and, clutching your cane with hands crippled by gout, laboriously make your way to your study. The walls of the bedroom are lined in black, and heavy black curtains cover all the windows. The only decoration in this room of mourning is a crucifix, a life-size ivory crucifix. That and your paintings. The Titians your Highness can never be apart from. There is a full-length portrait of Felipe. Another of the empress Isabel, and a third of your sister Leonor. Of the three, you like the one of Leonor best. And Don Carlos pauses in front of the portrait. He struggles to lift his head, bent by the years, and looks at the painting with a gray, almost empty gaze. Leonor is wearing a blue brocade dress in which gold and silver threads trace elegant arabesques. A coral necklace and a pair of coral earrings set in silver complete her modest attire. The single strand of her necklace intertwines with a lock of dark hair that falls to her waist, setting off the white of her throat and the red of the coral. She is wearing the rest of her hair tied up with ribbons the same color as her dress. The shading of her neck is done to great effect, as are the almost invisible freckles the artist has painted on her bosom. Yet it is the expression the master has succeeded in giving to her eyes which draws your Highness's gaze almost irresistibly. They show a meek sadness that is as deep as an abyss and makes you feel giddy. Which makes your prominent lower lip tremble. Then the music swells again, takes over the church next door, and fills your room despite the protection of the heavy black curtains. The music flows like a river, sweeping away old blame, ancient memories. And Don Carlos remembers how he gave his sister to the King of Portugal in a marriage negotiated for reasons of state. A woman who was opening like a rosebud. An old, hunchbacked king. A brilliant move which guaranteed that Portugal would become part of the Spanish Empire. A daughter. A widow. A sister coming back to Spain. An only daughter, left as a peace offering. A mother who would never see her daughter again. A good piece of business. A widow and a rosebud, a mother separated from her daughter, a wife for Francisco I, a gift to test his goodwill and to seal lasting peace with France. A masterstroke. Not a son, not a brother, a chessplayer. Now, only keeping himself on his feet with the aid of his cane, standing staring at her portrait, he would dearly love to be able to rewrite time. Or better still, to tear out all its pages and start again. Or even better than that, to be a chess piece rather than a player. A simple pawn. At most a bishop. From now on, his son will be the one moving the pieces. Partly relieved by that thought, Don Carlos continues on his way to his study. He slowly crosses the room draped for mourning. Walks between giant maps of the world which mean nothing anymore. Pays no attention to the portable organ he has taken with him on all his campaigns. Until finally he reaches his seat. There he pauses once more. He climbs awkwardly into it, like a child, his twisted, rheumatic fingers clutching the black velvet curtain behind it. His cane falls from his grasp. He supports himself against the chair back, and finally manages to settle into it. Sitting on the pile of cushions under the black curtain, he looks like the portrait of a newborn baby. One of those frail princes whose life drains away in the cradle. Whose portrait in dark sad colors is added to the collection in a forgotten gallery somewhere, alongside others that are equally anonymous. Something is weighing on his mind. He stares at the black walls in silence. The smoke from the incense in the church that seeps through the curtains makes him cough. He feels he is drowning. He takes out a handkerchief and wipes away the spittle stuck to his beard. I am disgusting, he thinks. All old people are a bit disgusting, you think. And you stifle the impulse to reach out and pick up the silver-handled mirror on the table to look at yourself. Your eyes are looking for something else among the untidy piles of papers and books on the desk. They search anxiously, until a sudden gleam lights them up. Your gaze has come to rest on Juanillo's bulky manuscript. You lean forward painfully and grasp it with trembling hands. Your gnarled fingers go through the sheets of paper until you come to the one where you stopped reading several hours earlier. As you pick it up, the blue of your eyes becomes deeper, like the color of the ocean. And in the monarch's weary pupils the shapes of three tiny ships appear. You close your eyes. Your nostrils flare as you think you detect a stirring in the stale air of your room. The oppressive odor of incense, the sickly smell of the velvet drapes, the vapors from medicinal herbs and potions are all swept away in a gust of sea breeze. A salty tang invades the room. The breeze ruffles the curtains. You can feel its fresh caress on your wrinkled skin. A strange mixture of sounds and voices fills your ears. You no longer hear the monks' litany. The organ music continues unheeded. Its music no longer flows through your past. Your ears are filled with commands, with the shouts of the men carrying them out, the slap of sails as they unfurl in the wind, the squeaking of pulleys, creaking of timbers from the ribs to the masts, the echoing sound of empty holds. His Majesty opens his eyes. But his Majesty's eyes no longer see the walls in mourning, nor Titian's paintings, nor the seat next to the window, nor the window onto the church, nor the portable organ which went with him on all his campaigns, nor the meaningless maps, nor the big globe someone has placed by the worktable, nor the table itself, with its jumble of papers, nor the bulky manuscript in his hands, nor even those hands, crippled by gout. What his Highness sees is something else. He sees the men on the yardarms, scampering up the rigging, tightening the ropes, loosening the sails. He sees the *Trinidad*, busy as a smashed anthill. Rearing like a colt. Sails suddenly bloom from every mast. Sails whose shapes had almost been forgotten. The whole ship has become a white pyramid rocking on the waves. And if your Highness puts on the eyeglasses he keeps like the richest jewel in his gold casket studded with precious stones, then he will see the men contemplating this display in mute amazement. As if this were the very first time. In mystic rapture, as if they were priests gazing on the magnificent face of their god. None of them looking down at the ocean. The ocean the sails are going to help us defy. All of us in the sway of an enchantment even your Imperial Majesty cannot elude. Because after three months' wait, the wind has started to blow again. The fleet is on the move. My story picks up speed once more. Fills with wind. With all thanks to Juanillo Ponce, erstwhile Count of the Spice Islands, your buffoon, your servant, your friend, your child. Your mother. The only one who can tear down the velvet curtains draping your walls with mourning. Who can open the blocked-up windows. Flood the tomb you live in with salt and sun. Drag you from your retreat. Take you far from there. Erase the past. Drive away death. As long as your sight lasts. As long as my life lasts. As long as this music goes on.

THERE WE were, kept apart from all that was going on. Because everything was decided and took place at the stern of the ship. And we were apart from it all. Silent. Furtive. On the lookout. For whatever snaked its way to us from the other end of the ship like a trail of gunpowder. And ignited into a rumor in one or another of the sick mouths. Twisted, incomprehensible. Like the news that we were passing close to two large islands. Cipangu, the pearl of the East. And Sumbid, or something like that, that was how it sounded in a rotten crimson mouth. The Captain General has said so. Or so they said. Quoting an explorer from Venice. Whose name was Polo. Cipangu. Or so they said. The most easterly of the islands in the Indian Ocean. The first we should have come across. Or so they said. And we were going to take on supplies. And water. Our hunger was over. We were traveling seventy leagues a day now that the wind had returned. And the Spice Islands were within reach. The Captain said so.

Yet there was nothing. Three days on the lookout. Nothing.

Hanging from the rigging like rag dolls. All ears for any shout from the crow's nest, where someone from the world of the healthy was posted, searching the sky for birds and the sea for any other signs. But nothing.

We did not see the islands. We had no way of knowing whether they really existed. Cipangu. Sumbid. Or even if we were on the right course. Or if the rumor was true, or they were making fun of us. Those in the other world. Cipangu. Sumbid.

Then one afternoon, there was something. We sat there staring at each other, trying to see who was still alive. And something crashed into the prow of the ship. One of us leaned over the side to look. And a sound came from his mouth, a mouth like a split pomegranate. A sound something like a laugh. So we all went over to him. Using each other to help us along. Dragging the weakest with us. And stared down in ecstasy at a branch. A branch that still had green leaves on it. And plump fruit. We stared and stared, until at last one of us staggered down the ship to the frontier between our two worlds. Shaking with illness and emotion. He waved to the men in the other world. Several of them gathered beyond the capstan. Stared at us perplexed. Advanced slowly toward us, but stopped at the invisible frontier. Looked at each other, unable to make up their minds. They stood there for a while, until the boldest among them asked what was going on. Shouted at us, "What's going on?" None of us had the courage to reply. So as not to show our mouths. Seeing the curiosity in their eyes, we lost our voices. Little by little, we fell back. Went to hide once more in the forecastle. Keeping our secret. Keeping the branch with its green leaves to ourselves. And its plump fruit. Sorry we had called attention to ourselves. Little by little. Ashamed. But before we could disappear, we heard voices at the far end of the ship. The curious group came to a halt. Turned their backs on us. Because there were more and more voices from the stern. So, little by little, we regained our space on the deck. Until we reached the capstan dividing the two worlds. Then ventured even further, because all the shouting made us want to see what was going on. Everyone was hugging each other on the poop deck. And staring up at the sky. We peered up as well. And saw seagulls, your Highness. Wheeling round the masts. Screeching in the wake of the ships. So then we hugged each other too. But we did not shout like the others. We kept our mouths shut. We just looked. Looked and looked until night fell. Silent. Furtive. Until night fell and the seagulls left us. We heard their last cries, then they left. And silence fell again. But this time only for an instant, no more. The men's voices soon rang out once again. Talking of cloves and cinnamon. Of turquoise green lakes. Of clear waters where fish swam like precious jewels among coral reefs. The chorus of voices swelled. On the far side of the capstan. At the stern of the ship. Under an indifferent, cold, unextraordinary sky. Snatches of phrases reached us in the prow. Disconnected words. Isolated sounds. Echoes that died away across the boundless ocean.

That night, excited by the closeness of land, we, too, had our dreams.

Silent. Furtive. Dreaming.

Dawn's pale glow caught us all dreaming.

In that hesitant first light of day we saw, for the first time in four months, the dark outline of islands. Harsh silhouettes against a white sky. High, pointed peaks. Wreathed in wisps of mist, like dribbles of night. A somber, desolate landscape. Entirely at odds with our dreams. And so we took advantage of the privilege of being sick and closed our eyes again. Went back to our dreams. Until the sun was high in the sky and the ships closer to the islands. We could see the reef. Waves breaking over it in a garland of spray. A huge, roaring, whiter-than-white garland. Breathing in salt water like an enormous gill. Spouting out a stream of water like a gigantic whale. Like a whole school of whales. Outside the reef, the seas were blue. A deep, violent blue. Beyond the barrier though, they were the soft turquoise color we had imagined them to be all night. And in our dreams.

What we hadn't seen in our dreams was what happened

next. One longboat full of heavily armed men shot out from each ship. Rowed and rowed until they had crossed the reef. Made for the beach. Gone to fetch food. Or so they said. If you kill anyone, bring us their intestines, we said. And start the bargaining so we can have spices in exchange for our trinkets. From the crow's nests they spotted a village on the beach. Not from down where we were. But there was a village, or so they said. Which meant fresh water for our feverish mouths. Or so they said. Fresh intestines are the best medicine for our ills, we insisted. But they said: You should try the local fruits, they are sweet and juicy. Hunger like a red-hot iron in the stomach. Try to think of something else. Kill this empty time of waiting. But that was impossible. How could it be done?

A short while later, more shouting. Beyond the capstan, at the stern of the ship, everyone was staring in the direction of the beach. Pointing. Gesticulating. Pressed against the rail. We could see them looking, but could not see what they were looking at because the ship was stern on to the beach. What we could see was thick black smoke rising from the island. Disappearing in the curtain of vegetation that began where the sand ended, then reappearing above the trees, and finally dispersing in the white sky. And beside the turquoise lagoon, in the midst of that black mass of cloud like a fish, we could see violet tongues of flame, licking the sky. But we could not see what was being burned. We had no idea what was going on. No one on the ship would talk to us. They talked among themselves. Pointed. Gesticulated. But they wanted nothing to do with us.

Time went by, and suddenly we heard the sound of oars shattering the crystal of the lagoon. And the clatter of some arquebuses. We saw the longboats heading back to the ships. Serrano standing in the prow of one of them. Hands stained with blood. The hands of some of the oarsmen, straining at their oars. All of them silent. Serious. Serrano and the other men from the *Trinidad* climbed on board the flagship. The others left. Nobody spoke. A weird silence. Those of us on this side of the border were unable to cross into the other world.

Unable to ask anything. Killing the empty time of waiting. Waiting for any rumor to pass through the invisible bars.

Some time after that, two men appeared with a bucket. A bucket of water. Fresh, clear water. With a slight smell of earth. Fertile earth. Of leaf mold. Roots. Pebbles. And a taste of water. Not the dark, evil-smelling water of our barrels. A real bucket of water. The men left it on the capstan, like an offering. Before they retreated again, I asked them, "Where is the water from?" "From the island," they replied. "What happened there?" I wanted to know. "Nothing," they said, without looking at me. Nothing happened. Flames still lit up the beach, but nothing had happened. And we set sail again because the Spice Islands were so close by, but nothing had happened.

Island after island in that first archipelago. Each time, a longboat full of heavily armed men shot out from each ship. And in the bottom of every longboat were sackfuls of mirrors, hawkbells and other trinkets. They rowed and rowed until they crossed the reef. Made for the beach. They have gone to fetch food. Or so they said. And to start bargaining for spices in exchange for our cheap trinkets. And some of them did return with fish. Oranges. Coconuts. Oil. Palm wine. Bananas. The occasional chicken. And with a handful of cloves. A pinch of cinnamon. No more than a hint of pepper. All sure signs that we must be close to the Spice Islands. Or so they said. The Captain General paced nervously up and down the deck. Because he was getting closer and closer to his goal. After two years roaming the seas. Blinder than a blind man thanks to Faleiro's calculations. But at last he was close.

Island after island in that first archipelago. They returned from some of them with food, from others with nothing. With their arms stained in blood up to their elbows. Leaving behind them on the beaches a thick black cloud of smoke that disappeared into the curtain of vegetation. And violet-colored flames licking the sky. But nothing had happened. Nothing happened on any of the islands. Even though the rumors ran like wildfire through the ship. That on one island the skiff tied to the stern of the longboat had been stolen. And that the Captain was so angry he wanted to teach them a lesson. So he landed with forty armed men. Burnt down forty huts. All there were on the island. And burnt the canoes as well, together with many of the islanders. All those who could not escape into the jungle. Because the jungle was impenetrable. Our men could not make any progress through it. And I asked when they brought us food, "Is it true what they say about what happened on that island?" "No," they told me. "Nothing happened." Even though sometimes at night the beaches were lit by flames. And Serrano washed his hands in the clear water of the lagoon before he came on board to talk to the Captain. And Serrano's hands stained the turquoise green of the lagoon red. And the only sounds were the tinkling of the bells on his hat brim and the crackling of the flames.

Island after island. And nothing happened on any of them. Or so they said. But I know that on at least one of them something did happen, because on one of the islands Gonzalvo de Vigo deserted. He was the one who always carried a bag of corn with him, if you remember. Gonzalvo, who had gone mad, chose to stay on an island. Or so they said. Mad ever since he had eaten the corpse of Gaspar Díaz, the *Santiago*'s storeman. Or so they said. But he wasn't mad. It was just that the air was so balmy and the beach so white. The palm trees so tall and graceful. Such sweet and juicy fruit everywhere. Ripening in the sun within your grasp. Then there was the gurgling sound of water rushing down between the rocks. Always fresh. Collecting in pools where they filled their barrels. Enough for a man to wash off all the salt of all the seas in the world. Or so they said. So Gonzalvo took off his breastplate and his helmet, his sweat-soaked shirt and his breeches and plunged into the water before anyone could stop him. To wash off the salt from all the seas. Even though everyone was shouting "We've got to go!" at him and staring at the impenetrable jungle around the pool. Gonzalvo, with water up to his neck, looked down at his own pale white feet under the water. And smiled. Or stared at the tiny fish swimming around him. With everybody shouting "We've got to go!" as they retreated away from the curtain of jungle they could feel pushing them back to the beach. Where the longboats were waiting for them. Waiting to take them back to the ships. But Gonzalvo didn't want to go back. Some of them threatened him. He just laughed, a madman's laugh. Others made him promises. He just stared at his feet, so pale and white under the water beneath him. Or they spoke of Basilia, of his grandmother's corn field. But he just played with some pebbles, letting them go on the surface and watching as they dropped slowly through the transparent water.

This went on for a while until Serrano, their commander, arrived. He ordered them to pull back to the beach, to leave Gonzalvo. Everyone obeyed Serrano, his hands as small as a young girl's but stained with blood. His face grimy under the black brim of his hat, with its jingling hawkbells casting their spell. So there they left Gonzalvo, naked, smiling to himself. Washing off the salt of all seas in the transparent water of the pool.

What could his fate have been in a place like that? Could he have managed to survive? What became of him?

For years I asked myself these questions, your Highness. And it was because I tried to answer them and a hundred similar ones that I was persecuted, shut in dungeons, and had my pension taken from me.

With the result that if your Majesty wishes to know what became of Gonzalvo de Vigo, I suggest you find out yourself. Juanillo prefers to stay silent about whatever he might have discovered, since he swore under oath that he knew nothing.

THE NEXT episode took place in Zubu and, like our first three weeks there, it is relaxed and made up of long sentences.

For the first time in the twenty months since we began our voyage at Sevilla, after all the misfortunes I have told you about and many more I have preferred to pass over in silence, we came into contact with a world similar to our own. A world whose nature and values we thought we understood. Less shut off from us than those we had glimpsed until then. Less hostile and ambiguous. More predictable.

At least, that's what we believed for the first three weeks, until one day . . .

But I'll tell you about that day later on, your Highness.

For now, the day is the seventh of April. The episode begins as we are sailing into the port of Zubu very early one morning.

The ships glided over the surface of the waters like the swans on your ornamental ponds, your Majesty. They moved silently across the still lagoon beyond the reef, passing one by one up the natural channel the pilots could recognize by its different color. They edged toward the beach, the wind from their sails stirring the palm trees, casting their shadows across the sleeping village, and then, when the soundings showed the water was too shallow, they turned majestically and formed a tight circle offshore.

Without a word, the men slackened the ropes, furled the sails. For once the pulleys didn't groan or the yardarms creak. The capstan spun in silence. The anchors slid into the crystal waters and hardly had they hit the bottom of the sea than clouds of trusting, curious fish swarmed round them.

The ships floated at anchor. The light increased.

The operation completed, the Captain ordered all our flags raised and all the guns to be fired in a volley.

The gunners made ready. They silently loaded their guns. They took a last look at the still lagoon, the deserted beach, the sleeping village, and, still in silence, lit their fuses.

Instinctively, we all covered our ears, but this did not prevent the explosion.

The jungle shook. Cannonballs smashed into the calm lagoon. Seagulls flew off in terror. Parrots escaped screeching into the undergrowth. The sleeping village turned into an anthill someone had trodden on.

A few moments later, when everything appeared to have calmed down, Don Fernando sent his slave Enrique ashore as an interpreter.

Enrique was from Sumatra and spoke the Malay tongue, which these people apparently understood.

The slave was lavishly decked out like a Moorish prince, and he took with him rich gifts for the village's king and his wives.

Yet there was something in his look that made me think he had other intentions.

And he did, your Highness, but he could not carry them out until much later on.

While waiting for him to return, wondering why Juan Serrano had not been sent this time and whether Enrique would come back with bloodstained hands like the Portuguese captain always did, I passed the time staring down into the lagoon.

The water was so clear that despite its deep turquoise color I could clearly see the bottom and everything that moved or lay on it.

I have no wish to overwhelm you with a complete list of what I saw, especially since neither of us has much time left; and yet I must describe some of them to you or I would be failing in the duties of this or any other narrative. How else could I give you a sense of the time that passed while Enrique was on the island?

There were sponges as black as the velvet drapes on the walls of your rooms at Yuste, and others the color and shape of the oranges in your Alhambra palace.

There were giant crabs that glinted blue like sword blades in moonlight; they darted back and forth, also like sword blades in the moonlight. And every kind of coral, your Highness. Some as white as snow, like the trees in our squares on winter mornings. Others as red as Barbara de Blomberg's lips, like the trees on the battlefields in Tunis.

But it was the fish that most caught my attention, your Majesty. Never in my life had I imagined such bright, extraordinary colors and shapes. They were exactly like jewels, Don Carlos. Jewels that would make the most elegantly bedecked lady grow pale with envy. Jewels finer than any worn by the empress or adorning any of your crowns. Jewels surpassing the fantasy of the greatest of the royal goldsmiths. Jewels too exquisite to be kept in any casket. Too intricate for any jeweler to copy. Jewels, from the French *joie*. And from the Latin *iocus*, meaning "game." Jewels of infinite value, a boundless range of precious stones. Green malachite. Polished azurite. Lapis lazuli as deep and hard as the ocean. Speckled jade. Amber. Cornelian as red as blood. Amethyst. Striped jasper. Porphyry, like the jar you keep your perfumes in. Rock crystal. Veined agate, in glorious settings. Mother-of-pearl. Ebony. Amaranth. Blue and pink fired diamonds. A few fish that looked like fish. A host that looked like jewels. Fish like Byzantine mosaics. Like the stained glass windows at Rheims. Italian bronzes. Enameling from Venice, with golden figures on a blue and white ground. Like Limoges porcelain, embossed on blue. Or on gray, with details picked out in gold. Or with glints of yellow and pink, like Moorish ceramics. Fish like Faenza pottery, with grotesque figures. Or a rich creamy color, like dishes from Florence. Fish like those Roman ivory sculptures portraying the animals of Paradise. And other more subtle ones, like ivories from Paris. Fish the shape of dragons. Or Venetian cameos. Chess pieces. Flame-haired angels. Unicorns. Chimerae. Winged griffins. Moorish pitchers. Brooches. Pendants. The double-headed imperial eagle. Golden scepters. Jewels for a day of joy.

All the lagoon was a jewel case, a precious turquoise casket, a liquid box for a liquid jewel. It was also a monument to a story no one wanted to tell. A shrine more important for your realm than the one containing the arm with which Charlemagne wielded his sword Joyeuse.

You don't understand a word? You'll come to understand what I'm talking about, but by then it will be too late, just as it is now. So be quiet and listen, because here is Enrique back from his visit on shore as our ambassador.

ENRIQUE'S MISSION was a great success, your Highness. The king of Zubu wished us to be his guests. He also wished to embrace the Christian faith, and was anxious to recognize you as his sovereign. Furthermore, he could locate the Spice Islands exactly, and said they were less than a day's sailing from his island. He himself would take us there after we had recovered from our voyage.

Don Fernando was overjoyed. He embraced Enrique in front of everyone. Called him "my faithful, dear friend." He gave him the turban and the velvet cape he had worn before the king of Zubu to keep as a gift. He also promised that when we returned to Spain he would make him a free, respectable man.

Everyone present greeted the news with loud rejoicing. Everyone that is except for Basco Gallego, who had been in the delegation as Enrique's escort.

That huge blond man, who somehow always smelt of cow's milk, was suspicious of the Moor's behavior. And since he was frank and direct to the point of brutality, he told all and sundry that Enrique and the king of Zubu were plotting something against us. But nobody believed him.

Basco Gallego said that at a certain point in their discussion, our interpreter had ceased translating and had launched into a long conversation with the king in their own language. The men in the escort had not understood a word, but they had not dared intervene.

When the mission had finished and they were about to board the longboat to return to the ships, Basco Gallego had confronted Enrique. "What did you say to the king?" he wanted to know. Enrique replied that he had told him that if he wanted peace there would be peace, but that if he was thinking of war, then he should remember we could destroy the island in the twinkling of an eye. "Was that all?" Basco asked. When the slave nodded, he added, "And does it take so many words to say that in your language?" Unperturbed, Enrique answered that it did. Then Basco asked if it was not true that smiles and knowing looks meant the same in any language. To which the other man, not yielding an inch, replied that they did not. And he told Basco to leave him alone, since he did not owe him any explanation of what had happened.

"You are a cunning devil," Basco muttered to him as they walked down the beach to the longboat. "A devil and a villain."

Once they were back on board ship, Basco told all this to anyone who would listen. But nobody paid him any heed.

Since he was no fool, he quickly shut up. He did not say anything more, and from then on behaved as though he had accepted the official version of events.

Whether or not he was right—we had no idea at the time, and I have no wish to anticipate what happened later—the fact is that the sly expression I noticed on Enrique's face when he left on his mission had completely changed. When he came back on board he was wearing his customary meek, submissive slave's mask. An expression as stiff and inexpressive as that of a Chinese porcelain mask. And equally inscrutable.

At first light the next morning the Captain sent the chaplain, Balderrama, and some sailors to prepare for the celebration of mass.

A short while later the longboats took the crews to the beach. They all wore full armor. Only the sick and a few men whose task it was to cover the crews' backs or any possible retreat were left on the ships.

It was a radiant morning, and by the time everyone was gathered in the spot the chaplain had chosen the sun was high in the sky. It was beginning to be hot.

The king of Zubu wore the same Chinese mask as Enrique.

He accepted the gifts Don Fernando had brought him without any show of emotion: a yellow and purple silk tunic, a red cap, several glass bead necklaces, and two beakers embossed in gold. He did not react in any way.

Nor did he react when Don Fernando ordered three men to strike him, their Captain, with swords and daggers, to show the king that he was invulnerable in his armor.

The king watched the demonstration impassively. When it was over, he told Enrique that a man like that could defeat a thousand of his own men.

Enrique conveyed this to Don Fernando, who smiled with satisfaction.

When mass had been said, Don Fernando explained the meaning of the Cross to the king, and told him of the mission the emperor had given him to plant one wherever we landed. He also asked the king, through Enrique, if he wanted an alliance with the emperor and if he wished to embrace the Christian faith. If that were the case, he himself would instruct the king in the Holy Scriptures and explain all the dogmas of our faith to him. Once he had undserstood everything, he would baptize him, which would make him our equal.

Without once letting his mask slip, the king agreed to everything.

The Captain was pleased at this, and instructed Enrique to tell the king that if he had any enemies his new allies would be glad to fight them on his behalf. This was another of the advantages of becoming a Christian.

The king replied that he would be happy to have the ruler of a nearby island, who refused to obey him, taught to pay him proper respect.

The Captain promised that he would personally see to it that the man was taught a lesson. He asked for only two things in return: that the king adopt Christianity with all his heart, and that he tell him exactly where the Spice Islands were to be found.

Without removing his mask, the king agreed to everything.

Then the Captain said that since they were in complete agreement, he would disembark his crews from the ships, as they were in bad shape after our long voyage. He said he had several sick men who needed special food and attention. And one or two dead to whom he wished to give a Christian burial.

The king answered that we would be his guests as long as we wished.

The Captain stepped two paces forward and kissed him on the cheeks.

The king of Zubu showed neither pleasure nor repulsion.

Don Fernando took two steps back, declared that this was a day of rejoicing for both peoples, and turned on his heel to walk down to the beach.

He had only gone a couple of steps when Enrique called

him back. The king wanted to know whether worshipping the Cross would make him invulnerable like the Captain.

Don Fernando turned back again and said with a smile that of course it would.

With that he walked off down to the beach again, commenting that the king of Zubu had seemed to him a sensible, trustworthy fellow. Everyone around him thought the same.

Everyone except Basco Gallego, who still did not trust the king. But he said nothing.

He did tell me of his suspicions though, thinking I might be able to make the Captain listen. But if the Captain didn't want to, it was all the same to him. He had warned them what had happened during Enrique's mission, and nobody had wanted to know. What more could he do? He was only sure of one thing: He was not going to fall into the trap. Basco Gallego was not going to be caught napping, he said.

I did not know what to make of it all. Perhaps it was simply another fanciful idea that had got into his huge giant's head. But I liked to listen to him. I felt good beside him. The smell of cow's milk that his vast body exuded was reassuring and awoke a strange tenderness in me.

He was also my only link to what was going on. Over the following days, while I was slowly recovering from the ravages that illness had wrought on my body, we became close friends. He came to see me at dusk every day, bringing me fruit and other food, and told me of the main events that had taken place. I anxiously awaited his daily visit.

We sick men were put in a large, cool hut surrounded by palm trees. It was a few yards from the beach and was sheltered by a spit of land covered in thick vegetation that jutted out into the sea.

Near the door of the hut grew a tree with enormous flowers that had white fleshy petals and gave off an exquisite perfume.

It was under this tree that I waited for Basco Gallego each afternoon.

I spent the rest of the day staring at the turquoise lagoon and listening fascinated to the distant roar of the reef.

The color of the water in the lagoon changed at every instant. It would sparkle or darken without warning. Sometimes it became milky like wormwood. At others, it turned as gray as a child's sadness, then suddenly became as black as adult despair. Most of the time, though, it was a transparent turquoise, as in a dream.

Beyond the reef, the color of the sea itself never varied from the deepest blue.

When the shadow of the palm trees began to lengthen, I went to sit under the tree in front of our door. Intoxicated by the perfume of its flowers, with the cool sea breeze on my face, I waited for Basco.

He plunged out of the jungle like an elephant, smashing branches and getting tangled up in the undergrowth. Then he stood there, frowning and menacing, on the edge of the clearing our hut was built in. Even though I was always sitting in the same spot, his eyes would search for me, and only when he had spotted me did his expression change. He paused for a second, like an actor getting into the character he is about to play. Then he stepped forward, smiling and looking unconcerned. His smile was forced, and the lack of concern did not come naturally to him, but he saw it as the way one should behave toward a sick friend, and I appreciated the effort he made.

Without a word he would place the day's offering in front of me: rice, pork, oranges, a squash, some garlic or a bowl of honey, and then study my reaction.

I had to devour whatever he brought even if I wasn't in the least hungry, pretending not to notice how he was spying on me. Once I had finished, he would slap me on the back encouragingly, the smile still on his lips.

Only then did he begin to tell me of all that had happened during the day. As he did, he gradually relaxed and became the Basco Gallego all of us knew.

He never beat around the bush, but always approached his stories in the same direct, frank way that he approached life, taking it for granted that I would be interested in what he had to say.

With the king of Zubu's approval, they had decided to make the main open space of the village into our cemetery.

The king told Enrique that since the Captain was free to dispose of the king's life and that of his subjects, he was all the more entitled to dispose of his land.

Enrique conveyed this to Don Fernando, who smiled contentedly. He ordered a cross to be put up first, to consecrate the ground.

They buried two men, then a third who had died in one of the holds of the *Victoria* without anyone noticing. His body was so decomposed they had to carry him out wrapped in an old sail.

Basco also said they had found human remains in all the ships' holds. They put them into sacks and opened a fourth grave.

The problem was that the inhabitants of Zubu went on using the burial ground as their main square. They went on buying and selling produce and any slaves they might have captured and all kinds of other goods. The women did their cooking there. The children played among the graves.

Then, when they found a pig rummaging in one of the graves, the Captain ordered them to build a stone wall around the cemetery. So now they spent the whole day breaking stone, even though there was so much wood available all around. It was useless work. But it was more useless still to complain.

The Captain spent the mornings teaching the king the Holy Scriptures. He told him about Moses and the Pharaoh of Egypt, the seven plagues, Job, Jacob and Jonas, Sodom and Gomorrah, Lot and his wife.

Never removing his mask, the king agreed to everything.

Don Fernando smiled with satisfaction. "He will make a good vassal," he said.

He had been told that there were huge black birds in these seas, similar to crows but bigger and heavier. They were said to follow whales; when the whales opened their mouths, the birds would plunge in and tear out the whale's heart to eat.

The islanders said they had seen several of those birds circling over the *Trinidad*.

The women of the island were very pretty and almost as white-skinned as Europeans, but not so prudish. All the men had tried more than one of them. The women preferred the newcomers to their husbands, who were less well-endowed sexually. So they slept with anyone who would have them, and so did our crews. Basco himself had filled several of them with his seed. In their vaginas. On their breasts. Even on their faces. At first he could not remember how it felt. It had been so long! But he soon acquired a taste for it again, and then he could not stop. He could not think of anything else. Except for the plot being hatched against us. But I was the only person he mentioned that to.

Andrés de San Martín also went around with a troubled look on his face. He had asked several officers for paper and ink, but they had refused to give him any. The Captain had ordered two men to follow him. They went along after him, erasing whatever he tried to write with a stick in the sand or by cutting into the bark of trees with a knife. So the astrologer roamed the seashore in silence. From time to time he stopped to draw signs in the sand with his toes. Signs the waves washed away before his guards arrived.

Basco had heard that every night the black birds he had told me about were seen flying over the village or settling on the roofs of the huts. That was why the dogs kept barking at the moon, he said. They went on until dawn, when the birds headed out to sea again, leaving the houses full of a strange, repulsive smell. The whole village was polluted by the stench.

He warned me: Something was happening or was about to happen. But they wouldn't catch him unawares. Not Basco Gallego. He could promise me that. And in the meantime he intended to enjoy the women. He would bring me one as soon as I was better. That would be sure to complete my cure.

They said that Juan Serrano went with one of the king's wives. She was young and beautiful and wore a black and white tunic with a palmleaf hat to keep the sun off. Her fingernails and lips were painted a bright red, which only increased her attractions. She was the most beautiful of all those he had seen, Basco told me. And the Portuguese captain slept with her. Still with his hawkbell hat on. The king knew about it, but nevertheless chose not to remove the mask he always wore.

Every morning he listened to the Captain talking about the mysteries of the faith, the Holy Trinity, the resurrection of the dead, the last judgment. And he agreed with everything.

When Don Fernando judged that he had properly understood all his teachings, he had him baptized.

Prior to that, as a demonstration of the benefits of conversion, he had sent his men to destroy a village on the neighboring island of Matán. The island was ruled by Cilapulapu, who refused to obey and pay tribute to the king of Zubu.

They burned the village down and put up a cross. Sebastián said they should build a column of stone to signify that their hearts had hardened against the place, as they did with Moorish villages. But their commander Juan Serrano would have none of it. He was sticky with blood up to his elbows.

They enjoyed their task a lot because the village was a large one. Basco came to see me late that afternoon and brought me a necklace as a gift.

The king of Zubu said he was very satisfied and that he was anxious to become a Christian.

The Captain had it announced that all the islanders who wished to embrace our faith should destroy their idols in the square, and from then on worship only the Cross.

The next morning there was a huge pile of smashed idols in the square. Don Fernando had a platform built and dressed the king all in white. The king was called Humabon, but he was baptized as Carlos, in your Majesty's honor. Then his mother was given the name Juana La Loca. The chaplain explained that La Loca was not a name, and that we should simply call her Juana. The woman with the painted lips and palmleaf hat was named Isabel. Juan Serrano, who was sitting next to her on the platform, gave her a small painting of the Virgin with the infant Jesus in her arms. She was enchanted with the gift, and promised that she would set it up in the place where she had kept her idols.

Then the two women sat on a heap of embroidered silk cushions and with great decorum the Captain sprinkled them and their followers with muskrose water.

More than eight hundred people were baptized that day.

One person who did not receive baptism was the king's brother, who was reputed to be a great soothsayer and was considered the wisest man on the island. He had come down with a mysterious illness.

One day the old man had begun to talk nonsense, words nobody could understand despite the obvious effort he was making to communicate. Then, on the very day of our arrival, he had started to emit sounds in a strange language which was not that of the island. Nor was it ours. Four days later, exhausted by his efforts and in despair, he had gone dumb. Now he was paralyzed as well.

Many saw what had happened to the old soothsayer as a sign, but of what they did not know.

Basco Gallego also thought that the presence of the menacing black birds, who now all clustered on the roof of the Captain General's hut, must have some hidden meaning. But he kept his mouth shut. He had said his piece after Enrique's mission and nobody had believed him. Now it was their problem. But as far as he, Basco Gallego, was concerned, he was not going to be caught unawares.

I spent hour after hour under the tree outside the door of the hut we were kept in.

The clearing where the hut stood was surrounded by thick jungle, except for a track that led down to the beach.

The jungle was full of strange birds and monkeys that played in the tops of the trees.

Sometimes the monkeys began to leap along the branches, swinging from one to another with deafening cries, a sure warning that an intruder was coming. Usually it was someone curious to spy on us from the safety of the jungle to see if one or another of the sailors had survived.

On other occasions, the hubbub in the treetops was followed

by the crackling of branches and leaves at ground level, which meant we had a visitor.

Once, Andrés de San Martín appeared in the clearing. He did not come crashing through the jungle like Basco Gallego, but emerged almost without a sound. Like a deer gliding through a wood. He stood nervously at the edge of the clearing, ready to flee at the slightest sign of danger.

He stared at the hut with those huge, velvety doe-eyes of his; then began to circle round the clearing at the jungle's edge. He took two timid, almost trembling steps, then stopped once more. He cast anxious glances in all directions, then went on.

I knew that if I called out to him or showed myself he would run away, so I pretended to be asleep.

He completed the circle then cautiously began to advance toward my tree.

When he reached it, he stood on tiptoe to gently pick one of the white flowers the size of a dove that hung from its branches. He bent a branch down but, just as he had grasped the flower in his fingers with the gesture of someone holding a cup of precious liquor, it flew up again. He fell over almost at my feet. I knew he was bound to run away, so I sat up.

At first he looked terrified, but when he recognized me he gave a spontaneous glad smile. There was no doubt he was pleased to see me. Perhaps that was what he was trying to tell me, while he still lay flat on the ground. But the empty cavern of his mouth produced no sound. A look of despair stole across his face. His smile vanished, and his head drooped into the dust.

I helped him up and motioned him to sit beside me.

We sat for a long while leaning back against the same tree, each pretending he didn't know the other was there.

He couldn't say anything to me, and I didn't want to make him feel even more incapable of expressing himself, so at first I said nothing either.

"It seems we've finally reached the Spice Islands," I eventually said. "I've heard the Captain is very happy. We'll soon be back home. We'll all be rich. The voyage was worth it. And I'll be a count."

I was talking quickly, without pausing between any of the

sentences, carefully avoiding any questions or anything that might be construed as one.

All of a sudden I stopped. I got up, went to look for a twig, and smoothed out the ground in front of us with my hands.

San Martín's face shone and a childish joy appeared in his usually sad-looking eyes.

He was tracing the first letters when two armed men burst out of the jungle. As soon as he saw them he dropped the twig and scrubbed out what he had written: "Don Fern . . ." Then he stood up. He gazed at me forlornly and strode off, disappearing back into the jungle from where he had appeared, closely followed by the two men.

One torrid noonday I was sleeping in the perfumed shade of our tree when I thought I sensed a strange presence. The jungle was silent except for the buzzing of insects, but a feeling I could not explain told me something or someone was prowling around.

Thinking it must be an animal, I opened my eyes and tried to keep still.

It was Sebastián, stealing across the clearing. He had emerged from the jungle as stealthily as a tiger, after slipping through the undergrowth without a sound. Not even the monkeys had detected his presence. Now he was advancing toward the hut, stopping with every stride to turn his head left and right before going on. Just like a tiger stalking its prey.

When he reached the hut he walked around it equally cautiously. First he peered in through the window and then through the door, then he walked around the building a second time and knelt down near one of its corners. He considered the spot, looking around him yet again, and then, with the casual ease of a tiger, plunged his hand in through the palm leaves of the wall. He felt around for a while, as if in search of something, stopping all the time to check that he was not being observed. He pulled his arm out and leaned forward. He seemed to be talking to someone through the wall. Soon afterward he swayed back again, looked everywhere around him once more, then began to creep away as cautiously as he had come.

He made for the tree. It was not particularly tall, but had a thick, bulky trunk. His calculated, measured movements suggested a muscular energy capable of bursting out at the first sign of danger. Just like a tiger, your Highness. His broad round face with a golden mustache and his short thick hair the color of old gold only made the resemblance all the more striking.

When I saw him approaching I pretended to be asleep, but kept track of his movements through half-closed eyes.

As soon as he became aware of me, he came to a halt. He stood motionless in the middle of the clearing, almost, or so it seemed, without breathing. He examined me carefully then moved off again, doubtless thinking I really was asleep.

A moment later I saw Juan Carvajo leave the hut.

When his son had fallen ill, the pilot had moved in with us to keep him company. Hijito, as I have said, was the apple of his eye. Carvajo was father, mother, everything to the boy. They were never apart, and lived for each other. So when Hijito became ill, Carvajo told the Captain he was abandoning the venture because there could be nothing more important for him than his son's life.

Touched by the attachment between the two of them, Don Fernando gave him permission to look after his son.

Carvajo did so with a mother's devotion; he never left the boy's side for an instant.

Yet here he was crossing the clearing beneath the merciless midday sun to go and meet Sebastián.

They both seemed nervous, casting glances at the hut and the jungle the whole time they were talking together.

Curiosity tugged at my innards, gnawed my bones. What on earth could those two be talking about? What could they possibly have in common now, when they had spent most of the journey hating each other? What were they up to?

I couldn't move in case they saw me, and they were too far off for me to be able to make out what they were saying. I was trying to think of how I could get closer to them when a shrill child's voice called out "Papa, papa!"

Juan Carvajo ran swiftly back to the hut, and Sebastián

melted away into the trees. I seized the opportunity to follow Carvajo.

I found him soothing the boy's brow and trying to get him interested in a small toy ship he had made for him during our stay at San Julián, a ship that looked as battered as the rest of the fleet.

"What happened?" I asked, going over to them.

Carvajo seemed surprised and confused, as if he weren't sure what the question referred to.

"The boy woke up and when he saw that his father was not beside him as always he became frightened," Antón, the man stretched out next to Hijito, said. "We tried to calm him down, but we couldn't," he added.

Carvajo himself continued to stare at his son, and did not say a word.

As the days went by, the easy routine, regular food, and balmy climate of the island helped bring me back to life.

I used to walk along the beach. The sand was fine and white. I collected shells and conchs of every size and color. I dug up turtle's eggs and ate them in the shade of the palm trees.

I also swam in the lagoon. The water was warm and transparent. I would float on my back and fish bright as jewels would swim over to inspect me. They were so fearless I could catch them. I lifted them from the water for a second to see them sparkle like gems in the sun, then dropped them back in.

Sometimes I pushed my way into the jungle. I stood there admiring the huge shiny wet leaves. The gnarled trunks. The creepers enfolding them in their snake's embrace. The orchids that carpeted the wettest spots of the rock walls.

After my excursions I would sit under the tree by the hut to wait for Basco Gallego.

One day when I had almost completely recovered, it was Don Fernando who emerged from the jungle.

Bulky in his suit of armor, he found it hard to make his way along the narrow track. Branches whipped against his bare face, big leaves were bent double as he passed by, he crushed rotten tree trunks underfoot, and creepers got entangled in the joints of his armor, yet he pushed forward regardless, as stubbornly determined as those giant turtles that struggle out of the sea to lay their eggs on the beach.

As he entered the clearing, the afternoon sun shot red glints from his steel breastplate.

Hijito, who was much better by now, crossed in front of him dragging his toy ship along on the dusty ground. Don Fernando halted, stroked his head, and whispered something in his ear. The boy laughed and walked on, still pulling the toy boat after him.

I went over to Don Fernando.

"Well, if it isn't the count of the Spice Islands!" he said with a smile. "How do you feel?" he asked, in a jocular tone I had never heard him use before.

His whole expression had changed completely since the last time I had seen him. No longer was he the taciturn, evasive man I had known on board ship. He looked happy, radiant even. Almost euphoric. It was plain he had managed to dispel all the doubts that had tormented him during the crossing.

"I'm pleased to see you well," he said, slapping me on the back.

I saw with surprise that he was not wearing his chain mail gauntlets. His hands seemed soft and delicate.

"Would you like to talk?" I asked.

"Let's go for a walk."

We went down to the beach. I did not know what to say. I could see he had changed, but did not know how to deal with it.

We walked by the sea's edge.

"Hijito is better. I'm glad for him and for Carvajo. His poor father would have gone mad if anything had happened to him. You know how close they are. The boy will become a good pilot. He's grown up with the sea."

"What about your son? Will he become a pilot too?"

Until now, any mention of his son would have disturbed Don Fernando, stirring up his feelings of doubt and remorse.

"I hope so. I'll bring him on the next voyage," he said without hesitating.

"You mean there is going to be another voyage?"

"There'll be lots more. You'll see."

"Oh no I won't. Don't count on me. Let's talk of something else. I've been seeing things again . . ."

"Within four days we'll set sail for the Spice Islands. We'll have a celebration first, in the king's honor. I'll need you to entertain us with your tricks."

"I'll see if I have any left. Don't you want me to tell you about your wife and children?"

"The king has said he'll lead us there. He's chosen a pilot for us. His younger brother will come with us, too."

"So your dream has come true. Is that why you're not interested in your family anymore? Or are you afraid of what I might have seen?"

"Don't start, will you? You haven't changed at all."

"But you have. You're like a different person."

He came to a halt.

"If you're going to annoy me, I'll leave you now."

I bowed my head shamefacedly.

"It's just that I've missed you," I murmured.

"And I you," he said, slapping me on the back again.

"We can talk about whatever you like. And if you don't want to talk, we can simply walk. The breeze from the lagoon is very pleasant, isn't it?"

He started off once more. The weight of his armor made it difficult for him to walk on the loose, fine sand. I walked beside him, stepping on his shadow.

"If you like, we can talk about our return. About when we arrive in port with the ships laden with spices," he said.

"It will be glorious, you'll see. We'll anchor in Sanlúcar bay because the ships will be so low in the water we won't be able to reach the docks.

"That morning everyone in the town will awaken with a shock. They won't know what to think. Their houses won't smell of cold omelettes, dirty pans, damp, cat's piss, sleep, acid sweat or even filthy sheets. Because the aroma of cloves and cinnamon will have invaded the town overnight. Seeped into all their rooms. Even taken over their dreams.

"And they will all go crazy, I promise you. They'll rush out into the streets half-dressed. Run down to the port in a crowd. And they'll gather on the docks to gape open-mouthed at the ships standing proud against the blue sky.

"The ships will sparkle like jewels. The fleet will be a diadem. To the crowd, the ships will seem as huge as the castle of Medina Sidonia. They will never have seen such pure white sails. Nor men who look so much larger than life as they move about the decks.

"A short while later, the duke himself will appear. With an escort of fifty pages, all dressed in satin and lemon-colored brocade. And the horses, every one of them black, will have trappings of the same color."

"On Friday we are going to crush the rebels on the island of Matán," Don Fernando said. "We'll teach their king, Cilapulapu, a lesson that will stand us in good stead with the Zubu ruler, because he wants to control the other one. I'll give him what he wants. I'll bring him the head of his enemy on a silver platter. Then he'll lead us to the Spice Islands.

"The king of Zubu thinks that all our strength is due to the suits of armor we wear. I'll show him what we can do without them. I'll lead the men, and I won't even put my armor on. The king won't have to do anything. He can simply watch."

"You mean to say you'll confront your enemies without any protection?"

"Have no fear, it'll be a fine sight. I'd like you to be there."

I said nothing, but stared at the lagoon which the setting sun was staining red. I thought of Basco Gallego. Of the black birds which he said settled on the roof of the Captain's hut every night. Of Andrés de San Martín tracing letters in the dust.

"Tell me about our entry into Sevilla," he said.

"I'm tired," I replied. "We'd better turn back."

"Let's sit for a while to enjoy the breeze," he said, struggling to settle in the sand.

I sat beside him. He picked up handfuls of sand and let them trickle slowly through his fingers.

"Well, what are you waiting for?" he said. "Tell me about Sevilla. What will it be like?"

"Like heaven, like paradise," I forced myself to say.

"Go on. Give your imagination free rein. What can you see?"

"The entire court will be there. I can see the king. He is wearing the crown, and has his ermine cloak around his shoulders. He is seated under a canopy that bears the double-headed eagle on a black ground. The queen is by his side. She is also wearing ermine with a hat to match. There are three strings of pearls on it, which set off her dark beauty."

"What about the ships?"

"The ships are just appearing round the final bend in the river. Anxiety grows in Don Carlos's bright blue eyes. His jutting lower jaw thrusts forward nervously. His aquiline nostrils flare and tremble as they catch wind of the aroma of spices that precedes the ships.

"At that moment the *Te Deum* begins, sung by no less a person than the bishop of Burgos himself. The organ music competes with the sounds of instruments playing in spontaneous street celebrations. The whole city is filled with rejoicing. People are dancing in the squares, making love in doorways. Bulls are let loose. There are fireworks in broad daylight. The fountains of wine his Majesty ordered built for the occasion flow without ceasing.

"The crowds flood everywhere. They swirl beneath the triumphal arches which, linked together by colored garlands, lead the way from the port to the royal palace. They spill onto the jousting ground where three thousand Spanish infantry veterans are set to engage in mock battle with a contingent of Moorish cavalry. They swarm onto the stands built as imitations of our ships.

"All of a sudden, the king stands up. Tall as a tower. Vast

as a cathedral. Radiant as the sun. White as snow. At a signal from him, all the music ceases. So does the shouting. The bullrunning. The kissing in doorways.

"In an instant, all the noise has died away. Nobody moves. Silence reigns over all the crowds. All mouths are sealed. Thousands of expectant faces turn toward the river.

"Now the huge sails are filling the sky. They hide the sun. They flit like a shadow across all the onlookers, who tremble as one. And begin to dream.

"The *Trinidad* draws alongside the quay. The first ropes are thrown onshore. The king is tense, his jaw thrusting forward. He is still standing, his eyes searching the deck of the ship as if he is looking for something or someone."

"Is it me he's looking for? Am I there?"

"I'm not a fortune-teller. And anyway, I'm tired. Let's leave it at that."

"You're not going now. Tell me what you can see."

"I can see Don Carlos, who takes a step forward. And the queen who is nervously biting her nails without realizing it.

"Then suddenly the king doffs his crown and waves it in salute. Like bullfighters do. He has seen you on the stern of the *Trinidad*.

"The crowd bursts into cheering. The castle cannon greet the ships. The *Trinidad*'s cannon roar in response and the sound echoes through the whole city. Beneath the royal platform, the musicians begin to play. The organ starts up again in the cathedral. Are you happy now?"

"You've committed an unforgivable mistake," he said. "You haven't put Beatriz and the children on the platform."

"I thought you didn't want to hear about them, that's why I didn't put them there."

"Well put them there now."

"Let me go back to the hut. I'm not completely well yet. I get tired very easily."

"Come on, put them on the platform, even if it's only for a moment," he begged me.

"All right then," I said. "Beatriz is beside the queen. She's wearing a brocade dress that is as blue as the sea. Her face is flushed with emotion and her moist eyes are staring at the *Trinidad*. By her side is a boy about three years old who is playing on the platform. He goes up to the queen and naughtily smacks her on the knee. Isabel smiles and stretches out her jewel-bedecked hand to stroke his head, but he runs away from her. He stops next to the emperor, who is still on his feet. The boy examines the folds of his ermine cape. He stares up at the snowy mountain rising to the sky. And when the emperor turns round, he runs away again. He rushes to his mother's lap for protection. She scolds him silently. Don Carlos smiles and his gaze alights on Beatriz. He must find her attractive, because his look changes: you know what a womanizer he is. A broad smile spreads across his usually severe features. He shoots a seductive glance at your wife, and holds out his hand invitingly to the boy. The queen gives him an icy stare, then turns back to gaze again at the river. Don Carlos lifts the child in his arms so that he can wave to his father."

"What about Rodrigo?"

"Can't you see him, standing there between his mother and the queen?"

"What is he doing? Tell me."

"He is watching all that is going on, his chest puffed out with pride. Just look at his face. It's obvious he is trying to control himself. He is determined not to shed a single tear. He thinks men shouldn't cry. I'm going to be a navigator too, he's thinking."

"So you can even see what the boy is thinking?" Don Fernando said.

"You know how I get carried away. And what about you? Are you going to laugh or to cry? I'd better go, I can't bear crybabies."

Night fell. A huge, blood-red moon rose over the ocean beyond the reef.

"Help me up," he said. "This armor exhausts me."

"Do you really mean to go and fight without it?"

Don Fernando did not reply. He shook off the sand then

walked over to the water's edge. His feet left a furrow in the beach. A furrow like the ones left by the turtles when they crawl back to the sea after they have laid their eggs.

He paused for a moment to stare at the moon, then walked off along the beach. The tide was rising and the waves soon effaced his footprints.

And can you believe, your Majesty, that I still weep whenever I recall the next episode in my story?

I still see myself cradling his head in my hands, while he stares up at me as though from the bottom of a well; and the truth is, Don Carlos, that I do not know where to begin. He is lying there stretched out, and his eyes are telling me he cannot believe it. No, this is not happening to me, his eyes say. It's all a dream; I have to wake up. Why can't I do so? they say. All this is so absurd it must be a dream. But nothing is as absurd as him stretched out there, with splinters of wood sprouting from his naked, bony chest. Jagged splinters of green wood. The aromatic wood of the clove tree. Splinters so green they look as though they will grow again. Plunging their roots into his chest to suck up the sap. Their perfume mixed with the smell of gunpowder and blood. Because there is blood all around. But not his blood. It can't be my blood, his eyes say. Eyes that show no terror, only utter disbelief. The blood staining the turquoise waters of the lagoon. His life ebbing away in that red stain darkening the clean sand of the sea bottom. A stain that dissolves and vanishes while the fish of the reef swim through it like jewels. All so absurd that it cannot be his blood. Yet it is his blood, and it is he who is stretched out in the waters of the lagoon. The waters of the lagoon are so calm he is convinced it must be a dream. So calm and clear it cannot be true. Perhaps beyond the reef where the ocean is roaring, he thinks. But not here. I have to wake up, he says. But he cannot. There is such a warm, gentle breeze, and it makes the palm trees sway so softly. But he cannot. Yet the air is scented with magnolia, with cloves and cinnamon. Above all, with cloves. He looks down at his chest and it is all so absurd it cannot be true. So he raises his astonished eyes and sees, as though in a grimy mirror, Serrano's face staring down at him. But it cannot be Serrano, because the face is weeping, and he has never seen Serrano weep. And the face is staring him as if he were a corpse. Why is Serrano staring at him like that, and not saying a word? It cannot be Serrano, and this is not me; it is all a dream. And that one further back who looks like Odoardo and who is staring at me just like this one who could be Serrano, and is kneeling as if glued to the bottom of the sea, as if he wanted to come closer, but cannot? It cannot be Odoardo. He is always so determined. Why is this person biting his fist and looking at me like that? It is all so absurd, he thinks. I have to wake up. And that other person staring at me over Odoardo's shoulder, his head bowed and his helmet cupped in his hands in an almost religious gesture? Or the other one kneeling behind Serrano, head in hands as if he could not bear to look? Why are they all doing that, his astonished eyes say. I have to wake up. So he struggles to get to his feet. But cannot. Wants to ask for help, but cannot. Everyone is staring at him without moving. I have to be able to, say his eyes, which begin to gleam with an absurd determination. His arm reaches back to push himself up from the sandy bottom. His body inches upward, his head lolls forward. His gaze encounters the beach, will have nothing to do with it, moves on to the reef where the waves are crashing, then to the ships beyond it. It pauses for a moment there, but then his head falls back again like a dead weight, shattering the calm surface of the lagoon. I rush to lift it and cradle it in my lap once more. He is lying stretched out, I am sitting beside him in the water holding his head up. As my arm darts forward, the bells on my bracelet tinkle and he says, "That's you, isn't it?" I say nothing, because I have no idea what to reply. His eyes seek me out, searching all around, and I would dearly love to hide so that they never find me. But find me they do. And he smiles and moves his lips, as if trying to tell me something I have no wish to hear. But I lower one of my big ears to his lips, I feel a cold breath and a voice saying, "Help me wake up." But I cannot help him, because there are splinters sprouting from his naked chest, and his blood is staining the turquoise waters of the lagoon red; the stain is growing, and his life is ebbing away. So I say nothing, watching doubt grow in his eyes. He is lying there stretched out, but his eyes have seen the ships out beyond the reef, so all this must be simply a dream. He can even hear the slap of the sails in the sudden silence. Since he is about to die, he can hear the slap of his ships' sails. Why then is there such a silence it seems everything is happening behind a pane of glass? Why have all the commands, the shouts, the noise of men rushing around suddenly ceased? Why is everyone so silent? Why such a silence? Why is everything so calm? Why has all the rushing ceased so suddenly? Why are they all motionless? Why are the waters of the lagoon so calm? And the breeze is so soft and perfumed. What had been happening before, which he cannot remember? Another dream? But if he cannot remember it, that must mean he is awake, and that cannot be so, because all this must be a dream. But it is not a dream. He is lying stretched out in the water, with splinters sprouting from his chest, and the stain has vanished, the water is crystal clear again, the sand on the bottom is glittering spotless once more. It cannot have been blood, say his eyes which seem calmer now. Less astonished. It cannot have been, because the fish of the reef swim by like jewels, and a shell is glittering like a piece of Chinese porcelain on the sand of the sea bottom. A motionless palm tree casts its shadow. And the lagoon is a pure turquoise color. There is no blood. It was all a dream. All of it. No, it is not. There is no more blood in the lagoon because it has all been carried out to sea on the current. The only sound is the slapping of the sails. Nothing else. I can see his lips moving so I bend over him once more, and he whispers in my ear, "You see, it was all a dream." I reply, "Yes, my Lord; yes, Captain. It is all a dream. And when you wake up, we'll head for the Spice Islands. Load all the pepper in the world onto our ships. And you'll make me a count. Remember that you promised me. And if we don't reach the Spice Islands, it won't matter. We'll be just as happy. What do the Spice Islands matter to us? Do you know what we should do? Throw all the parchments, compasses, quadrants, and hourglasses on the fire—especially the hourglasses! —and sail free of them all. As we please. For the simple pleasure of sailing. Without heading for anywhere in particular. Without searching for anything. Yes, Captain, it's all a dream. You'll see. We'll build a big stone house. All stone, with a huge hearth. And we'll work the land together. Turn the oars into plow-shares. We'll buy a good team of oxen. You can buy the best in Bustillo. Strong and gentle. It is only a dream, you'll see. Yes, my Lord; yes, Captain. It's all a dream; do you hear me?" But he can no longer hear me, your Highness. He cannot hear me. He is no longer there. He has ebbed away. All that is left is the turquoise, motionless lagoon, where there is no trace of blood. Only fish like jewels. The lagoon like a jewel case. A precious turquoise casket. A liquid box for a liquid jewel the color of rubies. Which has ebbed out to the ocean."

HOW DID it happen? I knew that as soon as you had the chance you would ask me that silly question. Everyone has. Ladies in their palaces, surrounded by silk cushions and Oriental per-fumes. Mule drivers at markets, watching the fire crackle with eyes dulled by wine. Children in village squares that stank of fish and rotten cabbages.

Everyone asked that same question, as if it were important. As if it had not been implicit in all that had gone before. As if it were not obvious to anyone who had been paying proper attention to the hints scattered throughout my story. As if it were not better to imagine the rest without needing it spelled out.

How slow you all are! And what a coward I am to satisfy your demands and tell you what you want to hear without protesting: It happened like this.

We left at midnight, after much eating and drinking. There were drums and dancing, voices and laughter all around (not the silence of the previous scene).

We made merry that night, but soon turned to the task at hand, putting on our helmets and armor to face the Tagalogs at dawn.

The Captain said he wanted three squads. Juan Serrano was to lead the left flank, taking the musketeers with him, while Sebastián was to command on the right, with the crossbowmen. He himself would be in the center. Each commander was to choose the men he wanted.

He picked twenty men for his squad. One of them was Basco Gallego, who said nothing but gave me a wink that meant: they won't catch me. Andrés de San Martín was also part of our group; he tried to say something, but no sound came from his empty mouth.

Once the squads were formed, Don Fernando spoke of the importance of our undertaking. The king of Zubu should see what we were made of so that he would never dare betray us. We had to wipe the people of Matán from the face of the earth, so that the king would realize the same thing would happen to him if he were lying about the Spice Islands.

Don Fernando said all this in a gentle voice that floated like a whisper across the still, perfumed night air.

Then Juan Serrano asked him whether he was really thinking of going to fight without his armor, shouting the question in front of everyone.

The Captain replied that he was, to prove his courage to the king of Zubu.

We left at midnight, guided by the king in his outrigger. We hove to in deep water off Matán to wait for day because we could not find a gap in the reef for our boats.

Day dawned at last. It still seems to me it must have been more than one day, because one day cannot have been so long, unless it was a day in a dream. But this was no dream.

At first light, we made our way up the lagoon, wading through water up to our thighs. It was so clear we could see our feet on the sea bottom. And the fish like jewels who came, curious, to see what we might be.

We waded through the water, and everything was still. So still that nobody could possibly die there. So peaceful that nothing could possibly happen.

The atmosphere was luminous. The light, pure. The beach

looked spotless. The palm trees graceful and slender. Nothing could happen there.

So when the first volley of weapons began to rain around us we thought nothing of it. We strode on confidently while clusters of arrows and clouds of stones blocked out the sun. They came from far off still, and our helmets and armor protected us.

At first everything took place in complete silence. It was like a painted canvas, full of braced helmets and raised shields, with pikes and pennants raised aloft, giant hands grasping sword pommels or lancebutts, glimpses of pain or fear on ill-defined faces fraught with tension.

I had the feeling I was looking at one of those huge tapestries which adorn your palace galleries, with warriors frozen in the threads of the design, silent battles gradually disappearing under layers of dust.

But suddenly it was as though someone had shaken off the centuries of dust, or as if a cold wind had made the tapestry flutter.

The first sign was the bloody face of someone fighting beside me who had been hit by a stone. Then a moment later I saw the first man collapse, as if he had crashed into an invisible wall. He fell in a heap on his back, then lay floating in the water, an arrow sticking from his forehead.

Soon everything was chaos. Commands. Shouts of rage. Cries of pain. The roar of muskets. The thud of bombs. The whistle of crossbows. The waspish buzz of arrows. Spears flying silently through the air. The acrid reek of gunpowder mixed with the cloying smell of blood, the harshness of armor. The smell of leather harnesses and sweat, of the excrement of wounded horses and men. And the warmth of the water round our legs. The taste of blood and bile in our mouths. The acrid aftertaste of the previous night's food. Our stomachs churning, our guts aching. The urgent need to relieve them. And people running everywhere. Rushing into each other. Trampling on the wounded. Crushing the dead underfoot. Starting to flee in panic because nothing had turned out as they had expected. As the Captain had promised them.

What more do you want me to tell you, your Highness? That in the midst of all that terrible confusion I went looking for Basco Gallego, but could not find him? That I ran from man to man asking for him, but nobody replied? That I finally found the great Basco Gallego swimming flat on his face, laughing at everyone? Or could it be that he was not swimming? His chest had a gaping hole in it. He still smelt of cow's milk, but now it was cow's milk that had turned sour. He had fallen into the trap. He had been taken by surprise, even though he thought he was so clever. He had been caught, like all the rest. What more should I tell you?

All this happened early in the morning, before Sebastián retreated. He shouted that there were too many of them, more than a thousand against the sixty of us. That we were an easy target out in the lagoon, while they were invisible, hidden in the jungle. He shouted all that to the Captain, while he gave his men the order to pull back.

Don Fernando was furious. He told him not to withdraw the crossbowmen. Told him he was a traitor.

But Sebastián just went on shouting for his men to hurry up, hurry up.

So then they pressed us on our right flank. The first to fall was Andrés de San Martín, who had remained isolated there. He was unable to move, rooted to the spot like a frightened deer. Then a spear sped noiselessly through the air and pinned him to the ground. It went straight through him, the point digging into the sand behind him. So he was left standing, leaning slightly backwards, with the shaft of the spear holding him upright. Pierced like that, still wearing his conical hat and black cape, he looked just like a scarecrow left in the stubble of a wheatfield. What more would you like to hear? That his face was turned up to the heavens from which he had so often sought answers, that his eyes were like those of the deer you hang as trophies in your palace?

That happened in midmorning, when the sun was already high in the sky. It seemed to me like another morning altogether, because it was impossible for so much to happen in so few hours.

Seeing how things were going, Juan Serrano told the Captain we had to retreat. That his musketeers were useless because they had no target to aim at. That we were the only target, and an easy one at that.

Don Fernando glanced back at the reef, saw the king of Zubu's boat beyond it, and refused to pull back.

"You'd better put your armor on," Serrano said. "Do it before it's too late."

But before he had finished saying so, it was already too late.

An arrow pierced the Captain's thigh. He stood there staring down at his leg, unable to utter a word.

Juan Serrano took charge. He gave the command for an orderly withdrawal. Told us to signal those on board ship to cover our retreat with cannon fire.

But when the men saw their leader wounded, they broke ranks. They fled, turning their back on the enemy. They ran in all directions. Threw away their weapons and shields. Flung off their helmets and armor so they could run more quickly. And no sooner were they out of range of the Matán islanders than they fell victim to our own cannon, because the ships were too far from the beach and could only hit our own men.

Now the islanders concentrated their attack on the small band around the Captain. Hopelessly outnumbered, all of them fought like lions. Don Fernando himself had recovered from his stupor, pulled the arrow from his thigh, and was fighting in the front line.

But they gave us no respite. Our ammunition was running out, and so was our strength. The Captain began to shout that we should all withdraw. Should leave him there. Could we not see he had an arm and a leg that were useless? He did not want to be a burden to us. We should think of saving ourselves. Go back to the ships to get more men and ammunition. We should listen to him. He was still in command, he was not dead yet.

But Juan Serrano shouted back that he would not leave him. And Odoardo Barbosa said he would not go either.

Juan Serrano threw down his weapons, grabbed the Captain under the arms, and started desperately trying to drag him away. Cristóbal Rabelo came running over to take his feet, but suddenly stopped in his tracks. A stupid grin spread over his features. He stared down at Don Fernando's feet, then fell over on his side, an arrow sticking out from the base of his skull. Rodrigo Nieto ran to replace him, turned to tell us something, and found he could not: another arrow had pierced his throat.

That left just four of us: Filiberto the Fairy, who was having a nervous fit and was crying like a little girl; Serrano, still trying to drag Don Fernando out of range of the arrows; Odoardo, doing his best to help him; and your Juanillo, who was quaking with fear and at a loss as to what to do.

"Cover us!" shouted Serrano in a rage.

The Captain struggled to push himself upright.

This was at midday. The sun was at its highest, and the lagoon was a blinding mirror. So no one saw the vulture carved on the clove-wood spear that was seeking out his chest.

Don Fernando toppled backward, a look of infinite surprise on his face.

What more would you like to know, Don Carlos? That we stood there like stone, dumb to what was happening in front of our eyes and deaf to all that was going on outside our tight little circle? That the distant voices and shouts, the last roars of the arquebuses, had all suddenly been stilled? That we could not even hear the sound of the waves, or the whisper of the breeze swaying the palm trees?

That we were like statues in an abandoned park? Like those granite figures carved on kings' tombs. Like the marble acolytes on popes' sepulchers.

I was cradling Don Fernando's head in my lap. Serrano was sobbing silently. Odoardo wanted to come closer, but found he could not. Filiberto, head bowed, was cupping his helmet in his hands in an almost religious gesture.

Serrano was the first to react. He took off his hat and with a delicate gesture used it to cover Don Fernando's face. In the midst of that boundless silence the hawkbells sounded like breaking glass.

"Nobody must know what has happened," he said, standing

up again. And when none of us replied, he went on, "We'll find the right moment to tell the others. But not now, after our first defeat. Not a word to the king of Zubu, who has seen how vulnerable we are, and could take advantage of the situation. Or to the Spaniards, who could try to take over the expedition again. Nobody must know," he repeated.

"What shall we do?" Odoardo asked, his weeping eyes still fixed on Don Fernando's body.

Serrano understood. He went over and put an arm round his shoulder.

N O W Y O U R Highness removes his eyeglasses and with trembling fingers carefully replaces them in their golden casket.

Then he picks up the heavy manuscript in hands crippled with gout and puts it to one side.

He stares anxiously at everything around him, like someone surfacing from a dream. The papers piled on his work table, the huge globe, the worthless maps, the portable organ that went with him on all his campaigns, the Titian portraits hanging from the walls draped for mourning, the chair next to the window, the window giving on to the church.

Everything seems strange to him. Vaguely unreal. Like the perfume of incense filling the room. Like the organ music swelling from the chapel next door. Music rising out of the past.

He stretches with difficulty across the work table to pick up his silver-handled mirror.

Now he is looking at his features in the tiny glass oval: Wrinkled, sallow skin. Toothless mouth. Twitching lips. A trail of spittle escaping from the right-hand corner of his mouth and dribbling into his white-flecked beard. His jutting chin made even sharper by age. White hair. And his eyes. Eyes that are no longer the same turquoise as the lagoon. Eyes that have lost almost all color. The dull pupils where an oval portrait has replaced the reflection of three ships. A portrait with the paint flaking off. Almost a miniature. A cameo perhaps.

Don Carlos puts the mirror face down on the table. Takes out a handkerchief and wipes his beard.

"I'm disgusting," he thinks. "All old people are disgusting."

With a heavy soul, Don Carlos stares at the black walls of the room. The smoke from the incense filtering through the curtains of his only window makes him cough. He feels he is choking. His crippled fingers clutch at the back of his chair as he tries to reach the ground from on top of the pile of cushions where they have placed him like a child.

He finally manages to stand on his feet, still leaning heavily on the chairback.

He pauses for breath before undertaking the slow, lengthy crossing of a room that seems as huge to him as it would to a child, although it is not.

Then the slow crossing of the mourning room. Between giant, meaningless maps. Without even noticing the enormous portable organ that once went with him on every campaign. Campaigns he makes no effort to remember. Campaigns he has forgotten.

Until he reaches Leonor's portrait, which for the first time seems too large. He finds it hard to recognize her gigantic figure. So he walks by, supported by his cane.

The figure of the empress also looks huge to him. What makes Titian paint such big portraits? he wonders. But Felipe's portrait seems smaller. He remembered it as being bigger, but it is not. In fact it is small, almost a miniature. Why did Titian paint him so small? he wonders.

Puzzled, he makes his way across the final part of the room. The organ has fallen silent for a moment, and in the silence of the night Don Carlos's senses come to life. His tired heart beats more rapidly as he thinks that his mother is going to speak to him. He will hear her voice, as he does every night. "I had a terrible dream," she will tell him yet again. "I dreamt a monstrous giant cat, white as ermine, was devouring my innards."

But tonight his mother's voice does not speak to him. He waits a moment longer and then, as the organ sounds again, he walks the last few steps separating him from the window giving onto the chapel interior. It was he who had that window built, and had the others looking out onto the fields and hills of Extremadura blocked up.

Exhausted by his effort, he clambers into the seat by the

window. Curled up on the cushions, shrunken by age, Don Carlos looks like the portrait of a newborn child.

Then with shaking hand he draws back the heavy brocade curtains concealing him from the eyes of the monks. He tries to concentrate on the holy office which he offers day and night for the souls of his mother and sister.

He thinks: "From tomorrow I will get them to say a daily requiem for my soul."

Then the organ music swells up again, enfolds him, and carries him far, far away.

PART IX

Aʀᴇ ʏᴏᴜ still there, Don Carlos? Is it raining on San Jerónimo de Yuste? Here in Bustillo the raindrops are bouncing off the tiles. It's a sad rhythm, don't you agree? But then, Bustillo is a sad village. The tiles are brown, and green moss covers them as soon as autumn arrives. Because it rains a lot here in Bustillo. It rains for weeks and months on end. Life vanishes from the streets and the village dies. The villagers turn into shadows, muffled figures flitting under the arches. The streets are deserted. The rain laps at the cobbles. Not even the melancholy clang of cowbells or the monotonous creaking of cart axles can be heard. The fields stand empty. There is nothing besides the earth and the rain. Everything is silent. A vast, ancient silence. A silence that remains indifferent to the sound of footsteps disappearing quickly into the distance, to a lonely bell that rings out from time to time, its echo rolling and dying across the deserted land.

Yes, your Highness, Bustillo is a sad village. But it wasn't like that when I was a boy and the light was so strong it intensified all the colors and blurred the outline of objects in a golden haze. As if it came from the very soul of things, making them all look brand new. As if they had never before been seen. The hours went by in constant discovery, those slow hours of childhood. Because you and I were both children. Or at least I was, in Bustillo. A rather sad child, perhaps. But still I ran through the streets and played in the squares of the village. Its streets are narrow, and its squares are tiny and dark. Yet to the boy I was everything was broad and sunny. I ran wherever I pleased, and my wanderings often brought me to a shop under the arches of the main street. Inside it smelled of lace and buckram, but also of cat's piss and stale food. The shopkeeper was a widower whose sad, gangling daughter spent the whole day staring out at the square through the dusty windowpanes. She was my first love, though she never knew it. I spent hours watching her stare out because, though her eyes were fixed on the narrow gap between two thick stone columns, it was obvious she was seeing far beyond the square. Her eyes were high-flying birds. They flew far from Bustillo. Only rarely did they settle on the things or people directly in front of them. And whenever they did, there was a long wait while her mind returned from heaven knows what distant realms. While she was absent in this way, her father endlessly checked the well-thumbed books where he kept each client's accounts, muttering to himself, "Let's see what we've got here." And then he would add: "You see, Isabel, there's nothing like well-kept accounts."

But Isabel couldn't hear him; she was flying far, far away.

One day she flew so far she lost her way back. The shop was closed for a few days of mourning. Then someone took away the sign, but the shop still stayed shut. People in the village said Isabel had died. I never believed it. I thought that someone had left the shop door open and she had simply flown away. Just like a bird. From that day on, I wanted to fly too. To escape far away from that village, which had begun to seem sad to me.

What about where you were born, Don Carlos? I have difficulty imagining it. And I find it even harder to imagine you as a child. Tell me, are kings ever children? Do they play with other child kings? Do they have to do penance? Do they escape out of the window into the fields while their parents are sleeping the siesta? Do they get up to mischief under the bridge? Do they have great loves who know nothing about it? Do these girls fly off like birds?

It is a shame we did not meet before. Just think, two lonely children like us. Two rather sad boys who could have played together, who could both have fallen secretly in love with an older girl.

Well, Don Carlos, little Carlitos, there's nothing to be done about that. Not even you, with all the power you have, can turn back time; and that being so, what is the use of being king?

I had better drop it there and get back to my own affairs, which means finishing this chronicle before someone leaves the window open and I fly off far, far away as well.

Now it was the evening of the day that was too long to be just one day. A warm, quiet evening where the horrible events of the morning seemed like nothing more than a dream. Such a peaceful evening that the prayers for the souls of the dead sounded like the buzzing of bees on a summer evening in a vine arbor. An evening with such a gentle wind that the prayers for the Captain's recovery sounded like the fluttering of poplar leaves in a spring breeze.

An evening that had known no morning. That no night would follow. Nothing but an evening.

An evening not to believe in anything. Not to believe that Odoardo was sending Enrique to the island to ask the king for permission to bury our dead there. An evening without any dead. Do you understand me, your Highness?

An evening to believe everything. To believe Odoardo when he told Enrique he shouldn't disturb the Captain if he wanted him to recover quickly.

Enrique wanted to go and fetch the cape and turban Don Fernando had given him after his first mission to Zubu. They were both under the Captain's bunk. The Captain was resting and recovering from his wounds on the bunk. Everything as it should have been.

An evening to believe Enrique when he insisted on seeing his master, and to believe Odoardo when he promised he would see him on his return from the island.

An evening where there was no room for Odoardo's booming, threatening voice, asking Enrique what the devil he wanted with the Captain.

An evening where Enrique's voice sounded a little odd when he said the Captain had promised him that he would free him when we returned to Spain or in the event of his death.

An evening when the word "death" had a hollow sound. Perhaps that was what upset Odoardo so much that he forgot the evening and began to call Enrique a black bastard, swearing he would never be free because Odoardo would personally hand him over to Beatriz the day the Captain was no more, and would make sure that Enrique and his descendants continued to serve Don Fernando's family through the generations.

The light was as gentle as Juan Serrano's voice telling them that the Captain was complaining because Odoardo's shouts did not let him rest.

As gentle as the shadow of the hat brim across the Portuguese captain's weatherbeaten face. As the words he whispered into Odoardo's ear. As the friendly way he calmed Enrique.

An evening as still and unmoving as Enrique's face. As crystal clear as the water the boats were floating on. As slow as the rhythm of the slave's oars as he rowed away from the ships. As inscrutable as the expression on Enrique's face while he explored who knows what abysses.

An evening when time stood still. Like the sun in the sky. Like the dead bodies in the hold of the *Victoria*. Like Enrique on the island. Like Hijito asleep on his father's lap.

An evening without voices. An evening for lowering one's voice without knowing why. For whispering in the other person's ear. Like Serrano to Odoardo. Like Sebastián to Carvajo. Like a serpent lying in wait.

An evening round as an orange. Deep as a glass of wine. Rich as a golden goblet.

An evening that contained its night but refused to die, Don Carlos.

Because, as you know, night is a different animal. At night, outlines and shapes grow in a strange, inexplicable way. Gaps suddenly appear. Walls rise up. Doors that did not exist fly open.

Night is another plant, your Highness. A rare plant indeed. Fleshy. Sticky. With huge leaves that are crinkled and downy.

I fled so as not to see the evening ebbing away into night, and took refuge in the Captain's cabin.

But I was too late, your Highness. Night had beaten me to it. Nobody calls it and yet it comes. Like death, it changes everything. It was cold in the tiny room. It smelled of damp and mushrooms, not of the *Trinidad*'s fragrant timbers. It was like entering a tomb that had been sealed for thousands of years. Full of objects that had lost their meaning. Become useless. Enigmatic. The remains of an ancient civilization. The hourglasses on the table were strange glass bulbs full of sand, like pieces from a mysterious chess game, mere ornaments. The engraved compasses were like the scattered bits of some strange artifact or crazy scheme; the hands of a kind of clock not yet invented. The astrolabe was a jewel, a weapon, a tin mirror once used by faraway ladies. And the suit of armor in the corner was an absurd piece of clothing no one could ever have used.

Under the Captain's bunk lay his empty slippers. On the bunk lay Serrano. It was night. Nothing was where it should have been.

We ought to have spoken to each other, but neither of us dared break the age-old silence that seemed to have the room in its grip.

Then there was the night. At night, any word could lead us somewhere totally unexpected. It could open doors we thought were locked shut. It isn't like the day, your Majesty. In the dark, words can fly out of their own accord. They can be like bats flapping fearfully in a cave. They can drive us toward ever deeper depths. We can lose ourselves in labyrinths we will be unable to escape from until dawn comes to our rescue.

In that silence both of us were searching for something concrete to say. Something that could guide us safely through the darkness. A sentence as precise as a lantern. One that would light our way but leave everything else in the shadows. A piece of timber as much as a sentence. Something we could cling to so as not to feel the night all around us or the sea beneath our feet.

But all I could think of were questions, Don Carlos, and he could only reply with doubts.

So we both sat there silent and absorbed in our own thoughts like two players at a chessboard. Each one pondering his opening move, trying to work out what the other might do in response, calculating the next move and what that might produce. And so on to infinity.

I could have asked him what he was doing there, but I already knew his reply. I could have tried another gambit (already a classic one in my game) and said, "The Captain and I used to have long conversations: don't you want to talk?"

He wouldn't risk everything in the first move by saying yes. He would be more cautious, and say, perhaps, "What do you want to talk about?"

I knew I could counteract a move like that. But he might also have made a different opening and replied, "I've got very important things to decide."

With a move like that, I would have risked being caught up in his strategy, not my own.

I might suddenly have found myself thinking the same things he was. Thinking we had to cope with a dead Don Fernando. That there were eight more bodies being watched over on the deck of the *Victoria* (the light from the huge candles gave the ship a ghostly look). Perhaps I could have brought him back to my own strategy by saying:

"Your father will be proud when he sees you arriving at the head of a fleet loaded with spices after sailing round the whole world. He must have been a great sailor too."

He might have countered by declaring that his father had never been to sea. That he had spent all his life behind a desk piled high with dusty papers. That he was a tax inspector in some remote province. Yet I would still have been thinking that among the dead on board the *Victoria* was the cosmographer Andrés de San Martín. That with him dead there was no one capable of linking a reading of the stars to Ruy Faleiro's woefully incomplete calculations. That there was no one who could decipher Faleiro's figures now that the Captain had taken the few clues he had with him to heaven. And that there was no one to lead the fleet to the Spice Islands, because the king of Zubu was certain not to keep his promise. Perhaps we would sail straight past them without recognizing them, and go on searching year upon year until the ships fell apart with their crews of old men. Without being able to return to Spain, because no one knew the route back now that the Captain was dead and so was Andrés de San Martín, the fleet's astronomer.

Perhaps instead I should have accepted his ploy and replied, "And yet your father enjoyed the king's favor."

Then he would have told me that for his father the king was no more than a portrait hanging on the wall above his head, and which needed replacing every so many years. The features of the kings never seemed to change, though their names did. His father was not concerned about such small details because he always referred to all of them as "the king." He turned even the most anonymous and widely circulated directive signed by the king into a personal message, a friendly request, an intimate confession. And whenever it was necessary, he exchanged one portrait for the next. Sometimes the new portrait took so long to arrive that he was merely exchanging the portrait of one dead king for another. But he did not know that. Or perhaps it did not matter to him.

That was how his father was. But he did not want to be like that.

Then it would have been my turn. I would have moved in the same direction. I would have said, for example:

"But I would have wanted to be like my father. The problem was, I didn't know who my father was. For me it was the same as with your father and the kings. Every one of the many men who passed through our house was my father to me. My mother replaced them as indifferently as your father changed the kings' portraits, but for me they all had the same face: the face of my father."

A move like that might have turned the tables. Made it as

though we had changed places and now it was he who would be playing with the black pieces and me with the white. So, while I wheeled out my orphan story, trying to win his sympathy and to center the dialogue on that square, he would be thinking the thoughts that had been going through my mind, moving the pieces I had been moving a few moments earlier.

Thinking that the new commanders of the fleet were himself, Juan Serrano, and the loyal Odoardo Barbosa. That there was Sebastián, plotting with the other Spanish officers to dislodge them. Sebastián did not think Don Fernando would recover, and he would do anything to become the new Captain General of the fleet.

And though I might go on to tell him how my mother had children with the gentlemen who visited the house, and how nobody knew where those children who were my brothers and sisters ended up, he would be thinking that Don Fernando was dead but he had to convince everyone he was still alive. That he did not know how long he could do that, or what would happen afterward. That the king of Zubu must be planning to get rid of us now that he knew that without our armor we were as vulnerable as anyone else. Thinking of the king of Zubu, your Highness, and how he was laying a trap for us. Of himself, Juan Serrano, and what he had to do. Of Enrique, whom he could not trust, but whom he needed as interpreter. Of the burials the next day. Of the king's invitation, and promise that he would lead us to the Spice Islands. Of whether he should accept the invitation. Of the fact that he ought to go because he was the Captain General now. Of the lies he would tell the king of Zubu about Don Fernando, because if the king thought the Captain was dead he would never keep his promise. Thinking that perhaps he already knew Don Fernando was dead. That perhaps the Matán islanders had found the body even though we had weighed it down with stones. Thinking of the body, so small and white without its armor, without life. Of the fact that they might not have recognized the body even if they had found it. That perhaps nobody would recognize it, and that this would be for the best; the last thing he wanted was for them suddenly to appear with Don Fernando's body. Thinking that only myself, Odoardo and he, Juan Serrano, knew the truth. Filiberto the Fairy was dead, which was a great relief because everyone knew his kind were all blabbermouths. But he knew he could trust a buffoon. And also his friend Odoardo.

Such were the thoughts going through our minds while the silence in the cabin deepened and it became harder all the time to find the right phrase to smash a way through it.

We spent several hours in silence, until Serrano made the boldest move of all.

"Help me put Don Fernando's armor on," he said.

When I heard what he was suggesting, a chill ran through my bones and left me like a stone statue.

"There's nothing to be done. Come on, help me on with it."

I looked at the pieces of iron armor piled beside the Captain's work table: a pile of scrap metal shining silver in the moonlight.

"He taught me many things," I said.

I had caught Serrano's attention.

"He taught me the importance of a dream. An impossible goal that made life worth living. And I encouraged him in his."

"You should be at peace with yourself then. And I can teach you other things."

"With all due respect, it will never be the same."

"You knew him well. You know the high regard he had for me," Serrano said.

I surveyed all the objects cluttering the room. The hourglasses, the compasses, the astrolabe, the sea charts, the slippers under the bed, Serrano on the bed. Nothing was where it should have been. And I wondered if I had really known him. I was afraid he might have been a character I invented. But I didn't say a word. Perhaps when dawn came that feeling would vanish.

"You were his favorite," I said.

"So were you," Serrano replied. "He really thought well of you."

We both lapsed into silence.

I stared at the armor, unable to make up my mind, while he watched me expectantly.

"I'll help you," I said in the end.

Then I stood up and quickly grabbed at the breastplate. As I did so, the whole pile of armor came crashing down, and Serrano sat up on the bed with a start.

I stared down at the breastplate glinting in the moonlight, then put my nose to it.

"What does it smell of?" he asked.

I would have liked to tell him that it smelled partly of the sea, and also of tar and the canvas of our huge sails. Of spices, too. And of apple blossom. But all it smelled of was piss and age.

"Of nothing," I replied. "Nothing. But we'll have to clean it and polish it a bit."

"Leave that till later. I only want to try it on."

"Do you want to wear all of it?" I asked, looking around for the chain mail suit. It had been thrown under the table, where it lay like the sloughed-off skin of a powerful snake. "Did you know that snakes change their skin each spring so they can continue to grow? When I was a boy I used to collect the tubes of transparent scales I found on the heaths. I used to be scared of picking them up, because I could not help thinking of the dangerous animal that left this skin behind to sun itself in a shiny new one. But soon my fear vanished and I would start playing with the old skin, trying to fill it in order to frighten people."

Beneath the hat brim, Serrano's eyes were glittering with their old malice.

"You were lucky you didn't pick up a live one," he said.

"There's no way to confuse an old skin with a live snake."

"But while you were playing with the old skin, the snake might have slithered up in its brand new coat and sunk its fangs into you. Just think of that."

"That's enough," I said. "Are you going to put the chain mail on?"

He nodded, swung his legs down from the bed, and held out his arms to me.

"Aren't you going to sniff it first?"

"I know what it smells of. It smells of acid sweat. And of the sand from those hourglasses," I replied, lowering it over his head.

"To me it smells of spices."

"Of spices too," I agreed, tightening the straps of the breastplate. Then I held out the gauntlets for him.

"Do you want to put the greaves on as well?"

He nodded again, and stretched out his legs for me.

"The helmet too?"

Serrano took off his hat. I went over to him, carrying the helmet as if I were a priest carrying the holy chalice.

He put it on, closed the visor, and struggled to lie back on the bed.

By the pale light of the moon he looked exactly like my childhood memory of the warrior's statue in the crypt.

I felt as if time were spinning round, repeating itself. As if the night were stretching out, joining other similar nights. As if morning would never come.

"Did you know the Captain kept earth from Oporto on board the *Concepción* so he could be buried in it?" I asked, trying to keep my bearings, trying not to become completely lost.

But Serrano had disappeared inside the suit of armor, and there was no reply.

I decided to take the plunge. I sat myself down at his feet like a loving mother and said, "Would you like to hear a ballad? Perhaps it'll send you to sleep so you can rest awhile."

I began to recite the verses of the *Infante Arnaldos*:

> Her sails are the purest silk
> And her rigging plaited gold
> Her anchors are made of silver
> Finest coral her timbered hold.
> The mariner who steers her
> Is singing soft and low
> Stilling the waves of the sea
> And making gentle breezes blow.
> His song brings to the surface

The fish who swim in the deep
And the birds who fly on high
Fold their wings on the mast in sleep.

"Fernando was stupid," Serrano interrupted me. "He should never have gone without his armor. He should have been more careful."

"He never took it off in the whole voyage," I said.

"Exactly. It was stupid of him."

"Anyone can make a mistake. An oversight."

"One mistake can cost you your life."

"That's true, that's true," I said, as dawn crept across the distant horizon and the *Victoria*'s stark outline emerged against a porcelain sky.

Now it was dawn, your Highness, and the preceding day's dead were being lowered from the deck of the *Victoria*.

Dawn is the hour of the dead, Don Carlos. The final hour when resurrection is impossible. The hour when families become resigned to death. The cold, cruel moment when the dead have become objects and the wind of forgetting has begun to wipe out their traces, their gestures, the sound of their voices, the smell of their skins, the warmth of their hands, everything.

It was an uncertain dawn, like the expression on the faces of the dead. Silent as the to and fro of the survivors preparing for the burials. Hard as Sebastián's face as he watched Serrano take charge. Cold as marble, like Carvajo's face as he spied on Odoardo out of the corner of his eye, his hands gently stroking Hijito's hair while the boy slept between his legs, wrapped up in a cape, oblivious to everything.

A dawn that slipped furtively between the ships, like Enrique along the deck.

A dawn that issued from the dead like a chill aura. That made the living seem unreal.

The living who, bleary-eyed and with stinking breath, began to load the dead into the longboats. Then set off like sleep-walkers in the boats.

A dawn made of finest crystal, like the surface of the water smashed to pieces by the oars. As short as the movement of the oars dipping in and out of the water. As subtle as the perfume of flowers coming from the coast.

A dawn like a chrysalis, with a sun inside it. A sun emerging and spreading its wings of gold and blue like a butterfly. A sun as glowing as Hijito's face after he has awoken, seen his father, and given a beaming, innocent smile.

The sun for the living. Darkness and blackness for the dead. A sun that put them to flight as it does bats in the depths of their caves.

The living had already reached the coast, and were busy digging the graves of the dead. The islanders of Zubu approached but remained at a distance, as if to say: Those are their dead.

A sun full of promises, your Highness. Like all suns. Like the look Serrano shot at the queen of Zubu. The queen of Zubu, provocative and sensual like the morning this sun was promising. Insinuating, like the look Carvajo shot at Sebastián, who was standing beside a grave. Conspiratorial, like the look Sebastián returned Carvajo. Treacherous, like the one Enrique gave the king of Zubu, who was watching Serrano. Devious, like the king's smile when he asked after our Captain General and said how much he admired him and was praying for his swift recovery. Lying, like the reply Serrano gave Enrique to transmit to the king.

A sun that gave rise to the chatter of birds in the jungle and the murmur of Latin in the square, where the chaplain was praying for the souls of the dead, who were laid out in rows next to their graves.

A sun that began to cast the shadow of the tall cross which Don Fernando had erected in the square, and to cast light into the sides of the graves, without reaching their depths. The dead were lowered into that darkness to the sound of sad bugles and furious screeching from the monkeys.

They lowered them on ropes, like someone drawing water from a well. Taking great care as they did so, as if they were alive. Or perhaps even greater care.

Then the chaplain blessed the graves from on high, without peering into them. All sound ceased, and the only thing that could be heard was the dull thud of the spades and the sound of earth falling on the dead like sand falling through an hourglass, amid complete silence.

The earth covering Andrés de San Martín's doe eyes. Consigning Filiberto, always so afraid of the dark, to utter blackness. Filling the mouth of Cristóbal Rabelo, that great talker. Stilling all the movements of the ever-active Rodrigo Nieto. Covering Basco Gallego's cow's milk smell with that of the earth, of dung and leafmold. Dirtying Francisco Espinoza's blond locks which he had always taken such care of because he foolishly believed they made him look like Gaspar de Quesada, whom he had always admired for his beauty. Filling Nuño's nostrils, the man who boasted he had the keenest sense of smell in the whole fleet. Clogging up the ears of Antón de Goa, who always listened to what he should not have, then trembled like a mouse without daring to tell anyone what he had heard.

The earth filling the graves with shadows, and the sun filling the land with light. Blocking up the caves of night. Unfurling the sails of dawn. Making life into one long sunny morning.

Because by now it was full morning, your Highness, and the dead had finally departed. Now it was the hour of the living, and there was no room for anything else.

A happy morning, Don Carlos. As blithely unaware as Hijito's face. As carefree as the way he dragged his toy boat in among the freshly covered graves. As loving as the look his father gave him, while he and Sebastián muttered together.

A morning to feel pleased in. To celebrate in. To receive gifts in. To eat a lot in. To get good and drunk in. To be aroused by the queen and her escort. To hear from the mouth of the king the exact location of the Spice Islands.

But only our officers, all twenty-four of them, were to attend the king's feast. The rest of us were already on our way back to the ships, at peace with the morning.

A morning as bright as the waters of the lagoon seen from the longboats. A morning gleaming like a jewel. Sparkling like a diamond. As brightly colored as the fish in the turquoise

302

lagoon. As spotless as the sand on the beach where the group of our officers was following the king. As still as the palm trees and the ships anchored close in to the coast. As clear as the clear blue sky. As fragrant as an early morning market. Pungent with flowers, fish, ripe fruit and the sea. A morning like those that follow a night filled with nightmares.

A morning to sit still in the sun on deck. To talk nonsense. To daydream quietly while the sun hardened into a ball and climbed the sky, and time passed without anyone noticing. As if it were flowing on far from us.

A morning for not lending importance to anything. Not even what we were saying to each other. Or what we were dreaming. Or Sebastián and Carvajo who were back on board the *Trinidad* and were casting anxious glances toward the island, as though there were some reason to be worried. As though something could shatter the warm crystal of the morning. As though the shouts we could suddenly hear might be cries of terror. As though they might be coming from the throats of our officers. Had they not said they would shoot to defend themselves if attacked?

Yet someone gave orders and others left the morning behind and began to turn the capstan and prepared to hoist sail. And the gunners were loading the guns. And the ships were making slowly for the shore.

And then the porcelain morning was cracked open, your Highness. The crystal of the morning was smashed. So too were the still waters of the lagoon. The clear morning air reeked of gunpowder, not flowers, and the huts began to burn as we fired on them, and out of the flames and black smoke we could see islanders leading the wounded Juan Serrano who shouted for us to stop firing because otherwise they would kill him.

The guns ceased firing, and there was a heavy, dead silence, broken only by the roar of the ocean crashing onto the reef, and Serrano still shouting for us to stop firing because they would kill him.

So then I, too, gave up on the morning and went to the starboard side of the ship. I shouted to him to ask what had happened. He struggled with his captors and replied that they had been caught in a trap. All the others had had their throats slit, he said, staining the morning bright red. It had been Enrique who had betrayed them. And they were demanding a ransom in return for his life.

"Send a longboat full of mirrors and some suits of armor," Serrano cried in desperation.

"We'll have to consult the Captain!" Carvajo shouted back.

"It's up to you to decide!" raged Serrano. "I order you to!"

But Carvajo wouldn't hear of it. He insisted that he could not put more men's life at risk without the Captain's consent. Sebastián nodded his head in agreement.

"You're the ones in charge of the fleet now!" Serrano insisted. "You can't leave me here! Pay the ransom, for the love of God! You can't leave me here!"

Carvajo held a long conversation with Sebastián. Too long, because now time was flying by. It had massed all around us, and we were in the eye of a hurricane. The two of them were very calm, while all around them the wind was destroying everything. They gave the command to put about and to head out to sea under full sail, and the wind snatched everything away. It snatched away Juan Serrano's words as he alternately implored and cursed Juan Carvajo, calling on God to make him pay for his crime on the day of judgment. It snatched away the smoke from the burning huts and the burning cross Don Fernando had erected. It snatched away the huts themselves, the palm trees, the beach, all of them receding in the distance as we searched for the channel out through the reef. It snatched away the figure of Juan Serrano, tiny as a doll. Snatched away the ships, by now out on the open sea. Piling on sail until the island itself was snatched away from us.

The wind also snatched away Juan Carvajo's inconsolable cries as he ran up and down the deck calling out to his son. He had thought the boy was playing on board, but he had been left on the island, where we dared not return. Someone remembered seeing him running after his toy boat close to the shore. The boat was keeling over in the wind. A gentle breeze blew it on toward the island and Hijito had chased happily after it.

I WAGER that it's still raining throughout the valley of Plasencia. That the summits of the mountains of Extremadura are lost in black clouds, and mud has made the steep mule tracks up to Yuste impassable. That the rainwater is sluicing off the slate roofs of the village of Cuacos and lying in puddles in the cloister of your monastery. That it has washed clean all the stone saints in the church porch, and brought out the scents of your hanging garden where it competes with the plashing fountains. It has stilled all the birds in their cages and has lent an edenic touch to the orange and lemon trees brought from Byzantium. It makes the fig trees from Corinth seem all the sadder and deepens the red of the carnations from India. It beats against the door leading to the kitchen garden, bounces off the tiles and courses down the stone guttering to the water tanks and the well. It impinges on your room like a distant rumble. The black velvet draping the walls deadens all sound, so that whatever is happening outside seems a long way off. Distant in time and space.

Shut off from the world, in the center of the gloomy room, Don Carlos is playing a solitary game of chess.

The board, a gift from a Persian king, is made of glass. The pawns are tiny warriors, there are miniature castles and knights.

Hunched over them, hardly able to distinguish one from the other, you remember far-off days when you filled your spare time with fierce chess battles against kings as powerful as you were.

In those days you were invincible. Nobody moved the pieces with such cunning. The game fascinated you. You savored each move leading to your inevitable victory. You enjoyed seeing your opponent's astonished face. You were flattered by the comments and applause of the people who followed the game for hours. You longed for the moment when you could shake your defeated opponent's hand with false modesty.

Things are different now. You can hardly see the pieces, and almost have to touch the board with your nose to work out which square they are on. You are bored of playing on your own. Without an opponent or an audience. Struggling from one chair to another to consider moves you already know by heart. Moves no one is going to applaud. To achieve a victory that is at the same time a defeat. That means nothing, and leaves you cold.

This solitary pastime of yours always ends the same way. You sweep all the pieces away with one hand, while the other taps feebly on the glass board.

You stare down at the polished glass, seeing the reflection of your tired face. Then you bend forward to survey the tiny figures.

There are fallen warriors, toppled castles, vanquished knights. Tomorrow your chamberlain will put them all back in their places. And when you are sickened by the game again, you will sweep them all off once more.

But your breath clouds the glass board, your eyes are troubled, everything becomes a blur. The knight fallen under the table reminds you of Don Fernando lying in the turquoise waters of the lagoon. That other piece, up against the edge of its square as if trying to escape, makes you think of Juan Serrano. A third one, still standing, looks like Sebastián. And in a toppled castle you imagine you see a ship.

Then you collapse exhausted onto the board, thinking that chess is a stupid game which you will never play again.

I MUST tell your Majesty that after leaving Zubu behind we drifted for several days at the mercy of wind and current.

In those two bitter days we had lost not only many lives but also the fragile sense of hope we had regained, and with it all our last vestiges of reason.

We found ourselves lost in a maze of islands that all seemed exactly the same, and all seemed as dangerous as Zubu.

Those were days of such tremendous confusion that even now, so many years later, I find it hard to distinguish what really happened from what were the projections of my own tormented mind.

Sebastián was in command of the fleet because Serrano never recovered his reason after his loss. He spent whole days sitting at the foot of the mainmast, staring up at the sky with a distant expression on his face, or carving another toy boat out of a piece of wood. The sudden, brutal death of all our officers in the king of Zubu's trap had left gaps he couldn't possibly fill. The crews spoke of the dead men as though they were still alive. They spoke of them in the present tense, then corrected themselves in amazement, leaving their phrases disjointed, half-finished. They tried not to mention the dead, and found that their sentences had no subject. Then the predicate or, above all, the verb they used, always in the conditional, gave them away.

Above all, we needed time to get used to the sudden absence of those who had been killed and to accept it as definitive. That was what was hardest. We had shared the cramped confines of the ships with them for twenty months. And the even more cramped space of fear and hunger. And the windowless room of doubt. The dungeon of anguish. The pit of despair. All of us piled in there together. But suddenly there were blank spaces, as in a sketch for a painting. Lines that showed the bare canvas underneath. Even worse, those blank spaces had been officers. People who gave us orders. People we were used to obeying. People in whom, fitfully and more out of necessity than conviction, we had come to believe. Even Sebastián and the other surviving officers were prey to the same sense of confusion, so that there was no one now to give any orders, and no one who had any idea of the next step we should take or the direction we should steer in. The fleet followed the winds, or an occasional, haphazard change of course taken by the *Trinidad*, the lead ship, which obliged the others to change course too, as soon as they became aware of it. But that was all. No one decided what sail we should put on. No one kept the rigging tight. No one read the compass, or took our bearings or soundings for depth. We simply fled. As far from Zubu as possible.

Not so much to escape from the danger, but rather to put as much distance as possible between us and the dreadful events that had taken place there. We sailed on blindly, directionless and out of control, like a man walking round his house in the middle of the night in order to forget a terrible nightmare: he keeps on and on out of fear that he might fall asleep again and find himself caught in the nightmare once more. To add to our confusion, the archipelago we were stuck in seemed to consist of an infinite number of islands, islets, and reefs. All of them very much alike. We were even afraid we might be sailing round in circles and would never find our way out. Nobody thought of using the astrolabe, and we didn't have the slightest idea whether we were in the northern or southern hemisphere. We might well have been among the Spice Islands, but no one even considered landing. At the very heart of all the confusion and ambiguity in which we found ourselves was Don Fernando's unresolved death. This gave rise to the most absurd situations. Sebastián, for example, grew very angry when he discovered the truth, although I think he had never believed in Serrano's lie. Yet it suited him to keep up the illusion, for his own protection. So he frequently visited the cabin, and filled his mouth with orders from the Captain that fooled nobody. There was no point in his trying to keep the secret, as the news had already spread throughout the ships, although not everyone believed it or could take it in. A lot of the men went on talking about the Captain's wound and of how everything would be fine once he was better. This attitude soon took hold like the plague, and everyone began to pretend that Don Fernando was still alive, even though they knew it was a lie. So much so that I even came to pretend it was true myself, and one night I had to go down to his cabin to rid myself of the delusion. The Captain General's presence seemed far more real and tangible now than during all the time when Serrano was trying so hard to make believe he was still alive. It was as though the hourglasses had become hourglasses again, and the same with the compasses and the astrolabe, not to mention his slippers under the bunk and his suit of armor on it. No longer were they objects that had outlived a person, or the remains of some lost civilization. It was as if their owner had simply stepped out, and could return at any moment. That sensation gave me courage. I sat on the bunk next to the armor and stared at it for a while. Then I touched the helmet with my fingertips. I caressed each of the pieces of the suit. I did not sniff them, because I was afraid that perhaps Serrano had left the imprint of his smell on them and I wouldn't be able to distinguish it from Don Fernando's. But I tried them on: first one part, then another, until little by little I was wearing the entire suit. I must say that despite my lack of stature it did not seem too big for me. The only thing I didn't put on was the helmet, because I was afraid of suffocating or of getting stuck inside it. If the visor were to fall shut, the outside world would disappear and in that deathlike darkness there might perhaps be some traces of the Captain's spittle, still damp. Or a hair from his head or beard stuck in one of the helmet joints, still growing. Or there might be some hint of his warm, living breath. I imagined that the helmet was a gourd, whose pulp was made of Don Fernando's ideas and feelings, whose seeds were his dreams or the germs of other ideas he had never thought out, other feelings or sensations he had never succeeded in living. As I lay stretched out on his bed, the temptation to put the helmet on grew despite myself. When I realized what was happening, I tried to fight against it, but I was already completely seduced by the idea. I knew I was bound to give in to it, so I threw off the armor as quickly as I could and fled from the cabin. I ran along the deck, stumbling over Carvajo who was, as ever, sitting beneath the mainmast, and flung myself into the forecastle without once looking back.

But your Highness should also know that the situation I have described above lasted only a few days, although I couldn't say exactly how many, before a change took place.

In this respect, I must admit that it was Sebastián who gradually freed us from the grip of the dead and began to take charge of the fleet.

His new authority stemmed largely from the determination with which he made a decision that was painful for us all. When we fled Zubu, the numbers of our crews had diminished so much that we no longer had enough men to sail three ships. As the days went by, it was plain to everyone that there was one ship too many, but nobody had the courage to say so or even to admit it to himself. This was because the ships were our only possible link with Spain. They were the only umbilical cord joining us to our placenta. Cutting that cord meant forever renouncing the world we belonged to, and instead opening our eyes at last to the cold, hostile, distant one we were in. The ships were our gateway back. They were Spanish animals, born of the same land as we were. They had left their roots in the soil there, like us. They had been torn from the land and thrown into the sea, like us. They had resisted even when we had given up hope. And although they were as battered by now as we were, somehow they were better, more important than us. And anyway, we had already lost two of them. Nobody was willing to think of losing a third. Nobody. Except for Sebastián. He said there was one ship too many, and that it would be better to go on with two that had enough men and provisions. His announcement started a bitter argument. On the first day, everyone was against an idea that was considered not only crazy but brutal. A great wave of rejection swept from ship to ship and continued well into the night. But the seed had been sown. Two or three days later, Sebastián calmly and coolly said we ought to agree on which ship was to be left behind. This time the uproar was between those supporting each different ship. There were fierce quarrels, which even came to blows. No one could agree, but all the while the seed was sprouting and growing. A few days after that, Sebastián held a meeting with the few officers who remained. Each one gave a report on the condition of his ship, but the reports were far from impartial, and the meeting broke up without any decision being taken. Then, after another couple of days, Sebastián announced his choice to Francisco de Albo, the chief pilot.

He intended to keep the *Victoria* because it was the most maneuverable. He would keep the *Trinidad* since it had been the original flagship. But the *Concepción* would be burnt.

"Burnt?" Albo queried.

"Make sure you collect anything that might be useful and transfer it to the other two ships. And share out the men as you think fit," was the other's laconic reply.

"Can we really not save the ship?" Albo insisted, disagreeing with Sebastián.

"When you see her, you'll know I'm right," Sebastián retorted.

Your Majesty, your servant Juanillo was one of the small group of experts who went with Albo to examine the *Concepción*.

We went over in the skiff, discussing what could be done to save her. As we looked at the dark hull from the sea, we all thought: there is nothing wrong with her.

And yet before we had been around her once, every one of us had fallen silent.

She didn't have a hull anymore. It was a rock. An upside-down promontory rising from the sea. The oaken beams had absorbed so much sea salt they had turned to stone. There was no sign of any joints between them, or any rivets, wedges or bronze nails. The hull was the prop for a strange world of seaweed and thousands of tiny creatures that had stuck to it during the voyage. There were big barnacles, pink as a young girl's cheek but as invulnerable as warriors inside their armor-plating. There were other barnacles too: the kind that cling to turtle shells, and others normally found on whales' backs. There were innocent-looking hat-shaped limpets, which were always the toughest to remove in any careening. There were waving goose barnacles, clinging to the hull as obstinately as a crusader to his faith. Some of these were white, others black, like chess pieces. There were tiny crabs as well, and more starfish than there are stars in the sky above Bustillo. And of course there was a plentiful supply of the kind of termites that burrow long and complicated tunnels into wood. While a ship tussles with the wind up above, below water its death creeps forward along these secret passages. But above all, the hull was covered in seaweed. Green seaweed and brown. Some small and crinkly

311

like young lettuce leaves. Some as hairy as beards. Some fleshy and dark. And some with huge wavy leaves that projected their shadow on the sand of the sea bottom. Adding a sinister touch to everything.

The *Concepción* lay keeled over, and this hidden, extraordinary marine world spread all over both sides of the hull, right down to the water line.

As I said, your Majesty, not one of us said a word as we climbed on board.

We found it hard to move about on the tilted deck, although the crew had grown so used to it that they seemed to have no trouble. When we were able to stand upright properly, we surveyed the remarkable scene before our eyes.

Everything was covered with green foliage. Creepers thrust their way out of the gangways, invading the deck. They entwined themselves round the masts, and pushed their way out along the yardarms. They carpeted the sterndeck and filled every porthole.

In the midst of this explosion of vegetation, the rigging hung limply like lianas in the jungle. All the metal and bronze fittings had disappeared under a green mold. The sails, which would never be white again, were covered with fungus.

The whole ship was like an abandoned park, with only the silent fountain and broken statue missing.

"How could this have happened?" I wondered. I myself had been present in Santa Lucía bay when Don Fernando had given the order to throw overboard all the plants which were threatening to take over the ship. I had seen the oranges glimmering underwater; lit by a gentle evening light, they seemed to have ripened, even though they were dead. The lemons though, I remembered, had looked paler on the sand of the seabed. And the olives had gleamed like rubies set in the gray branches of their trees planted in barrels that sat under the water beneath the hull.

All of which meant that what was happening now could not have anything to do with the floating kitchen garden that Gaspar de Quesada's ship had once been.

Besides, my Jewish nostrils no longer perceived the scents of a Sevilla garden. This time a much less subtle, more penetrating fragrance wafted over the stilled decks.

It was then that I saw the birds of the islands flying in and out of the hatchways. I saw the insects swarming in the portholes, and the bees building their honeycombs in the mouths of the cannon. I could hear a buzzing and the beating of wings coming from the empty stores. And I remembered the earth from Oporto.

That earth the Captain had ordered kept was the source of the miracle. Tilled by the birds, sowed with the seeds they dropped in their excrement and with pollen from flowers brought on the insects' legs, everything had germinated in the humid climate of the islands and the hot sun.

The *Concepción* had blossomed a second time. It had become a garden once more. A strange, fragrant vegetable creation. A creation that obeyed its own laws and would have nothing to do with ours.

Yet I did not have a clear idea of all that was happening until we went down to inspect the holds.

We found complete chaos. The empty barrels had broken free of their ropes and were floating or rolling around freely, causing untold damage. One of them had crashed into the store where the mirrors and other trinkets were piled, smashing nearly all of them. There were other compartments where the water reached up to our waists. Everywhere below decks stank of rotten seaweed and urine from the bilges. And yet life was teeming in this sordid darkness. Birds made their nests among the broken mirrors and glass necklaces. They fluttered in and out of the beams. Preened themselves on top of the empty barrels. Darted into every corner, searching for seeds and grain. Anything that had survived our periods of hunger. Anything we had loaded in Sevilla that had perhaps fallen from some split sack. Or had been carried there on the muddy feet of a cabin boy. Precious seeds the birds carried away with them to the islands.

How had we not noticed this transformation before?

You know what men are like, your Highness, and how they can look without seeing, especially if they put their mind to it. Take me, for example. As a boy, I always thought my mother was the most beautiful woman in Bustillo until I saw her laid out dead. Force of habit they call it, Don Carlos. I'm sure the same happened to you with the queen. Or that you were the most surprised of all of us to discover that Felipe had suddenly turned into a real king. I wager that until that very moment you had gone on seeing him as a child. And that even today you find it hard to see him any other way.

That is what happened with us and the *Concepción*. Only Sebastián, who was cold and calculating, could see the ship as she really was. And he ordered her burnt to free us of our illusion.

The ship that had first been commanded by Gaspar de Quesada, and then by Juan Serrano. That had carried Don Fernando's bucolic dream, his cows, his chickens, his oranges, his eggplants. That had been both a prison and a hiding place for the young virgins. That in one of its forward holds still transported some of the earth the Captain General had wished to be buried in. The *Concepción*, your Highness, despite its lovely name, was going to be burnt. Like a witch or a heretic. For a number of practical reasons. And because she had betrayed the will of her builders and given in to other powers, with the docility only wood possesses.

The chosen day was one of mourning for us all. Sebastián pointed to a reef for her to be driven onto and then, without even having her broken up, ordered her set on fire.

At first we thought she would resist, but gradually we saw the flames emerging from the hatchways and licking at the sails.

Soon the *Concepción* was burning like a giant firework. The sails burst into flame and fell in fiery tatters. More flames spread along the yardarms and the rigging, then leapt up the masts. The sterndeck was a blazing mass, the forecastle collapsed and scattered red hot timbers along the decks. It was the time of day when a shore breeze blew, and the wind that had so often filled her sails now fanned the flames.

A short while later, the hull, too, was on fire. The timbers crumbled to cinders, and flames snaked like a trail of gunpowder along the secret tunnels made by the termites. Thick black smoke poured out, enveloping the ship and rising in a plume into the sky, blocking out the sun. Smoke that smelled of the tar Sebastian had used to start the blaze with, but that also gave off hints of the fragrances soaked into the wood: the smells of an ancient woodland, far-off ports, the salty tang of the sea and a vague suggestion of jasmine.

The sight suddenly became too much for me. As I looked around, all I could see were men with tears in their eyes. I ran to seek refuge in the Captain's cabin.

I flung myself on his bunk and shut my eyes tight so I would not have to see the red glow of the flames. But the crackling of burning timbers became louder and louder in the darkness, until it was deafening. I could not bear it.

Suddenly an idea crossed my mind. This time I couldn't resist. I picked up Don Fernando's helmet, put it on, and pulled the visor down.

At first I was in complete darkness. I was scared: my heart was pounding in my chest and the veins on my neck pulsed wildly. I found it hard to breathe inside the iron mask. I felt I was suffocating, and was bound to choke and die. But after a few moments, my eyes began to get used to it. Through the visor I could make out parts of the room, bathed in the red light from the fire. I could see strips of the table and the window. I could see half an hourglass, the point of a compass, the rim of an astrolabe. And if I moved my head carefully, I could see the rest: the carved wood of the compasses, the tin disc of the astrolabe. Little by little I worked out what all the objects around me were, even those that were closest to me and so were most affected by the bars of the helmet. This calmed me a little. I regained control over my breathing and became less anxious. I realized I was not going to suffocate inside the helmet, so then I began to explore it with all my five senses. On the outside it was shaped like a griffin, and my hands drew back from the cold touch of metal. But inside it was warm. My nostrils picked out the neutral smell, like cold water, that the iron gave off, and this disturbed me. Previously I had always thought that this was Don Fernando's smell, and if it wasn't, what did he really smell like? When I licked the iron, it was harsh and sticky. Just like any piece of iron.

Now I had no more doubts: Don Fernando was no longer there. I stretched out on the bed with the helmet on and closed my eyes again.

"Would you like me to tell you about them?" I said. Nobody answered, but I went on pretending I was having one of the dialogues I used to have with him, when suddenly I was overwhelmed by a vision.

I saw a woman dressed in black who looked very different from the Beatriz I had imagined for the Captain. She was disheveled, with a wild staring look in her eyes. Like a madwoman. She was in a huge, bare room. A room that was too big and empty to be in a private house. She was seated in the middle of that vast space, rocking backwards and forwards as if she were cradling an invisible baby. Every so often, a boy aged about three or four crossed the room. He might have been playing, but if he was, it was a sad, unenthusiastic game.

Then a door opened. A shaft of light streamed across the floor, which I now realized was made of black and white tiles, like a chessboard. The dark outline of a soldier appeared in the rectangle of light, oddly magnified. The child ran from the far end of the room, taking an eternity to reach the door. The shadow held out a bowl to him. The boy dashed it away, then ran back to the opposite corner of the room for protection. The shadow moved agonizingly slowly across to the woman, and carefully placed another bowl and jug beside her. Without looking up, she said, "Has the fleet returned?"

The shadow did not answer. But it stood still next to the woman.

"Is there still no news of the expedition to the Spice Islands?" she asked again, this time more gently.

The soldier did not reply, but leaned forward and briefly stroked her gray hair.

"When my husband returns I will tell him how good you have been to us. He is a very important person and he is very rich, he will make sure you are well rewarded," she said, still not looking at him.

"You should eat," the shadow said.

"Have you heard of the Spice Islands?" came her reply.

He nodded, but she stared into the distance without noticing. Then she added, "The Spice Islands are . . ." but did not finish her sentence.

"You should eat," the soldier insisted. "If only for the child's sake," he added, looking down at the woman's empty arms.

She raised her eyes and looked up at the shadow for the first time. She smiled.

"He's almost two," she said. "He eats everything."

"Do you need anything more?" the shadow asked.

"The same as always. Just tell me when the fleet arrives. I'll have to smarten up. I can't go to the port like this. His Majesty and all the court will be there."

The dark shadow moved back toward the door. It paused an instant in the rectangle of light shining on the floor, then cast a final glance at the woman, who had begun rocking back and forth again.

"You'll see, when your father gets home . . ." she said to the boy, who had run over from the corner and was eating from her bowl.

The shadow disappeared, cutting off the phrase with the clang of the heavy door shutting. Then all that could be heard was the sound of the key turning in the lock, and the vast space once more became as silent and desolate as it had been at the start of the vision. Except that now there was nobody there . . .

"I see a square in Sevilla, and a woman walking across it with one child in her arms and another beside her. As they pass a corner, a dog barks, the older boy is frightened and clings to his mother's skirts. She smiles and . . ."

But it was pointless to go on. There was no reason for me to lie like that, because nobody was listening. Suddenly the idea

317

of the gourd and its seeds flashed through my mind again and I quickly snatched off the helmet.

By the time I returned on deck, the sun had set and the *Concepción* was no more than a glowing pile of ashes on the reef.

ALTHOUGH THE episode I have just related was a shock that to some extent restored our spirits and helped confirm the new Captain General's authority, the effect did not last long.

The *Trinidad* and the *Victoria* were still lost in a maze of what seemed to be identical islands.

At each island we sent ashore a squad of heavily armed men. It was always the same thing. We never heard voices, only the roar of arquebuses. They never returned with any information about the Spice Islands, only bloodstained hands. Always the same thing.

At first they would wash the blood off before they returned to the ships, but it still left traces on the oars and the sides of the longboat. Soon they no longer bothered to make the effort, and went around with dried blood under their nails and in the hair on their arms.

They usually returned with wild eyes and mouths clamped shut, so no one asked them any questions. Sometimes not all of them came back, but no one mentioned the missing person: he was simply replaced.

But they never brought any news about the Spice Islands.

Gradually we began to notice again the gaps left by those who had died, especially the captains. Sebastián's authority foundered in those bottomless wells. He did all he could to plug the holes, but found it was useless. Phantoms were everywhere and time, Sebastián's worst enemy, was on their side.

As the weeks went by, the feeling that the voyage was over began to take root in everyone's mind. So it came as no surprise when one morning, after many months of wandering, the squad came back from an island without us having heard their guns being fired and with their hands unbloodied, and informed us we were in Castilla.

After all, Don Fernando had always said that the world was round and by sailing west we would inevitably come back to the place we had started from.

"How do you know we are in Castilla?" Sebastián asked, nervously running his fingers through his once red hair.

And then the members of the squad, usually so silent, all began to talk at once and we could not understand a thing.

They had landed on the beach and almost immediately a group of islanders had appeared. They looked like Moors. The soldiers ordered them to halt, as usual. In fact, they looked more like the other islanders than like true Moors, but they seemed very friendly. The soldiers asked what the island was called, something they always did to see whether we had finally reached the Spice Islands. One of the islanders was a boy about ten years old. His skin was as white as ours. According to the boy, the island was called Castilla, his name was Serrano, and he had a letter for Don Fernando. He showed it to them, wrapped in a deerskin.

"There are so many ships sailing to the Indies nowadays; these must be people brought to Castilla by someone keen to show them to curious Europeans," Pigafetta said, with that knowing air of his.

But no one was listening to him, because we were all clinging to what the squad had said, words that still floated in the silence, the way that the fragrance of jasmine persists even after the flower has faded.

We all stared at the coastline. At first it did not seem anything like Spain, but gradually, as memories came back into our minds, we began to identify it more and more.

One man thought he recognized a place that was close to his home village. Another said that an object sticking up in the distance was the belltower of his town. And a third man remembered how he used to go fishing with his uncle up on the rocks we could see. One man in our group was worried about how he looked. Another was silently practicing a smile that he found hard to muster. Yet another was wondering what he would say. Everyone was very composed and restrained, as though waiting for a signal. Staring first at the coast and then at Sebastián, who was the person who had to give the signal, but who seemed confused, unable to make up his mind.

There was a pause, as long as the voyage itself, then finally came the sound of Sebastián's expressionless voice, which said: "We're home."

At once the celebrations began. Men hugged each other and danced around. Others started weeping. Still others were mute with astonishment. A few rushed down to the longboats. The gunners began loading the cannon to announce to the world that we had arrived.

Now tell me, your Highness, can you possibly imagine how we felt at that moment?

No, Don Carlos, the truth is that you cannot. First and foremost, because your home is the whole world, and though I take no pleasure in saying so, that means that you have no true home. All cities are the same for you, because you always see them decked out in garlands, with triumphal arches and Roman gods. And their people are always happy and celebrating, waving flags and shouting "Long live the king!" until your procession has passed by. After which they return to their usual routine. To their empty pots and pans, their domestic quarrels, the bawling child or the cat waiting for them curled up by the fireside. And they are happy to be there because, however poor they might be, they have a place of their own in this world, and all they have to do is shut the door and leave the weather outside and they will feel better, more in control of their destinies.

Whereas you, your Highness, find that at the end of the long avenues of paper garlands and cardboard triumphal arches, there is only an empty palace waiting for you. A palace the same as all others. With too many windows. Endless corridors. Doors that are always shut, with nothing behind them. However much people admire their magnificent exteriors, you yourself hate these mazelike buildings where ever since you were a child you have been terrified of getting lost.

That is why you cannot understand how we felt when Sebastián said, so unemphatically, "We're home."

Nor can you understand the emotion that overwhelmed us as we drew closer to the beach. Nor the feeling of solidity it gave us to land there rather than anywhere else. Nor the dejection which slowly took hold of our minds like a poison. Because the islanders were explaining to Sebastián in broken Spanish that their king had been awaiting our arrival for years and that he had changed the name of his island to Castilla in our honor. Their Spanish was so hard to follow our squad must have misunderstood what they meant. When they heard all this, some of the men drifted off; others tried to hide their tears. Perhaps they simply did not want to hear the questions Sebastián was asking. Or the replies he was given. The islanders knew we would come thanks to one Francisco Serrano, a Portuguese friend of our Captain, Don Fernando. Serrano had lived there nine years, in the service of the king of Ternate. He was in charge of their armies and their trade. And he knew we would come because that was what he had agreed with the Captain. Many years earlier. They had been shipwrecked together once, after they had put down an uprising by the sultan of Malacca. They had been searching for cloves and the Spice Islands when their ship sank. Don Fernando had saved Francisco's life, and had promised him he would raise the money to equip a fleet and come back. But we had arrived too late, because Serrano had died a few months before. He had left two children, one of them a girl, dark-skinned like the island people, the other a boy who was as white as his father. Serrano had taught them Spanish when he heard Don Fernando would be sailing under the flag of Castilla. The boy was nine by now, and had a letter for the Captain General.

While the islanders were explaining all this, our crews wandered off in all directions. Some of them walked down the beach. Others went round in circles. A few explored the paths into the island jungle. Marcos de Bayas, the *Trinidad*'s barber, waded out to sea, calling out, "What on earth is a barber doing here?" He never came back.

Little by little, Sebastián was left on his own with the boy. He was trying to explain to him that Don Fernando had died, like the boy's father, and that he was the new Captain General of the fleet, so the boy should give him the letter. The child showed him the deerskin it was wrapped in, but refused to hand it over.

I was tired of always hearing the same thing, namely that we had not reached home, so I drifted away from them too. I walked up and down, without knowing which direction to head in. Finally I stopped to examine a tall tree that stood out from the rest of the forest. It was about the width of a man in girth, and the top branches formed a kind of pyramid. Its bark was olive-colored, and its leaves looked like laurel. What most caught my attention, though, was that its newest branches ended in a bud made up of cloves, some of them red and others black.

I picked one of the cloves and put it in my mouth. It had such a strong taste that as I chewed it my tongue went numb. I pulled off a bunch and smelled them.

It was a clove tree, your Highness. The tree our spice grew on! And the island was filled with them as far as my eyes could see.

I could not believe it, but there was Joan de Acurio standing next to me, his huge, warm, dove-like hands full of the same tiny cloves. He had a look of utter astonishment on his face and held them as if he did not know what to do with them.

I ran back to Sebastián.

"Ask him what the island is called," I shouted.

"Spice Island," the boy replied. "My father called it the Spice Island."

DON CARLOS wakes with a start. Someone is talking to him, but he has fallen asleep slumped over the glass chessboard and it takes time for him to emerge from the mists. He opens his eyes and looks down between his arms, without straightening up. He can scarcely make out the tiny chess pieces. But Don Carlos knows they are there: fallen pawns, toppled castles, vanquished knights. And that the next morning his chamberlain will put them all back in their places.

He struggles to lift his head. He can feel a trickle of spittle drooling out of his mouth onto his beard, and he feels ashamed, so he stays in the same position.

He knows the servant is standing next to him like a statue, carrying the heavy silver tray in his hands. He can make out the smell of stale sweat coming from the page's velvet jacket, but cannot tell what is on the steaming tray. His sense of smell had once been as acute as a bloodhound's, and he had been able to distinguish every aroma. He could combine the different savors in his mind without ever getting them wrong. He had been the only person in all the court who could spot the subtle fragrance of nutmeg, identify ginger straightaway, distinguish white pepper from black, and discuss any recipe without even trying the dish. Anyone could tell if a dish had cinnamon in it, but only he knew exactly how much. And similarly with aniseed, cumin, barberry, musk, sandalwood used for perfuming white wine, and even ground ambergris. Of all the spices, the one he liked least was the clove. Its aroma was too strong, and he found its taste too vulgar and overpowering. He detested all dishes made with cloves, and his cooks soon learnt not to include them in their recipes. But that was long ago. Nowadays they paid him no heed. And if he protested and threw the plate on the floor, they treated him as condescendingly as if he were a spoiled child.

Don Carlos lifts his head, already annoyed. With a gesture intended to be majestic but which is merely childish, he signals for his tray to be left on the chessboard.

The servant obeys. He puts down the tray, and unceremoniously ties a big napkin round the king's neck. Then he leaves without a word.

His hands trembling, the king lifts the lid of a porcelain dish shaped like a fish. Inside it lies a steaming turbot baked with garlic, pepper and aniseed. Once, this was one of his favorite dishes, but now the mere sight of it revolts him. He prefers desserts. His lusterless eyes light up for an instant when they spy the bright scarlet of a small cherry tart. But the gleam of joy quickly turns to one of anger. The tart is decorated with a string of cloves, and to make things even worse, there is a whole bunch of them in its center. The sight of the fresh cherries overwhelmed by the cloying, overpowering smell of the cloves is more than the king can bear. So he pushes wearily at the heavy tray with his crippled hands until it reaches the edge of the board and slowly topples over, falling with a crash onto the rug. For a while he stares at what he has done. There are cherries scattered everywhere, and the ridiculous little cloves have even reached the bronze feet of the enormous globe at the far side of the room. Proud of his handiwork, Don Carlos rings his bell. Nobody comes. The organ has started up again in the chapel next door. Perhaps they cannot hear me, he thinks. Then his mind goes blank. He is trying to focus on something, but it keeps escaping him. He would like to sleep, but he is not sleepy. These days he dozes off at any time without warning, but at night he cannot sleep at all. This makes his nights long and empty. He peers again at the fallen tray. He sees the remains scattered all over the floor, and his gaze comes to rest on a handful of cloves mixed in with a jumbled mess of cherry tart. Suddenly he remembers Juanillo's chronicle. He tries to recall what he read that morning, but everything is blurred, like a landscape viewed through a dirty pane of glass, or like the chess pieces under the table. Yet he does not give up, because he knows that my pages are the only thing he has to help him through the night. He could go and get the manuscript, but it is at the far end of the room, which seems to him to grow bigger by the day, and he does not think he has the strength to walk all that way. Besides, the idea of the long trek, with both hands on his cane for support, fills him with dread. He will have to pass in front of the Titian portraits again, and he will have to stop and ask himself why the artist painted them so out of proportion. He will have to lean on the organ he took with him on so many campaigns—campaigns whose names and dates he no longer remembers. He will have to kneel in front of the ivory Christ and in order to get up again will have to clutch at the black velvet drapes the Cross hangs from. And he will smear his feet and the hem of his gown with the food strewn across the floor. So he chooses to stay at the chess table, trying to conjure up my chronicle in his mind. He cannot recall the exact words I used, but perhaps he will be able to summon up some of the events, or the sensations they gave him. He remembers the two ships left the Spice Islands so heavily loaded that the *Trinidad* sprang a serious leak. He remembers that the idiots threw most of their cargo overboard in an attempt to save the ship. The precious cargo. And that they wasted more of it by exchanging the spices for food, which they were once again running out of. Spices for food, the idiots, he mutters to himself. He remembers that we were forced to abandon the *Trinidad*, and that Juanillo was so upset that he ran to hide in the Captain's cabin once more. He remembers that the buffoon wanted to take the Captain's armor with him, but the others would not let him because it was so heavy. He cannot recall the Captain's name exactly, perhaps it will come back to him later. He does remember that Juanillo put the helmet on again but found it impossible to conjure up a vision of the Captain's wife and child as he had done before. He remembers that we then set sail through Portuguese waters, as our ship would not have withstood the journey back the way we came, and he thinks that was very foolhardy too. He remembers that we preferred to carry spices rather than provisions, and that over twenty more sailors died of hunger. He remembers that we were so demoralized that . . . But he can get no further than the that . . . Try as he might, he cannot remember anything more. His mind is a blank again. Exhausted, he leans his forehead against the chessboard, enjoying the cool sensation of the glass on his skin. His eyes search in vain for the chess pieces: the fallen pawns, the toppled castles, the vanquished knights—he cannot see them. The smell of cloves dominates the room and makes him feel sick. The organ music fills him with horror. He rings the bell again with trembling fingers, but again no one comes. He makes up his mind. He decides he will set out. He will cross the black room. He will sit at his work table. He will pick up my chronicle, and this time he will not put it down until he has finished.

———

JUANILLO WAS perched up in the crow's nest like a bird, when he saw the bluish outline of a promontory rising out of the monotonous gray of the horizon.

At first he gave it no importance. He was not the lookout; they had long since given up posting anyone to do that. He was up there simply to get away from the misery on deck. From on high, the men walking around the ship like shadows were the size of figures in an altarpiece.

Your Juanillo was amusing himself imagining that the deck was a theater where a handful of actors were rehearsing their roles before going on stage. And he admired how well some of them were simulating fear, others hunger, all of them despair. He also admired their costumes. Most of them had several sets of clothes on, one on top of the other, all equally filthy. Some of them even wore a battered moldy green breastplate on top of the rags, just to emphasize their wretchedness. They had also made up their faces remarkably. The whole company had painted them a dull white, almost gray color, with violet circles around the eyes that emphasized the cadaverous hollows of the sockets. Yet it was not only the way the actors had used powders and disguises that made their portrayal so convincing. Like the skilled actors they were, their every gesture was thought out. They were true artists in showing sadness, indifference, fear, and confusion. And they trod the boards, rehearsing these gestures over and over again, because the play was in mime, without dialogue.

Watching their act from his vantage point high above, Juanillo was so caught up in his thoughts he did not even think of the promontory again until the ship was much closer to it.

Then he thought that either his eyes were deceiving him or his mind was playing tricks on him, and he again tried to turn his attention elsewhere. But the still imprecise image of the promontory kept coming back to him. Finally he got to his feet. It was hard to remain standing in the crow's nest, as the ship was keeled over at a sharp angle, but he clung to the mast and stared at the promontory for a long while. By evening they had drawn so close he had no doubt anymore: it was the rock of Gibraltar that he could see in the distance, standing there like a mother waiting for her children on her doorstep.

So he began to shout and to draw everyone's attention to the port side. Nobody paid any attention to his cries. No one looked to see where he was pointing. Not one of them seemed to notice the huge mass of rock that grew and grew with each passing moment.

Juanillo came down to the deck as quickly as he could, and seized the first man he came across: "It's the rock of Gibraltar!"

But Juan de Santander, a cabin boy from the *Santiago*, went on playing with a rope without even looking up at him.

He ran across the gangway and bumped into Miguel de Rodas.

"Look at the rock, your Honor," he said. "It's the rock of Gibraltar!"

"Stop playing games," the other man replied. "This is no time for your tomfoolery."

Juanillo insisted, but Miguel went on his way, muttering to himself. So he decided to seek out Sebastián, whom he found leaning against the port rail, staring at the rock.

"This time we really have arrived home," Juanillo said.

Sebastián looked at him uncomprehendingly.

"It's Gibraltar, isn't it?" Juanillo asked.

"It's similar, yes," Sebastián replied in a friendly way.

"It's more than similar, it's the rock itself," Juanillo insisted.

"I wish it were as much as you do," Sebastián said, smiling broadly.

Juanillo wanted to hurl insults at him, to drive him wild so he would wipe the stupid grin off his face, but after watching him closely for a moment or two, he changed his mind. This was not the Sebastián of old. He had aged years in the past few months. He was almost completely bald and his cheeks were gaunt and sunken from lack of teeth.

With the same broad smile on his face, Sebastián explained to him that it could not be Gibraltar because all the charts and instruments said it was not. He agreed that it was very similar, but he had sailed past the rock dozens of times and would be the first to recognize it.

"Don't you worry," he said. "The real one will soon appear."

Juanill made no reply, but watched silently as the ship sailed on and left the rock behind.

An hour later they sighted a village on the coast.

Sebastián, whose brain was muddled from tropical fevers and from having to show more patience than Job, ordered them to drop anchor. They would attack the village at night, he said, and make sure to take on water and provisions for the rest of their journey. Spain could not be that far off.

"But we have already reached Spain," protested Juanillo.

Nobody answered.

A short while later he tried talking to Joan de Acurio, who he thought might still have his wits about him.

"We passed the rock of Gibraltar, and this is the Spanish coast," he told him.

But Joan de Acurio was no longer the man of a few months earlier either. Even his round, warm, dovelike hands had become bony and cold from rheumatism. He stood there at a loss, trying to find words that would not come.

After nightfall they came as close to the shore as they dared, and then set off in a longboat that was leaking on all sides.

Barefoot and dressed in rags, they looked like ghosts flitting through the shadows. Each of them took up his place according to Sebastián's instructions, and waited silently for the signal to attack.

They waited for an absurdly long time, as if the Captain could not make up his mind. The moon rose in the sky and bathed the sleeping village in its light.

The village had whitewashed walls; the doors and windows of its houses were blue. The belltower cast its shadow across the tiled roofs; moonbeams danced off the stone cobbles of the streets.

Juanillo went to find Sebastián, who was under cover, staring at the houses.

"Now are you convinced?" he asked him.

Sebastián nodded.

"It's a Portuguese colony," he said. "We had better retreat."

(To my mind, your Highness, Sebastián was never convinced we had reached Spain, even after we had arrived at Sanlúcar and gone on to Sevilla, or when he received the honors you bestowed on him in Valladolid. He was so obsessed with the Portuguese and their supposed plot to rob him of the spices that deep down inside he thought everything was a show especially put on by them. So much so that when, four years later, you put him in charge of another expedition to the Spice Islands, he confessed to his closest friends that this was a plan of his so that he might finally reach Spain.)

A few days after that absurd landing we saw the unmistakable outline of the duke of Medina-Sidonia's castle and, in its shadow, the white houses of Sanlúcar de Barrameda.

Without anyone saying a word or any spoken agreement between us, we all set to work lightening the ship's load. Your Majesty should know that the *Victoria* was in such bad shape that she progressed less and less each day, and indeed it was almost a miracle she was still afloat. She was also keeled over to such a degree, and had so few sails left intact, that she was well nigh unsteerable.

So that as soon as we came within sight of Sanlúcar we began to strip her bare. We cut down the fore and mizzen masts. We threw the capstan overboard and cut the anchor free. We got rid of all the hourglasses, the astrolabe, the compasses, and even the sea charts. We had already disposed of all the empty barrels, the officers' bunks, even the mattresses and blankets from the forecastle. All we kept on board were the sacks of pepper, cloves and cinnamon that filled the holds.

By evening, the *Victoria* looked like a forest that had been pollarded, an empty trunk, a platform deserted after a celebration.

But she still would not move an inch.

In one last frantic effort we dismantled the sterncastle. Night was falling, and Sebastián paced up and down smiling ironically at us. Sanlúcar seemed as distant and inaccessible as ever.

Our struggle was worse than useless. Freed from the weight of the sterncastle, the *Victoria* keeled over completely and slowly began to founder, just outside the harbor.

Our only hope was that someone would see us and send help, but the tiny figures we could see coming and going in the streets and on the dockside did not seem to notice anything. We were so alien to their world, so distant from their daily routine, that we had become invisible to them.

To make matters even worse, we had abandoned our skiff and the longboat. There was nothing we could do except pray and wait for another dawn in the hope that the winds or the current would take us in to the port.

Exhausted from our labors, we watched as the last lights in the village went out.

Around midnight, a strong sea breeze blew up. The wind wafted the fragrance of our cloves and cinnamon into the streets and squares of Sanlúcar. The smell drifted in through open windows. Seeped under doors. Built up in patios. Invaded houses. Perfumed the night. Took over the whole village with its captivating aroma.

A moment later, there were lights in every window. Even the usually gloomy duke's castle was lit up as though for a celebration. The bells began to ring out. The villagers rushed out into the streets, and a crowd ran down to the dock by torchlight.

Despite all this, the *Victoria* continued to sink inch by inch.

So we were forced to take a decision we had always put off, hoping it would never become necessary.

We had to throw overboard the cargo of spices it had cost us so much to find. The cargo we had suffered all kinds of hardship and torment for. The cargo we had been traveling for almost three years to bring back. The cargo we had sailed around the world for. The cargo we had been pinning our last hopes on, so that we could say it had not all been in vain.

I know it will seem ridiculous to you, your Highness, but we had no other choice. The *Victoria* would have sunk before morning, and then everything would have been lost anyway. Would have gone to the bottom of the sea with her. At least this way we would save our lives. It was not much, but it was better than nothing.

So we got down to the task of emptying the hold and throwing the sacks into the water.

Nobody said a word. Some were crying silently. Sebastián was laughing a forlorn, crazy laugh. Acurio surreptitiously slipped a handful of cloves into his pocket.

As we began throwing the sacks overboard, the people on shore started to leave the dock and to put out their torches.

By the time we had finished it was nearly dawn. The wind was still blowing from the sea, but it no longer brought with it the smell of cloves and cinnamon. The few remaining onlookers went home. The lights went out. Everything was over for them. As if it had been nothing but a dream.

Freed of its cargo, the *Victoria* recovered a little and, thanks to the favorable wind from the sea, we managed to put into the port of Sanlúcar at first light.

Shortly afterward, the eighteen survivors—out of a total of two hundred and fifty men who had set out in the five ships —began to climb the empty streets of Sanlúcar.

At the sight of this ragged-looking group of men who could hardly stand and had to lean on each other for support, all the windows of the houses slammed shut, and keys turned in all the locks.

The village was deserted, as if it had been invaded by an army of lepers.

None of us knew where we were going, but we kept on walking through the streets, aware that a multitude of eyes were spying on us from behind the shuttered windows.

Although we needed help, we did not dare knock on any door. So we went on wandering up and down in the hope that someone would come out and offer us some.

The smell from the *Victoria*, tied up at the dock, was nauseating, pestilential, choking.

Early in the morning of the next day we set off again for Sevilla, without setting eyes on a single inhabitant of that village of your realm.

THE WIND carried our shipboard smells out over the deserted countryside.

The ship stank of rotten timbers, dried-out cables, rusty bronze, sails covered in fungus, empty holds, urine and excrement. It also reeked of broken dreams. Of far-off islands. Of the salt of many seas. And of rage, fear, and despair.

Now the river was full of twists and turns, winding between low hills and olive groves. Windy Trebujera showed in the distance, surrounded by salt flats.

Further upstream we passed fields of dusty red earth, a plowman following his oxen. A grove of slender palm trees swaying in the breeze. A shepherd, who waved at us.

Next came shady La Puebla, peeping timidly through its willows and poplars at the junction of the Repudio and the main river. A bounding dog barked furiously at the ships; a young man in a tavern doorway stared at the fleet going by, then at the empty river.

We passed Coria, village of doves, before anyone had time to peer out at us. Only the loud cooing of the doves, the river making for the sea, the black ship gliding on like a moving shadow in the bright sunlight.

The wind puffed out our sails, the current caught our hull, and images of more villages and fields rushed by as in a dream.

Then open fields again, dotted with cattle, and soon the white village of Gelves, on the port bank. The river shallows forced us so close to the village we could almost touch its walls, sniff the fragrance filling its cool rooms, its wardrobes.

Our sails stirred the calm air; their shadow flitted across the walls, darkened every room.

The ship seemed to be gliding along the dusty main street of the village, lined with low white houses and their empty flowerpots. Yet no one was outside to greet our passage, apart from a group of old men dozing in the sun beside a stockyard wall.

An old woman in black was shelling beans, piling them in her lap, letting the pods drop into a basket at her feet. She followed the ship with her gaze for a while, her hands going on mechanically with their task . . .

Two more old men, seated at a chessboard, one wearing a homespun woolen cap, the other a battered leather hat. A third man leaning against the wall. None of them apparently aware of the presence of the *Victoria* only a few feet from where they were taking their ease.

If we had stretched out our arms we could almost have touched them. But even then we would not have impinged on their enclosed, shut-off world.

Then white Gelves was lost round a bend in the river.

San Juan de Alfarache, fertile in vines, also appeared on the port bow.

It looked deserted, apart from a few children perched on the ruins of an old Moorish bridge, fishing. As the ship passed, the children dropped their rods and ran to the top of one of the buttresses to wave. They stood there until the *Victoria* had gone by, then rushed back to their lines. We could see them larking about, laughing, without a care in the world.

In the vineyards outside the village, men with huge baskets on their backs straightened for a moment to watch us go by. Three youngsters treading grapes in a vat next to a wooden shed raised their arms in greeting, without pausing in their work.

Women among the rows of vines popped up one by one, their heads turned to the river; a moment later their black figures with white headscarves, like a flock of birds on plowed furrows, bent again to the grapevines.

Now the river slid beneath the ship; the earth turned.

Empty fields, with now and then a low hill. Dusty olive groves. Plowed earth. A solitary palm tree swaying in the breeze.

Then, round the final bend in the river, we saw the great cathedral, the fortresses, the hundred towers and spires, all the red tiles of Sevilla.

Everything appeared to stand still, your Highness.

The river stopped in its flow. The sun in its climb up the heavens. The clouds as they drifted by.

AND NOW, Don Carlos, consider all I have related to you, which is nothing more than the truth, and tell me whether there is or ever has been a fool, jester, mountebank, clown, mummer, minstrel, tumbler, joker, jackanapes, dwarf or, as the French say, buffoon, who has rendered greater service to your kingdom than Juanillo Ponce, Count of the Spice Islands.

Is there any comparison between me and that drunken, lecherous old woman Felipa, whom you gave to your daughters? Or with Doña Lucía, Diego de Rojas's fool in the days of their Catholic Majesties, your grandparents? Or Davihuela, jester to the court of Juan II of Castilla, whom the poet Alfonso Álvarez de Villasandino rightly put to shame for the absurd verses with which he tried to make himself seem erudite?

Would you compare me to that drunkard Borra of Aragón, whose obscene jokes so disturbed the court of Martín I the Humanist, and who was stabbed to death in the throne room by a hired assassin? Or with Don Guzbet, whose best trick was to empty his masters' coffers of their gold and jewels, substituting them for sand, so that he could buy himself a huge swathe of land around the monastery at Sahagún? What about that other one, Martíñiano, who dallied with his mistress whenever his master went off to fight a campaign, and was even stupid enough to leave her pregnant?

But why am I talking about historical fools when those of today are enough to make one ashamed of this noble profession of ours? Just look at Perico de Ayala, jester to the marquess of Villena, and a great friend of your favorite Francesillo de Zúñiga (Francesillo, on whom you lavished honors and precious gifts, when he was no more than a vulgar mountebank, and a circumcised Jew like me). Each of them was as bad as the other, and the way they ended up is proof enough of that. Gabriel, servant of your cousin Don Fadrique? I'm not sure whether he's still alive, but should he ever cross your path, watch out for your purse, because he is as adept at picking other people's pockets as he is hopeless at raising a laugh. And what of Valdesillo, buffoon—that was the title he liked to give himself—to Gonzalo Pizarro? Corrupt, gluttonous dwarf that he was, he delighted in making off with the gold from the colonies destined for your coffers.

In all truth, can any of these fools be said to compare with Juanillo Ponce in the services they have rendered to your Imperial cause?

And yet what have I received by way of reward? I have no land or titles, apart from the one bestowed on me by my master, and which I will not renounce for all the world. I have kept no fine costumes, no silverware, or any other possessions. My name does not even figure in any of the chronicles, and I have been erased from the list of the survivors of the expedition to the Spice Islands to which I made so great a contribution—because in sea voyages as in battles, some are there to wield weapons, others to keep up spirits. And as a final injustice, your son Felipe has stripped me of the pension which you saw fit to grant me in recognition of my contribution to that so noble undertaking.

Well then, Don Carlos, here's what we'll do. You call for Sepúlveda. Tell him about my chronicle, and get him to find out how much truth there is in what I have narrated and told you. And if Sepúlveda informs you that I have not been lying, then write to Felipe and instruct him to restore my pension.

Once I've received it, I'll come visit you at Yuste, and from there the two of us will set off to discover the world. In any direction. With knapsacks on our backs, traveling wherever our tired feet lead us. A fair here, a road there, a village, a pine forest, a feast with hams and good wine. You'll see what a time we'll have.

You'll have to hurry though. Both of us are riddled with the afflictions of age, and soon a walking stick will not be enough to support us on the highroads and byroads we set out to explore.

And people will look on us with scorn. Children will laugh at us, and everyone will say:

"Look at those two. One thinks he is a count, and the other an emperor. Their Majesties are a fine mess!"

But we won't care, because we'll be off to discover the world together.

APPENDIX

To his Imperial Majesty Carlos V, by the grace of God king of Castilla, León, Aragón, Navarra, Granada, Jerez, Galicia, Valencia, Mallorca, the Two Sicilies, Naples, Jerusalem, the East and West Indies, and many other kingdoms.

From his humble and true servant Juan Ginés de Sepúlveda.

Most excellent and powerful Lord:

In response to your communication of August 20, in which your Majesty requests my modest opinion about various matters related to the first expedition to the Spice Islands, and with the satisfaction of knowing that I have done everything in my power fully to satisfy the proper curiosity shown by such a munificent Prince, I beg to inform you that:

1) *Your Highness did send and finance an expedition to the Spice Islands which left Sevilla on August 10, 1519, and returned to the same port on September 8, 1522.*

2) *The aim of this expedition was to prove that the Spice Islands fell within the jurisdiction of Spain as established by the treaty of Tordesillas.*

3)   The command of this expedition was entrusted to one Fernando de Magallanes, a native of Oporto.

4)   Said Magallanes claimed he could reach the Spice Islands by sailing west, since he reportedly knew of the existence of a passage or strait at the southern tip of the Indies which would permit him to travel out and back without violating the line of demarcation established many years ago between the kingdoms of Spain and Portugal.

5)   To this end, your Highness equipped for him a fleet of five ships, on board which sailed two hundred thirty-seven men.

6)   The said Fernando de Magallanes apparently discovered the strait which many before him had searched for. This, at least, is what the learned monk José de Acosta affirms in the Historia natural y moral de las Indias, *recently compiled by him. However, this monk also states that the location and characteristics of this strait present such hazards to navigation that it has since been forgotten, to such an extent that its very existence is now called into question, the general opinion being that it has closed up again as the result of some marine accident or earthquake. Such is the belief of Don Alonso de Ercilla y Zúñiga, an expert on the region, who writes in an as yet unpublished poem entitled* La Araucana:

> For lack of pilots or weighty reasons
> We know not where the answer lies
> This secret passage once discovered
> Is once more hidden to our eyes.

7)   As regards the Spice Islands, permit me to remind your Majesty that according to the agreement signed in Zaragoza, your Imperial Highness sold these objects of so much strife to the king of Portugal, since, as Sandoval says: "The expenses the Emperor had incurred in past wars and those which would become necessary and unavoidable to finance any future conflicts, in addition to those of the imperial sojourn in Italy for the coronation, were so onerous that the royal revenues and services owed to him were insufficient, and he found himself so short of money that he was forced to yield control of the Spice Islands to King Juan III of Portugal for the sum of 350,000 ducats."

To which should be added, as Antonio de Herrera has it in his Décadas *(IV, book 5, chap. 10): "Neither king understood just what they were giving or what they were receiving."*

8) *As regards the interest shown by your Highness in the fate of various members of that expedition, and of others linked to it, the following are the details I have been able to ascertain:*

9) *The said Ruy Faleiro or Rodrigo Faleiro was in fact the originator of the course followed by the fleet, as well as of the calculations and measurements related to it.*

It apparently transpired that all his calculations were pure inventions, given the real dimensions of the world and the consequences that his ignorance of them had on the estimated length of the voyage.

According to Barros, the author of a set of Décadas *which he allowed me to see though they are as yet unfinished, Faleiro did not join the fleet because "being an astrologer, he could foresee the expedition's fatal destiny, and so pretended to be mad so that he would not have to reveal all his secrets; eventually, however, his feigned madness became real" (*Década II, book 5, chap. 8*).*

For his part Gonzalo Fernández de Oviedo tells us in his Historia de las Indias *(Part II, book 20, chap. 1): "Ruy Faleiro, being of subtle mind and a keen scholar, either because of this or through the will of God, lost his wits and became mad, lacking both reason and health. Our emperor ordered that he be cured and treated well, but he was unable to continue with the voyage and so Captain Fernando Magallanes became its sole leader."*

It would seem that the said Faleiro was held in the lunatic asylum at Sevilla, where he died raving mad. This version is to be found in both the Historia pontifical *by Ellescas (part II, book 6, chap. 4, page 534) and the* Crónica de los descalzos de San Francisco en Filipinas *by Juan Francisco de San Antonio (part I, book 2, chap. 4).*

In relation to the aforementioned Ruy Faleiro, I also discovered the following documents:

a) *Letter written in Sevilla on March 22, 1523, in which he begs your Majesty to send him his captain's salary. He says that various offers have been made for him to return to Portugal,* and he asks permission to send one or two ships to the Indies, at his own expense, promising that "one third of their cargoes shall be destined for the king."

b) Royal warrant of February 13, 1523, in Valladolid, ordering that the sick Ruy Faleiro be removed from the Colonies' Office in Sevilla and found a suitable place of residence.

c) Royal warrant signed in Granada on November 9, 1526, calling on the Colonies' Office to pay Eva Alonso, wife of Ruy Faleiro, the moneys due to him, "provided that she come to live with her husband, who is lunatic, not in his right mind, living in the dockyards at Sevilla. Said Eva Alonso claims that her husband is in the hands of his brother Francisco Faleiro, who pockets the 50,000 maravedis sent him each year by the Colonies' Office."

d) Seven items from the lawsuit between Francisco Faleiro and his sister-in-law Eva Alonso concerning the care of Ruy Faleiro, labeled "evidence" and dated in Sevilla, 1527.

In these items of evidence, Francisco Faleiro defends himself against the charges made by his sister-in-law, whom he in turn accuses of having abandoned his brother and of wishing to have his salary for herself. Among many other things of interest, item 17 states that "the witnesses were asked if it was true that the said commander Ruy Faleiro was often so mad and raging that five or six persons were needed to dress and undress him."

The witnesses replied that this was so, one of them adding that sometimes they had to arm themselves with shields to give him his food because he threw bricks at them, on one occasion hitting one of them and causing him great harm.

10) Concerning the aforementioned Fernando de Magallanes, I have established that he came to Spain in 1517 and married Doña Beatriz Barbosa. In 1519, the year in which the expedition to the Spice Islands departed, he left written authorization for his wife to receive his pay on his behalf, and a will dated August 24. I have personally seen both these documents and can vouch for their existence.

In this will he sets out that the Royal Appointment with which your Majesty honored him should pass after his death firstly to his son

342

Rodrigo, who was six months old at the time; secondly to the child or children that his pregnant wife might bear; thirdly, to his brother Diego de Sosa, and finally to his sister Isabel de Magallanes.

In the same document, he bequeathes part of whatever sum he earns to the monasteries of Santa María de la Victoria, Santa María de Montserrat, and Santo Domingo, in Oporto. He also bequeathes a silver sovereign to the Holy Crusade, and another for the liberation of a Christian prisoner from the hands of the heathens. He also disposes that on the day of his funeral three poor men be given clothes: a gray cloth suit, a cap, a shirt and a pair of boots to each, in order that they might pray for his soul. He also wishes that on that same day those three men and a dozen more be given food to eat, so that they, too, might pray for his soul, and that a golden ducat be given as alms for the souls in purgatory. He also sets free his slave Enrique, twenty-six years of age, and stipulates that he be given 10,000 maravedis to help him on his way. He apportions and guarantees him this legacy because he has converted to Christianity and in order that he pray to God for the good of his soul.

Also regarding the said Magallanes, I have discovered the following documents:

a) Royal warrant of May 5, 1519, in Barcelona, authorizing payment of all moneys due to Fernando de Magallanes to his wife Doña Beatriz Barbosa de Magallanes during his absence.

b) Letter from the bishop of Burgos to the officials of the Colonies' Office in Sevilla, dated May 1521, Burgos. This letter is a reply to one from the officials advising the bishop of the arrival of the ship the San Antonio, part of the fleet to the Spice Islands. In his reply, the bishop states: "Firstly, use whatever means seem appropriate to you to ensure that Don Fernando's wife and children are kept in a safe place, and without taking any dishonest measures, make sure that they are closely watched, so that they cannot find any way to get to Portugal until we see what all this is about and until his Highness gives further orders."

c) I learned from an official at the Colonies' Office that Doña Beatriz Barbosa was in fact pregnant when the fleet left, but that she lost the child. I also learned that her son Rodrigo died in or

*about the month of July 1521, in prison; and that his unfortunate
mother followed him in 1522.*

    *d)   Finally I would mention to your Majesty a document
entitled "Financial claims by Jaime Barbosa and his brothers, heirs
to Fernando de Magallanes" in which they ask for the agreement
made with him before the fleet left for the Spice Islands to be
respected.*

    *11)   Concerning the fate of Juan de Cartagena and the priest
Sánchez de Reina, marooned on the coast of Patagonia according to a
letter sent from Sevilla by Juan López de Recalde to the bishop of
Burgos on May 21, 1521, in which he informs him of the arrival of
the San Antonio, all I can tell your Highness is that measures were
taken at the time, but I am unaware of their outcome.*

    *For example, in a letter from Don Juan Rodríguez de Fonseca,
Bishop of Burgos, which is his reply to the previous one, we can read
(paragraph 4): "I think it would be wise to send a caravel to search
for Juan de Cartagena. To this end, use some of the 5,000 pesos which
have recently arrived from the isle of San Juan."*

    *For his part, in his work D'Asia, the Portuguese historian Barros
suggests that both men were picked up by the San Antonio on her
return journey to Spain after she had deserted the fleet headed for the
Spice Islands commanded by Magallanes.*

    *If your Majesty would like my opinion in this matter, I would
say that neither of them came back to Spain. I am led to believe this
by a royal warrant dated October 10, 1537, which authorizes payment
to Doña Catalina de Cartagena, daughter and heir of Juan de Cartagena, of the sum of 48,217 maravedis, which corresponded to her
father for having taken part in the expedition to the Spice Islands.*

    *12)   As regards Juan Serrano, your Highness issued a royal war-
rant on April 4, 1526, instructing the Colonies' Office to grant his
widow 5,000 maravedis in alms since she was destitute.*

    *Your Majesty also issued a royal warrant in the city of Ávila on
July 24, 1531, instructing that Juan Serrano's wife be given twenty
ducats in alms, "since, until it has been ascertained if he is alive or
not, she cannot be given any of his pay."*

    13)   With regard to the aforementioned Sebastián Elcano, on

whom your Majesty conferred—as he will most surely remember—
the title of Primus Circumdedisti Me *for use as the motto on his*
coat of arms, I have ascertained that following a short period of rest
in his native village of Guetaria to recover from the first voyage, he
put to sea again on July 25, 1525, heading for the Spice Islands.

I was further informed that on May 26, 1526 he again crossed
through the strait, and died shortly afterward in the middle of the
Pacific Ocean. His body was thrown overboard.

I also learned that, feeling he was soon to die, he dictated a very
strange last will and testament to the fleet's scribe.

14)   As for one Francisco Serrano, the friend of Don Fernando
who lived for nine years in the Spice Islands, Barros tells us (Década
III, book 5, chaps. 7 and 8) that he died poisoned on Ternate on the
same day that Magallanes was killed on the island of Matán.

It would appear that among Serrano's papers, recovered by Antonio
de Brito, there was a letter from Fernando de Magallanes promising
to meet him again within a short time, either under the flag of Portugal
or that of Castilla, and begging Serrano to wait for him.

15)   As far as the ships themselves are concerned, I can only
inform your Highness that:

a)   The Santiago *sank off Patagonia, near a river known as*
the Santa Cruz. All its crew and cargo were saved.

b)   The San Antonio *reached the port of Las Muelas on*
May 6, 1521. Her captain was in chains, and the ship was com-
manded by one Esteban Gómez. The captain, Álvaro de la Mez-
quita by name, was accused of having had a hand in the executions
ordered by Magallanes in San Julián, and was turned over to the
officials of the Colonies' Office for trial. All his possessions were
seized, but he was given an allowance to cover his needs for as
long as the trial lasted.

c)   The Concepción *was burned on the island of Bohol.*

d)   On leaving the Spice Islands, the Trinidad *was leaking*
at the keel. She had to be unloaded and careened before she could
be repaired. I cannot say what then became of her, your Highness.

e)   As far as the Victoria *is concerned, she entered the port*
of Sevilla on September 8, 1522, in such a sorry state that nothing

could be salvaged from her, and the poor of the city were allowed to use her for firewood.

Finally, with regard to the author of this chronicle which has aroused such a keen interest in your Highness, leading you to show again the lively curiosity which was so prominent during your reign, for the benefit and good of all your subjects, I can only state the following:

16) *That neither the reliable author Gonzalo Fernández de Oviedo, who met the survivors of the expedition, nor Juan Bautista Ramusio, who wrote about the voyage, nor any of the historiographers who have dealt with the subject mention the presence of any buffoon on board the ships. Nor is there one mentioned in the official list of the eighteen survivors.*

17) *That list makes no mention of any Juanillo Ponce; nor do any of the aforementioned chroniclers.*

18) *It is, however, possible that someone of that name was among the ships' crews, as there exists great confusion in this matter, since there are several different lists of the members of the expedition, in which their names and places of origin often differ.*

19) *I have not been able to discover anything with regard to the claim made by this Juanillo Ponce that his name was erased from the lists and his pension stopped, but your Highness is well aware of how discreet the Office of the Holy Inquisition is in these matters.*

20) *For all these reasons, I find myself unable to confirm or deny with any certainty that the said Juanillo Ponce served in the expedition to the Spice Islands either as a buffoon or in any other capacity.*

21) *Notwithstanding this, I should point out to your Highness that the dates and the names, the course of the voyage and the majority of the events described in his chronicle coincide with what we know of the expedition from other sources, although of course he may have invented the whole thing on the basis of the other chronicles or after having talked to a survivor he may have known.*

Whatever the truth of the matter, I must admit, your Majesty, that the author, whoever he may be, has taken great pains to write his chronicle, and if I might be allowed to express a personal opinion, he has afforded me great pleasure in doing so, and seems to me well deserving of the pension he requests.

At Sevilla, this twenty-first day of September 1558, from your humble and true servant who kisses your hands and feet.

Juan Ginés de Sepúlveda